Vincent Cade took a BA in US Studies at Reading. He spent over twenty years at the BBC and made short films on the side. He left to study counselling and currently works with children and young people. He has a passion for films and music from the late sixties. He lives on the edge of London with his partner and two daughters. *Sunset Collector* is his first novel.

For E.W.B. with love

Lyrics and quotes in Sunset Collector

Frank Lloyd Wright: "Tip the world over on its side and everything loose will land in Los Angeles."

Alexander Pope: "Good God! How often are we to die before we go quite off this stage? In every friend we lose a part of ourselves, and the best part."

Disney Tomorrowland commentary: "I am so infinitely small now that I can see millions of orbiting electrons. They appear like the Milky Way of our own solar system…" ('The Happiest Place on Earth')

Disney Primeval World commentary: "…the next leg of our journey will take us along the rim of the Grand Canyon. It's a mighty long drop to the Canyon floor so for your safety, stay seated with your hands, arms, feet and legs inside the trains…" "Quiet now, as we travel back in time, back to the fantastic primeval world, land of the dinosaurs…" ('The Happiest Place on Earth')

George Eliot – Adam Bede: ""No: people who love downy peaches are apt not to think of the stone, and sometimes jar their teeth terribly against it." ('Tremors' & 'La Cienega Waved Goodbye')

Raymond Chandler – As quoted in Hollywood Remembered: An Oral History of its Golden Age (2002) by Paul Zollo: "Hollywood… Anyone who doesn't like it is either crazy or sober." ('Woman with the Feathered Hat')

'Hold On' – 'A Pueblo Indian Prayer':
'Hold on to what is good,
Even if it's a handful of Earth.
Hold on to what you believe,
Even if it's a tree that stands by itself.

Hold on to what you must do.
Even if it's a long way from here
Hold on to your life.
Even if it's easier to let go.
Hold on to my hand.
Even if someday I'll be gone away from you.' ('Am I Craig, or Not-Craig?')

Ecclesiastes 3. 1–13: "There is a time for everything, and a season for every activity under the heavens; a time to be born and a time to die, a time to plant and a time to uproot, a time to kill and a time to heal…" ('Into the Sunset')

Vincent Cade

SUNSET COLLECTOR

AUSTIN MACAULEY PUBLISHERS™

LONDON ★ CAMBRIDGE ★ NEW YORK ★ SHARJAH

A CIP catalogue record for this title is available from the British Library.

ISBN 9781398441118 (Paperback)
ISBN 9781398441125 (ePub e-book)

www.austinmacauley.com

First Published 2023
Austin Macauley Publishers Ltd®
1 Canada Square
Canary Wharf
London
E14 5LAA

I would like to thank everyone at Austin Macauley Publishers, especially Ella Thomson, for all their good-humoured support, guidance and assistance in producing this novel.

From a stuttering origin of half-ideas and reflections twenty years ago to occasional chapters to the gradual realisation that maybe it was something worth taking seriously after all, to give some shape and possibly even an ending, many friends helped me to finally drag the piece over the finish line:

Thanks to Paul Batchelor who insisted on reading whatever I had and pressed for more, spurring me on to a productive spell that broke the back of the task and made it feel real.

Special thanks to Paul Granville for his language skills, precision, creative suggestions and for the generosity of his time over many months.

Thanks to Nick Crowe for his robust encouragement and also for his constructive feedback.

Thanks also to Adrian Daniels, Alistair Macdonald, Nick Machon, Rodney Breen, Rupert Williams and Ray Bonner who all read sections and laughed in the right places or kindly kept their doubts under wraps and urged me onwards.

Thanks to Liz Booth, lodestar and long-suffering partner and Lorelei and Eloise, our two brilliant and beautiful daughters for allowing me space and time out from the day job to focus on my scribblings.

Finally, very special thanks to Paul Lewis, for being an inspirational, free-spirited, ever-entertaining friend, comrade and muse.

Table of Contents

Return Flight

"Pete burst in, drunk & excitable. Said he found himself playing pool at the Bottom Line with Johnny G, the hitman from NYC, and decided to throw the game on purpose. Other gossip from the world of Piper's included Travis trying to sell Pete a 'Fuck Iran' t-shirt. Apparently, he has dozens of them in the back of his van.

Pat, the gigolo, had his car stolen yesterday and was ranting how if he found the cocksucker, he would take him out into the desert and chop him into tiny pieces. Also Angelo, the Piper's chef, supposedly had a part in a Cassavetes movie."

Craig grinned at the diary entry from April 1980, then placed the dog-eared little book on the fold-out table and sipped at his tiny plastic glass of Diet Coke with ice. Apart from a vague memory of Pete deliberately throwing a game of pool with a hitman, he did not recall any of it.

It was vivid details like these that brought the past to life, surprisingly, rather than the big stories which were overfamiliar from reliving them countless times. He felt lucky that he'd kept diaries for a brief period in the late '70s and early '80s and wondered why he so rarely dipped into them.

It had been 26 years since Craig had seen Los Angeles, but if anything it felt longer, by a couple of lifetimes. He'd been to New York once and to Florida a couple of times with the family, but that was different. It felt deeply strange to be going back again, and not just for the obvious reason. He tended to divide his life into pre-LA and post-LA phases, as if the few months spent there almost three decades ago formed a sort of liminal existential boundary.

He'd been barely 19 when they'd set off on their West Coast adventure: a naïve, passionate, angry, sensitive, and slightly earnest teenager. Now he was a settled, mature, unambitious, still slightly sensitive 45 year old husband and father of two. Looking back through a journal darkly, Craig's impressions of LA at the dawn of the '80s, were of a sort of hedonistic playground.

This was certainly the way he portrayed it to friends when the subject occasionally arose, but he was aware that this was not the whole picture. At some point, the adventure had taken a wrong turning and things had started to unravel. He had never been entirely sure how or why things turned sour, but felt the return to LA might provide some answers as well as closure, hence the diary.

Craig looked at the youth next to him in the aisle seat, gazing almost slack-jawed at some animated blockbuster (he guessed either 'Ice Age 2' or 'Over The Hedge') on the small screen embedded in the seat in front. He was probably in his late teens, around the same age as Craig back then. Although he hadn't heard the youth speak, Craig guessed he was American, mainly from the size of his girth, but also the t-shirt, long shorts and baseball cap combo.

He tried not to be judgemental but the huge flabby arm flapping over the arm-rest made this difficult. Craig wondered how his opinion of America and its citizens could have changed so radically since his LA days. Back then, he and Pete had the USA on a pedestal and were desperate to live there.

By the mid-80s, Craig saw only an arrogant, reactionary, charmless country obsessed with money. By the mid-90s, the pendulum had swung back a little, but he could barely believe that he once held the place in such high esteem.

He opened the diary again, thinking it might make sense of the seismic shift in perception. He opened it randomly and found himself reading about a Berlin gig at the Starwood. Shandy had put black eyeliner on him, and he apparently wore black PVC trousers and a hippy shirt. They met a few of Shandy's friends at the gig. John, the bass player, had put their names on the guest list as they'd become pretty friendly by then.

He'd already seen them at Club 88 & The Londoner, but this gig was the best according to the diary. During the group's first set, the lead singer, Virginia, had crouched right over his face, at the edge of the stage, causing him to spill beer all over himself. During the second set, by which time he was smashed, Virginia left the stage and danced raunchily with him during one number.

When Berlin set the world (and several crop fields) alight in 1986, with *Take My Breath Away*, from the 'Top Gun' soundtrack, Craig could scarcely conceive that it was the same new wave synth-pop band he'd taken to back in 1980; he'd also been confused that the singer looked so different and was called Terri, not Virginia. Thanks to the internet, he finally discovered in the early 2000s that Terri Nunn had temporarily left the band in 1980 to pursue an acting career when replacement vocalist Virginia Maccolino had joined them. It had felt good having his memory validated after so many years.

He flicked through a few pages. The entry for May 12 jumped out at him: "On the way from Barney's Beanery to the Odyssey club, I saw a large dead rat on San Vicente." The inclusion of this morbid detail made him laugh out loud, drawing a quizzical glance from his chunky neighbour, who was still wearing his baseball hat, despite clearly sweating profusely. Craig could recognise himself in the noting of a dead rat as he would do the same today if he still kept a diary.

His mind started to drift. He wondered if Shandy, or her husband, Doug, would be picking him up from LAX. It was kind of Shandy to put him up for his brief stay. It occurred to him that she was now the only person from the 1980 trip that he still had fairly regular, if infrequent, contact with. Of all the colourful cast of characters from that time, he never would have predicted that Shandy would be the longest lasting in his life.

He felt his eyelids twitch then close for a second. There was still an hour or so until they were due to land, so he shut the diary again and surrendered his grip on consciousness. He was soon being chased by giant rats through deserted Hollywood streets. He made it to a large black building which he felt would offer sanctuary.

The rats were almost on his heels as he raced up the front steps. A suited doorman was holding the door open for him and ushered him in then slammed the door shut behind him. He handed Craig a small business card that read 'Starwood Funeral Home' and gestured towards the stage.

Shandy appeared, wearing a veil, taking his hand and guiding him through the crowd towards the front; and he recognised the band, all dressed in black, were in fact Berlin, and they were playing a version of *Take My Breath Away*, which was very slow like a lament; and then he noticed an open coffin on the stage. John, the bass player, recognised Craig and beckoned him up on to the stage. He felt afraid and wanted to run away but the crowd had closed behind him and Shandy was urging him forwards.

"Wakey wakey, little Craigy. Welcome to LA. The '80s start here!"

A hand was shaking his shoulder. Craig groggily opened his eyes to see Pete next to him, grinning wildly and rubbing his hands together excitedly. "I ordered these to celebrate our arrival."

Craig noticed two tall glasses full of orangey-yellow liquid and some fruit protruding from them impaled on little sticks. He lifted his one up and smelt it suspiciously.

"What the fuck is this?"

"Tequila Sunrise, you philistine, for our new dawn. Geddit?"

"It does kind of look like a sunrise, doesn't it?" said Craig, admiring the gradated colour.

A stewardess passed their row and Pete called out, "Marcie, can I introduce my companion Craig?"

A pretty blonde stewardess turned around and flashed a smile even more dazzling than her bright red Laker uniform. He felt grateful in that moment to Sir Freddy for his 'no frills' airline model; at less than half the price of a normal economy ticket, he had made their trip possible.

"Well hi, Craig, I am so pleased to meet you. I was sorry to hear about your condition, I think you're very brave."

"Um, thank you," managed Craig, dreading to think what preposterous tale Pete had been spinning while he napped. He glanced sideways but his friend was avoiding his gaze.

"Marcie here lives in LA, and has kindly been recommending some top nightspots."

"Yeah, remember to check out P.J. Sloane's, you guys are gonna love that. OK, we are starting our descent now. Can you fasten your seatbelt for me, Craig, honey?"

As he buckled up, he looked out the window of the wide-bodied DC10 just as they emerged from the clouds, and he caught his first glimpse of the huge sprawling metropolis. He felt an undeniable ripple of excitement caused by the butterflies furiously waving their wings in his stomach. He turned to look at Pete at exactly the same moment Pete turned to look at him.

They were both in perfect synch, grinning like 6-year-olds at Christmas. As the engine roar grew louder, they both lifted their glasses and clinked them.

"To the City of Angels," said Craig.

"Fallen or otherwise," said Pete, and they both downed their cocktails in one.

The First Time

It was Saturday evening. Pete and Craig were standing at a bus stop on South La Brea Avenue waiting for a bus to take them to Hollywood, and buzzing in anticipation. They were still lapping up the natural splendour of this city ringed by mountains and shimmering ocean, under vivid blue skies. Drunk on the glamorous novelty of the massive cars and the way the sun's golden rays reflected off the shiny bonnets on the broad tree-lined roads. The sunbeams sometimes strobed through the palm fronds high above many of the buildings, each of which looked distinct. All around them strode proud striking Angelenos of every ethnicity. California girls with movie star tans and perfect teeth sometimes flashed by, like extras in a schoolboy dream.

Craig tried to make sense of a laminated timetable affixed to the bus stop when Pete nudged him. Craig looked around and clocked a raggedy-looking man stumbling towards them. There were three people sitting on the blue wooden bench in front of them. The street person, which was an expression Craig had picked up, walked around in front of the bench and mumbled something to each of them in turn, with a slightly grubby hand extended.

The first person who was only young, did not speak and just shook his head. The second person, who was a middle-aged man reading a newspaper, just lifted the paper to block out the beggar. The third person was an elderly woman with white hair, horn-rimmed glasses and a severe expression. Craig guessed the man might be in for a frosty reception here too, but he did not foresee what came next.

The man asked if she had any loose change in a slightly louder voice. The woman did not look at him. She undid the handbag on her lap and reached inside. The man leaned in hopefully. The woman pulled out a small aerosol can, raised it and calmly sprayed the man full in the face. He screamed out in shock and pain, whirling around with his hands covering his eyes, stumbling backwards into the road.

Craig and Pete stared open-mouthed at the old woman who coolly put the aerosol back in her handbag. The youth sitting on the bench sniggered. Just at this point, a loud horn blasted and the beggar just managed to stagger back onto the sidewalk out of the way of their bus as it pulled in. Everyone filed onto the bus and stood waiting to pay the fare. Pete shook his head and sniggered.

"It was like she was spraying a cockroach or something," gasped Craig.

"For an old dear, that was pretty brutal," agreed Pete.

They were still reeling from witnessing their first macing as they took their seats near the front. Craig felt bad that they had just boarded the bus without even checking to see if the poor man was ok. He peered out the window as they pulled away, he seemed to have already disappeared.

"Neat accent, boys, where are you from?" asked a little man with a grey droopy moustache, sat directly behind them.

"Aldebaran," replied Craig.

"Just off the North Circular," said Pete.

"London, I'd guess," said the man leaning forward on the back of their seat. He had beady eyes and a slightly stoat-like appearance, reminding Craig of Lee Van Cleef.

"Spot on, mate," said Pete, sitting sideways to take in this American with the rare ability to place a non-American accent.

"And where are you boys headed tonight?"

"Hollywood," answered Pete, "actually, could you do us a favour and tell us when we reach it?"

"I would, only it doesn't really exist."

Craig tutted and looked out the window.

"What, as in it's only a state of mind?" persisted Pete.

"No, I mean technically, there is no Hollywood on the map. There is a west Hollywood which may be what you're looking for."

Pete seemed unsure if he was being wound up but played along just in case, "We're looking for the centre of the action, you know, Sunset Strip, Hollywood Boulevard; where it's all happening."

"Hmm, I think I know what you are after. Don't worry, there's still a way to go yet."

They had both been buzzing with excited anticipation and Craig resented this stoat-like man interfering and bringing them down. He wished Pete would just ignore him. Just then, he became aware of a strange clucking noise from the back of the bus. He couldn't resist turning around to see who or what was responsible. As he turned however, the man's face loomed up with a big toothy beady-eyed grin.

"Hi, I'm Donald, pleased to meet you."

Damn, now he was offering his hand, there was no escape barring extreme rudeness.

"Craig," he mumbled, speedily extracting his hand from the clammy grip.

"Craig, ah…so Craig, how do you like it out here in sunny California?"

"It's great, so far."

"Your first time, I take it."

"Uh yes, that's right," said Craig feeling distinctly uncomfortable.

"Out of interest, have you considered getting into the movie industry?" Craig smelt a rat but before he could deny any such ambitions Pete leapt in.

"Craig Carter and Pete Lawes at your service. Yes, we have a couple of meetings lined up actually, Donald. Why do you ask?"

The man relaxed back in his seat, his baiting work done, now confident of a bite.

"Well, let's just say my job involves some scouting around for fresh talent for the major studios."

Craig glanced back out the window at the darkening sky and felt his stomach contract. Reality was threatening to break free of its moorings. His rational, cynical mind was suddenly struggling with the boundless power of dream, desire, ego. It couldn't possibly be but what if…?

"You're a couple of good-looking young guys. Bright and also English; that's a huge plus right now."

As he heard these words, Craig suddenly glimpsed the illuminated Hollywood sign for the first time, high up in the hills above the street lights and the neon. Just for a second then it was gone, blocked from sight by some large building. What if…? The omen was too powerful for Craig's rational mind to possibly compete. He felt a huge surge of energy which made him dizzy but he desperately tried to appear cool as he turned to face the ugly moustached face of destiny.

"Tyrone Power! That's who Craig's face reminds me of. It's been bugging me," said the man to Pete, who was trying to look more enthused than amused.

The clucking broke out again but louder this time. The blue-uniformed driver who was a couple of rows in front of them declaimed to no-one in particular, "Why do they always have to choose my bus?"

Craig's mind was elsewhere, but he took in a straggly-haired man on the back seat flapping his bent arms against the sides of his body.

"Now seriously that's an angle we could use, we could leak it to the press that you are the bastard son of Tyrone Power. Yes, we'd have to decide which English actress could have been your mother."

"Nobody here but us chickens!" screamed the man in the back row.

Pete suddenly spotted something out the window and bound to his feet.

"Hey it's Sunset Boulevard, Craig, get up!"

"Relax, Pete, the Strip's several blocks away. Sunset Boulevard is twenty miles long, you know."

"Is it?" said Craig, "Wow, I didn't know that. So, Sunset Strip is just a small part of Sunset Boulevard?"

"Yup, just a few blocks really, perhaps a mile long. So what do you guys do in England?"

Craig waited for Pete to answer this one, knowing some absurd or fantastic lie was imminent.

"We worked for the government, Donald."

Actually this was not technically a lie; until recently they had both worked at an obscure branch of the Royal Courts of Justice, called the Court of Protection.

"Jeez, you're not telling me you're some sort of spies."

Craig weighed in.

"Obviously we aren't in a position to divulge details or we'd be in breach of the Official Secrets Act."

"We both had to resign recently which is one reason we are here in the Land of the Free," added Pete.

"We may have a Freedom of Information Act but that sure don't make us free," said Donald.

"Anyway," said Pete, "suffice to say that our work necessitated skills similar to acting, if you know what I mean, Donald."

"I get you. The whole spy thing opens up a lot of PR possibilities too I guess."

"Uh, I don't think we would be wise, given the circumstances, to reveal that sort of information."

"Well, we can thrash around the details later. Would both you gentlemen be free to pay a visit to my office in the next few days?"

"I think we could manage that, Donald," said Pete, cool as a cucumber. "Do you have a card?"

"Of course," he said, fishing in his jacket pocket. "The Strip starts around here by the way."

Craig and Pete stood up gazing out the window looking for some sort of non-existent marker.

After much ferreting about in both inside jacket pockets, Donald apologised that he seemed to be temporarily out of cards but wrote his name and office number on a bus ticket and handed it to Craig.

"Make sure you call me now, Craig," he said and winked just as they jumped from the bus.

They both stood on the sidewalk laughing as the bus pulled away. Pete lit up a Marlboro. Craig noticed the man who had made the chicken noises had fallen asleep, sprawled across most of the back seat.

"I think you could say we out-bullshitted a master bullshitter," boasted Pete.

"So you don't think he was for real then?" said Craig feeling a little foolish.

"I doubt it very much, dear boy," said Pete winking, "I think he just wanted your arse."

They started walking up the Strip, not sure what they were looking for but hungry for experience. They drank in all the details as they walked—the preposterous stretch-limousines with blacked-out windows; the enormous billboards towering overhead; the young kids in expensive cars (probably their parents') cruising up and down over and over. Then there were the prostitutes.

Throngs of girls posed and sashayed in an orgy of leopard-skin minis, pink leather teddies, boas, fishnet and lace. What really startled them was how beautiful these girls were. On some of Pete's guided walks through the seamy side of London, they may have seen the occasional pretty working girl in Meard Street or Shepherd Market but nothing to compare to this.

The majority of these girls would not have looked out of place on the pages of Vogue or up on the Silver Screen. Most of them probably left home dreaming of this but ended up on the Strip. Tonight, however, the sadness behind the girls' lives did not occur to either Pete or Craig, only the sheer sleazy glamour. They felt an undeniable tingling excitement when passing these exotic creatures especially when they smiled seductively or promised a good time.

Pete sang or hummed Donna Summer's 'Bad Girls' each time they passed which made some of the girls giggle. Craig likened the experience to that of sailors being drawn to the bewitching songs of the Sirens and vowed not to be drawn in. Pete helpfully pointed out that a) he was being pretentious, and b) the danger of contracting some venereal illness, easily cured by a shot of penicillin, hardly compared to wrecking your ship and drowning. Craig had to concede on both points.

They were a little surprised at how few actual bars there were and how spread out they were. Craig felt a thrill of excitement run through him as they approached the dark red exterior of the Whisky A Go-Go. It had opened way back during the British invasion of the Beatles & the Stones and become a monument to the West Coast counter-culture. A band called Pearl Harbour & the Explosions were apparently playing tonight.

"Good name," admitted Pete.

"Let's check it out," said Craig, "the Whisky a Go-Go is like a West Coast version of the Marquee club: everyone who's anyone's played here."

"Nah, another night; let's check out the rest of the Strip," said Pete.

On the same stretch as the Whisky were two more semi-legendary rock establishments; the Roxy Theatre right next to the Rainbow Bar & Grill, both around since the early '70s. The Roxy was a cool intimate French Revival venue, which had played host to everyone from Aretha Franklin to the Sex Pistols, suitably painted black.

The Rainbow was an unlikely looking mock Tudor affair, sporting a 15 feet rainbow coloured oblong sign on the roof, but was known to cater to the excesses of rock 'n' roll. There seemed to be a party going on in the Rainbow car park, where there must have been as many kids outside as in.

On the other side of the road a little further up, a huge queue was forming outside a cinema called The Tiffany Theatre. As they drew nearer, they noticed that almost everyone in the line, male and female, was sporting unlikely black lingerie, black leather and make up.

"Blimey, quite a freakshow!" said Pete.

They were a little disappointed when the film turned out to be 'The Rocky Horror Picture Show', giving a straightforward reason for the crowd's attire.

Craig insisted on investigating a head shop called 'The Psychedelic Conspiracy' which was still open, but Pete said he'd be in a nearby bar he'd spotted called Hi-Pockets. The bar was surprisingly quiet considering the amount of people milling around outside. After a quick beer, they moved on.

When they reached Ben Franks restaurant, they decided that it must mark the end of the Strip or thereabouts, as things definitely looked more sedate beyond this point. They turned around and retraced their steps, feeling they were getting a handle on the place.

"Nice building," said Craig as they passed an impressive art deco tower.

"Yeah, what is it?… Oh, the Argyle, John Wayne used to live here."

Craig often found himself impressed by Pete's little nuggets. Just then an open-top car pulled up in front of them.

"What the fuck is that?" said Pete, astonished.

Apart from the lights and the license plates the car was completely covered in brown fur.

"One of the Banana Splits?" suggested Craig.

A large grizzly bear of a man sat at the wheel singing along at the top of his impressive voice to some Italian opera booming from the car cassette player. A slim young woman, at least ten years his junior, appeared from nowhere and climbed in next to the man and kissed him. She was wearing a Norman Wisdom style peaked flat cap which added to the absurdity of the scene. The fur-mobile roared off, and two blocks away Pete and Craig could still hear the man's rich baritone.

"Did I just see that?" asked Pete.

"Maybe someone spiked our coffees earlier," said Craig.

"Shall we get a bite to eat in that yellow train carriage?"

Pete was referring to Carneys, a hamburger restaurant, but in a former life it had actually travelled across America's railroads. They opted to sit out front at some picnic tables with stripy umbrellas in case they missed any action on the Strip.

Having filled up on low grade fuel, they went in search of a bar Pete recalled seeing near to the spot the bus had dropped them off.

"There it is," Pete pointed, "the Bottom Line. It looks suitably seedy."

The opaque boarding in the window was reminiscent of an English sex shop. They pushed open the door and peered inside. The lighting was minimal but they made out a few masculine shapes dotted around. The central feature of the bar seemed to be the pool table. A muscular man in a vest and tattoos on each arm was leaning across the table about to take a shot. He looked up at them and due to the overhead fluorescent strip, his baleful expression was clearly visible even through the reams of cigarette smoke.

"Mmm, perhaps not," said Pete and they both withdrew to the street.

"A bit gloomy," said Craig.

"No pussy," said Pete. "Hey, how about this place."

Next door to the Bottom Line, was an unremarkable-looking facade. One palm tree; a small bricked-off seating area; an uneven, mainly glass exterior with a pair of happy/sad masks painted on a fanlight window. A bland illuminated sign by the palm tree proclaimed in red letters, 'Piper's Pizza'.

"It's a pizza restaurant," protested Craig.

"Yes, but it's got a bar and it looks quite lively," said Pete.

With these words they wandered inside, little guessing that this place was about to become the epicentre of their universe for the next few months.

Pipers at the Gates of Dawn

The inside of Piper's was deceptively large. There was a horseshoe-shaped bar in the centre with barstools arranged all around at regular intervals. The kitchen was situated behind the bar out of sight. On each side, against the walls were rows of red leather chairs and wooden tables in booths for dining purposes.

Along the length of the left side wall was a lovingly detailed, though amateurishly-executed, mural of Chicago at night. The idea was obviously to mirror this design along the right side with a New York mural, but so far only a cluster of buildings, including Manhattan's Twin Towers, were in evidence.

Craig noticed once they'd perched on barstools and ordered their beers that there was a tiny raised performing area by the window (to the Chicago side) next to a desk-size jukebox.

"They must have live music in here," he observed.

"Yeah, some nights," said the attractive blonde barmaid, putting their glasses on coasters.

"And we have really cool improvised sessions every Sunday lunchtime where anyone with an instrument can join in."

"What style of music?" asked Craig.

"Jazz, of course," said the barmaid.

"Oh," said Craig, a little disappointed.

"Excellent!" said Pete grinning.

"You should come along tomorrow and check it out."

"We might well do that," said Pete with a sparkle in his eye.

Craig knew instantly that Pete fancied her. He decided to let Pete work his charm while he did a reccy on the jukebox. Since *99* by Toto was playing, he wasn't too hopeful.

Here we go, he thought, scanning the first column of typed white cards:

Boz Scaggs—*Middle Man*

Linda Ronstadt—*Hurt So Bad*

Billy Joel—*It's Still Rock 'n' Roll to Me*

"Vapid West Coast bollocks," he mumbled to himself despite never having heard either the Boz Scaggs or the Linda Ronstadt singles.

The second column was a slight improvement, what with *Brass in Pocket* by the Pretenders and a couple of Blondie numbers. By the third column, he'd detected quite a few jazz-oriented songs, some by artists he hadn't even heard of, in between the obligatory Bob Seger and Eagles tracks. There was a smattering of Frank Sinatra tunes.

It occurred to him that there were virtually no new English bands. He wasn't expecting any obscure or experimental new wave stuff in a mainstream US bar, but it was almost as if punk never happened! England was sadly represented by Queen's *Crazy Little Thing Called Love* and Pink Floyd's *The Wall*.

A couple of Stones classics on the last column just about saved the day, oh and a little gem by the Police, which Craig suddenly realised was appropriate this evening. The barmaid was serving someone else by the time he returned to his stool.

"Anything good?" asked Pete.

"Yeah, Foreigner, Bob Seger, and wait for it…Jefferson Starship."

"Bloody hell, it can't all be that dismal!"

"Almost," said Craig, "but you'll like my selection."

Toto finally drew to an end. After a few seconds, a simple, stripped down guitar and drum pattern, interrupted by laughter, changed the mood significantly.

"*Roxanne!*" said Pete.

"Mmm, five seconds, not bad," said Craig.

"A fine choice, my friend," said Pete.

As if by magic, the song had barely kicked in when two garishly dressed, long-legged beauties; one black, one white, cruised in and sat down at a booth on the left. As Sting warbled about a woman not wearing a particular dress or turning on a red light, Pete and Craig cracked up.

A few minutes later whilst Pete was bombarding the poor barmaid (who they'd discovered was called Mimi) with questions about LA, Craig spotted an unsavoury-looking character the other side of the bar, staring at them. His complexion was red and blotchy, and he was missing at least three front teeth. His looks were not improved by a wide scar that ran like a tramline from the side of his mouth all the way to the lobe of his right ear.

"Have you seen pizza-face over there?" whispered Craig.

"Yeah, I wouldn't fancy meeting him on a dark night," mumbled Pete, "or on a light summer evening."

"He looks like an extra from *The Texas Chainsaw Massacre*," said Craig, starting to giggle.

"Shhhh, he's staring right at us," hissed Pete, through the side of his mouth. Craig took another brief glimpse of the malevolent bloodshot eyes baring down on him and, spooked, turned in his seat so that he was facing the other side of the bar. Just then a large black guy with a shiny bald head walked in and sashayed up to the bar next to Pete.

"Hey, beautiful lady," he purred in a velvet Barry White tone at Mimi.

"Fuck off, Bing Bing," grumbled the Texas Chainsaw extra.

"Hey, Bobby, how ya doin'?" Smiled Mimi.

The large black guy smiled beatifically, his eyes twinkling, "Reality. Real people."

He raised the index finger of his right hand very purposefully, until it was a couple of inches in front of his nose, then said, "Bing Bing!"

"Uh huh, I guess you'd like a beer," said Mimi.

"Gracious lady," he beamed, settling himself down on the barstool next to Pete. Whilst she poured him a glass of Miller, Mimi said, "Bobby, these guys are just over from England. Guys, this is the one and only, Bob Atcheson."

"Very pleased to meet you," said Pete with perfect middle-class manners, offering his hand. Bob grinned from ear to ear, probably amused at this alien politesse. He grasped Pete's hand up to the crook of the thumb and raised it into the air whilst waggling his own thumb.

"Hey, little brother."

He repeated the same curious handshake with Craig.

"England, ooh, you're a long, long way from home."

"Um yes, I suppose we are," said Pete.

"Have you ever been there, Bob?" asked Craig.

Bob Atcheson looked a little baffled for a second, then murmured thoughtfully, "I've been here, I've been there…and I've been a few places in between. Bing Bing! You understand me?"

"Of course," said Craig, at a loss.

"What's your mission, little brother?"

Craig guessed this meant what is the purpose of your visit and was about to reply "We're on holiday," or something equally bland when for some reason a slogan from the Easy Rider poster came to mind.

"We're looking for America," he said, trying but failing to inject the same laid back gravitas to his words as Bob.

Bob nodded solemnly.

"It sure is lost. Maybe it's just around the corner, but then again, maybe it's around the corner after that. I ain't never found it, that's for sure…never even been close."

Bob's eyes had started to glaze into the middle distance.

"Bobby's one of my favourite regulars," said Mimi giving him his beer, "he's a sweetie and he has a unique take on life."

"Ooh baby, that's where it's at," said Bob, returning to Earth's orbit, with a sharp intake of breath and a shake of the head.

A familiar looking figure in a vest and baseball cap then burst into the bar, but holding the door open, still yelling at somebody outside, "Yeah, fuck you too, baby!"

He strode up behind Bob Atcheson, and pretended to spit on his shiny dome and polish it with his forearms without quite making contact. Then he leant over as if peering at his reflection:

"I'm looking good!" he exclaimed.

"For a horse's ass, Travis!" growled the Texas Chainsaw extra who then made a deranged guffawing noise, presumably amused at his own witticism.

With the reactions of a brontosaurus, Bob Atcheson finally sensed that someone was standing behind him and turned round, by which time Travis had walked on, leaving Bob looking very confused.

Pete nudged Craig, "That was the guy from next door who was playing pool."

"Oh yeah, of course," said Craig, thinking he didn't seem half as scary now.

"Hey, Mimi baby, get me a slice of pepperoni while I'm in the john," called out Travis as he disappeared around the back.

"On the tab, I suppose," called out Mimi with a tad of mockery.

"Yeah, but I got a feeling tonight's my lucky night," floated back the disembodied response.

"Wow, I think I just had a deja vu," deadpanned Mimi.

"Do you reckon he's a pool hustler?" asked Craig.

As Pete shrugged, Mimi tittered, "Travis thinks he's a hustler, but in actual fact, he's a joker."

She moved away to put in Travis's order.

Thirty minutes later, Pete was raving about his own slice of pizza and Craig was feeling a little intoxicated, as much by the atmosphere as the alcohol. The place had really filled out all of a sudden and was starting to buzz.

"Pimp at two o'clock," said Pete.

Craig span around to look behind him.

"No, *your* two o'clock dummy!" said Pete.

"Oh yeah, I see him," said Craig, now looking over Pete's shoulder, wondering how on earth he hadn't noticed the guy in the fluorescent green suit and floppy purple hat come in.

"He came in the back way," said Pete, his psychic antennae obviously having been dusted recently, "he seemed to be doing some sort of deal with the chef."

As Craig stared, an argument seemed to develop between this guy and a thin white blonde girl in a micro-skirt opposite him. Within seconds, she was in tears and the guy was berating her, seemingly over money. What amazed Craig and Pete was that such an amazing little scene did not really draw attention or even particularly stand out in this environment; just one striking splash of colour in a dense, vibrant action painting.

The man reduced the temperature fleetingly by kissing and caressing the girl's face and arms, whispering reassurances in her ear. Two minutes later, however, the girl was in tears again, her thick mascara running so bad she resembled a mime artist. Then she was on her feet, and storming out of the bar. The guy stood up and angrily yelled, "Two hours, baby! Make sure you're there!" then sat down again and resumed conversation with another girl next to him.

Pete and Craig had relaxed a lot since the Texas Chainsaw extra had left. Mimi told them that he was a 'real loser', his name was 'Cricket' (!?), that he worked in Piper's sometimes (a favour from Joe Junior, whose old man owned the joint); oh yes, and he lived in a cave somewhere up in the Hollywood hills.

"Where else?" said Pete.

They had two more bizarre attempts at conversation with Bob Atcheson, still sat next to them. The sentences were fractured. The dialogue was often incoherent. The gaps between words were large and answers frequently lacked any relationship to the questions asked. And yet, the man oozed charm, charisma, gentleness and oblique humour.

He seemed to imbue several levels to each subject broached, then shift gear randomly from one level to another. Craig could not work out if the guy was an eccentric mystic or a drug-damaged nutter, or both! In mid-flow, talking to Pete about the meaning of 'the eagle', he suddenly broke off. He bent over double as if in pain, his head beneath bar-level.

Then, abruptly, he stood up, turned round, and walked in slow motion towards the jukebox. Hunched over, his head turned to the right, with a hand cupped over his ear. Pete and Craig gasped at each other in amused bewilderment and even a few other customers looked up from their drinks. Only when the man put a hand either side of the jukebox, as if hugging it, and leant in with his head, left profile upturned, did either of them realise that he was enraptured by the music and not having a strange psychotic episode. Craig could not resist wandering over to the jukebox to see what music was responsible for generating this drastic effect on Bob. It was something called 'The Jody Grind' by Horace Silver, which meant nothing at all to Craig, but he made a mental note.

"I love this place," said Pete, slightly drunk by now.

"Ditto," concurred Craig, "you remember our fantasy of running our own bar?"

"Dream, not fantasy!" corrected Pete, blowing cigarette smoke at Craig, in admonishment.

"OK, dream. This is just the sort of vibe I'd want to aim for."

"I'm with you, but that would only work if we were able to set up a bar in the US."

"True," nodded Craig, "you just wouldn't be able to recreate this sort of atmosphere in London."

They delved briefly into practical ways to realise their dream, such as hospitality training, legal compliance, stock choices and getting a bank loan, but the multitude of potential obstacles soon brought them down, and they decided to kick that can down the road and enjoy the ambience instead. Pete drew his attention to a thick-set, soberly-dressed man in his late 40s who was helping himself to some fifty dollar bills from one of the tills.

He was greying at the temples, moustachioed, and wore a solemn, focused expression. Craig noticed he had large bruiser's hands. He turned to Mimi and said something in a low voice about her being late for her shift again. Something about the man's commanding presence made Pete and him sit up straight on their bar stools. Mimi looked respectful as she apologised, and then he vanished into the back of the bar somewhere.

"Was that the boss by any chance?" asked Pete.

"Yeah, that was Joe. Can I get you guys another beer?" asked Mimi.

"Ah, we were just pondering heading off so we don't miss the last bus back to Culver City," Craig said, feeling like a killjoy.

"Why are you staying out in Wheel Alley? There's nothing there, 'cept for tyres, oh and MGM Studios."

Craig smiled in recognition as he pictured the sun-faded donut shops, the weeds growing through the cracks in the sidewalks and the sad pile of tyres on street corners.

"Yes," agreed Pete, "we failed to research our options, and just asked a guy at the airport for his recommendation and he sold it as halfway between the beaches and West Hollywood."

"Trouble is, it's neither one thing nor the other," chimed in Craig.

"Sounds like this guy probably had an agenda, gets a cut from the hotel that he recommends or somethin'," Mimi grumbled with a sympathetic frown.

"We will be revising our address very soon, maybe to this neck of the woods…"

"Glad to hear it. So you guys want one more for the road?"

"Are you trying to get us trousered, young lady?" deadpanned Pete.

Mimi guffawed as she started pouring their beers "I ain't heard that one before. It's classier than blasted or juiced…"

"Or pissed as a newt," added Craig.

"Certainly classier than shit-faced," said Pete.

"My favourite expression for drunk is three sheets to the wind," smiled Mimi.

"Ah yes, the sailing reference," said Pete, "You have certainly outclassed us there."

Mimi passed them their glasses and they raised them aloft in tribute.

"See you again soon, I hope," said Mimi. "Safe journey back to Culver City," she said chuckling.

"I think she likes you," ventured Craig, after Mimi had turned away.

Pete beamed and clinked glasses with Craig.

"To LA," he toasted.

"To Hollywood," Craig zoomed in.

"To Sunset Strip," Pete went further.

"To Piper's," Craig said, reaching the limit.

They both downed their beers in one long go before reluctantly re-joining the outside world for the bus journey ahead. Craig sensed that their futures had just begun.

La Cienega and Sunset

La Cienega and Sunset. Even the names themselves sounded magical. Since they had relocated from Culver City to the Travelodge, a mile or so east of the Strip on Sunset Boulevard, this junction had for Craig become almost a sacred space. There was something about the view from this particular vantage point that thrilled him to the core. Somehow, the carpet of multi-coloured points of light below him lay open for him like a promise; a physical promise, in the pit of his stomach: a promise of freedom.

La Cienega Boulevard itself dropped away from where he stood, and stretched out in a straight line for a mile or two then veered left; searing across this valley of light, aiming for the horizon. Seen from this position on Sunset Boulevard, La Cienega felt like his own astral runway, revealed only to him, a launchpad for his dreams. Craig swayed his head from side to side and felt himself soaring out over this dazzling dreamscape.

He half-closed his eyes and blurred the coloured lights so the motion felt more real. He desperately felt like beating his arms and running towards the view, but couldn't quite blot out the awareness of how he might appear to those around him. This behaviour had become a sort of ritual for Craig ever since the first time the view had stopped him in his tracks. Tonight however felt different.

It felt like he was close to something special, something awesome. He sometimes ran soundtracks in his head to accompany the experience and sometimes to help kick-start it. The Doors were a favourite, perhaps because Jim Morrison's eulogies to his L.A. muse were so appropriate.

Erotic poetry about riding a seven mile-long serpent floating over a shamanic rhythm as he swooped low over Cienega, tracing the glittering lines in the balmy night. Tonight though, the Doors were not right. They seemed too specific, locked into a particular time and mindset. Instead Craig heard universal, timeless music of the spheres (he wasn't sure if he was creating it or merely picking up an existing signal). It touched him at a deeper level and seemed to be hurtling him towards a fate; perhaps, a place of total liberation. The intensity of his feelings suddenly frightened him. He felt himself pulling back and heard the music shift into a mellower phase.

Just at this point, a voice penetrated Craig's peripheral consciousness. A camp drawl but delivered in a high-pitched nasal whine.

"I want to go to London *soooo* bad."

The effect on Craig's psyche was not unlike a sudden introduction to a freezing plunge pool. He was pulled, or sucked, back into his body with a jolt. Irritated by this emotional whiplash, although simultaneously, a little relieved, Craig span around towards the face behind the voice.

"What the fuck for?" he spat, a little aggressively.

Standing next to Pete was a thin, louche-looking young black male with the sweetest of faces.

"Cos' LA's the pits!"

Less than ten minutes earlier, Pete and Craig had squeezed their way out of the rammed French discotheque-inspired Whisky a Go Go, beneath the dancers' cages suspended from the ceiling. They had crossed Sunset Boulevard and encountered this unlikely, sad but graceful, figure sitting on a mailbox and clutching a blue balloon. He was an apparition, a refugee from some hip alternative Neverland.

Being more than slightly bombed this sight struck both Pete and Craig as absurdly comic and they'd both started to laugh. Fortunately, the lost boy with the blue balloon did not take exception to this. He just smiled broadly at them and asked them for a light. Pete was more than slightly suspicious after several dubious encounters in recent days but offered his lighter anyhow. On hearing their voices, the figure gasped theatrically then sprang like a cat from the mailbox.

"I just *looove* those accents."

Here we go again, thought Craig semi-wearily, although if truth be told, he still delighted in the stir caused by their home counties vowels. Pete and Craig were by now taking for granted the quasi-celebrity effect bestowed by their accents (They had passed through the phase of exaggerating them for greater effect).

"Yeah we're Australian," deadpanned Pete, having already been mistaken for an Antipodean twice that day.

"You guys sound English to me. My name's Duane."

Duane accompanied them on their late leisurely stroll back to the Hollywood Travelodge. Duane told them he was a dress designer and before long he'd won over Pete and Craig with that effortless, easy going and wide-open Californian charm they'd seen displayed so often of late. Duane regaled them with tales about famous actors he claimed to know (they were always suckers for that particular game) and spontaneous bursts of falsetto singing.

He twisted himself around lampposts like Gene Kelly and promised to show Pete and Craig around all the cool places in Beverley Hills. Pete grilled him with all the customary questions about clubs, music and women. Duane was apparently bisexual and had many women friends. Craig found himself drifting off into thoughts of Betsy, the barmaid at the Piper bar, then realised they were about to cross La Cienega Boulevard.

Craig instantly regretted his harsh tone in admonishing Duane but could not comprehend how someone could think so highly of London and not appreciate the heavenly virtues of his own home. The irony of the situation did not escape Craig's still-addled brain: Duane's desire was the mirror of their own. Whereas they both longed to be free of England and move to California, he dreamt of escaping LA to live and work in London. Craig gestured vaguely at the magical view south of Sunset Boulevard:

"I mean look at all that, man," (he was increasingly lapsing into hippie patter when stoned) "London's got nothing to compare to this!"

Duane followed Craig's gaze but could find little of interest.

"All I see is a bunch of roads. London's got all those cute shops."

"But..." Craig floundered a little, "La Cienega. La Cienega fucking Boulevard, man!"

His accent vanished as he repeated the Spanish name like an incantation.

"Even sounds beautiful: Cienega and Sunset Boulevard."

Unimpressed, Duane spun his balloon in the charged night air and shouted at the top of his voice, "*Buck in Ham* Palace! Hoo whee, I'd love to go there! What's it like?"

Pete and Craig groaned in unison.

A few hundred yards further down the Strip, Craig gazed up in wonder at the fairy-tale turrets of the Chateau Marmont. He and Pete loved the huge range of architectural styles on Sunset, from Italian Renaissance Revival apartment buildings to modernist glass boxes to art deco towers and Googie diners.

"Street harlots!" screamed Duane.

Craig looked down and realised that Duane was addressing two black hookers on the opposite side of the Strip beneath a gigantic billboard advertising the controversial new Friedkin movie, *Cruising*.

"Come on over here and meet my new friends," yelled Duane.

The two women shimmied their way across the many lanes, giggling as they came. Pete smiled conspiratorially at Craig, "Things are looking up, including my penis!"

Craig gazed across at the girls but the focus of his attention was drawn to their epic backdrop. The Hollywood hills thrust up proudly beneath a resplendent starry sky. Duane introduced them to Nancy and Roxanne. Nancy almost made Pete's night when she pointed at him and announced, "I want this one."

His 'freebie' fantasy was destined to be frustrated once more however, as the girls were on their way to work. They parted ways and Pete watched wistfully as the two gorgeous creatures disappeared into the Imperial Gardens Japanese Restaurant. Duane, who had been enthusiastically encouraging Pete's carnal ambitions, laughed and his eyes shone mischievously as he twirled his blue balloon.

"They was boys."

Bethany

On their first foray to Santa Monica, Pete and Craig had mainly explored west of the pier. This second visit from Hollywood by bus, they ventured to the east side and found themselves on Main Street, parallel to the ocean but set back about three blocks. They had been disappointed by the lack of promising nightspots until they had walked almost the entire length of Main Street before happening upon an intriguing bar called The Oarhouse. Raucous bluesy rock announced the bar half a block before they reached it.

"I wouldn't get your hopes up, I'm sure it's just a bar," teased Craig.

"But the name might be a coded indication that it's pussy central!" Pete boomed, whilst rubbing his thighs vigorously.

Through a window they could make out a chaotic junk collage suspended from the ceiling. This included a bicycle, birdcage and what looked like a stuffed crocodile whilst a sweaty throng of enthusiastic dancers writhed below. The downside was a sizeable queue to get in, which put Craig, who was tired from all the walking, into a negative frame of mind but Pete who had been determinedly upbeat all evening, just saw this as proof it was popular.

After ten minutes standing in line, they were denied entry due to Craig's lack of Californian ID. He waved his fake student card, obtained by his mate Karl from his university, the London School of African and Oriental Studies.

"What's wrong with this, it has a photo?"

The bouncer, however, had clearly not just swallowed the rulebook but had it tattooed on his ample buttocks: The security at the Oarhouse seemed to contradict the bacchanalian spirit of the bar itself.

"I'm sorry sir, but I can only accept a passport or driving license if you don't possess any Californian ID."

"Obviously I don't have Californian ID as I'm English. I don't have a driving license as I don't drive, and I didn't want to risk losing my passport in a nightclub!" moaned Craig, "my friend has his driving license, surely that's enough…"

The man's vacant but implacable stare suggested this was not the case. Something about the obese bouncer's squeaky-voice in tandem with his rigid inflexibility made Craig snap, "I only want to buy a fucking drink for God's sake," he virtually snarled, "I bet I'd have less hassle than this if I wanted to buy a gun!"

A cool looking couple behind yelled support like "wooo, right on!" and "tell the man!" but the only indication of a reaction was a slight raising of one eyebrow, before resuming with a robotic reiteration of the door policy.

"Medication time," said Pete in a singsong voice as he guided Craig away with an arm over his shoulder.

"Sorry," mumbled Craig, "that fat android really wound me up."

Reluctantly they retraced their steps back along Main St.

"There was another bar a couple of blocks down," said Pete.

"Right here in fact," said Craig, stopping in front of Willie Tiffany's, "Hmm, looks a bit dull compared to the Oarhouse…"

The long narrow bar was an elegant parade of ornate mirrors, tiffany lamps and polished chrome.

"Oh well, it's packed," mused Pete, "it can't be all bad. Plus, I spy a babe spying on you."

"Huh?" murmured Craig, before clocking an attractive woman, thirtyish, standing inside near the entrance, smiling right at him. "Oh yeah."

He grinned sheepishly then looked away at Pete who looked like the Big Bad Wolf, virtually licking his lips.

"Mmm, an experienced older woman, my little Craig fish! I think she wants to chase the boy in you away."

Craig couldn't help laughing, simultaneously surprised at his friend's knowledge of Bobby Goldsboro.

"Shut up! Are you coming or not?"

He strode in across the black and white checked floor, trying to look nonchalant but was pretty sure his face had turned a bright shade of lobster. Suddenly, he felt possessed by Woody Allen and felt sure he was going to trip over a table at any second and spill drink down a woman's top. Pete ordered them a couple of Buds at the bar.

'In this vision he showed me a little thing, the size of a hazelnut, and it was round as a ball. I looked at it with the eye of my understanding and thought "What may this be?" And it was generally answered thus: "It is all that is made." I marvelled how it might last, for it seemed it might suddenly have sunk into nothing because of its littleness. And I was answered in my understanding: "It lasts and ever shall, because God loves it."'

The Lady Julian of Norwich

from her Shrine Church: St Julian's, King Street, Norwich

"Were you guys watching the fireworks?" asked the friendly barman with a Village People moustache as he poured the drinks.

"What fireworks?" asked Pete.

"Down at the beach. Quite a big display."

"It's not July 4 already, is it?" said Craig.

The barman laughed, "No, that's a way off; sounds like you guys have been partying hard!" he said, putting the beers down on paper coasters.

"Dedicated hedonists, dear boy," said Pete.

"I love the accents. Are you Australian?"

At this familiar juncture, Craig zoned out and turned around to check the woman was still around. She was smiling right at him which threw him somewhat. He grinned back timidly then turned back to Pete to update him but he was in full flow running down London compared to LA.

He glimpsed back towards the door again. This time she was speaking to another female, with shorter blonde hair, that Craig hadn't noticed before. She was cupping her hand to the other woman's ear, with her mouth almost touching it, probably due to the volume of *Glass Houses* by Billy Joel.

Then they both turned, smiling towards Craig. The friend said something and they both laughed hard. Craig felt a nervous thrill of anticipation and again turned to Pete. He was asking the barman for recommendations for clubs in Santa Monica but luckily another customer needed serving.

"That woman by the door is definitely interested and she has a friend with her."

As Pete turned to assess the friend's finer qualities, she was kissing the longer-haired woman on the cheek and seconds later she was gone.

"Curses," complained Pete, "she looked quite passable as well. I am going to point Percy at the porcelain. Try and strike up conversation with the other one as she clearly thinks you are toy-boy material."

No sooner had Pete vanished into the horde at the far end of the bar than Craig's thin bravado started to evaporate. She was smiling directly at him again and he returned the look for a couple of seconds before once more taking refuge in his glass. He felt angry, almost bitter, at himself for his pathetic shyness.

She obviously likes the look of me and I fancy her, he thought, *so what's the problem?* He guessed it must be down to fear of rejection and tried to reason with himself that it wouldn't be a big deal if they just talked and it came to nothing. He blamed that hideous all-male grammar school for his complete lack of confidence with girls.

Ok he might have been a little shy even in his primary school but at least he could talk to girls in his class then without shrivelling up like a spineless jellyfish. No, it was that hell-hole of a single-sex grammar school that had turned him into a social cripple. Thank God, he'd finally escaped its clutches last year, but how long would the mental scars take to heal? He might be scarred for life.

She was smiling again with a sort of questioning look, as if to say don't you want to talk to me? Where the hell had Pete got to? Craig wished he had some charlie. A line or two in the toilet would be bound to relax him. He desperately ran through some opening lines of patter but they all sounded ridiculous to him.

It didn't help that Craig had an inbuilt loathing of clichés, but would it matter if his first line was a cliché, as they'd soon get beyond this and he could gradually start to reveal his real personality. Maybe he could use the chessboard floor; walk up to her along a diagonal line and say "checkmate": No, too pretentious. Come on, think!

The more he forced himself to think of something, the more his mind became a void. Pete's suggestions would probably all be filthy and unusable, though perhaps if he understood Craig's anguish, he might empathise and come up with something witty or amusing. What on earth was he doing back there anyway? He scanned the heads of those at the back of the bar but no sign. He glanced back in her direction. She was still smiling at him but hang on, what was she doing?

She pointed at him then at her own chest, touching her black silky blouse, then mouthed something with her head to one side, wearing an inquiring expression. For a second, Craig was bewildered and wondered if she was deaf and using sign language. Seeing his confusion, she tried again; pointing at him then doing a sort of circular movement in front of her then opened her hands palms upwards, fingers splayed, in a clearly questioning manner.

The angle of her eyeline made him glimpse down. Straight away he realised she had been pointing at his t-shirt and asking him who was on it. Craig had forgotten he was wearing his Malcolm McDowell shirt, an image taken from his favourite movie *If*. He mimed hitting his head for being so dim-witted and mouthed 'Malcolm McDowell'.

She evidently couldn't lip-read. He realised that she had given him the perfect opportunity to break the ice without the need to resort to a questionable chat-up line. He walked over to her, his head in the here, and now so his anxiety was side-lined for the time being.

She said, "Hi, sorry for the charades, I was just wondering who was on your t-shirt as he looks familiar." She spoke in a gentle Californian drawl as she opened his suede jacket wider to get a better view of the image.

"No, I'm sorry, I finally realised that's what you were asking. It's Malcolm McDowell, from a film called *If.*"

"Oh yeah, Malcolm McDowell' I saw him a while back in a movie called *Oh Lucky Man.* I thought he was really cool actually."

Wow, thought Craig, *she watches Lindsay Anderson films, this is a sign!*

"That was made by the same director. He was sort of playing the same character a few years later on."

"Oh OK, I must check that out. *If* did you say?"

"Yeah, it's probably my favourite film actually about revolution in an English public school."

Oh, oh, thought Craig, *put the brakes on, don't babble, but it was too late*; the mouth was speeding faster than the brain. "McDowell's character ends up mowing down teachers from a roof with a machine gun. I used to identify with him all the time at school."

"So you're English, right?" she interjected, luckily not seeming to assume he was a nutter likely to go on a gun rampage.

"Yes, that's right, my name is Craig by the way."

"Pleased to meet you, Craig, I'm Bethany, call me Beth. Your friend looks slightly like him doesn't he…"

His heart sunk briefly, thinking it was really Pete she fancied and she was using Craig to get to him.

"Pete, I suppose he does a little bit, it's probably the insolent expression."

Beth laughed and said, "I did briefly wonder if you were wearing a t-shirt with your friend's face on!"

Craig laughed uncertainly, "I might be a little strange sometimes but not that weird, Beth! I think Pete looks more like Michael York actually."

A look of mild concern crossed Beth's pretty brown eyes and she brushed his hand.

"Where did your friend go?"

"He went to the, er…rest-room, but that was ages ago."

Beth looked over his shoulder and said, "Oh, there he is, talking to David."

"David?" queried Craig.

"The barman, he's a friend of mine. Shouldn't we ask him to join us?"

Another flicker of doubt, but Craig quickly banished it. He surprisingly now felt quite confident on his own. "Oh, I'm sure he's fine chatting to David. Let me get you a drink and I'll check on him."

"Well, thanks, Craig, I'll have a beer please."

He surfed on over to the bar, riding a wave of teenage optimism and excitement, grinning like a loon. David was serving someone else, so Pete was on his own.

"Wow man, she's great. She seems to think you look like Malcolm McDowell."

Pete beamed, "Hmm, clearly she's using you to get to my dick."

Craig flinched as his own doubt was voiced aloud, "Shut up, you old tart, do you want a beer?"

Pete slapped him on the shoulder and rubbed his hands together characteristically, "I'm proud of my little protégé; he's found a Mrs Robinson. Don't blow it droning on about obscure post-punk nonsense!"

Craig felt a surge of warmth for his comrade.

"She asked if you wanted to join us…"

"Certainly not, I'd cramp your style, or blow her away with my McDowellesque charms. Buy me a beer and get back in there!"

Two beers later, Craig was convinced he'd found a soul mate. Beth was warm, funny, clever and also very lithe. She was wearing a pretty loose black top fringed with colourful flowers over her silk blouse and skin-tight satin black trousers which Craig tried not to stare at. Also it turned out, she was into post-punk herself, almost as much as he was, having grown weary of the three chord limitations of most LA punk bands.

Whereas most English girls he'd known had a brittle, sharp but reserved manner and were often casually cruel, Beth made him feel special, flattering him slightly and making him laugh. She was full of interesting, strong opinions. He wondered how much of this was down to her age which he guessed was between 28 and 32. She had a mature self-awareness and self-confidence that made him feel at ease and soothed his insecurities.

Beneath the surface, he also sensed a vulnerability and softness which prevented her self-assurance from being too daunting and which attracted him. He reflected on Pete's Mrs Robinson comment whilst Beth bought more drinks and laughed to himself. He had often daydreamed about older experienced women who made him feel comfortable, whilst seducing him with unashamed directness and that was just how this felt but even better than he'd imagined.

He looked back to the bar and Pete caught his eye then gave a crude impression of cunnilingus involving his tongue and hands. Craig looked nervously around to check that Beth wasn't looking. She was turned the other way ordering their drinks; he relaxed and laughed at Pete's Carry On antics.

The more Craig talked to Beth the more in awe he became. She had run away from home aged sixteen and gone to live in Haight-Ashbury for a while, dropping acid with freaks almost daily. She'd also been friends with the Seeds and Iron Butterfly and even Ray Manzarek back in the day.

She suddenly asked him if he wanted to come back to hers which was nearby. He said he'd love to, realising it must be quite late and that he'd lost sense of time. Then he remembered Pete. Reading his mind, Beth said, "Your friend is welcome to come back too."

"That's very kind of you, I can ask him."

He caught Pete's eye within seconds, even though he was ensconced on a bar stool talking to a young couple. He appeared to be saying goodbye in fact and kissed the female then waved goodbye to David the barman. He walked over to Craig. Craig introduced him to Beth. Beth said, "Pleased to meet you."

Pete raised her hand and kissed it theatrically, saying "The pleasure is all mine."

"I apologise for him, Beth," said Craig.

Beth laughed, "Why, he's charming."

"You have no idea…" said Craig ominously.

"I've just invited Craig back to mine which is only a few blocks away and wondered if you'd like to join us."

"No thanks, I'll be off," said Pete quite briskly. *He'd obviously pictured this coming and prepared his exit*, thought Craig.

"Are you sure?" queried Beth. "Aren't you staying miles away in Hollywood or something?"

"Yes, but that's fine, I'll walk or get a bus back."

"I could drive you back in the morning. You could sleep on my couch…"

Pete was already walking away, his mind evidently made up.

Craig wasn't sure if he detected a hint of resentment or even jealousy in his tone.

"I'll be fine. See you tomorrow, Craig, at some point. Have fun."

After a couple of seconds, he turned back and called out, "Be gentle with him."

Craig cringed but was also relieved it wasn't something more embarrassing. Beth, sweetly, seemed genuinely concerned for Pete's welfare.

"Do you think he'll be OK? The buses won't be very frequent and he'll probably need to switch and catch another. It might take him hours. Do you think you should go after him and try to change his mind?"

"Nah, he'll be fine, he loves walking. Don't worry." He wondered if he was sounding a little cavalier about his friend's welfare.

"OK," she smiled, "it's this way," she gestured towards the Oarhouse and Venice, and held his hand, which made Craig feel warm and gooey inside like candy floss, or cotton candy as he'd recently learnt they called it over here. *I am floating on a cotton candy cloud*, he thought.

*

Wow! What a way to lose my virginity, thought Craig, nestling up to Bethany's naked body. He gazed at the row of exotic candles, almost burnt out; a reflection of the spent passion they had lit for several hours. The first grey hints of dawn were creeping around the edges of the Roman blinds. He stared at Bethany's face, beautiful in repose and looking younger in the soft light without any make up.

He gently kissed her long graceful neck. He felt utterly sated and more truly relaxed than he could ever remember feeling before. *It was hard to know how much of this was down to the lovemaking and how much to the grass; they formed a perfect symbiotic relationship*, thought Craig, *each feeding the other*. Never had he experienced such powerful hallucinogenic cannabis before. The effects were similar to LSD without the full relinquishing of control.

They hadn't even smoked much of it…had they? Last night was already beginning to blur like a fabulously vivid dream slipping away, sinking beneath the conscious depths. Craig had imagined and dreamed about his first full intercourse whilst stoned numerous times so it seemed fitting that that the encounter itself was undergone in a chemically heightened state of awareness. So, in this moment Craig felt that sex and drugs were now cemented together forever.

There was also the scent of a mystical rite about their coming together, the strangely patterned candles, the incense, the ornately designed pipe they had smoked from (until they grew frustrated by it going out and resorted to rolling joints) and there was the music. He had looked through Bethany's impressive record collection in awe and she let him choose the soundtrack to their sexual union. He was amazed that she owned his two favourite albums of all time; the Stones wildest, most experimental album, the criminally underrated *'Their Satanic Majesties Request'* and Love's sparkling masterpiece *'Forever Changes'*, both products of 1967s altered states.

There were times when the sex became so intense and abandoned, and the music sounded so strange through the doped haze, that Craig was not sure who, or what, he was making love to. Beth seemed to shape shift as they fucked; one second a serene high priestess and the next a carnivorous wild beast. He vaguely recalled briefly glimpsing her past as a giggling young girl and her future as a doddery white-haired old lady.

Bizarre images had reared up like a ghost train bursting out through her left ear, turning around sharply and disappearing back inside. He'd seen seahorses in her hair and galaxies forming in her eyes. As she straddled him, bucking wildly, sweat glistening above her cleavage, he recalled fearing for a moment that she was a witch or sorcerer, sucking his psychic energy dry, whilst candle shadows danced woozily on the walls in the red glow of a scarf-laden lamp, to the beat of a swampy tribal jam.

The music did not follow the script laid down in the etched grooves but roamed far outside their vinyl remit, improvising and forever changing. He must ask her if the records changed for her too when she woke up. He smiled as he remembered his initial nerves, his pained embarrassment and lack of confidence all being swept away by Bethany's warmth and his own desire.

He did not feel that his Mrs Robinson episode had made a man of him so much as set his soul free. Now he was forever changed. He drifted off to the mournful cries of seagulls outside.

Shandy and the Silver Flask

Walking back east down Sunset, having cashed some traveller's cheques late one morning, Craig was trying to keep up with Pete's long strides. He reflected that everything in LA seemed to dissolve into the distance. Even stuff that was close up like the blue trashcan in front of them.

Back in London everything was sharp and in focus as if seen through a wide-angle lens. Bethany would probably say it's a smog thing, though to Craig there was just a pleasant haziness to things that encouraged a dreamy train of thought.

"So Craigness, over breakfast we need to focus on the issue in hand, to stay in Hollywood or move out to the beach. Let's go to Denny's for a change."

Denny's was almost opposite the Travelodge so it was odd that they had not tried it out before. The large yellow and red sign ahead of them looked warm and reassuring, underlining Pete's practical and optimistic mood. The airy uncluttered '50s interior with its sharp clear lines made it easier for Craig to focus his thoughts.

They sat on leather swivel-chairs at the long curved counter, and Pete contemplated the oversized leather-bound menu. An attractive blonde waitress, probably in her late 20s, smiled warmly at Craig as she passed.

"Be right with you guys."

Seconds later, Pete had ordered coffee, eggs 'over easy', bacon and hash browns.

"Don't get excited, dear boy, they're not what you think!" Pete said smirking at the waitress.

She said coolly, "You never know, if you play your cards right…" and turned beaming at Craig once more.

Craig coughed and glanced at his friend with raised eyebrows before ordering a coffee and a round of toast for himself. She scribbled on her little pad then looked at him again.

"Were you at the Whisky last night by any chance?"

"Yes," he said surprised once more. "Were you there?"

"Nah, I had to study."

Letting us know she's bright, not just a waitress, thought Craig.

"So, are you psychic then?" he asked.

"I just recognised the stamp on your hand," she said, nodding towards the red ink blotch on the back of his left hand.

"Ah yes, I clearly didn't wash very thoroughly this morning." She's observant too.

"How were X then?"

Impressive, Craig thought, *she knows what's happening, locally at least.*

"Very good, especially when the keyboard player from the Doors joined them for a few songs."

"Oh crap, I missed Ray?"

Craig was even more impressed that she knew Manzarek's name, but at the same time slightly put off by the way she called him by his first name as if they were personal friends. Unless they were of course…

"Sorry to interrupt the fascinating musical banter," piped up Pete, "but I wonder if you might have a pen we could borrow…"

Craig wondered fleetingly if he was reminding her that she was a waitress, perhaps a little jealous that she seemed to be more drawn towards him.

"Oh sure," she said and moved off in the direction of the till.

"Bit full of herself, but not bad," he pontificated, then added with a grin, "think you could be in there…"

"Just a new wave connection," he said dismissively, whilst secretly buoyed up that his friend shared the same instinct.

"Thank you, my dear," said Pete when she returned with a biro.

"So, you guys are English huh?"

"No, Canadian," replied Craig straight-faced.

"He jests, Shandy," said Pete, indicating that he'd clocked her little plastic name tag. "We are indeed from that sceptred isle."

"Sceptic isle," mumbled Craig, "from London actually." This always sounded hipper than an obscure suburban town in Essex.

"Oh really, which part?" Shandy enquired. This made it trickier as he didn't want to have to expand the fib, so he obfuscated: "Oh, the Eastern end of the Central Line."

"That's the red one right?" She was obviously on the ball about London too.

"Pete's from Finchley…on the black line," he added with a hint of mockery.

"Like Camden Town," she drawled, "I love that place."

They learnt that she and a friend stayed in London for a few years back when they toured Europe. Engrossed in the conversation, Craig barely noticed the thin grey figure in a crumpled suit jacket and dirty checked shirt slouch onto the swivel chair next to him, until he blew cigarette smoke into his face. The man was clearly eavesdropping on the conversation.

Shandy broke off her reminiscences with a rather obvious sigh and took the man's coffee order curtly after reminding him that they didn't serve alcohol. Judging by his breath, he'd already consumed a fair amount that morning. He managed to knock Craig's elbow twice within a minute, and apparently laughed at him and muttered something under his breath before dropping his cigarette packet on the floor.

"You are such a nutter magnet, Craig; they flock to you," grinned Pete as the man lurched sideways at a precarious angle to retrieve them.

Using a napkin they started on a list of pros and cons of moving to the beach.

"Nearness to Bethany," suggested Craig, kicking off the pros.

"Craig crumpet on tap," translated Pete verbally and in writing.

"The pier," ventured Pete.

"Counter-culture ambience," said Craig.

"Weird hippy shit," wrote Pete.

The man surreptitiously pulled out a silver hip flask from his jacket pocket and poured something into his coffee.

"That camera obscura thing."

"Agreed," said Pete.

"Hey, you look like the Queen of England," proclaimed the drunk out of the blue, staring at Craig. Pete laughed loudly as Craig glared at the man, more offended by the royalist sentiment than the gender issue.

"How about cons," he said turning back to the list.

"More bars," started Pete.

"And more venues," said Craig.

"Closer to the action," said Pete, "and those delicious ladies of the night."

"More glamour I suppose," concurred Craig.

"More glaaamour," mimicked his neighbour in an exaggerated English accent.

Pete laughed aloud again, annoying Craig further. He turned to his left.

"What's your problem mate?"

"Haha, maaate…" slurred the man in tortured Dick Van Dyke vowels.

Craig felt fury rising and was on the verge of spitting out an acerbic putdown when the man suddenly slapped him on the shoulder in a seemingly affectionate manner. Craig's anger deflated like a burst balloon.

"I met Montgomery once. He was a bit of a fag."

Craig noticed a broad smile spread across Pete's face.

"Now General Patton, he was a real man. He liked me; he gave me a cigar."

"Tell us more…" purred Pete, offering his lighter to the man whose cigarette had gone out.

Before long, they were caught like flies in the man's preposterous web of tales about his colourful exploits in World War Two. The American Spike Milligan had apparently spearheaded a successful mission to destroy Hitler's personal communications network along with the fabulously named Dr Saxx. When Pete asked if these fantastic adventures were immortalised in print, the man merely made vague reference to state secrets and national security.

Shandy came and refilled their coffee cups. Pete pointed at the man's almost empty cup and she reluctantly refilled this too.

"Do you want to hear how me and Dr Saxx smuggled gold bullion out of Germany?"

Shandy tutted loudly and flounced away down the other end of the counter. The silver hip flask made another reappearance and Pete smiled at Craig. After a couple more minutes of listening to Captain America, Craig began to think he should have put more effort into chatting up Shandy.

Disappointingly, she seemed to have disappeared. Just as he was about to learn how General Patton had stepped in to prevent our hero being court martialled, she reappeared out of uniform and kissed a female colleague goodbye. She looked across and he caught her eye. He waved a dollar bill and said, "Don't forget your tip." She laughed and walked over and thanked him.

"Are you guys staying in LA long?"

"For a while," he said hoping it made them sound mysterious.

"You know this guy's full of shit right?" she sounded halfway between arrogant and protective.

"Ha, one or two of his tales were on the tall side," he whispered back, "but he's amusing us."

Pete realised she was making an exit and called out, "Farewell, Shandy, my dear. I hope we meet again."

"Likewise," she laughed and said to Craig, "your friend's a riot."

"He should be arrested, certainly."

"Perhaps we could catch another gig," Shandy said in a throwaway fashion, "Anyway, see ya later."

"I love you, baby," said the man in a sing-song voice, then blew her a kiss and burped.

She stuck out her tongue at him, then threw her bag over her shoulder and walked out.

"Hey, Craig," said Pete, "shall I add Shandy to the reasons to stay in Hollywood column...? What say we all adjourn to Piper's as the sun is clearly over the yardarm?"

Floating in the Void

So this is heaven, thought Craig to himself as he squinted up at the cobalt blue splendour. This was possibly the bluest sky he had ever witnessed, untroubled by even a fleck of cloud. Not even the hint of a fleck. The temperature felt somewhere between 80 and 85 degrees Fahrenheit. Just right. Hot but not too hot. The air unstirring and yet vibrating.

The day was positively rhyming. Craig languidly pushed the airbed away from the side of the pool with a slight rotating motion. The sun suddenly appeared in his line of vision, momentarily dazzling him. He paddled across the perfect circle and stretched out for his black wraparound shades that were perched on 'The Crucible' atop his towel-laden sun-lounger.

That was better, the sparkling myriad of reflections on the water was softer now. He lay back and gazed up again at the majesty above him. *I am The Graduate*, he thought to himself as an image of a young Dustin Hoffman in shades floating in a Californian pool slid into his mind's eye.

This quickly dissolved into Bethany in seductive black lingerie but he consciously banished the image; he didn't want to get a hard-on out here in a scanty pair of Speedos! He looked down as the 'Sunset Travelodge' sign span slowly into his field of vision. 'Doubles/Twins—$30, Singles—$20.' Craig frowned at the large red plastic numerals as they reminded him that they hadn't paid for that day's board yet.

The strange little old lady might pop out of her office and harangue him at any moment. Pete probably had enough cash on him but he had gone for a walk to the 7-11, further up Sunset, for some fags.

The trouble with Pete was that he got restless very quickly. He had managed to sit by the pool for thirty minutes browsing through an *L.A. Weekly* and a book about the Irish potato famine (The range of Pete's reading always impressed him). This was pretty good going for him, but he hadn't quite got as far as taking a dip or indeed taking his shirt off.

51

Craig, on the other hand, was sinking gradually into a state of extreme relaxation; wallowing in the unbelievable luxury of having the pool to himself on a day like this. Not only that, someone had left a fully-inflated airbed by the side of the pool. *Perhaps it belongs to the manager*, he thought idly. *Who cares? I'm not harming it.*

The pool was unusually situated at the front of the motel in a raised area to one side of the lot. It was divided by a tall wall from the side road flanking the motel, but the view of Sunset Boulevard at the front was unimpeded which suited Craig fine. To many people, such as Craig's parents, the notion of an idyllic pool would have to involve a quiet exclusive setting, preferably overlooking the sea.

Craig had nothing against such a notion however, he had discovered paradise on a large noisy and hectic road, bang in the middle of a huge built-up urban environment. He loved checking out the activity on the Strip, be it ridiculously large stretch limos and glamorous blondes in shiny sports cars, or at the other end of the scale, winos rooting through trashcans or bag ladies wheeling along all their sad possessions in supermarket trollies. He heard a few bars of music from a car radio somewhere.

The melody sounded familiar but he couldn't place the tune until he heard the flute. Of course, *California Dreaming* by the Mamas and Papas. He could clearly recall an Essex bedroom 5 years earlier, when he'd listened over and over to the same song trying to conjure up images of the golden State. He chuckled aloud at the irony.

He glided back into the centre of the pool. The water must have been close to body temperature as Craig kept losing his sense of touch. This must be similar to laying in a sensory deprivation tank he thought. He had to waggle his hands in the water or kick his feet to restore his sense of feeling.

He smiled and felt his body relax even more, travelling deeper, further into himself. He felt rootless and free. As he gazed up at the firmament, he imagined he was becoming gradually weightless and was rising up like a hot air balloon into the ether, drifting higher and higher, elevating him to a new level of calmness and peace, in the serene silent void. He paddled gently with his right hand only so that his airbed started to spin in slow-motion circles.

This circular motion seemed to take on a life of its own and another cinematic image bubbled up into his consciousness. Now he was Kubrick's circular space station, elegantly wheeling and pirouetting in space to the graceful strains of 'The Blue Danube'.

He imagined looking down at himself from a great height. The pool was a beautiful blue eye and he was the pupil dilating at the centre. This image triggered a memory from junior school days when he and his friend Keith had walked over the fields and laid face up on a mound.

They had tried to imagine that they were in a helicopter looking down, and the sky was in fact the sea way beneath them. When the image had felt real enough to both of them, they had shouted out "Geronimo" and both leapt out into oblivion. The sense of excitement shifting gear into an icy terror felt surprisingly fresh to Craig. He felt goose pimples ripple across his arms and shivered.

The sky above him suddenly seemed too far away. A wave of reverse vertigo hit him and his stomach convulsed slightly as he felt he might fall at any second into this boundless sky. He looked back down at the row of motel chalets to restore his sense of perspective and equilibrium, but his eyes were soon drawn back to the deep blue vastness which was no longer just awesome but oppressive and frightening in its sheer scale and blankness.

His sensitivity to space and distance led him to contemplate how far away from home he was, 8,000 miles or so away from his family and friends. He tried to keep this as just an abstract thought but his jolt of anxiety had darkened his mood; thoughts were mutating into feelings and he was powerless to stop it. Moments later, he was missing his mother's smile; backgammon games with his father; even the 1000cc purr of his cat Merlin.

Tears filled his eyes. He felt so far away from everything he really loved. As he realised this a deeper pain welled up in him. He felt compelled to grant this pain a name; the word 'Rachel' left his lips a cracked whisper and hovered in the air above him. The word itself seemed to create a huge painful lump in his throat.

Why hadn't he phoned her? Now he would never see her again. He couldn't stand this sense of loss, it was still a raw open wound which surprised him; he had thought he was getting over it. He took a deep breath and with an effort he swallowed the pain back down.

After a while, all his anxiety and personal feelings became more distant, leaving a drained mood as desolate and hollow as the empty sky above him. It did not matter to him that he was clearly insignificant in the immensity of it all. He knew beyond doubt that he was face to face with eternity, that all human pursuits, ideas, emotions, all human endeavour would be sucked up into the merciless blue abyss and annihilated utterly.

Craig felt a profound but removed wave of sadness for humankind which could evaporate in the blink of an eye whilst the indifferent sky would not even register its passing. Rather than a self-pitying sadness, it was an impersonal sort of melancholy that inhabited him, permeating the core of his being.

"Hey lobster-face!" a remote voice called from another galaxy. He felt like an astral traveller exploring the distant frozen wastes of Jupiter, only for his umbilical silver thread to suddenly snap like an inertia reel seat belt set to warp factor nine; yanking him back through the Milky Way and crashing into his physical body. His first sight on re-entry was Pete standing at the poolside holding a brown paper bag and wearing an enormous grin.

"I think I'm in love. She works at the 7-11. She's so cute you wouldn't believe it and she talked to me for ages, at least five minutes. I think I'll ask her out. Where should I take her? We could go back and pretend we forgot to buy something so you can check her out."

During this barrage, Craig sat up on the airbed dazed with a sort of astral jet-lag. He scratched his head and wondered what on earth all that was about. How could he possibly veer from ecstasy to misery to epic melancholia in so short a time?

"Guess what I've got!" said Pete as he dipped a hand into the bag and slowly, teasingly produced a familiar blue bag of chocolate chip cookies. In perfect harmony, they both sang out the brand name, "Chips Ahoy!" like a pair of camp sailors from a Carry On film.

Craig was too shell-shocked to analyse his experience further so he pushed it for now under the magic carpet called Los Angeles.

Beyond Baroque

Craig laid back his head on the head-rest and started to giggle. Beth looked across at him.

"What is it?"

He was hopelessly, beautifully stoned. Great smeary washes of red and green neon flashed upon the drizzle-flecked windscreen. Every new turn revealed another dazzling impressionist view of the Hollywood night. To the left, dozens of elongated pillars of white light were ghosting on the shiny asphalt whilst they followed the parallel reflected forest of red brake lights.

Tall streetlights threw soft blue-white splashes over the ever-changing canvas, blurrily refracted in the new sheen of raindrops. Craig found the shifting colour shapes fascinating and disorientating. Every now and then, when the rain built up on the windscreen before being smeared by the intermittent wipers, he became unlocked from his spatial sense altogether and just perceived blocks of colour and light.

Sparkly red, white and blue crystals of light exploded in kaleidoscope. A stylised 'Stars and Stripes' was forming itself in front of him out of headlights, brake lights, streetlights and the rain. This is what caused him to laugh.

"I just hallucinated the US flag from all this red, white and blue light," he offered.

"Oh yeah, I've had that when it's raining," Beth said. "I thought you might have been laughing at my driving."

"No way," he stressed, "I'm amazed that you can drive at all in this state."

"It's mostly instinct right now," she laughed, pulling up at a red light beneath a towering billboard poster for 'The Empire Strikes Back'.

"Remind me where we're going," said Craig.

"Right now?" said Beth, changing into first gear.

"As opposed to yesterday, yeah." Craig started to giggle again.

Beth grinned across at him then swung a left turn.

"I thought you might've been talking on a more um…broad scale."

"What? Like we as in mankind?"

"Uh, possibly…or just you and me."

"Oh I see," said Craig, "are you worried then?"

"Huh, no, I just thought you were after a status check."

Beth's forehead crinkled slightly in a nervous frown which struck Craig as absurdly cute. She sat upright, almost huddled over the steering wheel, her chair pulled as far forward as it could go. His own seat was inclined such that he was almost horizontal and from this laid-back position, he gazed at her.

"So, where are we going?" he said, an involuntary laugh in his voice.

"Right now?"

"Yes, right now, in a purely geographical sense."

"Actually I've forgotten," she admitted sheepishly and they both burst into guffaws. Craig had a flashback to earlier on when they had both found the sight of a large revolving chicken on a supermarket roof painfully funny. Beth almost swerved into a Chevy in the next lane, causing an angry-looking bespectacled driver to sound his horn.

Craig spotted a small orange ball perched on the top of the car aerial. He wound his window down a little and yelled, "Hey man, at least our driving isn't so bad that people are throwing fruit at the fucking car."

The man looked a little confused. Craig pointed at the little orange blob by way of explanation but by then, the man was braking and looking at the car in front.

"Fruit? I don't see any fruit," said Beth, looking as confused as the Chevy driver.

"I was referring to the ridiculous satsuma stuck on his aerial."

"Oh, the 76 ball," Beth said before starting to shake with laughter again.

"The what?"

"Ah, you do make me laugh. They give those balls out at gas stations as a dumb gimmick. Lots of people have them. My mum has one. Hey, I've remembered where we're going, 'Beyond Baroque'."

She abruptly changed lane, waited for a gap then did a reckless but impressively smooth U-turn.

"Beyond Baroque…Rococco perhaps? Kitsch?"

"Weird name, isn't it. Sounds a bit faggy. I've only been there once. It's a bit of a dive but there's an interesting sounding band on tonight. Mind if I put KROQ on?"

"Sounds!" he enthused, "good idea."

Craig immediately recognised the frosty tones of Siouxsie Sioux.

"The Banshees, *Christine* I think," he said, showing off.

"Impressive," said Beth. "It sounds good."

She turned up the volume, and Craig let the ice-maiden drape his addled mind with lurid crystal shapes – or were these just the neon smears? The sounds were becoming indistinguishable from the patterns on the windscreen. Beth put the wipers back on full and it did not surprise him that they were in perfect synch with the drums. His eyes were drawn to the jerky motions of the spots along the edges that didn't disappear but ran in long unpredictable streaks, and his mind tried to trace the twisted path the evening had taken to reach this point.

Like the view through the windscreen, however, his recall was a little blurred; he could remember two or three clubs or venues and one bar, maybe two – or were these the bars inside the venues? Beth was clearly well versed in the ways of the LA rock circuit and had introduced him to a couple of musicians and a DJ they'd run into somewhere along the way. She knew all the back and side entrances of the clubs and if they were locked or manned; and if it came to playing the guest list game with security she was a smooth operator.

At the Starwood, or it could have been the Troubadour, she had bluffed their way in, employing her wide smile and feminine charms to the hilt only for them to both detest the band and leave again within 20 minutes. They had taken in the Rainbow on the Strip as well at some point, because Craig remembered them taking the piss out of 'rock god' Van Halen standing next to them at the bar in ridiculously tight leopard skin-print lycra pants, flanked by two young simpering blondes.

He became vaguely aware of a thin nasal voice droning on the radio.

"This is Rodney Bigenheimer," said Beth. "He plays some great stuff, especially the latest English new wave records. He always dug the English scene; in the '60s he got behind the Beatles and the Stones and the whole British invasion thing, and even opened a club on the Strip called 'The English Disco' or something. He's got a thing about young girls though…like Kim Fowley."

"How young?" asked Craig.

"Barely legal," answered Beth.

"Have you met him?"

"Oh yeah, loadsa times. You can't go anywhere in this town without running into Rodney."

"I'm Rodney on the ROQ," announced the car radio, "and this is P.I.L."

"Excellent!" said Craig.

Religion was almost two years old already but it had never sounded so fresh or powerful before. The instrumentation on the track had always sounded sparse but now there seemed to be a 500 yard gap between each instrument. There was a depth and density to the song Craig had never appreciated before. Lydon's theatrical venom, still intact from the Pistols, was harnessed into a vicious diatribe against the Church complete with sanctimonious priests compared to animals.

The scabrous couplets spat out like phlegm. Craig sat transfixed by the sheer intensity of the acerbic attack ending on the notorious blasphemy about the new inhabitant in heaven.

"Phew, rock'n'roll eh?" he said as the song reached its conclusion then segued into an anti-disco message.

"For sure," said Beth, "I'd love to go back and play that to my Sunday school teacher. Ah, here we are and it's stopped raining."

They had turned into a sideroad and Beth almost overshot the sole available parking space before swerving into it at 20mph and luckily hitting the kerb rather than the car in front. The bump jolted Craig out of his reverie.

He was dimly aware of being in a semi-residential neighbourhood as he squelched unsteadily across a grass verge with Beth. Loud raucous waves of noise reverberated out towards them from a curious looking building down the street. Was it a converted church or just some modernist weirdness?

In fact, as the shape kept shifting and distorting around the edges, Craig could not be sure if it really was an unusual building or if this was just his current perception of it. Perhaps, the last joint had suddenly caught up with him or the jolt as they parked had scrambled his senses further.

"Oow! Don't worry, it's only a foot; I've got a spare one," deadpanned Beth. Craig apologised and put some real energy into maintaining a straight line except that several large puddles kept sabotaging his plan. The front door swung open and even from 20 yards away they could make out a dense sea of people squirming inside.

"Jeez, it's sardine city!" said Beth.

One beefy po-faced man with a very black moustache stood outside. What is it with all the moustaches in this town, pondered Craig. You could go for days at home without seeing one, outside of a whiskers and beard combo. Surely not all these men were gay.

Somebody from inside pulled the door closed again. Craig hung back as Beth approached the bouncer.

"Mary, plus one," she said confidently.

The guy looked at the two lists attached to his clipboard and said, "Sorry, it's not here."

With a convincing look of disbelief and dismay, Beth said, "Do you mind if I take a look?"

"Help yourself," he shrugged.

Scanning the lists quickly she said, "Oh here we are, it's OK." The bouncer followed the direction of her extended index finger with his eyes.

"But this says Marcia plus one."

She just said, "Yeah, that's my real name but no one uses it usually."

Just for a second the moustache bristled and Craig thought he was going to argue the point, but then just nodded and stood to one side, even wishing them both a good evening. Craig managed to stifle his laughter until they were through the door and into the maelstrom.

"That was great. Why Mary?"

"It's a common name. There's a good chance there'll be one on the list or a Mary-Lou or Mary-Jane or something. Anyway what are you drinking?"

As they squeezed their way forward the noise level threatened to flatten them. It was ear-bleedingly loud. This, the suffocating heat and the fact that there were far too many people in too small a space gave Craig the sensation he was wading through quicksand. They decided to give up after less than 20 feet then Beth peeled off and inched her way to the right towards the bar. Craig asked a young, bouncy, gum-chewing teenager next to him who the band was.

"Huh?" was the response. He didn't know if the noise or the accent were impeding the communication most. He tried again through a cupped hand.

"Wha...oh, the band, they're called Human Hands!" the youth virtually screamed in his ear from point blank range. His head recoiled automatically with the pain but he covered this up with a thin smile and a raised thumb. As the song wore on he wondered why he'd bothered to find out.

The band were aggressive in a vaguely punk style but the music just seemed to lack any shape or subtlety. Perhaps, it was the poor acoustics of the venue but the next song sounded just the same, thudding repetition and no discernible melody.

Beth tunnelled her way back through the throng clutching two bottles of Heineken.

"Cheers. Bit on the pedestrian side, aren't they," he said discreetly, in case Beth loved them.

"A real crock I'd say."

"What was that?" he asked then moved his ear dangerously near to her mouth.

He needn't have worried, Beth was clearly well practiced in these conditions and kept an audible but pain-free distance, "A crock of shit. The next band should be better. The Wall of Voodoo, I've heard some good things about them."

The band soon lived up to the promise of their name. They looked quite new wavey with their short hair, neat, mostly black clothes and austere expressions. The lead singer particularly fascinated Craig from the start. He wore a brown suit although the jacket didn't last long, unsurprisingly, as sweat was dripping off the walls.

Over a black shirt, he sported an unlikely red country and western shoestring necktie. He had piercing eyes that exuded a cool intelligence and a whole ragbag of facial tics, squints and crooked-mouth mannerisms which strangely complemented the quirky angular sound of the music. He often spoke the lyrics rather than sang them in a wry, sardonic style, sounding like a hip young Raymond Chandler delivering sour film-noir vignettes on the emptiness of LA life.

"I like this guy, he's cool," said Beth, echoing his thoughts.

She produced another laughing cigarette from the little leather bag slung over her shoulder. *Just as I was beginning to straighten out*, he thought. Still, it would be churlish, improper in fact to turn down grass this good. She had a toke and passed it to him.

"This next tune's called *The Call of the West*," announced the singer.

Craig inhaled deeply during the synth-drum intro. Then the guitars and the keyboard came together for a hook line that took the roof of his head clean off. It sounded like a Morricone spaghetti western soundtrack played by the Doors.

A dark ominous sound but with a hint of country twang that fitted the mood like a glove. Lyrics jumped out of the song and ambushed Craig. A reference to a road winding through the hot Mojave and the Jericho signalled the hostile territory the song was heading into. Craig was sucked straight into the heart of this mythic western soundscape.

He strained against the poor sound system and could only make out certain words about a western savage, whiskey, rifles and an unarmed man. Did the singer just say "like you" pointing violently right at Craig? Either way he could feel goosebumps and the little hairs on his arms stand up.

The singer yelped and pulled bug-eyed expressions as he loped and stalked the small stage, cracking the mic-lead like a whip, his body twisting with sudden jerks reminiscent of Ian Curtis. The words he imagined he could hear just kept getting better, blowing Craig like a tumbleweed through the ghost towns of the old West; the singer mentioned spokes of a wheel and spinning around as he whirled his right arm around in large loops and Craig could almost see the stagecoach hurtling through Monument Valley; as he heard the call of the west.

A few yards in front of him, Craig noticed a man with dark straggly hair and beard, turning his head around slowly and staring intently at the crowd. He seemed removed from everyone around him who were either dancing, talking or watching the band. He eventually turned 180 degrees away from the stage until his malevolent gaze fixed just for a moment on him.

Craig shivered. The man continued to survey the crowd. The singer shrieked something about the wilderness.

"Hey, Humphrey Bogart! Don't forget me."

He turned to Beth, bemused for a second then realised she was referring to the fast-shrinking joint in his hand.

"Sorry, I was getting lost in the song," he said, passing it to Beth.

"This is their best number yet," she said with conviction.

"Have you clocked the Charlie Manson clone?"

"No. Where?" she cast her eyes around the crush.

"In front of us, down there…oh, he's gone now. Looked like he was casing the crowd for his next victim."

Craig shut up as he wanted to be reclaimed by the song. The singer was now delivering a rapid-fire stream of consciousness, leaning off the stage, mowing down people in the front couple of rows.

Craig's body which had been vaguely swaying now felt like it might rise up into the air and soar out into the night sky. ...At a line about taking drugs and having some craaaazy sex, Beth squeezed his hand tightly. He looked into her eyes which were sparkling, on fire. The words kept coming, random imagery about chilli, gas stations, plastics, gynaecologists.

Her eyes were sparkling, on fire. As the singer gyrated more and more fiercely, sweat spraying from his matted locks, Craig was being possessed by the music. He felt ecstatic, orgiastic; on the verge of losing control when rant suddenly ended, the tension discharged, and the song swung into the final verse. His body started to relax a little but he felt utterly charged and liberated. He heard someone behind him says, "He does the words differently every time."

Craig could believe this as the rap felt very improvised and spontaneous. He couldn't make out all the words of the final verse but was already looking forward to hunting down the album, assuming there was one, and decoding this transporter of a song in its entirety. The repeated title of the song was gradually overcome by, and drowned in, evocative native American-style chanting.

Beth dropped the butt of the joint on the floor and Craig twisted his suede shoe on it.

"Give America back to the Indians eh."

"You could do a lot worse," said Beth.

Voodoo Reprise

"I can't wait to feel you inside me," said Beth hitting the gas.

Craig slid his hand further up Beth's thigh as they roared down Santa Monica Boulevard heading back to Santa Monica. *It's a shame she's wearing trousers*, he thought as he started gently rubbing her crotch area. He recalled some graffiti they'd seen earlier sprayed across a brick wall—'Don't Wear Underwear'. He'd laughed and said it sounded like a political campaign.

"I haven't worn panties for 3 years now," she'd replied.

Sure enough, he could feel the soft contours of her pussy through the thin black cotton trousers. *It doesn't get much better than this*, he thought to himself. Just as he detected definite signs of moisture seeping through and darkening the fabric, he felt the car steering jerk a little.

"Much as I'm enjoying this, I think you'd better hang fire for a few minutes. I'm a bit nervous of making out at speed since an old boyfriend once came off the road while I gave him a blowjob and turned the car over."

"Whoa!" exclaimed Craig, rapidly but reluctantly retracting his hand.

Partly to distract himself from the ache in his groin, he wound the window down and stuck his head out. The sci-fi metropolis Century City loomed on his left and the elegant manicured lawns of the Los Angeles Country Club tapered off to his right. The rain had passed and now there was a beautiful cool breeze rushing at his face and rifling his hair. He twisted his neck to gaze up at the night sky.

The stars shone with uncanny brilliance behind the teasing veils of scudding clouds and the occasional palm frond in the foreground. He could feel his blood pulsing in his temples. There was a rhythm there. He listened intently then realised it was the Wall of Voodoo song that had possessed him back at the club. He started drumming along to the rhythm on the dashboard.

"Da da da da, da da da da…"

"Call of the West," joined in Beth. "That was just running through my mind too."

Craig loved the spoken word section at the end of the song, but as he couldn't remember any of the lyrics he started improvising.

"People come all the way out here to play chess on the beach, to hop freight trains, stay up all night in Ben Franks, turn right at a red light, try 99 flavours of ice cream, to take acid in the desert and commune with Comanche ghosts then rob a drive-in bank and maybe start their own religion, hunt Grizzly bears then have an orgy in the hot tub… you'll spin round like a wagon wheel…"

"A thousand dreams of the West," bellowed Beth and they both burst into laughter.

Beth turned on to Main Street in Santa Monica.

"Hey, I'm an exile on Main Street," Craig shouted out the window.

Piper's Politics

One afternoon in Piper's something extraordinary happened. Politics sneaked its way into the bar and stirred itself a cocktail. Pete and Craig were seated on their usual barstools listening to Travis relate another of his romantic exploits. This one concerned a bored housewife who found him irresistible, and a jealous husband coming home early to find her feasting herself on Travis's "pocket Cyclops".

The climax of this particular tale involved the husband going for his gun and Travis resorting to jumping off a first floor balcony to escape, wearing only "a shirt and a hard-on." Travis suddenly broke off from his swashbuckling narrative, "I can't believe some of the fucking flakes that walk into this joint!"

Intrigued, Pete and Craig turned around to see what manner of creature could evoke such passionate disapproval. All they saw was a slightly frazzled, washed out looking blonde, in her early 30s; strolling in from Sunset Strip in a hippie skirt, berber jewellery and bare feet. She ordered a Michelob and sat at the bar a few feet away from the others and stared blackly at Travis.

Robert Madigan, the barman, served her. Robert was slim with well-defined biceps. He had a severe receding hairline and a light brown well-trimmed beard that seemed to underline his piercing but compassionate green eyes. His obvious but understated intelligence and dry sense of humour had already won the pair over.

"Don't worry about Travis, he's harmless."

"Brainless more like," she retorted, winning laughs from everyone at the bar except Travis, who just grunted.

Everyone got talking and it turned out the woman was in town to catch the Timothy Leary lecture with Gordon 'Watergate' Liddy. This ignited Craig's interest as she seemed to be a genuine 18-carat original hippie, and in 1980 they were a dying breed. Robert slated Leary for turning into a 'fink' and appearing as a prosecution witness in a drug case against his own lawyer and hippie friends.

The woman, who introduced herself as Sunshine, insisted that he was an underground hero who, along with the Brotherhood of Eternal Love, almost succeeded in transforming the world with LSD. Robert took his customary cynical line and said the Californian counterculture had totally failed to change the world, and instead had turned into a hippie mafia. Through setting up an illicit drugs industry the supposed idealists had instead just descended into crime and links with international terrorism.

Craig had never really trusted Leary, but looked up to other '60s luminaries like Ken Kesey and Abbie Hoffman so he felt obliged to join sides with Sunshine, and praise the achievements of the counterculture like helping to end the Vietnam War. Fuelled by the pitcher of Budweiser he was sharing with Pete, he started to drift into an unfocussed tribute to the legacy of the '60s, the free, laid-back, hedonistic lifestyle of California compared to the grey repressive climate in England with its new far right leadership.

Robert said Craig should wake up and smell the coffee. America would shortly be voting in its own fascist president. Ronald Reagan—a man who, as governor of California in the '60s, wanted even more bombs dropped on Vietnam, and had ordered the police to turn water cannons on hippies who were peacefully protesting in the 'Sunset Strip riots'.

"And a man who was once out-acted by a chimpanzee in a b-movie," added Pete.

Sunshine said she couldn't believe America would really be stupid enough to vote for a man who last year claimed that 80% of air pollution comes not from chimneys and exhaust pipes but from plants and trees. Craig almost choked on his beer laughing. Robert backed up Sunshine's claim, confirming that Reagan had said this in a radio broadcast, and that some opponents had hung posters on trees saying: 'Cut me down before I kill again'.

Travis revealed his deep understanding of US politics, "At least Reagan would sort out this fucking Iranian hostage bullshit, unlike that pussy Carter."

"Sure, Travis, by dropping bombs," chided Robert.

Travis soon warmed to his theme, downing an almost full glass of beer in one gulp and claiming that he could rescue the hostages himself.

"All they gotta do is send me to Iran in a chopper with a handful of goddam grenades; I'd sort that shit out in minutes, man, no problem."

66

Venice

"Portobello by the Sea, I'd call it," said Pete as they passed another palm reading stall.

"Yeah, those mime artists were like a scene out of *Blow Up*," enthused Craig.

They stopped for a while to watch a bronzed guy in cut off jeans spray painting a t-shirt with the ubiquitous image of local god, Jim Morrison. Although the image belonged predictably to the famous session where Jim looked at his Alexander-the Great best (moody, topless, a single string of beads), the shirt looked amazing. The guy was subtly adding delicate splashes of pink, blue and orange via a thin strand of tubing attached to a gas canister beneath the easel in the sand.

"I'm tempted," admitted Craig, pulling out the crumpled wad of dollar bills from his jeans pocket and counting them.

"That's a night less you can afford to stay here, Crayman," smiled Pete smugly.

"S'pose you're right," sighed Craig, burying the cash back deep into his pocket.

"Some of them are a bit gaudy, aren't they," said Pete, nodding at some of the other t-shirts hung up surrounding the artist. *He's right*, thought Craig, casting his eyes over lurid pink Michael Moorcock style warriors and psychedelic Mickey Mouse designs. This made it easier for Craig to walk away.

"I can smell weed again," Pete noted.

"Really?" asked Craig, sniffing the air like a bloodhound, "I can only smell the sea."

"Blimey, look at this one!"

Pete had to sidestep out the way of the oncoming apparition on wheels. They both stared open-mouthed at the tall black figure on roller skates playing an acoustic guitar. He wore kneepads beneath what looked like a white chiffon nightie and lots of chunky jewellery topped off flamboyantly with a sort of skullcap festooned with ostrich feathers.

"How ya doin', boys?" he said as he glided past them, smiling broadly. By the time they'd managed to formulate polite replies, the man was out of earshot.

"I like this place!" said Pete loudly over the roar of surf and the bebop jazz from a nearby cafe.

"I'd have thought it was a bit tacky for you, all this crystals and read-your-aura stuff," mocked Craig.

"No, it's got a genuinely bohemian feel to it…and lots of pussy!"

Craig followed his friend's eyes up Ocean Front Walk, and immediately recognised the pert young behind in tight little blue shorts as the source of the distraction.

"Look at her! She could have been the muse for that Aphrodite painting."

Pete was referring to the well-known Venice mural they'd paid homage to earlier which was a parody of Botticelli's *Birth of Venus* updated to the Venice Boardwalk itself, where the heroine sported a skimpy top, shorts, leggings and roller skates. Craig found it depressing that some moron had spewed ugly black graffiti across Venus's leggings. The mural had impressed both of them as great street art, exactly the sort of vibrant cultural statement lacking in London.

A little further up Ocean Front Walk they passed a fire-eating stand-up comic whose act was coming to a close judging by the storm of applause and the excess of bows.

"Please don't throw money; it might blow away, if you get my drift!"

Pete laughed loudly at this. Further on a woman in a turban was performing acupressure, according to her sign, on a sunburnt comatose man. Just beyond them was a little photographic shop with a 'Models Wanted' sign above the door. In front of the shop, a photographer and assistant were shooting an unlikely applicant: A tall, thin, angular-looking man in outlandish tight white bellbottoms and long pink and rainbow-patterned Doctor Who scarves posed foppishly. Perched precariously on long tangled locks was an undersized cowboy hat studded with sequins.

"This place is wall-to-wall weirdoes," exclaimed Craig.

"I hope that doesn't include us," murmured Pete, gazing at the man's large guitar case crammed into the panier of a tiny bicycle. "Let's take another look at Muscle Beach."

"If you insist," sighed Craig, "but I can't see the attraction myself."

Muscle Beach was an outdoor gym which prided itself on being the birthplace of the Physical Fitness Boom. As this was situated in Santa Monica this meant they had to walk all the way back to where they started from. Craig was used to long treks on foot in London with Pete leading the way, criss-crossing the city from one watering hole to another (the Intrepid Fox in Soho to Blushes in Kings Road, then back to Blackout in South Molton Street…).

Craig could never quite figure out why they couldn't just take the tube like everyone else but he'd secretly grown fond of this ritual. There wasn't a tube option in LA of course, but today's jaunt was nothing, even in the hot sun, after Pete's punishing training programme.

They decided on the twists and turns of the Boardwalk for the journey back which crossed the beach parallel to Ocean Front Walk. There were less of the weekend crowds on the Boardwalk though cyclists, roller skaters and skateboarders were even more prevalent.

"Uh oh," mumbled Craig, looking down.

"What is it?" asked Pete.

"That guy over there, by the side of the skateboarders; I think it's Brad, I met him last week."

"Is he a tosser?"

"No, he's OK, just a bit intense, and I'm not in the mood. Do you remember the day you hired the Caprice Classic?"

Pete furrowed his brow, "Hmm, don't remind me." He'd managed within 3 hours, to somehow crash it into a kerb while turning right at a red light, which immobilised the car, and he'd had to call the hire company and wait an hour for them to pick him up. Craig hadn't even set eyes on the car, let alone had any use out of it.

"Do you remember me telling you that day I went on a bit of a bar crawl in Santa Monica when I met all these strange people…?"

"Vaguely," affirmed Pete.

Craig tried to shield himself from view behind Pete as they passed him, but Brad looked preoccupied and not really paying attention to his surroundings. Craig relaxed.

"Brad was the pool hustler guy with a supposed IQ of 180, he was like some Bukowski barfly philosopher. He sort of took me under his wing and took me to a rich client's place in the Valley. It's hazy as I was totally wasted by then. I vaguely recall these amazing chandeliers and we went in the hot tub in the garden. There was a 16 year old girl there, bit of a spoiled brat, who was wearing a dress made out of paper…"

"Wow!" whispered Craig, stopping dead in his tracks.

"What?" said Pete, eyes darting around for the superbabe.

"That!" said Craig, gesturing to their left at the stretch of Pacific Ocean framed by three stately palm trees.

"Oh, that," said Pete, "what about it?"

"Jesus Christ, Pete, don't you see…"

He stopped mid-sentence as Pete's smile told him he had risen to the bait once more.

"You're not the only one with a soul you know."

They both stood staring in silence at the tray of diamonds spilt across blue polished glass. Craig felt hypnotised. Pete was first to break the spell of the dancing light.

"Did you know Aldous Huxley used to walk along this beach?"

"No, I didn't," said Craig, intrigued.

"With Thomas Mann on one occasion."

"Who?" asked Craig, feeling stupid.

"You should spend less time listening to the Soft Boys and more time reading the classics, my boy."

Craig laughed, momentarily astonished that Pete had even heard of the Soft Boys before he recalled dragging his reluctant friend to a gig at the Hope and Anchor a few months ago.

"Christopher Isherwood lives a few blocks from here you know," Pete went on. Craig felt he must keep up with this intellectual game and ransacked his brain for a literary name to drop. Luckily, a trivial sliver of knowledge acquired whilst studying 'The Rainbow' for English O Level sprang to mind.

"D.H. Lawrence strolled on this beach a few times too," he said casually.

"Lawrence, are you sure?" asked Pete sceptically.

"1923 I think it was. He was trying to get a boat to Mexico."

"Oh yeah, Mexico, where he wrote *The Plumed Serpent*, of course!"

"Not one of his best," said Craig dismissively, feeling distinctly vulnerable as he'd only reached page nine before consigning it to the bookshelf. Pete was obviously convinced this time as he changed the subject.

"I wonder if that Mexican girl in the pink bikini is still working out."

Pete was in luck. Amongst the exhibitionists flaunting their oiled muscles, was the itsy-bitsy pink bikini girl who made Pete's day with a series of stretches and contortions that left little to the imagination. As she bent forward in a right angle clutching the heel of her right foot in the air above her, Pete, who was leaning on the wire pen surrounding the gym just a few yards from her, exclaimed a little too loudly, "Just imagine what she could do to you in bed!"

She pulled her foot even further back over her head until her powerful legs were in a splits position then turned to look at Pete and stuck her tongue out. Craig laughed. Pete yelled, "She likes me, she's flirting with me, look!"

The girl tried to conceal a smile as she bent her body back to something resembling a normal shape. Craig wished he had the sort of easy manner to tease girls like this. In Pete's position, he would probably have cringed and slunk away assuming that the tongue-out meant a firm rebuff.

Pete's hopes were raised but apart from a couple more smiles he failed to get a positive response. Craig eventually lured him away to the more highbrow site of Chess Square where a multiracial group of men sat at four benches frowning over chessboards, stopclocks at their sides.

"A cerebral gym; this is more my scene," said Craig.

Pete's mind was clearly still possessed by the pink nylon bendy-doll.

"She was so hot," he purred.

"I don't know," said Craig, "I find well developed muscles on a woman a bit off-putting."

"No way, they're more exciting than those pale delicate little flowers you go for."

Out of nowhere, Rachel flashed into his mind in all her pale delicate balletic glory, then vanished as quickly as she came. *Like a white queen in a game of speed chess*, he thought to himself, *or a game of fool's mate.*

"You all right, mate?" asked Pete.

"Um, yeah. I could do with a drink though."

Barking Spider Cloud

I'm on a bus sitting next to a young guy in a baseball cap, chewing gum. We get talking about jobs and stuff. I ask him what he wants to do. He says, more than anything, he just wants to be on the Johnny Carson show. The bus pulls over and the driver turns around and stares at me.

It is Lee Van Cleef. He says "Hey, Craig, this is your stop." I am suddenly filled with dread and don't want to leave the bus. The young guy stares at me and says, "Hey man, don't be a loser, this is your stop." I feel all eyes on the bus are on me and expecting me to get off. So I do.

Later, I am walking through a park by the sea with Pete. There is a beautiful blue sky. Suddenly, I spot a tiny lone cloud through a tall palm tree. I shout, "Look at that!"

I whip out a camera from my jacket pocket and take a snap of the cloud. Pete says he is jealous of my eye for an unusual shot. Then as we watch it the cloud seems to change shape and grow legs. It becomes spider-like then, as if gaining weight or substance (perhaps because we are looking at it), it sinks slowly to the ground. We lose sight of it behind a large bush.

Further into the park, I am on my own now (Pete has disappeared) though there are several people around. Suddenly, a man approaches me on the pathway with a huge spider on a lead like a dog. Its body alone is about 6 feet long. I am freaked out by this but everyone else acts like it is perfectly normal.

I try to cover up my horror by acting normally, but the man and his spider can sense my fear and make a beeline towards me. The huge black spider barks at me and strains at his leash. I cower by a tree. The man maliciously toys with me by pretending his 'pet' is just being a bit playful lurching at me and barking (others smile as they pass), but I know that really the hideous black thing aims to get me.

"Uurrghh, it was really vivid," says Craig, looking up from his notebook. Pete was in the bathroom with the door open, brushing his teeth. He'd listened abstractedly as Craig read out the details of last night's dream from the notebook.

"Barking bloody spider! You're the one who's barking. You need help, mate. At least, we're in the right town for shrinks."

"I guess the cloud turned into the spider," mused Craig, lying back on the bed. "I suppose the park was inspired by the walk by the beach yesterday…"

"Perhaps, the spider was actually that gangly bloke in the hat by the photographers," opined Pete who was staring intently at his reflection as he combed his hair, "though I thought he looked more like a daddy-long-legs."

"I don't think the spider was a person…" said Craig, staring up at the motel ceiling.

"Time for breakfast, Doctor Freud," announced his freshly groomed friend leaping into the bedroom, like a jungle cat in his stripey t-shirt.

"Schwabs or Ben Franks?" asked Craig.

"Schwabs today I think."

Schwabs Versus the World

Schwabs Pharmacy was a large rectangular building on the Strip conveniently near to Piper's. You couldn't really miss Schwabs as its name was scrawled across its upper concrete exterior in 10-feet high swirly letters that lit up in pink neon after dark. Pete bought a Los Angeles Times from a magazine stand outside the store. Craig noticed that the neighbouring stand held rather fewer copies of what appeared to be a pornographic newspaper.

"Looks like 'Screw West' has more readers than the Times," he observed.

Inside they sat at the counter and immediately ordered coffee from a friendly middle-aged waitress.

"Why is there a dining area in a chemists anyway?" asked Craig.

"Dunno, said Pete, but it's been here since Leon Schwab opened it in the early '30s."

Craig laughed.

"How the hell do you know that?"

"Bob Madigan was telling me about it the other night. Apparently it's a really popular hang-out for movie business people, writers and technicians as well as actors."

At that very moment, Craig noticed a familiar looking face on a stool by the window.

"Pete!" he whispered loudly, "I think that's Jean-Paul Belmondo."

"Where…? Oh there. Mmm, could be but he looks a bit too old."

"Well it's probably a few years since you last saw him in a movie."

"True," admitted Pete. "Why don't you ask him?"

"Maybe later," said Craig, overcome with shyness.

As they tucked in to their breakfast, Pete got chatting to a thin, greying, heavy-smoker next to him, in rolled-up shirt sleeves who revealed that he used to write for TV. His credits included *Kojak, Starsky and Hutch* and *Baretta*. He didn't like TV work but needed the money for alimony payments to his third wife until she died and he was able to quit. Pete bummed a cigarette from him, and optimistically asked about job opportunities in television for two young English guys without work permits.

They were impressed by the way customers treated the diner as an office, taking business calls and using the waitress as a secretary. Schwabs seemed to have its own distinctive sense of humour too; customers would frequently wind each other up, though not in a malicious way. There seemed to be a wry detachment to most of the conversations, even the gossip which often revolved around the insanities of the town and the motion-picture industry in particular.

Quite a few ex-New Yorkers seemed to hang out there where they could touch base reading their beloved New York Times, often out loud to each other, and feel superior to the phoney tide of tinsel and tack just outside the door.

The man who may or may not have been Jean-Paul Belmondo paid his bill and left without uttering a word, keeping Craig in the dark.

"What a drag."

"Yeah, just as you were about to leap up and speak Froggy to him."

"I was working on a good question, like how difficult was it working with Godard or…"

"Did you fuck Anna Karina?"

"Maybe…once I'd bought him a croissant."

Pete immersed himself in yet another article on Ronald Reagan. Craig sat picking at the crumbs from his blueberry muffin and drinking in the atmosphere; the endless teasing of the waitress; the anecdotes; the yearning nostalgia for a younger, more innocent and smog-free Los Angeles; the constant free refills of coffee; the clever one-liners; the hustling on the phone and the laughter ringing like music. Craig consciously filtered out the language in his head (a trick he'd learnt from years of smoking dope), until he just heard the tone and pitch of the voices.

Every few seconds came a chuckle, a giggle or a chorus of guffaws. In this slightly removed state, he also became aware of the extraordinarily tactile body language; hand-shaking, back-slapping, hair-ruffling, it was going on all around him. There, to his left, two burly men giving each other bear hugs.

Craig felt himself smiling like an idiot. He was tapping into a real sense of community he hadn't experienced for some time. Schwabs suddenly felt like a pocket of warm, vibrant but level-headed interaction between people seeking sanctuary from the loneliness and the craziness outside.

"Hey, Pete, I've just had…"

He turned to share the moment with Pete but he'd vanished right under his nose. He'd probably gone to 'the john' or more likely the cigarette machine. Then right out of nowhere, there was a loud thump as a big fierce looking dog outside lunged at the glass window, barking and straining at his leash.

For a second or two, the animal seemed to be staring right at him before the owner wrenched it away, and as suddenly as it appeared it was gone. So was Craig's sense of inner warmth. Schwabs was just a place to get breakfast, full of nondescript people. *A burst bubble*, he thought and shivered a little.

The Starwood

Craig had staggered out of Piper's leaving Pete to try his luck with a glamorous black diva who'd been in the bar once before and had "smiled beautifully" at him. Craig felt very light-headed. The beer may have contributed, but however much Budweiser, Michelob, Schlitz or Miller he poured down his neck he could never seem to get really drunk, at least not before feeling too bloated to drink more.

No, the floaty, semi-abstracted state of mind was definitely down to the joint Bob, the barman, had rolled him. Craig had gratefully smoked it out in the car park behind the bar and felt a rush almost immediately.

Craig reached the junction with Fairfax and stepped out dreamily. Somebody hooted, and in the back of his mind Craig guessed he may be jaywalking but he was beyond caring. One of his frequent minor spasms of irritation with the American way of life shot through him. Jaywalking! What kind of officious, Big-Brother mind dreamt up that ridiculous law, or that ridiculous name for that matter?

Craig felt smugly rebellious as he strutted across onto the sidewalk in front of the gigantic pharmacy building. Actually, it was more of a saunter but Craig had a vivid mental picture of himself strutting. The pharmacy building looked a peculiarly intense shade of pink this evening he noted.

He grinned at the 'Disco Sucks' message graffitied on the brick wall. His irritation already a thing of the past, Craig was composing more of his mental eulogy to American dope. Unlike the beer, the weed (for it was always weed; he had not come across a whiff of hash in the country so far) was vastly superior to its English equivalent.

He wondered how much this strength was down to the American custom of smoking grass pure. Until a few weeks ago, he had never smoked a joint that wasn't rolled with Silk Cut or Old Virginia, but here the mere concept of polluting your j. with tobacco seemed to be an anathema. Craig felt a twinge of embarrassment as he recalled a recent Hollywood party where he'd committed an obvious social faux-pas by offering people joints rolled with Marlboro cigarettes. Not only had several people declined the offer but he was sure he heard a bearded surf-bum type whisper, "Why the fuck's he using tobacco?"

Once Craig had gotten used to the idea of smoking pure grass, he thought it was great. He didn't smoke cigarettes after all so this way you get high without paying the price. The main drawback to this was keeping joints alight; it was a pain having to tug really hard on pure joints and constantly have to relight them.

He wasn't sure about smoking single-skinners. He could see the sense in only smoking small joints when the dope's pure, but being a creature of habit he felt attached to his system which used three papers (or more, as they frequently required reinforcements). He didn't yet feel confident rolling a joint with only one paper but was prepared to give it a go.

Tweezers on the other hand were a no-no. Americans seemed to favour producing tweezers to hold the joint as it neared the roach. This may well have been a practical device but to him it just looked comical and affected.

Faggot!

Craig looked up just in time to see a large Buick filled with sneering blonde (and probably blue-eyed) males pull away. Two of them were still leaning out their windows making obscene gestures at him. Without thinking, Craig stopped and blew them an extravagant kiss with a studied effeminate flourish.

This seemed to enrage the muscle-clad blondes judging by the contortion to their features, growing small in the distance. Almost immediately, Craig wished he'd yelled 'Nazis' back at them. He always found the right riposte in retrospect rather than in the moment. He had to make do with an action replay of the improved scenario in his head.

Do I look gay tonight, he pondered before remembering he had opted for his white silk scarf and black leather jacket. In Hollywood, this was obviously tantamount to sporting a leather cap and handlebar moustache. Craig had a feeling he had to take a left turn around here somewhere in a couple of blocks.

The night had kicked in by the time Craig had finally found himself queuing up outside the Starwood with a battery of LA punks. He gazed up at the large uninspiring shed of a building, painted black in a vain attempt to conceal its blandness. In front of him, a guy with peroxide hair and a white 'X' painted on the back of his leather jacket was arguing with a large black guy at the door. He was insisting that he was on the guest list whilst stumbling backwards and forwards.

Craig dodged the cowboy boots for the second time, and wondered if Zena would be there. He'd met her a few days ago at a bus stop in Century City. She'd told him about Exene's sister dying on Saturday night just before X's second show. He'd liked her, especially the way she swigged whisky out of the bottle and aimed acid remarks at the disapproving onlookers.

She was petite and fairly plain-looking but her punkette clothes and spiky manner attracted him. She had a sort of brittle vulnerability which was not quite disguised by the layers of attitude. She was on her way to see a band called 'Ecstatic Stigmatic' and said she might see Craig on Tuesday at the Starwood.

He trawled about in his jacket pockets for a flyer he'd picked up in Rhino Records the other day. With this, it only cost him 3 dollars to get in. He argued half-heartedly with the black guy about the necessity of getting his hand stamped to get a free drink then entered the throng.

The first band were just finishing as he queued at the bar. He hadn't even heard enough to form an opinion which irritated him. Still, he hadn't missed any of the Weirdos, and then there was The Gears; potentially a good solid punk double bill. As he ordered his Michelob, and showed the barman his stamp, a girl next to him, pricked up her ears then asked if he was English.

"I'm impressed," he said, "an American who doesn't assume I'm Australian."

The girl's face lit up as she laughed. She had short boyish blonde-brown hair and was wearing what he imagined must be a jumpsuit. She asked if he was in a band. He almost made up a tale but couldn't be bothered.

"No, it's one of my biggest regrets," he sighed, "I'm just a ligger."

"Do it, if you want it that bad. I did."

He was amazed to find he was talking to the lead singer of the Go-Go's, an all-girl LA punk/new wave band, that he'd actually heard of, but as yet hadn't heard anything by. Craig almost nervously blurted out, "So you must be Whisky," but thought better of it and coughed instead. She introduced him to two companions who were fellow bandmates though he failed to catch either name.

The singer said she asked if he was English as they were all excited about starting their first UK tour in a couple of weeks. One of the bandmates asked about decent venues in London. He mentioned Dingwalls in Camden and they said they were already booked to play there. He was a little confused if they were asking about venues to play in or to watch other bands in.

He was on firmer ground when the singer asked him for some recommendations of new English bands to check out. There were laughs when he suggested Echo and the Bunnymen and the Teardrop Explodes based on their atmospheric debut singles and good reviews, and also The Cure. They knew of The Cure but not the others.

They were all friendly and bubbly with a good teasing sense of humour. He would have liked to chat more but the Weirdos were about to start their set judging by the rising noise of anticipation around them, and the Go-Go's wanted to get near the front.

"See ya later, Craig, come and check us out in London!" one of them yelled out as they disappeared into the throng.

The Weirdos weren't bad at all. It was a bit like going back in time 3 years, the songs being short, sharp, angry Clash-like bursts. Their clothes had a flamboyant glam rock flourish to them which made them look more like a British band in Craig's mind. He was twitching rhythmically to a song called 'Happy People', and wondering whether to get a bit nearer the stage and dance, when he suddenly felt the warm smack of lips against his left cheek.

"Are you still asking chicks to marry you for 500 bucks?" a slurred female voice shouted painfully in his ear.

Craig laughed, dazzled by dilated pupils, sweat-streaked mascara and violently red lippy. He pulled back to take a proper look at this grinning, nodding creature in an orange boob tube and black bomber jacket. She looked like a quirky, interesting, kind-of-attractive mess, but not at all familiar.

And yet she clearly knew him; she had just referred to his and Pete's masterplan, cooked up in Piper's, to marry a Californian girl, get a green card and stay in the City of Angels. *This plan had sometimes doubled up as an amusing drunken chat-up line, which is presumably what happened here*, he thought.

"I can't believe you don't remember me!" she wailed dramatically. "You were loaded on vodka and ludes at the time I guess."

Ah, a clue!

"The Odyssey!" he exclaimed. He did recall having one or two quaaludes with some smuggled-in vodka at a cool booze-free new wave disco called The

Odyssey on Beverly, a couple of weeks back, but worryingly, he still had no memory of this wild child.

"I enjoyed our little head to head out on the veranda. I might consider it for a thousand bucks by the way."

"Would that include marital privileges?" Craig asked flirtatiously, surprising himself.

"Mm, maybe for two grand," came the quick-fire reply.

"Remind me of your name," he said.

"Tammy, which you found very amusing."

"Did I? Sorry…"

"Like a doll's name, I think you said. You were right though, I hate it. So, Clay, do you wanna get high?"

"It's Craig actually, and yes, I'd love to get high. What are we talking?"

"Bitchin' black beauties," she said, opening her palm to reveal two large, seductively shiny, black capsules.

"Very nice, I love those," he enthused, assuming they are the same as the English ones, he thought. A couple of friends and he had stumbled upon black beauties in the Finsbury Park Tavern last year, whilst trying to buy hash from some rastas, and they had sent two nights blissfully buzzing. Stronger than blues, but less of a comedown.

Tammy swallowed one of the tablets dry which was impressive given its size, then said, "Come and get it," popping the other one onto her tongue. Craig pushed away a slight feeling of unease and locked lips with Tammy, gently probing her wine-tasting mouth with his slightly elongated tongue. He wasn't sure if she was deliberately playing a game of oral hide and seek with him or if it was just difficult to get a hold of.

They both laughed and started to enjoy a tongue dance to a punk version of 'Jungle Rock'. Eventually, he located the tablet, she held her tongue still then sort of tipped it from her tongue to his, which he then retracted and swallowed quickly with the last of his beer. Tammy suddenly grabbed his wrist and pulled him forwards until they reached some more animated punters, then started dancing.

He joined in, wishing he had another couple of Michelob's inside him. Before long though, he was being possessed by an infectious rhythm, and was shouting "We Got the Neutron Bomb" along with most of the Starwood. Tammy

81

was losing herself to the music, whirling around frenziedly, her head thrown back, eyes closed, laughing like crazy.

Craig admired the spirit but realised that she was beginning to seriously annoy people around her, treading on feet and spilling drinks. When she triumphantly punched the air and managed to clip a guy's ear, he apologised for Tammy, who remained oblivious, and gently tried to guide her back to where there was some more space. He managed to achieve this with some difficulty, but then wondered if they'd swapped the frying pan for the fire, as she started groping him through his trousers.

This was now more visible than it would have been in the mob. He shook her off a couple of times, but disguising this as dance moves, but then she thrust a hand down the inside front of his trousers and grabbed hold of his genitals. Craig wasn't sure if he was not getting into it due to being less drunk than Tammy, or due to doubts that the flaky look in her eyes might actually be an indicator of genuine mental illness.

He also wasn't sure but felt he might be experiencing a twinge of guilt. It wasn't like Beth had ever mentioned any bourgeois expectations of fidelity and after all, wasn't hedonism the game plan here, the *mission*, to exorcise the ghost of Rachel? Whatever the reason, he could hear alarm bells in his head and decided to distance himself. He told Tammy he needed to go to the john, prying her hand out of his trousers.

"Do you want me to come with you?"

"No, you're ok."

Tammy stuck her tongue in his ear and said, "We could get out of here and find somewhere quiet…"

"Er, I was really looking forward to seeing the Gears, but maybe later…"

Luckily Tammy was too out of it to register any rejection, and he was relieved to see her dancing happily on her own when he looked back over his shoulder.

He could feel his heart beating hard against his chest as he stood at the urinal vainly trying to pee. A smiley guy next to him was making conversation.

"I've seen the Weirdos four or five times. They always deliver man. I'm Jeff by the way."

Craig wasn't sure if Jeff was talking slowly or if he was just thinking faster than usual.

"Hi, I'm Craig, yeah I like them. They have a lot of energy. Maybe they are sticking a bit rigidly to the punk formula, if you know what I mean…" He was gabbling.

"They're one of the very first though. Been going since…ooh…'75."

"Oh really, I didn't know that," Craig said. "Respect; I didn't know any LA punk bands started that early. That's even earlier than the Pistols or the Damned!"

Jeff sighed, turned to stare at Craig, smiled, and nodded, all in slow motion.

"I'd sure loved to have seen those guys."

"Same here," Craig assumed from the past tense that Jeff was referring to the Pistols, "actually I did see the Damned last year."

He was just doing his zipper up, having resigned himself to another toilet break quite soon, and Jeff was making a sort of impressed whistling sound, when Craig suddenly felt a hard shove in the back, causing his face to smash into the white tiles above the urinal.

"What the fuck?" he groaned, feeling his sore nose and realising there was a warm trickle emerging from his right nostril. As he turned to see who was responsible, he felt a powerful punch in his right side, near his kidney, which completely took the wind out of him.

"Whoa, buddy, back off!" he heard Jeff pipe up.

Craig, doubled over in pain, took a deep breath then twisted his head sideways, finally managing to get a look at his persecutor. The looming figure was tall but quite thin, almost gawky, in ripped t-shirt and jeans, probably twenty one or twenty two: by no means invincible. The thing that struck Craig though was the lip-curling sneer, nostrils flaring, eyes blazing with sheer hatred.

"Why…?" was all he could manage.

"You fucking limey shit!" he hissed, raising a clenched fist.

"Hey hey," Jeff shouted, stepping in between them, hands raised, palms open, trying to calm the situation down.

"What has this guy done to enrage you so much, man?"

"Mind your own fucking business!" he barked then launched himself at Craig who was still bent double. Jeff, who Craig noticed was pretty well-built and probably no stranger to the gym, blocked the advance then threw the guy back against a cubicle door with some force which dropped him to the floor. Craig noticed a growing number of spectators massing around the doorway. He took a deep breath and straightened up.

83

The attacker scrambled back to his feet. Now sounding somewhat wary of Jeff, he growled, "He was feeling up my girl."

Oh God, thought Craig, *is he Tammy's boyfriend?*

"Any truth in that dude?" asked Jeff.

"Absolutely none," insisted Craig, "I've never seen this idiot before, or met his girlfriend."

"You saw this happening?" queried Jeff.

"My friends saw him, a limey in a leather jacket, all over her," he snarled.

"There are probably several English guys here tonight," Jeff pointed out in his slow deliberate drawl, "and a leather jacket ain't exactly rare at a rock gig, man."

Unable to contain his anger, the guy then spat across the room in Craig's direction, but the thick globule of phlegm actually narrowly missed Jeff before splatting against the wall. Jeff looked at it gradually sliding down a tile, his face a grimace of disgust. Craig couldn't help seeing the irony in Jeff's revulsion at spitting, whilst being a keen fan of punk gigs. He turned back then suddenly kicked the guy hard in the balls, causing him to howl in pain and crumple like a thin can of root beer.

"I was trying to be reasonable but you've made me angry now, you scumbag. Get outta here before I kick the living shit out of you!"

The guy teetered out, mainly on all fours, like an ungainly wounded deer, but paused at the door to threaten Craig, "If I see you outside, you're fucking dead!"

Craig felt his self-control snap, "Crawl back under your stone, you pathetic piece of shit."

All of a sudden he wanted to chase this low-life and lay into him viciously. Jeff asked if he was OK, putting a hand on his shoulder. His touch and his humanity brought Craig back to himself. The anger and darkness evaporated and was replaced by a real sense of warmth for Jeff, who had really gone out on a limb for a complete stranger.

"Thanks, Jeff, I really appreciate your help. Let me buy you a drink."

"Nah, you don't have to do that, man."

"Please, it's the very least I can do…" asked Craig, desperate to show his gratitude.

They chatted by the bar, downing their beers fast as the Gears were due on at any minute. Jeff seemed like a genuinely nice, down to earth bloke. He was a native Californian, born and raised in Sacramento. This was a nice environment for a kid but grew 'kind of boring' as a teenager, and eventually a couple of years ago he moved down to LA and found a job at an auto-repair shop.

He asked a lot about England and said he'd like to visit one of these days. Craig couldn't help rudely scanning the crowd whilst listening, for both Tammy and his assailant. He struggled to picture a free spirit like her in a relationship with that individual. It was probably a case of mistaken identity as Jeff had suggested.

The speed in his system seemed to accentuate the lag between Jeff's slow manner of speech and his own gabbling twelve to the dozen. This made it hard to concentrate on Jeff's words, together with paranoid thoughts he'd be jumped again at any moment, although Jeff's presence did offer a sense of protection.

An attractive woman, with bright red hair, was passing, then stopped dead in front of him.

"Hi, Craig, how nice to see you again."

Uh-oh here we go again, he thought, another female I don't remember, but then the bright green eyes and delicate features locked into place.

"Oh, Charmian, sorry I almost didn't recognise you with the red hair."

"Ha, I keep forgetting I've changed the colour. How are things with you?"

"It's turning into quite a night actually. Oh sorry, this is Jeff. Jeff, this is Charmian."

Charmian was the charming wife of Ian, the lead singer and guitarist with the Differentials, who Craig saw at Club 88 a week or so earlier. She was a very elegant woman, a little older than Ian, perhaps in her early 30s, and a businesswoman too, with her own fashion shop on Melrose.

"Is Ian with you?" he asked.

"Not tonight, I'm having a night out with a couple of girlfriends, but as I've run into you, I know Ian would want me to invite you along to the next Differentials gig on Saturday 19 at the Londoner. I have a flyer here somewhere and I'll make sure Ian puts you on the guest list."

"That would be great, Charmian, thanks." He turned to Jeff. "Have you seen the Differentials yet, Jeff?"

"No, I've seen their name around though."

"I think they are probably the best new band I've seen in LA so far. Really edgy and dramatic. Very powerful songs."

Charmian laughed, "You should be their manager, Craig. Jeff, let me give you a flyer too, just in case."

She finally located a couple of small white photocopied sheets and gave one to each of them.

"Thanks, Charmian," said Jeff, "I will try and come along on the 19."

"I'd better get back to my friends, I think the Gears are about to start," she said, then kissed Craig on each cheek before hurrying off.

"Classy lady," said Jeff, approvingly. "Come on man, let's get down the front and have some fun," he enthused.

"OK, why not," laughed Craig.

The next 45 minutes or so was a whirl of very loud, aggressive rock'n'roll or rockabilly, pogoing, anger, sweat, screaming, danger, laughter, ripped black jeans, silver studs, whooping, chanting and a lot of spilt beer. Craig was horizontally charged or smashed into, seemingly deliberately, a number of times. He got annoyed the first couple of times until Jeff pointed out that this was known as 'slam dancing' or just 'slamming' and was becoming a staple at most punk gigs.

So Craig relaxed and went with the flow, and after a while realised that he was finding the knocks, shoves, pushes and general physicality kind of liberating more than threatening, although there were two or three guys seemingly intent on causing maximum pain. Luckily, there was no sign of the jealous restroom psycho. The Gears songs didn't sound that special and most sounded pretty similar.

He vaguely made out certain songs like 'Baby Runaround' and one about high school girls that reminded him of Beth's criticism of the band as 'misogynistic', but the relentless chug-a-chug beat and infectious riffs were winning him over. He could not deny the sheer excitement, no doubt fuelled by the speed, that he was experiencing.

During the particularly frenzied finale, Craig wiped his brow for the umpteenth time as he was drenched in sweat, then realised that his vision was now blurry in his right eye. He must have wiped his contact lens away. He was dismayed as he only had the one pair of extended wear lenses, meaning that he'd have to resort to wearing his back up glasses for the rest of his stay.

He could not help his vanity railing against this scenario as the glasses were more functional than flattering. Desperately, he dipped down to floor level, amidst the heaving, jumping, stamping, mass of feet, searching for a tiny see-through piece of soft plastic in the dark, on a debris-strewn dance floor. He was knocked flying sideways but persisted, cupping a hand over his left eye, so he didn't lose the other lens too.

He could barely see down here. It was like diving down to an unfamiliar subterranean depth where the sound was muffled and the view had a surreal perspective. The wooden floor was literally pulsating as the boots, pumps and sneakers bounced, twitched and quivered in between the crushed plastic glasses, cigarette butts and candy wrappers. He was about to give up the search when a male head joined him down at floor-level.

"Have you lost a contact?" he shouted.

"Yes, that's right. I think it's hopeless…"

He realised the head belonged to a huge bear of a man who was one of the most zealous slammers, that Craig had been trying to avoid, but here he was, looking through the filth for a stranger's contact lens. Talk about a lesson in not judging a book by the cover. He was throwing himself into the task and pushing away any feet that got in his way.

He even enlisted a friend's help. A nearby girl, guessing what was happening, helped out too, concentrating on keeping people away from their little patch. Jeff, having only just noticed Craig's absence, knelt down and offered assistance. Incredibly, the huge guy struck gold.

"Here you go, man!" he said, gently picking up the contact and passing it to Craig.

"Wow, amazing, thank you very much," said Craig, then the big friendly bear hauled him to his feet, patted him on the back and resumed slam dancing. The lens was a little dried out and probably dirty but not obviously torn. He put it inside a tissue in his jeans pocket and hoped for the best.

Jeff said something about being lucky but the rest of his words were completely drowned out. Craig shook his head, shrugged, then threw himself whole-heartedly back into the fray, followed by Jeff. He was now riding a wave of good-natured camaraderie that he could feel pulsing underneath the wild surface.

It all ended too soon after just one more number and before long he was stood outside the club as the human tide rolled past, giving Charmian's flyer to Jeff to write down his phone number on. They agreed to meet up at the Londoner on the 19.

"Hey, loverboy, where did you go to?"

He looked up to see Tammy, swaying about in a questionable state, but being physically supported by two or three other girls.

"This is my fiancé!" she said to the others, who did not seem overly interested. They pulled her along with them but she screamed, "Wait, I have to give you this, Clay," and pulled out a packet of Starwood matches and thrust them into one of Craig's leather jacket pockets. "Call me," she ordered tapping the side of her nose, before being led away.

Jeff looked at him questioningly.

"That was Tammy," he grinned, "the one I told you about. Seems like she wasn't paired up with our friend, so I think you must have been right about mixing me up with someone else."

"Yeah, keep your eyes open on the way back, Craig. Perhaps, you should get a cab…"

"Can't afford it, mate," he said, "don't worry, it's only a few blocks away."

The quiet, balmy stroll back to the Travelodge felt refreshing and was mercifully uneventful. His body felt somewhat battered, his head was starting to ache from the uneven vision and his ears were ringing, but he felt satiated. He was happy to passively review the blurred faces and scenes from the evening's kaleidoscopic parade that his mind's eye conjured up. The only anxious thought that nagged at him was that he must not forget to put his lens in solution before crashing out.

Bruised

"Fucking hell! What happened to you last night? Did you get beaten up?"

Craig's eyes shot open before his befuddled brain was ready. The woozy sight of Pete standing, staring at him, already dressed, at the foot of his bed with an open suitcase in front of him, made no sense to him; but an anxious dream, he was wrenched from seconds earlier, carried over and his mind started forming a vague narrative that his friend must be deserting him in this motel room; and he, Craig, must have done something really bad to cause this.

"Earth to Craig; did you get beaten up last night?"

The fog started to clear a little. He sat up, scratching his head.

"What…? No, well actually, almost… Why?"

Pete laughed; "Check your reflection," and nodded to the large mirror on the wall. These words fed into the anxiety and he had an ominous feeling that he wouldn't recognise himself. Taking a deep breath, he pushed his fears aside, picked up his glasses from the bedside cabinet, and swung his legs around to the side of the bed.

He stood up, but promptly collapsed back on to the bed again.

"Ow!" was all he could articulate.

His legs were made of jelly, his mouth was full of sand and someone was pile-driving rocks in his skull. He stood again, more carefully this time, holding onto the wall as he edged towards the mirror.

"Jesus!" he exclaimed, not at the hair matted flat with sweat, or the stained black jeans he was still wearing from last night, but at the pockmarked naked torso. A plague victim's pustules came to mind as he surveyed the trail of dark blue and purple blotches on each flank and on one shoulder.

"There's a big one on the back too," said Pete, unable to fully disguise his amusement.

As Craig twisted his neck to look down over his left shoulder, he felt a sharp twinge of pain, and abandoned his efforts, instead hobbling back to the bed and delicately arranged himself on it with a groan.

"I hate to break it to you, leopard-boy, but we have to be out by 10."

"What, that's today?" his head span with recent jumbled memories of looking for alternative quarters further up the Strip, and settling on a place, booking a few days in advance.

"And what time is it now?" he asked warily, dreading the answer.

Pete looked at his watch, "9.35 and about 40 seconds."

Craig just groaned again, but louder and longer.

"So who did you shoot your mouth off to?"

"No one. These are just battle scars from punk's frontline," managed Craig, pleased that his brain had located first gear, gently tracking the painterly splodges down his left side with an index finger.

"Punks did this?" asked Pete confused.

"No, well yes, I suppose so, but not on purpose; it was just some over-enthusiastic slamming which is like a horizontal pogo."

"Mmm," commented Pete with distaste, "perhaps you should start frequenting some black dance clubs with me, they are a lot more civilised."

"Oh shit, my contact lens, it's still in my pocket!" Craig stressed, thrusting his hand into his right jeans pocket.

"No, you put that in something last night when you got in, at least I think that's what you were doing, in between falling over and bumping into things. Look, on the dresser."

Pete was right, there was a vial of solution on the dresser underneath the mirror. He hauled himself up again to investigate.

"One of them came out last night, in front of the stage, right in the middle of the action. I thought I'd lost it then, unbelievably, one of the hardest-looking blokes got down on his knees and found it for me."

Craig took the lens out of the solution and held it up to the light streaming in through the window. It looked ok; no obvious splits or nicks around the edge.

"Tell me over breakfast, man, we have to clear out of this place or the old lady will charge us for an extra day."

"I really need a shower," whimpered Craig, "I don't suppose you could…"

"Yes all right, you ponce, I'll pack for you while you shift your bruised arse into the shower, but make it quick."

At 09:58, they were stood, with their suitcases, in the little old lady's office at the front of the Travelodge. Her Jack Russell, Louis, was sat in his basket by her side.

"Did y'all have any extras?" she asked.

"I didn't realise extras were available," teased Pete, "a massage would have been very welcome."

"Not that kinda extras," shrieked the old woman, "newspapers or food orders…"

"Oh I see, in that case no, my dear," said Pete, handing over the pre-counted wad of dollar bills.

"I knew I had to watch this one, I seen the way he was lookin' at them bad girls on the street," she said addressing Craig.

"Yes, I'm afraid he is a terrible reprobate, I have an awful job keeping him on the straight and narrow."

The old woman laughed, relaxed now that business was out of the way.

"You is more of a good boy, I can tell."

"Yes, my mother brought me up that way," he said.

Pete could not resist shocking her.

"Actually, I caught him masturbating last night, make sure you give those sheets a thorough wash."

"Say what? He did what? Wash your mouth out, young man," she admonished Pete, also slapping him on the arm.

"I think you need to get Louis to pray for him," suggested Craig.

"I done that once already. Now Louis, you say goodbye."

The cute brown and white dog with pointy ears, sat up straight when she mentioned his name.

"Y'all shake hands with Louis," she instructed.

They took it in turns to bend down, hold out hands and shake the little white paw that was offered.

"Goodbye, Louis, it's been a pleasure knowing you."

"Come back again soon, boys."

They heaved their suitcases across all six busy lanes of Sunset Boulevard to the Denny's opposite.

"Did you ask Shandy if she'd be able to give us a lift up the Strip?" asked Pete as they struggled with the door.

"I didn't get around to it. I'm sure she won't mind though."

91

Unfortunately, Shandy was not on shift that day. They sat at the counter with their cases by their feet. Pete had a full Denny's breakfast whereas Craig could only manage some toast and coffee. The two paracetamol he'd had earlier were just kicking in, thank goodness, but he still felt a bit shaky and physically aching all over.

He filled Pete in on the highlights and lowlights of the evening at the Starwood, using items in his leather jacket pockets as aides-memoire, such as Tammy's number scrawled on the pack of matches and Jeff's details added to Charmian's flyer. Pete seemed vaguely impressed that Craig had chatted to the lead singer of the Go-Go's, as even he had heard of the local all-girl punk outfit, but he mainly focused on the rest-room altercation, wanting to know every detail.

"You haven't told me how it went with the gorgeous black woman!" Craig blurted, feeling guilty for being so self-absorbed.

"Ah, Chantal, the heartbreaker! I thought it was going really well; all smiles and even a little touchy-feely flirting, then she suddenly mentioned a long-term boyfriend."

"That's a drag," sympathised Craig, "but not necessarily a deal-breaker…"

"My thoughts entirely, but she said she couldn't possibly be unfaithful to Antoine."

"Sound like she was sending out mixed messages," noted Craig.

"Uh huh. I asked for her number just in case, but she said was sure we'd meet again in Piper's soon."

"Strange place for a girl in a committed relationship to hang out, isn't it."

"Quite. I have a feeling she may not be all she seems," Pete said with a forlorn sigh.

After paying the bill and giving their new address on a napkin to Carmen, to pass on to Shandy, they picked up their cases again and continued on their journey, heading west up the Strip. The sun was hotter now as they neared noon. Craig was soon driven into taking off his leather jacket which made negotiating the suitcase even harder, as he was having to swap hands quite frequently.

"I think the bloke at Park Sunset said we couldn't access the room until 3," said Pete.

"Shall we kill time at a certain watering hole on the way then?" asked Craig.

"Good man, I thought you might be feeling too fragile."

"Hair of the dog," Craig mumbled, coming to a halt to wipe his forehead.

As they stood taking a breath outside the All American Burger, Pete hissed at him:

"Twelve o'clock, quick!"

Craig took a second to process that this was an instruction, rather than a time-check, then looked straight ahead. The middle-aged chubby blonde woman, trying to hail a cab, immediately looked very familiar.

"Is it Bette Midler?" he asked, but sensing this wasn't right.

"Shelley Winters," said Pete.

"Oh yes, of course it is."

She was frowning, probably late for a meeting, but suddenly a grin lit up her face as a cab saw her gesticulating and pulled in.

"Underrated actress," Pete opined, as she climbed in the back of the cab and was whisked away. "Did you know she has two Oscars?"

"No, presumably not for *Who Slew Auntie Roo*?" smiled Craig, recalling a deranged horror movie he'd seen on TV a while back.

"Rumour has it that she used to be quite wild, maybe still is…"

"I can believe that, she has quite a tough, take-no-shit vibe," mused Craig.

They continued at a snail's pace up Sunset Boulevard. The hangover and the coffee had dehydrated Craig and the strain of lugging the heavy case felt like it was exacerbating his injuries from last night. He found himself counting the tall slender fan palms that they passed every 15 or 20 yards.

They had grown extremely large; their height and spindly appearance brought to mind Dali's elephants. The only fronds nestled high up at the very tips of the trees. They were staggered either side of the Strip, forging ahead of them into the distance, as far as the eye could see; quite possibly all the way to Pacific Coast Highway.

Dazzled by the light, Craig had to look down then close his eyes until his dizziness faded. He was regretting letting Pete do his packing as presumably his sunglasses were in his suitcase somewhere.

It was Pete's turn to stop, this time for a fag break. Craig soon realised that there was an ulterior motive though when he caught sight of the peroxide blonde vision flouncing towards them. Surely one of Sunset's finest ladies of the night, in broad daylight. It was still just about morning in fact.

"Hi boys, where are you headed?" she stopped and gestured for Pete to lend her his cigarette. He did so with one of his wolfish grins.

"Chateau Marmont, my dear."

"Oh really," she said taking a deep drag then blowing smoke up skywards, "Why aren't you in a cab then? Or a limo?"

"Because we are English eccentrics and we love to walk," Pete countered.

"Has anyone ever told you, you bear an uncanny resemblance to Debbie Harry?" asked Craig. This was no mere flattery either, although the red thigh-high boots, reminiscent of the ones she wore performing 'Denis' on Top of the Pops, may have underlined the similarity.

"One or two, but thanks all the same, honey, I like Blondie." She handed Pete back the cigarette. "I would love a drink with you guys in the Chateau Marmont bar…or maybe from the mini-bar in your room…"

"You are working early today," deflected Pete.

"Girl's gotta make a living," she said.

Pete passed the remainder of the cigarette back to her then pulled the lining of each of his trouser pockets inside out to show how empty they were, and pulled a sad face. Craig laughed at his friend's Chaplinesque mime, with all his worldly belongings, on the street beside him.

"Sorry, I lied, we are almost skint," he confessed sheepishly, "otherwise we would love to buy you a drink."

"I kinda guessed you guys weren't loaded, but it's a shame as I think it would have been fun. I ain't rich enough to offer discounts though."

She blew a kiss as she departed, mirroring Pete's miserable expression.

"Have a nice day now," she called out in a sing-song voice.

"Missing you already, Debbie," shouted Craig, which prompted a laugh.

"She is one of the hottest women I've ever met," reflected Pete, "and she isn't even black."

They picked up their cases once more, buoyed by this brief encounter.

"Perhaps, we should have asked her to join us in Piper's…" speculated Craig.

Craig insisted that he buy a cold can of Coke at the 7-11 and persuaded Pete to take five while he played one game on the Space Invaders machine in the corner. He only scored 4,000 which underlined how rough he felt, then it was once more unto the breach.

Before long, Craig was virtually begging for them to break their no cabs, money-saving policy, but Pete claimed that it wasn't worth it now as they were almost there. This may have been true if they were going their usual walking pace, but encumbered by heavy luggage, it took almost another thirty minutes to reach their oasis. Craig pressed for a side booth rather than barstools, so he could recover in relative comfort.

Betsy came over to them, as if Piper's had become waitress-service. Having clocked the suitcases she approached with a pained expression in her smoky-blue eyes.

"Are you going home?"

"No, we're just relocating," answered Craig.

"Nearer to Piper's in fact," added Pete, "so you'll see even more of us."

"Oh good, I'd have missed you; I like you guys," said Betsy sounding uncharacteristically sentimental. In fact, they had tended to think of her as quite aloof and even spikey until now.

"The ice queen melts!" commented Pete as she went back to the bar to pour their beers. "Don't get your hopes up though; Gregg told me the other night that she's a lesbian."

"Really?" exclaimed Craig, who had not even considered this possibility.

"So, we should save a little bit at this new gaffe."

"Might give us an extra week in LA," suggested Craig hopefully.

"Well, at least a couple of extra nights in Piper's," Pete said then got up and headed to the jukebox.

"What, again?" said Craig as Pete sat back down, recognising the intro to Donna Summer's *Bad Girls*.

"I can't help it, it just feels so right for Piper's." He grinned and rubbed his hand together gleefully, always a sign that he was in high spirits. Craig idly surveyed the Piper's clientele and noticed Joe Senior sat tucked away, almost out of sight on the other side of the bar talking conspiratorially with an intense looking, smartly dressed, black guy.

"That's Chuck apparently," said Pete, following his line of vision; "bit of a mystery man by all accounts." At that moment, Joe Senior handed Chuck an envelope which he put in his inner jacket pocket, nodded, stood up, and made a discreet exit.

A twinkly-eyed, guy in his 40s, with receding red hair and a neat pencil moustache, had come in with a younger, pretty Chinese companion and they had taken up residency on Craig and Pete's usual barstools. They seemed to want to display their love to the world, constantly kissing and stroking each other.

"Get a room!" commented Ernest from the other side of the bar, but it failed to register.

The guy made a wisecrack that made Craig smile as he stood waiting for at the bar for Betsy to serve him again.

"Gordon," he said proffering his hand, "and this is Jennifer."

He shook Gordon's hand saying "how do you do," and did the same to Jennifer. A young couple wandered in, seemingly in mid-argument, the guy who had the physique of an American football player was scowling and intense although the girl who looked like a slightly spaced-out, jaded, prom queen was not really paying attention. He virtually pushed her into a seat in the booth next to Pete, then tried to lecture her with his finger wagging in her face but she pushed this away saying "fuck you." He then barked "don't move," at her then disappeared back out into the street.

"He's been to charm school," said Gordon.

"Two Buds right?" said Betsy as she popped up in front of Craig.

She continued to surprise Craig as she poured, talking about how she was stuck on an ending for a poem and it was really bugging her.

"I didn't know you wrote poetry, Betsy. If you want a different perspective, I'd be glad to look it over," he offered, "not that I'm any kind of an expert but I do dabble occasionally myself."

"Thanks a lot. I might take you up on that. It is Pete right?"

"No, that's the other one. I'm Craig."

"Craig. Ok."

She moved away to collect some glasses. Gordon leaned over and in a hushed conspiratorial tone said, "If she wants to show you her scribblings, she must have the hots for ya, pal."

"I dunno, I think I'm the wrong gender for her," whispered Craig.

His girlfriend chimed in a little too loudly, "I thought I picked up a vibe too. Perhaps, she's not exclusively one gender…"

"You could be right. It was only hearsay."

"Ah, uncorroborated rumour eh?" said Gordon, "I'd put more weight on personal observation if you know what I mean. Looks like your compadre is knocking on the door too," he said, looking in Pete's direction.

Craig turned to see the girl who was under orders not to move had already moved, to the next booth, and was chatting animatedly to Pete.

"He might not wanna get too interested; her boyfriend seemed like the 'you're with me and don't forget it type'."

"Yes I sensed that too," said Craig, and judging by Pete's furrowed brow, he may have been thinking the same thing.

"Why don't you two join us?" Craig invited, partly to defuse the potential sexual time-bomb, and partly as Gordon and Jennifer seemed like an interesting couple.

"Sure thing," said Gordon.

"That's nice of you, thank you," said Jennifer.

He led them towards their booth.

"Pete, this is Gordon, and this is Jennifer."

Pete looked pleased to have the extra company.

"Hello, and this is Apple," he said, introducing his new friend.

"Ah the Windy City," said Gordon wistfully, gazing at the mural on the wall beside them as they sat down, "that makes me feel nostalgic."

"Are you from Chicago then, Gordon?" asked Pete.

"No, but I practiced there for a few years."

"He's a criminal lawyer," explained Jennifer.

"Very interesting. Are you in the same field, Jennifer?"

"God, no, I'm a physiotherapist," she laughed.

"How about you, Apple?" smiled Gordon, "Are you a model or an actress?"

"I'm an actress!" Apple exclaimed, "How did you know?"

"Just a wild guess, honey. Movies, TV, theatre? Anything we might have seen you in?"

"Well, I'm trying out for a role in a soap next week."

"Exciting," said Gordon, his face deadpan. He turned to Craig; "So what are two young guys from London doing in a place like this?"

"Impressive ear for an accent, Gordon," Craig replied, "we're just travelling, soaking up the culture and enjoying the colourful characters," he said nodding at the bar in general.

"Slumming eh," translated Gordon, "I'm hoping not to stumble across some of my clients in here as it goes."

"We may well have conversed with one or two of them," said Pete grinning.

"What's with the cases?" said Jennifer, peering under the table, "You haven't robbed a bank, have you?"

"Ha ha, no, nothing like that…just a liquor store," said Craig.

Gordon and Jennifer laughed but Apple stared at him in confusion.

"You robbed a liquor store?"

"He was fooling around, Apple," said Gordon.

"Oh yeah, of course," she said then turned to Pete and asked him if he'd buy her a beer. Craig intervened and suggested he order a carafe for everyone.

"Great idea, Craig, let me pay half…" Gordon said, pulling out his wallet.

By the time Betsy brought over the carafe of Budweiser, Gordon had moved on to international affairs, which for Piper's was a bit of a novelty.

"So, how do you guys feel about losing the last corner of the British Empire?"

"Do you mean Rhodesia?" asked Pete, on the ball as usual.

"Now known as Zimbabwe, yeah," said Gordon.

"I'm happy it's gone. We had no right to it in the first place," asserted Craig.

"The people might be happier with British rule rather than this Mugabe guy," pondered Gordon. "He claims to be a Marxist."

"Good for him," said Craig, the Bud loosening his tongue, "I imagine most black farmers would rather Mugabe was in power than Ian Smith," the name of the arrogant white former leader of Rhodesia came to him just in time.

"You may be right. Time will tell," said Gordon equitably.

"Why are you talking about this?" asked Apple.

The abject lack of curiosity or awareness behind this remark stumped Craig. He had no idea how to respond. Gordon stepped up.

"Strange as it may seem, Apple, some of us are interested in life beyond the Hollywood bubble."

Pete stifled a laugh and Craig too, although he felt a little sorry for Apple, but she seemed to be oblivious to the put-down.

"Why? It's boring."

Gordon studied her as if he were examining a lab rat.

"You might want to go easy on the coke there, Apple, it can shrink the brain."

Jennifer slapped his arm. Craig realised Gordon was right, she was high; he hadn't paid attention to her hyper-active foot or her dilated pupils.

"It's speed, not coke," she said, narrowing her eyes at Gordon.

"Oh my mistake, I thought you might have been doing some damage to yourself."

"Apology accepted," said Apple.

Gordon looked at Craig with raised eyebrows and shrugged his shoulders, which caused Craig to start giggling. Luckily, Apple had already returned her attention to Pete and told him she thought he had a cute accent. The boyfriend chose this moment to reappear. He stood by the door, his expression even surlier than before.

"Hey, Apple, we're going!" he said loudly, glowering at Pete.

"Is there a dog in here?" said Gordon quietly, pretending to look around for one. This set Craig off, giggling again which probably did not alleviate the boyfriend's paranoia.

"Apple, come on, now!" he shouted.

"Sieg Heil!" said Craig, disguising the comment as a sneeze.

It was Gordon and Jennifer's turn to start giggling. Pete threw him an admonishing look but it seemed to be struggling to compete with a smile.

"Gesundheit!" Gordon almost choked.

Apple sighed theatrically; "I'm having fun with my new friends," she moaned.

"I won't tell you again," the boyfriend said balefully.

Apple tutted and reluctantly got to her feet then kissed Pete on the cheek, but nobody else. *Uh-oh*, thought Craig. Pete looked distinctly uncomfortable but the boyfriend kept his position, maybe a little intimidated by the group.

"You can be such a jerk," she told him.

He grabbed her arm roughly and frog-marched her out the door.

"Bye everyone," she called back blowing a kiss.

"Bye, Apple," yelled back everyone, including Betsy and even Ernest.

"Sweet but inane to the core," commented Gordon.

"I just hope Apple doesn't get bruised," said Jennifer.

"Like this you mean?" said Craig, pulling up his t-shirt and turning each way to show both blemished sides.

"Whoa!"

There was a collective gasp which made Craig question his action. He noticed Pete shaking his head and quickly pulled the shirt back down.

"Who did a number on you?" asked Jennifer.

"Oh just a little S&M, no big deal. He gets carried away sometimes," Craig said, looking at Pete.

"He deserved it," said Pete, straight-faced, back in the game. "He'll be in for worse tonight now."

"Ha, you guys are too much!" laughed Gordon.

"You are joking, aren't you?" checked Jennifer.

"They are just some LA punk bruises. I was introduced to slam-dancing last night at the Starwood."

"Ah, it can get pretty brutal down the front, can't it," said Gordon with feeling.

This led to a long dissection of the LA music scene between Craig and Gordon, whilst Jennifer, from what Craig overheard, asked Pete about London, jobs and girlfriends. Pete then asked Gordon if there were any jobs going at his law firm.

"As I work for the State, you'd have to have a proper working visa," said Gordon, dashing Pete's hopes, "I could ask around some friends of mine though if you are serious."

He wrote down Pete's number and gave each of them one of his business cards. Jennifer reminded him that they had to get going or they would lose their reservation at Le Dome. Standing up, she hugged both Craig and Pete warmly, saying how much fun it had been to meet them, and Craig suggested that they meet up again soon for drinks or maybe a gig.

"Right on, we have numbers, let's make it happen," enthused Gordon who then high-fived Pete and then Craig, who tried to mimic the move, wondering what was happening. Pete explained it to him later on. Jennifer started to physically drag Gordon towards the door.

"Hey, now I know what poor Apple felt like!" he proclaimed as they melted into Sunset Boulevard.

"I like them," said Pete, downing the last of the beer from the carafe.

"Gordon is sharp, isn't he?"

"Definitely, and funny, the way he ripped the piss out of Apple. Fingers crossed, one of his contacts has a job-lead. Right, I'm going for a slash then I suppose we ought to hit the road."

Almost as soon as Pete left for the restroom, Betsy came over and sat down next to Craig.

"Do you need to talk to someone about what he did to you?" she said as if she were a priest asking for his confession.

"Huh?" he was blank for a second then realised she must have seen the bruises earlier. "Oh, no, I was joking."

"Are you sure, Pete?" He didn't correct her as she looked so serious. "I have friends who have been victims of domestic violence. The first step is to open up to someone about it, which I think you have done." She stared at him intensely at him, clearly not believing his story.

"Honestly, Betsy, it was just a tasteless joke; the bruises are just from being barged into repeatedly at a gig last night."

Pete reappeared from the restroom and Betsy quickly pulled out a sheet of paper from her pocket and handed it to him.

"This is the poem I was telling you about. Let me know if you have any ideas on where to take it."

She got up quickly, avoiding eye contact with Pete.

"Is this a copy, Betsy?"

"No, but you can hold on to it. Bring it back next time."

"I will look after it."

Pete pulled out his suitcase from under the table.

"Is she OK?"

"Um yeah, I think that might be my fault," Craig admitted, "she seems to believe you gave me the bruises."

Pete laughed, "I quite like that she thinks you are my bitch."

Craig speed-read the poem entitled 'Dust in the Wind'.

"If you don't move your ass, I may have to whip it again," loudly, so that Betsy might hear.

Craig folded the poem up and put it away in his pocket, then pulled out his own suitcase.

"Dream on, you are the one in for a whipping, from Apple's boyfriend. He popped his head in and looked around while you were in the bog. I think he was looking for you!"

"Seriously?" questioned Pete.

Craig could not keep up the pretence: "Gotcha! Ha ha ha."

Pete grinned and feigned swiping Craig around the head.

They embarked on the final leg of their journey, recharged by the Piper's pit-stop. *For once, the hair of the dog actually seemed to have worked*, thought Craig although it was only a couple of blocks before his aches, pains and dehydration were back in force.

"You should have seen your face when Apple kissed you!"

"I wasn't relishing the thought of a kicking from that psycho, especially over someone I didn't even like!"

"Fair enough," acknowledged Craig, in between huffing and puffing.

"What on earth possessed you to take off your shirt in there?"

Craig had to stop walking to get enough breath to answer this one; appropriately enough outside the all nude strip joint, the Body Shop, leaning for support on the base of a tall wooden sign reading 'Live Nude—Girls Girls Girls.'

"I really dunno. In the moment, I just felt it would be funny," was Craig's attempt to explain his behaviour. I think my sense of judgement is being increasingly hijacked by drugs and alcohol."

"You don't say," came the sarcastic reply, possibly fuelled by impatience at their slow progress. "Did those bruises really come from being beaten up in the toilet last night?"

"No, why would you say that? Betsy didn't believe me either, though at least she was sympathetic."

Pete picked up his case again and started walking.

"Sorry. Sympathy and poetry. Was it an ode to Sapphic joy?"

Craig reluctantly picked up his case too with his less blistered left hand and followed his friend.

"I only skimmed it but didn't notice any obvious lesbian references."

"Any good?" asked Pete.

"Not bad. Pretty language and at least one clever metaphor. The content was maybe slightly formulaic…"

"What was it about though, Mr bloody A Level English?"

"Sorry," Craig said, then paused to take a deep lungful of air, "I'd say it's about impermanence and death."

"Inspired by a dead parent, do you think?"

"Hard to say. Could be drawn from a personal loss or it may just be a meditation on the concept."

"I presume your feedback will be glowing…in case she's not a rug muncher after all."

"Such a cynic. I have to admit it's a relief that the poem is fairly good so I don't have to lie through my teeth."

Carney's came into view on the other side of the Strip with tree-laden hills rising up behind it. The yellow train carriage was so familiar to them by now, it no longer looked out of the ordinary.

"What's the address again?" asked Craig.

Pete pulled out a card from his pocket and read out, "Park Sunset apartments, 8462 Sunset Boulevard."

"Carney's is 8351. Thank God, we are almost there!" called out Craig.

Sure enough, 2 minutes later they were stood outside the unprepossessing building.

"This is it," said Pete.

"Yes, I remember the sign," said Craig, gazing up at the bright red letter P and the neat grey lower case 'park sunset', almost lost in the outsize rectangular crazy paving sign.

"Wow, we really are in the heart of the Strip! Look, just a stone's throw from the Riot House," Craig nodded over the road towards the modernist 14-storey multi-balconied Hyatt on Sunset.

"That's the debauched rock'n'roll hotel you were telling me about, right?" queried Pete.

"Uh huh, I guess you could say it's a Stones throw of a TV set away," quipped Craig.

"The boy's a wit," said Pete, impressed.

The formal little man in reception; Ted, according to his name tag, told them their room was ready and ran through some swimming pool rules and how the outer door should always be locked after 9. Then he led them around to the right and up a dimly lit corridor. *Thankfully they were on the ground floor*, thought Craig, passing the case back from his sore left hand to his right for the last time.

Ted opened room 42 and stood aside for them to enter. The room was certainly not glamorous, and it was smaller than their Travelodge room, but he could live with that. It was the double bed that presented the problem.

"I think there must be some mistake," said Pete in his posh voice. "We requested a twin room…with two single beds," he added in case Ted was unclear.

"I'm very sorry, I didn't have a note of that," said Ted sounding flustered, "and I'm afraid we only have this room and another on the first floor, currently available, both with double beds. One may well become available in the next day or two, then we could switch you."

"Yeah, this will do for a night or two, Pete, it's no big deal."

He was fearing Pete was about to cancel the booking and they'd be back out on the street with those bloody suitcases and nowhere to go, and in his 19 years, he had seldom felt so exhausted.

"Fine." Pete shrugged.

Ted pointed out the facilities, which took about ten seconds, gave them a set of keys each, apologised again for the mix up, then mercifully left them in peace.

Craig flopped onto one side of the contentious king size bed and Pete did the same on the other. He pulled out Betsy's poem to read more thoroughly but then put it down and cackled.

"What?"

"This is going to feel like the Morecambe and Wise sketches where they share a double bed."

"With me in the Eric role of course," smirked Pete.

"With those short, hairy legs? I don't think so."

"Are you looking for a new bruise for your collection?"

Count

Joe Junior was serving today, wearing his trademark black buttoned shirt and black jeans which emphasised his slight resemblance to Joe Strummer. Craig guessed he was about 21 or so, in the same age range as his friend Gregg.

"How do you do," he said in a passable English accent, grinning at Craig.

"Spiffing, Joseph. May I sample one of your splendid ales."

Joe chuckled as he poured Craig a Budweiser. He had a cool but friendly demeanour, so far inheriting little of his father's gravitas. Craig sensed that he wouldn't suffer fools gladly however.

He sat at the bar reading *The Crucible* and was barely two sips into his first beer of the day when he noticed the lean, cool-looking young black man sat at a table to his right in front of the New York skyline mural. He was dressed in a mildly flamboyant, expensive looking brown leather jacket over an open-necked red shirt. He was playing with a thick gold chain around his neck as he talked to Ernest, probably not about the delights of translating Italian operas.

Craig realised he must have been staring at the man, who suddenly beckoned him over. Apprehensively, Craig carried his glass and book over to the table.

"How's it goin', man? Pull up a chair."

Craig relaxed and said hello to Ernest. The young man introduced himself as Count Fitzgerald something or other. Craig had vaguely noticed Ernest behaving a little obsequiously to this young man.

Craig was fond of Ernest but he was an oddball in many ways. He was overweight, had unkempt hair, oversize glasses, and poor dress sense. He moaned a lot, in his high-pitched voice. There was something in his manner that could bring out the bullying side of certain males in Piper's, a slight trace of Piggy from *Lord of the Flies*.

"What are you reading, man?" asked Count.

"Uh, it's by Arthur Miller," mumbled Craig self-consciously, "it's called *The Crucible*."

"Hey, I've heard of that," chimed in Ernest, "S'all about them Salem witches 'n shit."

"Yeah? I never read it," said Count, "is it good?"

"So far, it's quite powerful. I think it's really an allegorical thing about the McCarthy communist witch-hunts."

"Say wha'?" said Ernest, his eyebrows shooting up his forehead like frisky tadpoles.

"Hey, Craig, you's an intellectual man, I like that. Let me buy you another beer."

Ernest soon had to leave, an important aria no doubt awaiting his return. Craig recalled Mimi telling him that Ernest lived downtown and his daily journey to Piper's took him over an hour. Craig sat chatting to Count about all sorts of things.

Count asked him if he was going to stay in the USA. Craig said he wanted to but he'd have to find a job or get a green card somehow. Count said "I can get you a job man."

At that point, a smartly dressed woman in her mid to late thirties walked over to their table and asked Count how much he wanted for his gold chain. He said he'd sell it for a hundred bucks. After some debate, Count let her take it over the road somewhere (Craig hadn't noticed a jewellers nearby) to get it checked out.

A few minutes later, she was back again, bristling with self-confidence and saying she would pay $75 but no more. Count laughed and agreed with barely a protest. She said she'd have to draw the money out the bank, so Craig and Count accompanied her in her silver BMW.

On the way, the subject of employment came up again and Count said he was looking for a new career. The woman offered them both phone numbers at Paramount and CBS where she knew jobs were going. It also transpired that all three of them were Capricorns and that Count shared the same birthday as Craig which seemed to be a very significant omen to Count.

They all went into the bank together. Count flirted vaguely with the woman but got nowhere as she disappeared fast once she'd obtained the gold chain.

Count suggested they continue their conversation back in Piper's. On the way, they passed a call box and decided to try the job leads while they were still hot. Count told Craig to do the talking and he produced the necessary dimes.

Craig felt a little disappointed when both CBS and Paramount only offered to send them application forms to be submitted in the usual way. Count was nonplussed. As they were passing Cliff Raven's Tattoo Parlour, they encountered a large sullen looking black guy whose face suddenly lit up when he recognised Count.

"Hey, you inky dink motherfucker!" he exclaimed loudly and slapped Count's upturned palm.

"Hey, bro', where you bin'?" asked Count. Craig gathered that the ensuing brief exchange was about a coke deal but he felt very stiff, English and unhip all of a sudden as he could not fathom much of their street jive. It ended with the other guy saying, "I'll be on the scene, wearin' the green," and a punching of fists.

"Do you think you could get me a little taste of coke, Count?" he asked cautiously as they continued on their way.

"No problem, Craig, I can get you anythin' you want, man." Craig was pleased to hear this but simultaneously felt a little wary. Perhaps, because the last time he heard that expression it came from a sleazy cab driver who picked them up at LAX when they first arrived. Within minutes, he had turned and leered at Pete saying, "How about some pussy boys? You wanna hand-job, you wanna blow-job? I can get you anythin' you want, man."

Maybe it was just that there seemed to be more to Count than met the eye; he seemed to be making deals everywhere. This impression was reinforced back in Pipers over a carafe of Michelob, beneath the twinkling night-lights of Chicago, when Count revealed that he used to earn $1000 a day.

"Really?" gasped Craig, slightly alarmed but spellbound by the revelation that Count used to be a pimp with, at one point, seven white women working for him and he used to cruise around in a Rolls and a gold-painted Mercedes Benz. Count seemed to intuit Craig's uneasiness over the pimping and insisted that this was ancient history and that he was a reformed character who had learnt his lesson.

Apparently, Count had found a beautiful blonde who he decided would become the prize jewel of his collection and potentially the best money-spinner. Unfortunately, she also turned out to be an undercover policewoman who, despite falling in love with Count (Craig did suspect some creative embellishment at this point), eventually busted him. The consequent spell 'in stir' gave Count some time to reflect on his life and focus on what was important to him. Craig never discovered what this amounted to as Count went off on a female tangent.

"Do you know this bitch over here, Craig, beating up her gums?" he nodded over towards Frenchie who was sitting at the bar, in full flow, but surprisingly for the time of day, still sober.

"Yeah, she works in the bar here sometimes. She's French."

"French eh," ruminated Count. "Hey baby, venez-ici," he called over to her.

She exhaled Gauloise smoke in a perfect movie-star pose before turning to face Count with a look that would freeze mercury and said, "Fuck off." Count laughed then turning to Craig he stage-whispered, "That dusty butt ain't no spring chicken anyway, man."

Craig's mind drifted back to a conversation with Pete a couple of weeks back in Ben Franks, just a few blocks west of Piper's. They both loved the vibe of the coffee shop which was a semi-legendary rock'n'roll hangout since the '60s. They had both been praising the clever modernist architecture with its tilted asymmetrical A-frame and the way it slanted upwards to the front. Craig was looking out the window at the space-age signpost, saying it made him think of the Jetsons, when he noticed an angry old woman gesticulating wildly, on the sun-bleached sidewalk.

He stopped mid-flow and Pete soon noticed why. They could make out her tirade of abuse even with the door closed, over the general hubbub. The woman was middle-aged but had extremely long hair, like a child's, though it looked in serious need of a wash. She seemed to be wearing several layers of colourful scruffy clothing and a bobble hat, despite the heat.

She kept throwing her arms around wildly. They both strained to see who she was arguing with so vehemently, then they realised there was nobody else, at least physically. Pete shook his head, looking baffled:

"Why is it that all the weirdos and nut-jobs seem to gravitate to Sunset Boulevard?"

"Who knows. Magnetic fields? Ley lines? Maybe they are just caught in a spider's web?"

"Ha, maybe that's what we should call them…'Sunsets'."

The term coined by Pete had since expanded to include the whole of LA, and now embraced all manner of wild, whacked-out and colourful, larger than life characters. Once encountered they were deemed 'collected'. The 'Sunset' list was already growing fast when Craig decided, mentally, to add Count, as he wove his way to the Piper's restroom.

Possibly distracted by the motley selection of soft-core porn adorning the walls, Craig realised he was drunk when he collided with the door frame as he walked out. Stumbling back to his seat, he just caught sight of Frenchie stalking away from their table, presumably after rejecting another crude come-on.

Towards the end of the carafe, Craig heard himself explaining to Count the fatal mistake of underestimating the importance of pawns and came to an abrupt halt, disorientated. How did he get onto chess and why on earth was he talking to Count about it? Count, assuming that this was a meaningful pause, nodded slowly then leaned across the table and in a husky tone whispered conspiratorially, "You teach me to play chess Craig and I'll teach you how to play chess with people."

The heavy line and stylised delivery would probably have caused Craig to smirk if it wasn't for the unnerving penetration of those dark dilated eyes. They were like laser weapons piercing his warm alcoholic cocoon, reaching right down deep inside him. Just for a flash he imagined his soul was trapped in a vice then Count laughed and switched the lasers off.

"I like you, man; you could move into my apartment and I could teach you to drive. You have to drive in this city."

"Not so far," countered Craig.

"Yeah but y'all's just a tourist up till now; you dig what I'm sayin'? I'm cracking but I'm facking."

The warm glow soon returned and Craig decided (or was it Count's decision?) to stroll back up the Strip to their apartment to get the cash for the charlie.

Twenty minutes later, the sun had lost most of its heat as they approached 'Park Sunset'.

"You'd love my pilch, man, it has a roof garden where you could sunbathe naked and work up that Californian tan. Or is your white English ass not ready for that?"

Craig laughed as he trawled for his keys. The outer glass door onto the street was already open and he held it ajar for Count. Count paused on the threshold.

"Seriously, Craig, I think we were meant to hook up today. It's like a fate thing, man. Shit, we even have the same goddam birthday, you know what I'm sayin'."

"Yeah," mumbled Craig, thinking, *No, I haven't got a clue.*

They walked through the spartan foyer with the sofa and the pot plant and into the corridor on the right.

"Home sweet home," said Craig as he stopped outside the first door on the right and fumbled his key into the lock. Before he could turn it, the door was pulled open from within, wrong-footing Craig who almost fell into the room. Pete was standing at the door stony-faced.

"Where have you been?" he asked staring at the stranger behind Craig.

"Uh, in Piper's mostly," replied Craig, wondering hazily if there had been some arrangement he had overlooked. It seemed unlikely; the order of an LA day tending to be loose, lazy and spontaneous.

"Pete, this is Count," announced Craig cheerfully. Pete stood blocking the entrance to the room.

"Hi man," said Count.

"Oh yeah?" snapped Pete, "Is this one a pimp or a drug dealer?"

"What?" stammered Craig, taken aback, not least by the accuracy of the throwaway remark.

"Hey, Craig, does your friend have a problem?" asked Count whose laid-back drawl had adopted a rather steely edge.

"Yes he does," said Pete. "Craig, I want to speak to you alone."

"Um ok. Sorry about this, Count. Do you mind standing out here for a few seconds?" asked Craig, feeling very awkward.

"Shine it on, man. Why don't you just get me that money? I'll be on the couch out front."

Pete almost cut him short by pushing shut the door.

"Jesus Pete…"

"What the fuck are you playing at, bringing lowlifes back to our apartment?"

"Shh, he'll hear you," admonished Craig.

"So what!" thundered Pete.

"Calm down, I'm just scoring some coke off the guy. He's ok. Why are you so pissed off?"

"He knows where we live. If he comes back in the middle of the night with some gangster friends, you can deal with him, ok."

Craig suddenly felt strangely sober. He found the money, and took it out to an angry looking Count in the foyer.

"You oughtta teach your friend some manners; he's got a bad attitude. Oughttaa whip it to the red. Fuck this shit."

Craig apologised and assured him that Pete's behaviour was bizarrely out of character and that no offence was meant by it. They arranged to meet in Piper's in a couple of days when Count would have a gram for him: Craig thought that under the circumstances Piper's would be a wiser rendezvous point than their apartment.

Back in the room, as daylight drained away Craig sprawled across the unmade bed listening to Pete develop his theme that he was inviting danger.

"Count!" he sneered. "Could be Count fucking Dracula for all you know!" (Craig almost said, "Don't you mean Blacula," but thought better of it) I mean, he looked like an extra from Starsky and fucking Hutch; he only needed the wide-brimmed hat!"

"Actually," admitted Craig with a grin, "he was playing with a gold chain when I first met him."

They both started to laugh, and Craig went on to reveal the details of Count's alleged past as a pimp.

"He's a classic 'Sunset' man; a real dayglo character. I can't see what your problem is."

Pete was laughing now. "Oh, Craig, you're so naive, it's why I love you, you idiot."

"What do you mean, naive?" asked Craig defensively.

"He probably wanted to put you on the street. His little English fag: a star Hollywood attraction," said Pete as he disappeared into the bathroom.

"Don't be ridiculous!" shouted Craig, whose turn it was to have a sense of humour failure. He turned over burying his face into the pillow. His anger was exacerbated by his friend's arrogant big-brother posturing. Pete was 22, 3 years older than him, and considerably more streetwise, but he had a tendency to milk these factors in their friendship.

Craig was often charmed and moved by Pete's genuine protectiveness then alternately he was irritated and frustrated by it. The more he thought about Count however ("…I'll teach you to play chess with people…"), the less absurd Pete's theory grew.

The Happiest Place on Earth

When Bethany got back from work, she feigned shock to find Craig still laying in her queen-size bed. He had woken up around midday, watered Beth's 'one hundred plants', read some of her underground '60s magazines she'd dug up to show him, including one from the first Human-Be-In, then drifted back to sleep. He mumbled sorry, pulled the covers back and started to get up.

She pushed him back, saying, "Well, since you're here…" She pulled off her top and trousers and dived in with him. She laughed as she showered him with kisses, "You thought I was serious, didn't you?"

"I wasn't sure," Craig admitted.

"It's a lovely surprise; I was sure you'd have left long ago," she said, craning her neck so he could nibble it more easily. They made love. It was less frenetic and intense than usual, but none the worse for that. Craig felt it had a tender, relaxed, idyllic quality. Still basking in the afterglow, he asked if they could go to the beach and watch the sunset.

"Sure, though it might be kinda windy."

Beth was not kidding; within 30 minutes they were on Santa Monica beach, laying on one of her native American rugs, kissing and caressing, but the wind was blowing fine sand into their faces and hair. On the plus side, they virtually had the beach to themselves. The pounding surf looked majestic in the long slanted golden rays. A few small boats with white sails festooned the horizon.

Nearby, a cute pair of black kids, brother and sister, were trying to sell their mum's sweet potato pie to occasional passers-by. Whispering and giggling, the pair were clearly also spying on the couple, no doubt intrigued by the kissing and fondling. This made them laugh, but inevitably put a brake on their more raunchy behaviour.

Craig was amazed to hear that Beth probably only visited the beach three or four times a year, despite it being almost on her doorstep. It made slightly more sense when she revealed that she'd never learned to swim. Beth had brought an LA Weekly in her bag and looked through the gig guide.

"There's not a lot on, apart from The Plugz at the Starwood and I'm bored of them. Oh, The Last are playing Madame Wong's West. They aren't bad…"

Beth had also brought her cassette player, and Craig was playing her a C90 with the first two albums by The Only Ones. She was loving it, but then she had to put it back in her bag as she was worried that sand was blowing into the mechanism.

"Aw, look at those cute little guys," gushed Beth, pointing at a couple of brown, long-billed spindly-legged birds splashing about in a puddle to their right.

"Weird-looking, aren't they," said Craig.

"Sandpipers I think," said Beth.

"Like the Taylor and Burton film!" declared Craig. "Actually, that was set by a beautiful Californian beach come to think of it."

"Hey, I know that movie, where she has an affair with a married priest. My sister and I used to love watching that movie. I think they shot it up at Big Sur."

"I suppose the title, *The Sandpiper,* was referring to the Liz Taylor character…"

Craig looked pensive as he stared at the birds, enjoying the last rays of the sun. Then he grinned.

"I might start calling you my little sandpiper…"

"Oh really…" laughed Beth, before throwing a fistful of sand at him. "So I look like those weird-ass birds, do I?"

"No, no of course not…" soothed Craig reassuringly, "well, apart from the pipe-cleaner legs, I guess…"

Beth shrieked and hurled more sand at him.

"Put this in your pipe, you…!"

"I was only joking, honest, your legs are absolute perfection," he said and underlined this sentiment by trying to kiss every inch of them, to the accompaniment of children's giggles.

He flicked his tongue around in her ear lobe then whispered, "I want to make love to you as the sun sets, then in the future, I can always look back and recall the best sunset of my life."

He kissed the tip of her nose and couldn't help noticing her eyes were welling up.

"Are you OK, Beth?"

"Yes, I think I just have some sand in my eye."

Craig felt something unidentified turn over in his chest, but he put it down to the melancholy cry of a seagull flying overhead.

"Hey, I know," she suddenly exclaimed, "why don't we go to Disneyland…"

"Tonight?" Craig laughed, "Will it even be open?"

"Yeah, until midnight I think. My friends and I often used to go just for the evening."

Craig had secretly fancied checking Disneyland out, but as Pete had zero interest in it and Craig didn't want to go on his own, he assumed he would miss out on it.

"Why not, I'm game."

"It's already 6:30 and it will take an hour or more on the freeway. Do you mind missing out on your sunset?"

He noticed she was shivering slightly.

"Nah, there's always another one around the corner isn't there."

On the long drive to Anaheim, Bethany entertained Craig with tales of dropping acid at Disneyland with her friends in the late '60s and early '70s.

"It always felt like the place had been custom-made to trip in. I've never had a bad one there either."

They compared notes on bad trips although Craig had only had a handful of lysergic adventures compared to Beth's hundred or so. On one of them, she said a friend tried to steal her boyfriend in front of her and it took a long while to realise it was real. The bad-trip story that really stuck in Craig's mind was a desert journey at the end of the '60s with a few friends.

It was beautiful until she came across a rattlesnake that reared up at her; she was terrified of snakes in general. For some reason, she drove back while still very high and started to see rattlesnakes landing on the windscreen, dozens of them, causing her to swerve off the road at one point. *They would have to make do with two pre-rolled joints for psychedelic enhancement tonight*, Craig thought, *although they were made from Beth's mind-blowing grass.*

They smoked the first number in the car park. The place was so big that they had to board a shuttlebus to the amusement park itself. They passed a big sign, modestly welcoming them to 'the Happiest Place on Earth'.

"If it feels a little hokey, just go with the flow," Beth sensibly advised. In fact, Craig did not need to suppress any cynicism as his inner child responded in kind to the positive sense of wonder radiating from the hordes of excited, smiling faces. Perhaps, it was just down to the dope but Craig even found himself hugging Pluto (or Goofy, he was never sure which was which) in New Orleans Square, to Beth's delight.

Being an avid fan of ghost stories, ghost movies and even ghost trains, Craig asked Beth if they could check out 'The Haunted Mansion' first. He loved the locked room with no-way-out scenario and the campy Vincent Price impersonator who proclaimed *unless you take my way* before a shock crack of lightning revealed a corpse hanging from the domed ceiling above their heads. Everyone screamed, even Beth, who had seen it several times before.

Even better was the 'doom buggy' ride past an 18th century hall where semi-transparent figures danced or flew in through windows and circled a chandelier. Craig guessed they were looking at state of the art holograms, but Beth said in fact they were simply carefully arranged reflections. Either way the effects were infinitely superior to any Craig had seen in the UK.

They had to queue for 30 minutes for 'The Pirates of the Caribbean' ride but the sophisticated animatronics, the level of painterly detail and the humour involved more than made up for this. Their 'tour guide' was an unexpected bonus too; genuinely engaging and amusing rather than just loud or crass. As time was of the essence, they fast-forwarded into Tomorrowland.

Beth suggested they smoke the second joint before going on the 'Adventure through Inner Space' attraction. They found just enough cover behind some bushes.

"I love that name," said Craig, coughing as he exhaled, "is it a simulated LSD trip?"

"Not quite," said Beth, "though it did open in 1967. You are shrunk to the size of an atom."

"Oh OK, like in 'Fantastic Voyage'," he ventured, but judging by Beth's blank look, she hadn't seen it. They were both distinctly wobbly as they made their way to the back of the very small queue. The visuals were a little dated with rows of basic sphere shapes and giant snowflakes but the hammy gobbledegook from the unseen scientist was priceless: *I am so infinitely small now that I can see millions of orbiting electrons. They appear like the Milky Way of our own solar system...*

Also the carriages had a peculiar hypnotic motion that Craig found pleasing. Beth said she and her friends went on this ride over and over again when they were tripping.

After popcorn for Craig and cotton candy for Beth, they boarded the Skyway to Fantasyland which had some great illuminated views. As they flew serenely over the heads of the throng, Beth looked at her map of the park and realised the attraction they were after next was back in Tomorrowland. Great name for a song thought Craig.

They ran or jogged most of the way back. Beth was keen to try the space-themed indoor steel roller coaster called 'Space Mountain'.

"It's only been open for a couple of years and it's supposed to be a real blast."

There was another long queue even though it was now almost 11; testament to the popularity of the ride. They both laughed at the ride's extensive health warning that you had to be free from high blood pressure, heart, back or neck problems, motion sickness, pregnancy, etc. Craig did wonder however, what they were letting themselves in for, trying not to think about his intermittent back pains.

Beth looked as though she might be having doubts herself, when an obese know-it-all behind them started talking loudly about the woman who fell unconscious on the ride last year then fell into a coma and died. They held their nerve though and both loved the experience; a very fast thrill-ride in the dark, apart from some flashing red lights, with sharp turns, sudden drops and stops.

Their pulses were racing as they staggered out the other end, and in Craig's case a pain in his lower back throbbed. He kept quiet about this as he didn't want to come across as a killjoy. Beth suggested a quiet finale in the Disneyland train as the park was due to close in less than half an hour.

Eventually, they found the station in Main Street and got on board a train bound for the Grand Canyon and Primeval World. They had a carriage to themselves and as there was little in the way of lighting, they were free to fondle, but instead, this time they opted to talk, often competing with an excitable voiceover that burbled away in English and Spanish.

...the next leg of our journey will take us along the rim of the Grand Canyon. It's a mighty long drop to the Canyon floor so for your safety, stay seated with your hands, arms, feet and legs inside the trains...

"Thanks for treating me Beth, I've really enjoyed it."

Beth leant into him, resting her head on his shoulder.

"I'd forgotten what it was like to feel really happy."

"Did it take Mickey and the gang to remind you?" grinned Craig.

"No," she said, hitting his arm, "it just took Craig on his own…well perhaps, his worldview too."

"You seem like a happy person to me," he said quizzically.

"Ha, that's 'cos you're here with me, dummy. I've actually been in a pretty bad place for a few years now. I was diagnosed with depression and was on tablets for a while but they just seemed to make things worse."

"I'm really sorry to hear that, Beth, I had no idea."

He squeezed her as they passed some lifelike deer perched on a 3D precipice in front of an epic painted Canyon backdrop. The sky became a graduated fiery orange then red.

"Looks like you haven't missed your sunset after all."

They kissed passionately as things turned dark rather abruptly and Arizona retreated behind them. Craig asked Beth if she knew what had caused her depression.

"Well, you know I told you I'd had lots of boyfriends; not all of them were assholes, but several were. I guess I got treated in a pretty crappy way. Come on, I don't wanna drag your mood down, droning on about old stories…"

"I want to hear," said Craig sincerely.

Quiet now, enthused the voiceover, *as we travel back in time, back to the fantastic primeval world, land of the dinosaurs…*

Beth sighed and gave a quick run-through of the motley sounding men in her previous life, most of whom either cheated or left her, one stole from her, and another used to hit her. "I guess there is another reason for my depression, which I have tried to edit out of my mind…" Primeval World's overblown dramatic music was helping build the suspense.

"A few years ago, I was walking in Beverly Hills of all places, in broad daylight, at 8.30 in the morning, when I was grabbed from behind then dragged into the back of a van and raped…quite violently."

"Jesus, that's horrible," murmured Craig, as they passed by a tall long necked dinosaur chewing on some long stringy blood-soaked parts of an unseen victim.

"I never went to the police; I know I should have but I didn't feel strong enough. I just wanted to blot it out."

Craig felt like he'd been punched in the solar plexus. He tried to imagine what horrors Beth must have been through.

"I don't get flashbacks anymore, mercifully, and I can forget for days even weeks at a time, but then I get a really vivid nightmare where I'm right back in that fucking van…"

Craig didn't know what to say; what could he possibly say? So he just hugged Beth tightly and kissed her tears away.

They stayed like this, hanging on to each other, in a sad but tender cocoon, for what seemed like days but must have just been minutes. The train stopped and a loud and chirpy pre-recorded female voice told them that they were at Main Street station, then an equally chirpy live male voice cut in, saying that Disneyland was now closing for the night.

Craig realised that despite going around the whole circuit about three times, he hadn't actually seen Tomorrowland, which Beth had described as really pretty with thousands of multi-coloured lights.

There was a tangible depth to their intimacy as they walked back hand in hand to the shuttle that took them back to the car.

On the journey back, Beth insisted it was his turn to talk about himself. She wanted to know everything about his family, friends and lifestyle across the pond. Craig was afraid she'd see through him and realise he was actually quite boring, but she refused to be deflected even by French kissing at every red light. He described his family as nice enough but a bit shallow and materialistic.

He told her he thought he was a disappointment to them as he had no ambition, and still had no idea what he wanted to do with his life, unlike his older brother who was a chartered accountant and his younger sister who was already pursuing the same path.

"My mum and dad don't take me seriously. Apparently, hating the Royals, the Establishment and the Tories is just a silly phase. 'Anti-everything' my mum calls me."

"Ha, that sounds just like my folks," sympathised Beth.

Craig told her about his friends who were the only thing that kept him going through his dreary, oppressive all-male grammar school. He gradually relaxed and stopped worrying about what sort of spin he should put on his stories to impress her, and even started to enjoy opening up. He made Beth laugh with tales of teenage rebellion like smoking dope in the school bogs, but also drew her sympathy when he disclosed how his group of friends were verbally and physically bullied for being different.

"We were a group of misfits really, but we became united in loathing for the narrow-minded disciplinarian teachers and the moronic sheep they brainwashed. It felt like us against the world."

"Phew, that sounds pretty alienated," said Beth, pulling out to overtake a painfully slow station wagon.

"Yeah," agreed Craig, remembering Beth was a teacher, albeit of younger kids, and hoping he hadn't offended her, "I had a dream the other night set in school where everyone was a vampire and trying to kill or recruit me. I managed to escape and ran home to safety, only my family turned out to be vampires too, and I locked myself in the bathroom trying to keep them at bay."

"Just 'cos you're paranoid doesn't mean they won't get you," laughed Beth.

Craig tried to persuade her to drop him off somewhere that didn't take her too far out of her way as it was now gone 1.30 and she had work in the morning. She wasn't having any of it though and insisted on dropping him all the way back to Park Sunset.

"I would suggest a quickie in the back," she said, "but I'm aware a lot of sand made it into every nook and cranny earlier, so it probably wouldn't feel too comfortable."

He laughed and kissed her one final time.

"Thanks for a truly special night…my little sandpiper."

"Get outta here!" she pretended to push him away before pulling him back to face her and fixing him with a serious stare, "Thank you for being a truly special person."

On the sidewalk, he waved goodbye as her maroon AMC Pacer started to pull away, then she lowered the window and called out, "Check your pockets!"

The Sentence

As Craig unlocked the door to their apartment, he was slightly surprised to find it dark and empty, although it was only 1.45 after all, and bars stayed open until 2 in LA. He threw his jacket onto the chair and flopped onto the bed. Automatically, he reached for the TV remote control on Pete's bedside table and pressed the power switch.

He soon regretted this since despite there being loads more channels here, as usual there was nothing on worth watching, unless you happened to be a fan of *I Love Lucy* or '50s B movies. His finger paused briefly over the channel up button when *Get Smart* appeared as he did find the '60s spy spoof quite amusing, but he just wasn't in the mood. He had noticed that there were more adverts than programmes on every time he flicked through the channels, and that meant waiting to see what programme was being interrupted or just going round and round the options until something halfway decent hopefully broke through.

After a fruitless few minutes of channel-hopping, Craig became exasperated, hit the off button and threw the remote control across the room. He lay his head back on the pillow and closed his eyes. His mind fluttered moth-like over the events of the previous few hours, alighting on a memory for a few seconds, tasting it, then restlessly moving on. It seemed to be searching for something.

A train carriage caused his heart rate to increase. Little wings beat frenetically above two heads locked together, illuminated by rays from the dying sun.

"I was diagnosed with depression and was on tablets for a while…" Crazy rock formations whizzed past. "…I was walking in broad daylight…I was grabbed from behind then dragged into the back of a van…" A guttural roar then a giant monstrous reptilian head burst through the train window and swallowed both of the lovers whole.

Spat out onto a beach at dusk. Alone, naked and shivering as the wind cut through him. A brown spindly-legged bird was digging in the sand next to him.

He stood up to leave. The bird seemed to move around him nervously, as if it didn't want him to leave. It squawked what sounded like a single word 'pocket' then bit him on the toe.

Craig opened his eyes wide and sat up straight. A moth was circling the light bulb above his head. He reached over for his discarded jacket on the chair and rummaged around in the pocket. He pulled out a tiny miniature red envelope with his name on.

He swallowed hard, opened it, a wave of foreboding washing over him. Inside, the lip-shaped card was just one sentence in pretty red ink, 'I think I have fallen in love with you'. His hunch, if that's what it was, was correct. He shivered as he really felt he had experienced this moment before.

For a few seconds, he felt nothing more, as if suspended in a bubble outside of time. He put the card back in the envelope and returned it to his jacket pocket. Then the bubble burst.

A tear rolled down his cheek and, for the next hour, his head played pinball with his heart.

Ping!—A surge of happiness. Ping!—A burst of aching tenderness towards Beth. Ping!—A lurch then a knot of guilt in his stomach. He realised he was starting to hyper-ventilate and his palms felt sweaty. He breathed in deeply and tried to get a handle on his emotions.

The bubble must have been made of glass as dozens of sharp fragments and shards had dispersed in all directions. It was some time before Craig could even tell if he felt more positive or negative at the disclosure: He fleetingly wondered if he had the power to choose but gradually his feelings seemed to follow their well-defined old tracks, and he sighed as he recognised that his heart must be half-empty rather than half-full.

He felt genuine affection for Beth and this had grown, perhaps more than he'd realised. He was not just fond of her, he did love her…to some degree, but ultimately, he was not *in* love with her. Unless he was holding himself back, not allowing this to happen. More than once he felt a spike of regret that Beth had broken the unspoken rules of their relationship.

When things started to calm down, he knew that this was just surface stuff and that Beth was merely being honest about the unexpected direction of her heart. Craig became aware that he had known their bond was strengthening but had suppressed the knowledge as it was inconvenient. He had decided before he even landed at LAX that he was going to stay free and untethered.

This was his time to throw himself, if not headlong into hedonism, at least forcefully into unfettered, free-wheeling experimentation. Beth had in many ways represented this freedom for him, and it was hard to reconcile this concept with bourgeois aspirations of falling in love and forming a couple.

A key turning in the lock interrupted his ruminations and a slightly drunk Pete half-danced in. He dived onto the bed and launched into a stream of Piper's gossip.

"Guess what, we are now officially known as 'the old chaps'. We have arrived, dear boy!" Apparently, this was a term coined by Joe Junior that had spread into general usage.

"Also, Frenchie asked me where my 'cute friend' was."

Craig only semi-registered the stream of news. A hooker had thrown a full glass of beer over Cricket for leering at her and asking for a freebie. Neil, the English guy, had invited them to one of his club gigs in Westwood. Bob, the barman, had opened up about what it was like to kill a VC in Vietnam. Pete took a breath and asked what Craig had been up to.

"We fucked, then went to the beach, then went to Disneyland," was the compact reply.

Eventually Pete noticed his friend's downbeat mood and asked if he was ok.

"Yeah, just a headache, I think I'll turn in."

He needed to continue processing, so whilst Pete read an article in Playboy, Craig lay with his back to him and continued to chew on the significance of the nine words in red ink. He didn't think he could, in conscience, reciprocate Beth's words and lead her on. Ironically, he sensed this was only because he felt a lot for her; if it had been a girl he didn't really care about, he could probably mouth the words and live with the uncomfortable feelings.

He fleetingly wondered if Beth could accept a fundamental imbalance in their relationship. He knew she would want him to be honest about his feelings for her, but he also knew she wanted him, more than anything, to fall in love with her. He sighed and pulled his knees up to his stomach, causing the Playboy magazine to rustle.

He pictured going out with her, having ruined her hopes but with her putting a brave face on it, and it was unbearable. Her words on the Disney train about her bad luck with men came back to haunt him. He loathed the thought of being the latest bastard on the list, putting her through new suffering.

He realised he was stuck between a rock and a hard place; if he pretended he felt the same as her she would be bound to find out eventually and it would cause her pain but if he called it off, because he was not in love with her, he would cause her pain too. Gradually, it dawned on Craig that that he had to do the right thing and stop seeing Beth; she would probably respect him for this decision one day. It was not an easy decision as he loved seeing her and she had opened up his world.

He wouldn't only miss the sex, the gigs and the amazing grass, but also the warm easy intimacy, the humour, the exchange of ideas. It would be a profound loss, the thought of which kept him awake most of the night. By dawn, his exhausted mind had digested the dilemma and accepted the necessary decision to move on.

The only aspect he did not pore over was how and when to tell Beth. He decided to kick this can on down the road for now. Finally, sleep swallowed him.

Sleep did not bring peace however. Craig dreamt he was back on the beach. The sun was going down and he was shivering, looking everywhere for the spindly-legged bird. He walked along the foamy edge of the vast ocean, scanning every piece of driftwood and seaweed, as darkness fell and with it a sense of dread.

Then a small wave deposited the bird at his feet, its neck twisted and its eye glassy, still beautiful in death. He cried out in horror and in grief. It felt like he had been delivered a life sentence. He turned and ran but he could hear the waves pursuing him.

The Magic Pan

"Phil, you make the best strawberry daiquiris in this city," announced Pete.

"Gee, thanks, Pete," answered Phil, the pale baby-faced barman at The Magic Pan Creperie in Westwood Village.

"He's just after another free one, Phil," said Craig, biting into another large, impossibly red strawberry from the silver bowl Phil had kindly placed in front of him.

Shandy, the waitress from Denny's sat between them at the bar. She had kindly picked them up from the Travelodge and driven them there in her beloved blue Beetle 'Flash'. Pete had been doubtful of the potential merits of an upmarket pancake restaurant but Shandy lured him with the 'free daiquiri' carrot and was true to her word.

Shandy's sister, Candice, sometimes worked there which was how she met her 'great friend', Phil the barman. They sometimes went out clubbing together.

"How come your skin is even paler than ours, living out here?" Craig asked Phil as he started to mix another cocktail.

"Oh I hate the sun," said Phil, "I avoid it wherever possible. I don't want skin cancer by the time I'm 30."

"Or have an old leather face like Candice," remarked Shandy bitchily about her kid sister, who to Craig's way of thinking, was pretty hot.

"The weather's so boring here," Phil went on, "it never rains, it's always…"

"Perfect?" suggested Pete.

"The same," said Phil. "I'd much rather live in England where you actually notice the seasons change."

"It's usually winter over there actually," snorted Pete.

This exchange led to Craig and Pete predictably running down various British institutions, like the monarchy, the Tory party, transport and the state of broadcasting (with exceptions like 'Play For Today' of course) in comparison to the, in their opinions, superior American equivalents.

124

"London has no tubes or buses after midnight. No need as there are no pubs open after 11. It's a joke," whinged Craig.

"It's as if we are stuck in the '50s, still recovering from World War Two," added Pete.

"Only 3 TV channels, they usually finish before midnight too. The BBC even closes down with the bloody national anthem!" Craig protested.

"Some idiots even stand and salute it in their own living rooms," sneered Pete.

"That is weird," said Shandy.

"Whereas you guys have bars open until 2, God knows how many TV channels; well over 20 to choose from, 24-hour shopping, drive-in banks for fuck's sake…"

"We also have too many guns, too many flags, and it looks like we will soon be saddled with Ronnie goddam Reagan," countered Shandy.

"OK, but we've had to put up with Maggie Thatcher, the milk-snatcher for a year now, which has to be worse."

Phil looked bemused: "Why does she snatch milk?"

"It's an obscure reference to her cancelling free school milk a decade ago," explained Pete.

The wholesale slagging off England didn't seem to dent Phil's enthusiasm for all things British. He was yet another anglophile it seemed, with a keen interest in the British post-punk, new wave music scene. Shandy was more of a Europhile, who proudly saw her Beetle as a status symbol in LA. Craig suspected that her 'two cute English boys' might primarily be a fashion accessory to show off to friends like Phil.

"Do you like the Psychedelic Furs?" Phil asked Craig.

"Yeah, I love the album. I saw them at the Lyceum just before we left. They were like a cross between the Pistols and the Velvets: a real wall of sound!" enthused Craig.

"Don't you recognise us?" interrupted Pete, "we are the Psychedelic Furs!"

Phil and Shandy looked understandably lost.

"I think he's referring to an incident in McDonalds the other day," explained Craig. "A girl cleaning the tables asked if we were a band, because of the accents I suppose, and Pete told her we were the Furs, on our first US tour."

"He even autographed her bloody napkin," laughed Pete.

"As Butler Rep, naturally," added Craig.

Shandy laughed.

"Ahh your English humour slays me. I'm a real Python fan you know."

Quick as a flash Pete nudged her in the ribs and said, "Does your sister go?"

Shandy looked blank.

"Go where?"

The other three all laughed at her but obliviously she turned and pointed to a dark long-haired man over to the left in the main seated section of the restaurant.

"That guy's really cute, isn't he?"

"Looks a bit faggy to me," said Pete, continuing to make fun of Shandy.

This was only their second evening out with Shandy but Craig was beginning to detect certain traits like an affected narcissism and obsession with people's looks.

Shandy swept her perfectly straight 'Julie Christie bangs' away from her face.

"Actually I think you two look slightly faggy."

Her blatant attempt at goading fell a little flat when Pete grabbed at Craig's crutch, proclaiming loudly, "That's because we are rampant homosexuals darling; I have him every night."

This was a familiar routine of Pete's usually employed to liven up a tedious queue in the bank or shock onlookers on the tube. Shandy managed an expression of admirable indifference although Phil seemed to be amused. Grinning, he looked up from drying cocktail glasses.

"Hey, you guys, we should all go to a club together, it would be fun. They play great new wave stuff at Studio One."

"Oh no!" moaned Pete, "not more skinny white blokes. Take us somewhere black. Soul food and disco music, that's what we need."

"Pete has a 'thing' for black women," Shandy said, by way of an explanation to Phil.

This was true of course, but Craig couldn't help wondering if Pete had been exaggerating the preference in order to guide Shandy in his direction.

Greyhound Man

A greyhound bus bound for Las Vegas. *This is what it's all about*, thought Craig as they settled down into their seats. Pete had wanted to get a plane but Craig insisted on the romantic, if somewhat slower alternative. Pete sat at the back where he could smoke.

Craig found himself a window seat where he could enjoy the desert scenery. He had dreamed of the jaded panoramic vistas of Death Valley as far back as the first form in grammar school. Unfortunately, they were travelling quite late in the evening so it was dark but Craig was still buzzing with anticipation.

Just before the bus departed, a large shambling figure shuffled on board and gravitated straight towards the empty seat next to Craig. Craig felt a little irritated at having to relinquish the extra space, and was soon cramped by the man's sprawling bulk. Craig glanced back at Pete who had clocked the new arrival and made an exaggerated grimace that made Craig smile. He knew what Pete was thinking.

"You nutter-magnet! They cross the road to talk to you."

The man-mountain was wearing loose colourful shorts and a 'Nashville' baseball cap. He had a large unruly beard and his breath smelt of stale beer. The bus had barely left the depot before Craig had learnt that he was unemployed but travelled around from state to state courtesy of a complicated welfare fiddle, and had once lived in a cave in the Great Smoky Mountains.

Somehow this subject set off a neural connection in the man's brain to a mystical experience in San Diego a few years back involving a vision of a 'lady'. This account led into a conversation about spiritual awareness and psychic phenomena; always one of Craig's favourite subjects. Craig was not sure why but he launched into an account of a recent Ouija session at a party in Santa Monica. The experience had not been particularly dramatic; the glass had been painfully slow in spelling out its oblique message, but the words still intrigued him.

'Sharon Tate. Slaughtered. 1969. Innocent.'

Perhaps, for Craig, the fact that the killings had taken place there in Los Angeles lent some significance to what otherwise seemed to be a rather pointless and obvious message. The man, however, became noticeably more animated and leaned nearer to Craig, his watery eyes gleaming. In a conspiratorial whisper, he said he wanted to tell Craig a secret by way of a story that he wouldn't usually relate except that the coincidence seemed to call for it, if not demand it.

Back in 1969, when the man was just an impressionable 16 year old (*You haven't aged well*, Craig thought to himself, who had taken the man for forty), he and a friend had gone up to L.A. to check out the hippie scene. Two attractive young hippy 'chicks' had approached them and come on to them. They tried to entice the guys into coming back with them to their place in the desert and meet an 'amazing guy' they lived with.

His friend thought they were weird and left to go home. The man hung around a little longer, almost persuaded by wild offers of free sex and drugs. He had been getting into the occult via an Ouija board, and tried to impress the girls with tales of these experiments. He even went so far as claiming he had made an allegiance with the Devil through the board. He also found the girls a little intimidating however, and before long backed out, made his excuses and went home.

One week later, he was hitching up Sunset Strip when a green and white Cadillac pulled over and offered him a lift. He accepted. The passengers, he found out later, were Charles 'Tex' Watson, Susan Atkins and Linda Kasabian. The driver's name was Charles Manson.

He thought they may have been looking for him, as the two girls were the same ones that came on to him a week earlier. Almost straight away, they revealed that they were going to kill some rich people that night and they wanted him to help them. He remembered being unsure whether they were serious at first. Their intensity soon started to freak him out.

Sensing his reluctance, the others started to lean on him. Then Linda Kasabian pulled a knife on him. She pressed it into his ribs and threatened to kill him if he didn't help them. Then came the crucial moment.

He suddenly underwent a staggering transformation: he was hit by a lightning bolt between the eyes and Jesus spoke to him, or rather through him. He denounced what they were doing, knowing it to be evil and wanting no part of it. He barely recognised his own voice, it sounded deeper and stronger than normal and he felt removed from it. As he spoke, Manson's body reacted violently as if physically repulsed by his words. He stopped the car abruptly and ordered the others to throw him out.

He was dumped somewhere in a remote part of LA. He was frightened but convinced that the others meant business so he found a call-box and phoned the LAPD. He told them about the car journey and the crazies who boasted that they would kill someone that night.

The police wanted to know the number that he was phoning from but it was scratched off the phone. They asked where he was but he didn't recognise the area at all. He said he'd find out and call them right back. Once he'd hung up though he started feeling really 'spooked'.

What if Manson came back for him because they'd told him too much? Night was falling. Scared out of his wits, he made his way home. By the time he finally made it back, he was shattered but in a calmer frame of mind. He wondered if he'd got the whole thing out of perspective. Manson and the others would be long gone now anyway.

The next morning he awoke into a nightmare. Screaming headlines about the brutal Hollywood murders and the famous actress victim, Sharon Tate. He tried to delude himself but knew it was no coincidence. He phoned his grandfather, who happened to be a retired LAPD officer, and asked his advice.

His grandfather told him to keep quiet and forget all about it (*perhaps*, thought Craig, *because he was more aware than most of the dubious reputation of the LAPD, who might try and implicate him*). For a long while after, this the man wrestled with his conscience. He wanted to give the police his information but his grandfather was adamant that he stay silent.

Sometime later, an advert was circulated asking the man who had phoned in before the crime to come forward. Eventually, he did contact the prosecutor's office. At this point Craig, who had been listening spellbound in suspended disbelief, felt his brain switch into sceptical mode. He had read the book 'Helter Skelter' on the Manson murders and knew he could use this to check up details of the story later.

He asked who the man spoke to in the prosecutor's office. The man said Bugliosi's assistant had interviewed him but he couldn't remember the name. This was inconclusive thought Craig; Bugliosi's name, like the suspects, was fairly well known to anyone with more than a passing interest in the case. What came next was potentially more substantial: The man said his testimony was not used in the end as it put Linda Kasabian in a bad light. Despite threatening him with a knife, she was to be the key witness for the prosecution, informing on the others in return for immunity from prosecution. Bugliosi understandably believed that the knife story would destroy any sympathy the jury had for her, so the man was never called to present his evidence.

The recounting of this tale was increasingly punctuated by bursts of violent coughing and asthmatic wheezing. He interrupted his narrative to stumble to the front of the bus and fish out some tablets from his bag. Craig gazed out at the desert darkness. Unfamiliar and often sinister outlines of rock formations floated past.

The eerie emptiness and vastness of the place sent an involuntary shiver down Craig's spine. He wondered if the jagged and deformed cactus silhouettes would have looked quite so menacing if he hadn't heard the man's story. Out of the blue, it occurred to him that Manson's ranch hideaway in the '60s was somewhere in Death Valley, here in this very desert somewhere.

Craig felt a pang of icy dread. It seemed to open up a huge cavernous space in his chest. He could taste the desert in his mouth. The man was groping his way back towards his seat. He bent over as he hacked and spluttered, spraying nearby passengers and causing a small commotion.

Craig noticed the drivers' eyes cast a wary look in the rear view mirror. The man pulled himself upright, using the back of chairs either side of the aisle. Just at this point everything went black. There must have been some sort of electrical fault as all the lights in the bus went out for a second or two.

During this brief moment, Craig saw the man's twisted shape in silhouette, arms outstretched in a ghastly parody of crucifixion. The image remained etched on Craig's retina like a strobe effect long after the lights had returned. The visual distortion, the ghostly desert backdrop, the Manson story; they all seemed to be blending together like a piece of Gothic wild-west theatre. Craig felt his hold on reality slipping.

Could the mountain-man somehow be orchestrating all this? Craig felt a subdued but rising panic, and turned back towards Pete who was frowning, engrossed in the sports section of a newspaper he'd picked up and nearing the end of another Marlboro. This broke the spell; a reassuringly familiar and friendly face instantly restored his sense of reality and gradually reduced his heartbeat.

The man sat back down heavily and smiled at Craig. He had spittle on his beard. His chest made a peculiar rattling noise then he dry-swallowed a couple of large tablets. The man said he hoped Craig didn't mind listening to such a long story. Immediately, Craig felt ashamed and embarrassed to have been scared by the man. He might be a little flaky but he seemed to be sincere and genuinely friendly. Craig assured him that he found the story fascinating.

"You see, I think now, it was the Ouija board that drove me directly towards Atkins and Kasabian the first time, and then towards Manson himself. The board kinda opened up a door and something evil came through it. You can't control what comes through that door once it's open."

"That's why I'm telling you all this. The story you told me was too much of a coincidence; I think maybe you were meant to find me and hear this as a sort of warning about messing with Ouija boards."

Craig wanted to smile inwardly and dismiss the man as more of a fruitcake than a flake after all but he couldn't. He must still be in the shadow of that sense of unreality he had experienced. The man was clearly being serious. Maybe he was mad, but maybe…just maybe not. Craig could sense warmth and compassion in him, and decided that he was a gentle giant even if his lift didn't quite reach the top floor.

As a sort of epilogue to this story, the man related how the event scarred him and ruined the next 7 years of his life. He had been unable to shake off the guilt he felt for not revealing what he knew that night and possibly saving lives. He was unable to get on with his life and out of this frustration and anger he drifted into delinquent behaviour and petty crime.

In 1977, he was in a courthouse awaiting trial for one of these offences along with twenty or so other prisoners when again he was shot through with a vision of a being of light. Jesus spoke to him and he felt the weight that had ground him down being lifted. He noticed that both his hands were bleeding from the palms. Several other men around him saw this.

He felt inexplicably happy and was smiling as he passed an armed guard who asked him what he had to be happy about. He explained about the vision and his wounds. The guard asked what had happened to the blood as there were no visible wounds on his hands. He pointed to the sink where he had washed off the blood. The guard checked the sink and was surprised to find traces of blood all around the bowl still.

Craig had always disliked and distrusted what he called the 'God Squad' but this man was different in that he did not seem to be a zealot, and mercifully did not try and convert him. After chatting about some lighter topics, the man went to the toilet at the back of the bus, and Craig pretended to be dozing when he returned so they didn't speak again. Having soon fallen into a real sleep, Craig woke on the outskirts of Las Vegas and the man was gone. Craig felt bad for not saying goodbye, and realised that he didn't even find out the man's name.

Minutes later, Craig and Pete were startled by the 80-90 degree heat that hit them as they walked off the bus. It had not occurred to either of them that it might be hot during the night. Just as Craig was going to launch into a condensed version of the mountain-man's story, Pete excitedly said, "Guess what? I was having a smoke at the back of the bus and got talking to this guy."

"Yeah."

"He used to work at Piper's last year, and knows everyone there. He was friends with Gregg and had some amusing stories about Ernest, but get this…"

"Go on," said Craig, wondering if his thunder was being stolen.

"He confirmed our theory that the place has mob connections and does shift a lot of coke. Joe's uncle was a major player in NYC…"

"The scary one that Ernest told us about?"

"Correct. He tried to take over a massive drug-trafficking operation there which upset the New York crime families who got official mafia approval for a contract to take him out. He was whacked last summer in a restaurant in broad daylight!"

Pete reached for a ciggie and looked like he was gagging to spill some more Piper's beans. Craig thought he'd hang fire on the mountain-man's story for now.

"I'll buy you a beer, Craiglet, and you can teach me how to play blackjack."

Circus Circus

As their luggage had been sent ahead in an earlier bus to the downtown depot, for some unfathomable reason, Craig and Pete decided to pick them up tomorrow. They felt pleasantly light and unencumbered. Although it was past 2, the place seemed to be buzzing. They agreed they might as well stay up all night and save on the hotel bill.

They wandered about 3 miles down the Strip, dazzled by the neon from all sides. The central area of the Strip seemed to consist mostly of casinos, clubs, motels and quickie-wedding chapels. As they stood outside one of these chapels, laughing at a grotesque neon cherub, a police car slowed down and a fat-faced double of Rod Steiger from 'In the Heat of the Night' glowered at them. The sincerity of his baleful stare chastened them into silence.

By 3.30, Craig's feet were aching and he felt himself starting to wilt. Even Pete, with his French Foreign Legion stamina, felt 'a bit knackered', and suggested they have a look inside Circus Circus. They passed under the gigantic creepy illuminated clown sign and entered the humungous stripy mock circus tent. They marvelled at the sheer scale of the place, the Big Top being several stories tall.

"Circus Circus, so big, they named it twice," said Craig.

There was even a slide for gamblers to get from the midway to the gaming floor. It was all a little overwhelming. There was a show involving performing poodles going on in the background. The air conditioning was a relief and so was the fact that Craig's fake ID did its job.

Pete bought a Time magazine and was soon immersed in an article on the Soviet invasion of Afghanistan whilst Craig purchased a booklet on how to play blackjack, to brush up, and check for any different rules in the US. They sat at a bar reading and sipping beer, looking up now and then at the aerial trapeze artists soaring high above their heads or beholding bevvies of showgirls dancing in enormous feathered headdresses and skimpy sequin-studded outfits.

For once, they were too tired to flirt with the statuesque cocktail waitress in a sexy majorette uniform, but she seemed a bit on the snooty side anyway. They soon realised that the beers were a mistake and switched to coffees.

A very smiley and friendly black croupier called Joanne managed to charm them into playing Keno, a sort of variant on Bingo, where you chose numbers on betting slips then 20 numbers were drawn via a random number generator and stand to win up to $25,000. Craig lost and went back to his blackjack book, whereas Pete won $8, and feeling confident, or possibly just attempting to chat up Joanne, had a few more attempts, before also losing.

Round about 6, when they were both feeling slightly spacey from lack of sleep, a thin, deep-tanned man in his late 20s or early 30s, wearing an expensive suit, sat next to Pete, and ordered a gin and tonic. Pete must have detected his accent as he asked the man if he was English. Craig soon wished his friend had bitten his tongue.

Hugo was indeed English, gay, and a confirmed admirer of Margaret Thatcher which put Craig's back up straight away. He had evidently gone to a posh public school and top university, judging by his self-assured manner, which came across as arrogance to Craig. He was in 'Sin City' on business, and was scathing about the American abuse of the English language, bemoaning the 'poverty of nuance' in even the most intellectually sophisticated American.

Pete seemed to find him interesting enough to while away half an hour listening to. Craig might have found some of Hugo's arch observations amusing if he wasn't running on empty, but instead he found the man's jaded and petulantly spiteful manner grating, so he returned his focus to the finer points of blackjack. He kept zoning out, then being jerked awake by the flying bodies in the periphery of his vision. He wondered how early one might rent out a room in a motel.

Hugo was expounding, in a loud voice, on the vagaries of foreign travel. Tokyo would have been nice apparently 'if it wasn't populated by drones'. Thailand had been ruined by a severe bout of diarrhoea due to insanitary conditions. Rome was a total nightmare 'because of the strikes'. His main complaint, however, seemed to be about the poor quality of men everywhere, except for London and the civilised parts of the United States.

Judging by the scorn poured on last night's sexual partner, who Hugo had left snoring in his hotel room, Las Vegas did not qualify as one of these parts.

He paused in his monologue to order another G and T, in an irritatingly brusque tone. Pete turned to Craig and quipped, "Around the World in 80 Assholes."

In another context, Craig may have found the comment offensive but in this moment, it caused him to almost choke on his coffee, laughing and spluttering at the same time. To Craig's relief, this seemed to induce paranoia in Hugo who made an excuse then took his drink elsewhere.

Craig went back to reading how players can split their hands three times to make up four hands and can split any pair of cards over and over. He found himself reading the same sentence over and over, too tired to absorb the words in front of him. Somebody then raised the volume and brightness of his surroundings in the mixing desk of his brain. The flashing, blinking lights of the slots started to strobe.

The clinking of coins and glasses and plastic chips formed a dense rhythm. The swooping figures arcing backwards and forwards above his head constructed a vast pendulum that swung between the waking state and dreaming. He dipped in and out of a reverie where ghosts flew above him, and around him like the transparent spectres from Disney's Haunted Mansion. He dimly realised he had started to levitate from his barstool and was floating upwards like a helium balloon.

Figures swished back and forth through the air as he rose. Beneath him two tiny figures were perched on stools at a bar, reading, 'players can split their hand 3 times to make up 4 hands…'. Upwards he floated, higher and higher. The scenes far below were like brightly coloured moving figures in a child's toy set.

Eventually, he felt the canvas of the Big Top pressing down on his head. He moved his head down so that his chin was resting on his chest and canvas now pressed down upon his neck. He thought he could make out a topless tattooed bald man molesting a female croupier on a green baize gaming table. Was that Travis!

People were crowded round, still betting. With a blissful release of pressure, he swam away through the air using breast stroke motions. He tried to swim down for a better view but could not control his movements. A female ghost in a pale Victorian gown flashed past then a pirate, mocking his efforts.

Eventually, he managed to pull his way through the thick air until he was hovering over an enormous woman sat feeding a slot machine from a bucketful of coins. Just then, she must have hit the jackpot as a torrent of shiny gold coins streamed noisily, Niagara-like out of the machine, until she disappeared completely beneath the golden flow. Dismayed, he tried to propel himself away. Two cowboy ghosts flew up to him and took an arm either side and helped escort him. They picked up speed and followed a trail of other ghosts down and out the entrance doors.

He felt a surge of horror as he simultaneously realised he was now a ghost like them, and also that they were hurtling towards Lucky, the clown sign outside. He was feeding on the ghosts, and they were seemingly drawn towards that appalling, lipsticked hole. Resistance was futile and he screamed as he was ushered towards the gaping maw that opened extra wide to swallow them all whole.

The black hole felt infinitely silent and devoid of light, but mere seconds later they all seemed to be spat out into the dark desert sky. The cowboys laughed as they jettisoned him, then they vanished. He now seemed to have gained the fledgling ability to fly like them. In a jerky fashion, he circled round and round above the Vegas skyline, reluctant to stray too far in case he could not get back but with a growing yearning to be free and to disappear into the Nevada night.

Then everything lurched, and he got a flash of Pete's face up close before he was pulled back, rather than flying back, at great speed, down to the Circus Circus sign and back through the mouth. After another pause of utter black nothingness, he opened his eyes to see carpet, shoes, and blinking lights at a strange tilted angle, then Pete's face filled his vision, asking if he was ok.

"Where am I?" he asked.

"You dropped off and fell off your chair. You're lucky the carpet broke your fall," said Pete, helping Craig to his feet.

Craig barely even registered the pain in his arm and his side. There was a small gaggle of staff and curious gamblers gathered around. His head was still reeling with images of ghosts and the feeling that he could fly. He babbled a bit about his experience but Pete was not listening. He spoke over Craig, telling him he was OK whilst hoisting him to his feet.

"Come on, you need some fresh air."

Unsteadily and with Pete's assistance, they soon made it outside, except of course it wasn't fresh but much warmer than inside. The early stages of dawn took them by surprise too, as it had still looked like night inside the casino. The sun was just below the horizon, colouring the sky orange and yellow. Looking up at the grinning Lucky sign, Craig said, "I've gone right off clowns."

Ant World

They could not believe the heat at 7 in the morning. According to a large sign that displayed the temperature as well as the time, it was already 86 degrees Fahrenheit. Combined with tiredness and for Craig, aches down his right side, they both felt in a slump.

It was mutually agreed to book into the first, reasonably-priced, hotel or motel they could find. This turned out to be the 'Holiday Motel' which had a small pool to the side. The price was not cheap for a slightly run-down looking establishment in need of a substantial refurb. Neither Pete nor Craig really registered any detail of their surroundings however, as they were both just pining to hit the sack.

The manager was a grey-haired man with glasses, in his 50s. His accent sounded German or possibly East European, and yet he introduced himself, incongruously, as Pedro. He had a gentle vibe but he was also very thorough and painfully slow in booking them in. Craig could sense Pete's grumpiness growing and feeling this might trigger some rudeness at any moment, he tried to offset this with excessive amenability.

Pedro struggled to pronounce Craig's name; it came out more like Cleg, which did cause a flicker of a grin from his friend. They paid upfront for one night and Pedro gave them their room key. Pete immediately started to walk off although Pedro was still in mid-flow about money-off deals with certain restaurants and casinos via a voucher system of some sort. Once Pete had disappeared out of sight around a corner, Craig apologised for cutting Pedro short and hurried off after him.

The room which overlooked the pool, was basic but a reasonable size. Pete laughed out loud.

"Haha, get a load of the pervy bed!"

Craig could not see anything out of the ordinary with the double bed and sat on it, half expecting a water bed, but it felt solid enough, when he bounced up and down on it.

"You have to turn it on first," said Pete.

He was reading some instructions taped to a black, clunky-looking piece of kit attached to the wall, above the bedhead.

"What does it do," asked Craig.

"It vibrates. Costs a quarter a go. Do you want to test it out?"

"Maybe later, I just want to kip right now."

"Me too, I'm shattered," agreed Pete.

Pete took the side nearest the door. Craig pulled the curtains as it was already bright out and only going to get worse. He was just about to flop onto the bed when he noticed something moving on the little bedside cabinet. He opened the curtains again, just a little, to see more clearly. It was a couple of ants scurrying about on the dark wooden surface. Hang on, there was a third, and a fourth…

"Urgh, bloody hell!"

"What?" mumbled Pete, not even opening his eyes.

"Ants," Craig said, succinctly summing up the problem.

He noticed one vanish over the edge of the cabinet and followed its progress over the side, gasping as he came across a dense line of comrades going in both directions and stretching down to the floor.

"I think the trail may continue under the bed," he said leaning down to take a look then suddenly realising Pete was stood right behind him, taut like a spring.

"It's in the bed I'm worried about," he snapped before whipping back the blanket and top sheet. Sure enough there was a breakaway faction, albeit smaller, snaking their way across the white sheet like a rogue platoon on a wintry mission.

"Fucking unbelievable!" he thundered, turning the cabinet towards him then picking up one of Craig's trainers he inflicted a massacre, whacking the heel against the invaders on the cabinet and on the bed, over and over. Then he ripped back the entire top sheet, screwed it up and threw it through the open door into the bathroom. Cowed, Craig watched the outburst in silence. Then Pete peeled back the undersheet from the corner, exposing an ugly selection of multi-coloured stains on the aging mattress.

"Urrgghh, that's revolting, but at least there's no more ants," breathed Craig with a modicum of relief.

"I don't even want to think about what caused those stains," said Pete, as Craig hurriedly replaced the sheet, but then went on to do just that. "I wonder if somebody could have died here…"

"I'm supposed to be the one with the wild imagination," said Craig, to break the tension, as he examined the inside of the pillow case.

Having vented his anger, Pete was now done with the ant situation and turned his back on the carnage, walking around the bed and throwing himself back onto his side. Craig fiddled around wiping both survivors and the dead from the chest with some toilet roll then flushing everything, before he would allow his desperately tired body to relax.

Sometime later, Craig heard a clicking noise like a key turning, and opened his eyes. Why was the room so dark now? He could barely make anything out. Perhaps, they'd slept right through to the following night. Then he heard breathing; deep laboured breathing, coming not from beside him but from the other side of the room. It was a slightly raspy, wheezy sort of sound that literally froze him in fear.

He couldn't even speak to alert Pete. Gradually, his eyes started to adjust to the dark and he could just make out the shape of a man stood against the far wall. Then the figure started to slowly approach the bed. He may have had a limp as there was a slight dragging motion. Time stood still as Craig's breathing paused.

The figure chose to come around his side of the bed. He thought he could just make out short scruffy hair and glasses. It was the manager, Pedro! He couldn't really see for sure but felt he just knew somehow. Once he reached the cabinet, he paused staring down at Craig.

Then he slowly reached out his large hand, wrist extended, thumb protruding, parallel to the four bunched curving fingers, as if he was holding a mug. For a millisecond, Craig wondered if Pedro might have brought him up a cup of tea for some reason, before his mind clicked into another more likely scenario; the hand was in a strangling grip. Very slowly, the arm extended towards his throat.

Craig couldn't move a muscle, he couldn't even blink. His heart felt like it was about to explode in his chest. Suddenly, a loud ringing noise erupted. A bedside light switched on and for the briefest of flashes as the hand was mere inches from his throat, Craig made out a trail of dark ants scurrying from a hole in the palm, pouring out and away up the arm, another burst of light then the figure was gone.

The noise stopped as Pete had picked up the phone next to him. Craig gasped for breath now the hold on him was released. There was a sharp pain in his chest and he wondered if he was having a heart attack. He sat up, fighting to get air into his lungs, whilst at some level aware that Pete was speaking to someone on the phone, oblivious to his plight.

"Yes, he's here. OK, I'll tell him. Yes, I'll get him to come down for them."

Craig was reeling in confusion. His brain told him that the episode with the intruder must have been a dream, but his body was giving him the opposite message. It had felt so vividly real, whereas this scene now with Pete on the phone felt thin and unconvincing. Pete hung up.

"Norman Bates wants you to go down and see him in his office."

Pete making a reference to 'Psycho', after what he'd just experienced, felt like too much of a coincidence; he asked himself if he was still dreaming.

"Why Norman Bates?" His voice sounded hollow, like it belonged to someone else.

"I dunno, he just strikes me as a bit of a weirdo," yawned Pete.

"I just now had a nightmare about Pedro coming into this room to murder me."

"Ha ha, really? Let's hope it wasn't a premonition."

Craig's heart rate was beginning to decrease. He took a long deep breath which seemed to stabilise him to some degree.

"Just as he was about to kill me, the phone rang and it was him, wanting to speak to me."

"If you're not back in 10 minutes, I'll call the cops," laughed Pete, then closed his eyes again and turned onto his side.

Craig felt a little hurt that Pete was being so cavalier about it all but as each second passed, the anxious sensation was fading and he began to feel slightly daft. He didn't relish going down to face Pedro but if he ignored the request Pedro would probably come up to the room which was worse as it might resemble the dream. Going down to see him break the stupid dream or put it in perspective. He went into the bathroom and splashed cold water onto his face then headed down to reception.

Despite an absence of natural light and a broken bulb on the staircase, the ugly brown and orange '70s stair carpet still managed to assault his sense of taste. It probably disguised any stains well though; this thought brought back the memory of that hideous mattress and then the ants. It suddenly occurred to him that the image in his nightmare of the ants emerging from a hole in someone's palm was inspired by a scene in Bunuel and Dali's silent surrealistic classic, 'Un Chien Andalou' which he saw at the Roxy in Wardour Street a few months ago.

This film itself famously used Freudian imagery to help convey the essence of real dreams and had now ironically helped create one of his. He also reflected that the man on the Greyhound bus with his tales of Charles Manson, not to mention the stigmata story could well have fed into the dream, as well as Pete speculating about someone dying in their bed. Deconstructing the dream took some of the sting out of it, and by the time Craig walked into reception he was feeling almost restored to normal.

Pedro looked up from reading the National Enquirer and smiled through very thick lenses in his metal-rimmed glasses.

"Hello, Cleg, I have sometheeng for you."

The open smile and gentle tone made him feel guilty for entertaining such dark thoughts about Pedro. He got up from his chair and beckoned Craig to follow him through a door behind him into a little office. Craig noticed that Pedro limped slightly, dragging his left foot, just like in the dream and yet he did not remember seeing Pedro move when they booked in, so how had he known that?

They continued on through the office into a small kitchen beyond. There was some awkward small talk. Pedro asked where he was from and how long he was staying in Vegas. He turned on a kettle by the fridge, then asked if Craig would like a cup of tea or coffee. Wanting to get this over with as soon as possible, Craig said no thanks.

Pedro persisted in his slow deliberate way, offering alternatives such as apple juice and water. Craig realised it might be easier to accept some hospitality and asked for water, knowing he could swig it down quickly. Pedro opened the fridge and took out a glass jug of chilled water then took an age decanting some into a glass. He talked about touristy things like going to see the Riviera and the Stardust.

Craig half-listened and nodded and said "aha" a lot. Pedro shuffled over to the side door of the kitchen which seemed to lead out to the pool area, and produced a key from his pocket and locked it. He launched into giving Craig all sorts of information about his discount vouchers and found a pile of them in a kitchen drawer.

He stood next to Craig, not giving him much personal space, showing him each voucher in turn. Craig noticed with distaste, a couple of small flakes of dandruff floating down onto his own arm. Pedro explained where each casino or restaurant was and which were thought of as the ones not to miss.

Craig stifled a sigh, thinking this was becoming tedious and how to make an excuse and leave, when Pedro's free hand dropped down between them, brushing Craig's trousers. He instinctively moved a step to the side but did not think much about it, assuming Pedro did not have good spatial awareness. Pedro kept on talking and shuffled right up next to Craig again.

"Here ees one you will like I think: 15% off the Folies Bergere show at ze Tropicana. It is a revue show based on a famous show in Paris," he said tapping the voucher, then his right hand dropped once more and fell against the front of Craig's trousers this time. "The Tropicana ees very nice place, only renovated last year."

Craig sidestepped again but was now up against the kitchen wall. He downed the rest of his glass of water in one and looking at his watch, he said, "Well thank you for these, Pedro, we really ought to make a move though now or we'll miss the day."

"Oh, just one minute please; I have sometheeng else in ze office."

He padded back into the office, almost closing the door behind him. Craig followed him this time. He stood looking through some paperwork in a tray on a filing cabinet, effectively blocking the narrow pathway through cluttered office equipment. Craig noticed a wheezy sound as Pedro breathed and impulsively swerved neatly around him, saying, "Thanks again but I really must be going."

Pedro looked crestfallen and slightly irritated.

"Please, it will only take a second."

Craig merely called out, "See you later," without looking back and hurried out through reception and back upstairs. Pete woke as he let himself in.

"Urrgghh! Cleg," Pete shook his head to wake himself up, "how was he?"

Craig wondered whether he should voice his doubt as to whether Pedro might have deliberately tried to fondle him or whether it was just clumsiness. He didn't fancy more piss-taking about how naïve he was, like when he brought Count back to Park Sunset, so he decided to embellish and play it for laughs.

"Well he didn't try and strangle me, which was a plus…but on the downside, he just touched me up in his kitchen."

"What? Seriously?"

Pete sat upright, his shocked expression giving way to one of anger rather than amusement as Craig had expected.

"Under the cover of showing me his bloody vouchers, he touched my dick through my jeans, with his other hand, making it seem accidental."

"I knew there was something up with him! Bloody nonce!" Pete sounded furious. "Do you want to report it to the police?"

"Nah, it'd be a waste of time: just be my word against his. It's hardly child-molesting anyway, I am an adult you know."

"Just…" said Pete, still seething.

Craig stretched his arms; "I'm just going to have a quick shower. Then I guess we ought to go to the downtown depot and collect our luggage."

By the time they left the motel, a quarter of an hour later, the temperature had climbed to well over 100 degrees Fahrenheit. Not being experienced travellers, neither of them had felt this kind of heat before.

"Jesus, I've just had a shower, I've gone about 20 yards and my shirt is sticking to my back," moaned Craig.

"I thought I liked the heat, but this is like having someone blasting you in the face with a hairdryer."

"We are going to have to take a cab," said Craig, expecting Pete to scoff and insist they use a bus, but surprisingly he agreed.

Craig zoned out in the back of the cab, staring at the hazy mountains surrounding the city, whilst Pete in the passenger seat talked with the driver about the current level of mafia presence in Vegas. Melancholy thoughts about Beth were hovering and he had to consciously push them away. The driver pointed out 'Glitter Gulch' which was the casino area in downtown Vegas.

After what seemed an interminable wait at the inhospitable depot, Craig couldn't find his luggage receipt and realised he must have left it back at the motel. There was zero chance that the jobsworth dealing with them would be swayed by Pete's assurances or Craig's description of his case, and Craig decided that he would make do without it, borrowing essentials from his friend. They took another cab back to the motel for Pete to drop off his case then decided to have a quick dip in the pool to cool off.

The water was icy but for once Craig had no complaints about this. They didn't linger as they were quite peckish by now.

Back out in the oven, Craig was so relieved they weren't going to have to walk for miles, and it was only a block before they came across a McDonalds. After eating they lingered, savouring the air conditioning. Finishing off his milkshake, Craig picked up a free map left on a table and looked to see what was in the vicinity.

They decided that Caesars Palace was not too many blocks away and as it was the biggest and most luxurious hotel and casino on the Strip, that they ought to check it out. A family of four, sitting next to them, had evidently been listening to their conversation as the dad blurted out, "You guys are gonna love the Palace. Best joint in Vegas. We saw Sinatra there a couple of years ago, spectacular!"

Pete and Craig nodded politely without actually encouraging further conversation.

"Liberace too, hun," prompted his wife.

"Yeah, he was something else," said her hubby.

"Don't forget Tom Jones, he was my favourite. We've seen him three times here, haven't we."

"He got so many panties thrown at him, it was kinda wild," he confided, which drew a disapproving look from his wife. Craig looked at the terminally bored looking son and daughter and felt sorry for them.

"So what's the best thing you've seen in Vegas so far?" the dad asked.

"Yeah, been what's your favourite sight or activity?" asked the Mum.

Both adults fixed on them with such keen, earnest interest that neither Pete nor Craig could bring themselves to be sarcastic. Pete blew his cheeks out and frowned, looking like he was struggling to choose between so many contenders. Craig thought he might as well be honest:

"For me, I think it is the desert location, rather than the city itself."

The couple looked a little confused and disappointed. There was silence for a few seconds.

"So who do you think you'll go and see? Wayne Newton is playing I think…" said the dad.

"Ooh yeah, they call him Mr Vegas don't they, hun…"

"This place is an old crooners' graveyard," said Craig to Pete outside, as they once more battled the fierce desert heat.

"I want to go home," said Pete in an affected little boy's voice.

"Home?" echoed Craig in surprise.

"LA," Pete clarified.

"Of course. Shall we cut our stay here short then and maybe just stay one more night?"

"I was hoping you'd say that," said Pete sounding happier already.

The entrance way to Caesars Palace was set back from the street. They turned into the long luxuriously landscaped driveway and filed past the grand row of fountains that Evel Knievel almost died jumping over, back in '67. They were both struck dumb by the sheer scale of the place.

Both of them felt disenchanted in general by the transformation of a desert town for mobsters and gamblers into a decadent escapist theme park for American tourists. A Disneyland for adults but without the childlike sense of wonder. Although there was an undeniable surrealism to Las Vegas, it struck them both as tacky rather than exciting. Although many derided LA as fake or phoney, it felt like a real city to them rather than this artificial desert folly.

They passed through throngs of gladiator greeters and waitresses dressed as Cleopatra, into the main casino building and wove through marble statues avoiding beer-soaked hot-dog stalls. Craig could not take his eyes off the crystal-studded ceiling. They sat at a relatively quiet blackjack table where Craig hoped to put his rekindled knowledge of the game into action. Pete chose to just spectate, at least until he worked out how to play. He ordered beers from a passing Centurion.

Unlike his father, Craig was not a gambler by nature, but was quite cautious, at least in that sphere. He gave himself a firm $50 limit to play with. Things started surprisingly well, and after 20 minutes he was up by 75 bucks. Craig noticed Pete become quite involved in the game, smiling and laughing for the first time since they had arrived.

Inspired by Craig's modest winning streak, Pete bought $25 worth of chips to join in, saying, "When in Rome…" but somehow lost the lot in just three or four hands. Craig enjoyed playing but the novelty was already wearing off by the time his luck inevitably ran dry. Craig recognised this was the time to call it a day while he was still over $30 up.

They decided to abandon the bacchanalian pleasures of ancient Rome and search instead for a good ol' twentieth century American dive bar. The day was no longer young but the sun was still a demon. Within 10 minutes, they compromised and settled for the Holiday Inn hotel as they were passing.

Back in London, they had enjoyed a sedate drink in the moodily-lit Holiday Inn on Park Lane not long ago and pictured a similar experience, but this was a mammoth hotel with a huge brightly-lit busy bar and a gigantic TV screen. Nevertheless, there was air conditioning and more significantly, it was 'Happy

Hour', when all drinks were half price. They decided that this was the right time to road test a couple of cocktails.

"The perfect way to dispose of my winnings," announced Craig.

"We might as well go to town as it is our last night in Vegas," said Pete.

"Is that the royal 'we'?" asked Craig.

"Yes, clearly I meant you might as well go to town."

Pete chose a Blue Hawaiian for starters whilst Craig opted for a White Russian. They were pleasant enough but on scanning the contents in a cocktail menu, Craig spotted the drink for them.

"Long Island Iced Tea, man, that's the one. Check out the spirits in this!"

"Wow," said Pete, "vodka, tequila, rum, triple sec, whatever that is, *and* gin. You're right, it has our names on it."

They managed to fit in two iced teas each before Happy Hour ended then followed them up with a couple of beers.

It was dusk by the time they staggered out of the Holiday Inn and headed back for the motel.

"That's the strongest tea I've ever had," proclaimed Pete.

"Ha, yeah, they were nice. I could get used to them," said Craig, "in Happy Hour anyway."

Alcohol had restored their sense of humour, and they laughed about Piper's characters most of the way back. A sign outside a small chapel reading 'Jesus Christ is fire insurance' tickled Craig's funny bone. They even saw an amusing side to Pedro, albeit mostly portraying him as a potential psycho killer.

They were still giggling like schoolgirls when they reached the motel. They hadn't given their room key in when they went out, so they tried to sneak past Pedro who looked deep in concentration at his desk, but he saw them and his face lit up.

"Ah, Mr Cleg and his friend. Good evening. Were you using any of the discount vouchers?"

Craig said no at the same time that Pete answered yes.

"Umm, I meant yes…" mumbled Craig.

"Just the one so far in the Riviera. Very satisfactory," smarmed Pete.

"Good, very good, I am happy," beamed Pedro. "I think I find another one or two that have interest."

"Excellent," smiled Pete, "I will send Cleg down for them shortly. Au revoir."

Craig punched Pete in the arm as they tumbled up the stairs laughing. The bed had been made in their absence but there was a familiar camel train of little black figures traversing the hills that were Craig's pillows.

"They're back," he sighed. "Why is it always my side?"

"Sweeter blood, or maybe semen," suggested Pete.

Craig pulled back the cover and top sheet to reveal a dozen or so more scurrying for safety.

"We could go and demand he give us a different room…"

"We could…" Pete grinned, "or, we could trash this shithole then get a night bus back to dear old Hollywood…"

"Tonight?" Craig pondered the pros and cons, as far as his smashed state allowed.

"Think, we could be back in time for breakfast at Ben Franks then spend a leisurely day in Piper's."

As Pete said this he wandered to the window and tugged gently on one of the curtains. Craig looked at him with an uncertain expression. Pete nodded, as if to say it will be OK, then gave a hard yank at the curtain, pulling it down amidst a flurry of curtain hooks.

Craig shrugged, said, "Fuck it," then joined Pete at the window and followed suit with the other curtain. They stood howling with laughter. Craig put on one of the curtains like a cape and circled wildly with his arms outstretched. Pete started pulling out drawers from the chest and throwing them onto the bed.

Craig picked up the plastic bin, which was empty and drop-kicked it across the room. Pete lobbed it back at him. Craig picked up a Gideon bible on the bed, which must have been in one of the drawers.

"Do you think I could reach the pool with this?" he asked Pete, and opened the window as far as it would go.

Pete surveyed the 10 feet or so of swimming pool visible to the side and the oblique angle involved.

"A buck says you can't."

Craig steadied himself, put his arm behind his head then hurled it as hard as he could. They both whooped with joy at the resulting splash.

"You're going straight to hell, boy!" screeched Pete in a southern accent.

They waited to see if Pedro would appear, but all remained silent. Pete turned to the bed and started using his fag end to burn holes in one of the pillowcases. Craig picked up his bedside cabinet which was small and light, carried it into the bathroom and placed it in the bath. Pete asked him to help him turn the empty chest upside down which tickled them anew and inspired further creative furniture arranging, such as placing the TV in the freestanding wardrobe, then turning this around so it faced the wall.

Craig was almost crying with laughter and was doubled up as it was actually making his stomach hurt. Pete repeatedly kicked the bed massager unit on the wall, moaning that it was fixed too firmly. Then the phone rang and they froze.

"Shit, that will be Pedro complaining about the noise."

"He's going to come up here and take an axe to us," mocked Craig in a quavering voice.

Pete cleared his throat and answered the phone.

"Carter and Lawes waste disposal service, how may I help you?… Oh hello Pedro, no this is Pete… Oh you've found some more…how delightful. Cleg will be down once he's finished snacking on these ants. Bye for now."

"More vouchers?"

"Yep. Perhaps you should collect them and we'll turn them into a nice artwork for him."

Craig decided to wrap the wall mirror completely in toilet roll and whilst enacting this he reflected that he could not recall a time when he had felt such anarchic abandon, such liberation as this. He felt truly alive. Pete had rolled up a sheet into a thin tubular shape and tied it to the bedhead then threw the other end out of the window.

"We can use this to escape if Pedro does come up," he said and Craig was not sure if he was joking or not.

Pete found a biro and wrote on the bed massager instructions: 'Beware. Danger of electrocution when ejaculating'. Craig went into the bathroom again and fashioned a nice large picture of an ant out of toothpaste, over the mirror.

"Hey, Keith Moon," he called out to Pete, "you might want to rein in the damage as I just remembered Pedro took your passport details when we booked in."

"Oh yeah," called back Pete, sounding nonplussed, "Still, this is only a bit of light redecoration really, isn't it. We should bill Pedro."

Winding up with an appropriate parting gesture, Craig scooped up a few remaining ants and placed a tumbler from the bathroom over them on the upside down chest, and wrote a little note on one of Pedro's vouchers saying, 'Please feed the ants.' There was just enough of Pete's toothpaste left to write 'The Ant

Suite' on the outside of their door as they left. They crept down the gloomy staircase and peered around the corner. Pedro was sat at his desk as usual.

They stood no chance of sneaking out without him seeing, and they didn't fancy a protracted explanation as to why they were leaving early. They walked through the corridor leading towards the back of the building and soon found a back door. The fact that it was alarmed seemed neither here nor there given the circumstances so they opened it and walked out.

They seemed to have no choice but to go around the side by the pool in which the bible was still floating. They then ducked down under Pedro's window, trying to suppress more laughter, and hurried back on to the main road.

"Ah poor Pedro, I feel sorry for him now, he's kind of sweet really," said Craig.

"Only you would feel sorry for someone who tried to molest you," was Pete's sharp retort.

"I may have exaggerated the fondling slightly. I'm wondering if I could have imagined it altogether."

They ignored their no cabs rule once more and within 15 minutes were back at the downtown Greyhound depot. Craig had found his receipt and reclaimed his luggage. Then they bought tickets for the next bus to LA but this wasn't until just after midnight so they had almost 90 minutes to kill.

Their high spirits were rapidly wearing off now, along with the alcohol in their systems. The seating was very uncomfortable and the depot seemed to be full of edgy or aggressive people; they witnessed an attempted mugging and a minor fight as well as several bad tempered arguments. A grumpy policeman patrolling the area, kicked out anyone sleeping on benches unless they could produce bus tickets and completely ignored a potentially violent argument going on under his nose, before crossing the road to buy a snack.

"Good riddance to Las Vegas," said Pete when they finally boarded their bus.

"I should have listened to Beth; she warned me we wouldn't like it," said Craig.

They were both asleep before they had even passed the city limits sign.

Night Visitor

It felt good to be back in LA again, where the heat was pleasant but not overwhelming, where their bed was ant-free and there were no Centurions in the lobby. Here they were, back in Park Sunset at 3 in the morning, out of their heads on high quality coke from Piper's and a couple of black beauties each, sprawled across their dishevelled double bed, romanticising the City of Angels once more; especially the denizens of Piper's where of course they had spent their first evening back.

Pete had been reading aloud from the LA Times an account of a recent riot in Bristol, of all places.

"Typical," moaned Craig, "the first bit of excitement the country gets in years and we're abroad!"

Neither of them had been able to concentrate for long enough to finish the article. Pete had just completed 20 press-ups by the door and was now dancing around the bed singing *Uptight*. Craig distractedly joined in on the chorus from the bed, whilst scanning the gig page in the LA Weekly.

"Fear are playing the Starwood tomorrow night with The Screamers. That's a decent double bill. What do you say, Pete?"

Craig looked up, his friend was lost in Wonderland, outtasight in fact, but it had to be said, was looking quite sharp with some of those moves. There was a snake-hipped, loose-limbed abandon he could not recall noticing before. Craig felt semi-reluctantly sucked into the rhythm and started to clap along. Pete pranced up alongside him on the bed, grinding and thrusting like James Brown on steroids.

"Gimme some lovin', white boy!" he howled and grabbed Craig's head with both hands, pulling it towards his gyrating crotch.

Craig merely pushed him away and resumed clapping, long since used to such behaviour. Pete strutted back towards the foot of the bed, when a loud bang outside caused him to freeze.

"Whoa, was that a gunshot?" said Craig, the hand claps abruptly halted.

Pete said nothing, poised mid-step in a game of musical statues, but his eyes and ears were focused and alert like a Dobermann that's just heard a cat.

"I suppose it could have been a car back-firing," mused Craig doubtfully.

"Beretta, 9 millimetre," murmured Pete in a grizzled world-weary cop kind of way.

"Blimey!" said Craig, impressed, "how on earth do you know that?"

"I don't, you dork!" Pete grinned then threw himself on the bed next to Craig and reached for a Marlboro from amidst the clutter on his bedside cabinet.

"You know where Filthy Mcnasty's is…"

Craig looked baffled for a second; "Oh yeah, the club by Larrabee…"

"Ted was telling me it used to be a real gangster hangout."

"Who the hell is Ted?"

Pete laughed; "The desk guy."

"Oh, Mr Charisma. Your new buddy has hidden depths then, does he?"

Pete burst back into *Uptight*, employing a halfway decent falsetto, then interrupted himself: "Anyway, Mickey Cohen, who worked for Capone and Bugsy Siegel, and became LA's biggest mafia boss used to run his extortion racket from a haberdashery shop just up the road, near the Psychedelic Conspiracy in fact. He survived several assassination attempts on the Strip, including one at Sherry's…"

"Which is now Gazzari's, I know. I've been doing my homework too," said Craig, returning his attention to the gig page.

"You know that guy in Piper's tonight who asked us if we had any grass…"

"Uh huh, the new wave band…" grunted Pete as he fiddled with his lighter.

"The Visitors, yeah; I think I saw them a couple of weeks ago with Beth, playing Madame Wongs West. They are playing there again on Sunday. They were pretty tight."

"Why didn't you tell him you'd seen them?"

"I dunno really," said Craig scratching his scalp, "the thing is he said they were called the Visitors, plural, but the band I saw were billed The Visitor, singular, so I wasn't sure it was the same crew, plus I didn't recognise any of them."

A loud wailing siren put a full stop to his sentence which had not really been going anywhere.

"See, Beretta 9 millimetre," smirked Pete.

"Just like Finchley eh," said Craig.

"Maybe Bristol, the way things are going," he inhaled deeply.

Craig leant his head back on the lumpy pillow.

"What was Bob Atcheson going on about earlier? Bigfoot?"

Pete roared with laughter.

"Yeah, he swears he saw him on the Universal lot!"

"Did it occur to him that they might be making a Bigfoot movie or TV show there?"

"I doubt it," smiled Pete, "ah, I want to adopt him."

Just then, there was a tap at the door.

"Who the fuck is that?" asked Pete loudly, "it's almost 3:30."

"Probably someone complaining about the noise," mumbled Craig as he got up from the bed.

He cautiously opened the door a few inches. There in the dimly-lit corridor stood a tall, slim, stunning looking black girl with a neat Afro, in a shiny fur-trimmed bomber jacket, grinning from ear to ear.

"Er hello…" said Craig awkwardly as the girl was not saying anything. "Hi," she drawled in what sounded to Craig like a slightly southern lilt. "Sorry to bother you guys. I was looking for a friend. I'm not sure what room he's in and I heard laughing and thought it might be him."

"I'm afraid not…" started Craig.

"Come in, my dear," Pete intoned in a Terry Thomas kind of way, pushing Craig to one side and flinging the door open wide.

The statuesque beauty laughed and glided in to their room. Craig felt a little dislocated, but Pete took control and closed the door behind the visitor then grinned wolfishly and in an absurd theatrical aside to Craig, whispered loudly, "Pussy from heaven!"

Craig cringed instantly as she must have heard this remark but she merely said, "These accents are cute. Where y'all from?"

A mere 10 minutes later, and this lithe creature who called herself Candy ("how apt," said Pete), was laying on the bed between them. Craig could not quite work out how this had happened. She had fearlessly entered the room of two excitable male strangers in the middle of the night, giggled a lot, flirted with them and was now sharing their bed and her life story. She hailed from a large impoverished family in South Carolina apparently, but was lured away from home a couple of years ago by the glamour of Tinseltown.

She seemed to have the gift of the gab, and Pete almost dribbled as he lapped up every word. He had been literally all over her from the outset, emboldened by the chemicals coursing through his veins. Candy seemed completely unfazed by him, possessed by a powerful self-assurance. She took Pete in her stride, teasingly egging him on one moment then holding him at bay the next.

Craig somehow sensed trouble. From the moment she appeared, he had felt uneasy. He watched Pete and her, who were now french-kissing next to him, and told himself not to be a killjoy. Did he feel jealous? Perhaps. After all, she seemed to like him just as much, but Pete had simply assumed Craig would move aside because of his thing, his fetish, for black women.

A thought flickered dimly and briefly in the shadowy parts of his consciousness that perhaps he was jealous of Candy rather than Pete. Was he really worried that she would break up their cosy bachelor party and turn their feelgood buddy movie into a dramatic love triangle?

Candy suddenly announced she thought she ought to leave. Pete was immediately distraught that this fantasy woman might disappear as easily as she arrived and pleaded with her to stay. Craig asked if she had anywhere to go. She vaguely replied that she would be all right then looked at him piercingly and said, "Do *you* want me to stay, Craig?"

He was aware of Pete behind her making frantic affirmative gestures.

"Well, you can't walk around Hollywood by yourself at this time of night."

"Thank you for your hospitality, boys," her 'girly' voice returning, "I will stay then."

"Yes!" Pete punched the air.

"On one condition," she continued, turning towards Pete, "no one tries anything tonight, and maybe, *maybe,* they'll get what they want in the morning."

Pete rubbed his hands together gleefully.

"Did you hear that, Craigy? Oh I love this city!"

Craig had to laugh: Pete was like a little boy with a tenner in a sweetshop.

The sun was beginning to creep around the edges of the dingy curtains by the time Pete and Candy had finally shut up. Candy had even sung a few gospel songs she remembered from her childhood. These might have moved him in other circumstances, but he was shattered now the Charlie had worn off, and he just craved sleep.

It had been agreed that Candy would sleep in the middle. Everyone was under the sheets in their underwear. Craig realised he must have dropped off because now he was jolted awake by a hand sliding up the inside of his thigh. He turned away so he was facing the wall, his back towards Candy.

A minute or two later, as he was beginning to think she may have got the message, the hand was back and this time it went further. I'm going to have to put a stop to this, he thought or I will get turned on, then Pete will notice and be very upset, or livid. Although Candy was striking looking with beautiful eyes, he was not particularly attracted to her so it was not a massive hardship to be selfless. He gently but firmly removed her hand, turned around to face her again and whispered, "I'm gay."

"Wha? You ain't gay!" she hissed back.

"I'm afraid so."

"Why're you with him then?"

"We're friends. He doesn't have a problem with it."

There was a pause.

"I don't believe you."

"Why do you think I'm pushing you away?"

"Maybe you's a racist…or maybe you want me an' your friend to get it on."

Another pause while Craig tried not to show any reaction.

"Or maybe I'm gay."

Candy giggled briefly.

"You is a dark horse, Craig."

"And it's time to hit the hay," he whispered, turning over once more to face the wall.

He was not at all sure she had bought it but as seconds turned into minutes, with no more activity, he began to relax. Just before his consciousness slipped away, he wondered if he had seen Candy before, in the foyer of Park Sunset talking to someone on the couch… So what anyway.

Bird Trouble

"Craig!"

"Unnnhh", Craig murmured clinging on to his dream of Rachel performing ballet in the Debenhams kitchenware department (where they had met, doing seasonal Christmas jobs).

"Craig!"

A hand shook his shoulder. Debenhams vaporised as Craig's eyes opened. He was looking at a patch of sunlight on a light green wall. His head was a cement mixer full of cotton wool. He felt disorientated for a couple of seconds, and realised it was because he was on the other side of the bed to usual.

"Craig, wake up!"

He sensed that Pete's voice had been urgently calling him for a while now. He dopily turned around and was startled to find himself staring into the sleeping face of a girl, just inches away. The whole bizarre scenario of their visit in the dead of night came back to him with a jolt. Behind Sleeping Beauty, Pete was mouthing something and gesticulating.

"What?" he whispered.

"Get up and leave us alone," Pete rasped.

Craig felt a flush of irritation and resentment at being told what to do and especially being told to get out of his own room. The feeling quickly faded as it used up too much energy, and also Craig dimly comprehended that it was a significant threshold moment for Pete.

"Where should I go?" he whispered feebly.

"I don't care. Get some breakfast or something but don't come back for a couple of hours."

Craig carefully slipped out of the bed then pulled on his black jeans that were lying in a heap on the floor and found a fresh t-shirt. He forced his feet into his trainers without bothering to unlace them first. He checked he had a few dollars in his pocket, splashed cold water on his face and ruffled his hair in front of the mirror before giving Pete the thumbs up sign.

Pete was wearing a pools winner smile and rubbed his hands with glee once more then mimed squeezing Candy's buttocks. Craig tried to open the door quietly but the lock inevitably made quite a clicking sound, causing Candy's eyes to open. He hurried out pretending that he didn't hear her say groggily, "Where you goin'?"

The sunlight on Sunset hurt his eyes and he wished he had picked up his shades. His head started to throb as he slouched towards Crescent Heights and he could feel his t-shirt sticking to his back already. As he passed Cliff Raven's Tattoo Parlour he recognised John Hurt walking towards him. He was sporting an absurd moustache, presumably grown for a role.

If Pete had been there, they would have probably egged each other on to say something, if only an abusive comment about the facial hair, but as Craig felt fragile he merely nodded on passing as if greeting an old friend. This star spotting reminded him that he was living in the glamorous city of angels and lifted his spirit.

Craig walked a long way down Sunset past their old haunt the Travel Lodge, then crossed over to the Denny's on the corner. Shandy was nowhere to be seen, meaning it must be a shift day off. Over toast and coffee at the front counter, Craig gradually pieced together a plan for the day as the caffeine chased the cotton wool clouds away.

He would now have to phone Shandy, and invite her to the Starwood to see the Fear and Screamers double-header. That way, he could go back and stay at hers afterwards and not have to play gooseberry all night. It occurred to Craig that he hadn't picked up his fake ID card either which meant he might have trouble buying beer that evening.

Thinking about it, he also didn't have his contact lens solution which meant another headache as he would have to sleep with his lenses in for another night. Sighing, he resigned himself to returning to the love nest after all, to collect some essentials plus some spare clothes. Pete had said to stay out for a couple of hours. Craig looked at his bare wrist: there was another thing he'd left behind.

He must have already been out for a good forty five minutes. He decided to kill some more time productively by summoning the muse. He asked the waiter for a pen, and before long he was scribbling down some lyrics on the back of his paper napkin.

'I get so far out I no longer see the bars.

And emotions are distant like the stars.

But the man in the mirror beckons me.

He says pain is a friend of memory.'

He recognised that the melancholy words were connected to Rachel. Last night's dream of her was still fresh. He could see that he had been trying to block out his painful feelings for her but his conscious mind could not police his dreams.

'I still wear her words like scars.

I don't believe in life on Mars.'

He felt better for releasing the feelings even though he winced a little at the clunky melodrama of the words.

'Twigs snap like bones in my December wood.

I would leave my body here if I only could.'

He almost crossed out the last couplet but decided not to censor himself, to stop resisting and go with the flow.

'I locked horns with the Beast in bed.

Now dreams are gone and love is dead.'

Embarrassed, he became aware that his eyes were welling up. He took a sip of lukewarm coffee and put down the pen; the spell was broken. He folded the napkin and stuffed it into his pocket, intending to add it to his all-purpose notebook later.

"What were you writing?"

He looked around to see who had spoken. Two stools along from him was perched a petite figure in black with a brown blouse. Two dark glittering beady eyes fixed him.

"Me?" he said. His voice quavered oddly. "Oh nothing, just a shopping list."

"Shopping, ha!" she chirped loudly.

He wasn't sure if this meant she didn't believe him or that she didn't like shopping. Or maybe she just found his accent amusing. He was relieved that she didn't pursue it but instead jerked her head towards the waiter.

"May I have a fresh glass of water, this one is dirty."

The waiter said nothing but took her glass away. Craig observed the woman discreetly. Something peculiar about her look and manner intrigued him. Her body was the size and shape of a twelve year old child though judging by the face and grey hair she had to be in her 60s.

She wore an implausibly short black skirt for her age and black tights that emphasised the scrawniness of her legs. She made lots of abrupt darting movements with her head and clutched a large black handbag tightly on her lap. When she leant forward and daintily pecked at a toasted muffin, Craig suddenly grasped what she had reminded him of and almost snickered out loud causing the beady eyes to shoot around in his direction.

She is just like a bird he thought, in fact not just any bird but a tiny sparrow, in her brown and black clothes. He wondered if she qualified as a Sunset. Was she strange enough? Random forthright comments to strangers might qualify as eccentric behaviour in England, but here it was virtually the norm.

Hang on though, he thought, *what's she up to now*? She was peering into her oversized bag and ferreting around in it for something. She produced a 6" by 4" photograph and smiled broadly. She turned to show the large man on her left and in a sing song voice said, "That's me!"

The man seemed oblivious to her, leaning forward, squinting at his newspaper; possibly having trouble reading it through the fog of cigar smoke that enveloped him. He had a huge bullneck covered in short frizzy grey hair which reminded Craig of an elephant's hide. The woman tried again, this time placing her photo on top of the article he was reading.

"That's me!" she trilled.

"Unnghh!" grunted the man, his bullneck bristling. He flicked the photo aside as if it were an irritating fly, without even looking up. The woman became all agitated until she had safely retrieved the photo from the other side of the counter. Disappointed by the lack of response, she turned towards Craig and repeated, "That's me!"

"May I see?" he said with politeness but also genuine interest.

Beaming with pride she placed the photo carefully and squarely in front of him. It was an old black and white print in reasonably good condition considering it probably dated back to the '20s or '30s. A young girl of 10 or so, and a boy of similar age in old fashioned but reasonably fancy clothes were standing in front of a large detached wooden house. The girl's hair was windswept but she was smiling shyly for the camera. The boy looked hesitant, even a little nervous.

"It's a very nice photograph," he said. "That's a pretty dress you had there."

"Sunday best!" she chirruped then gave a high pitched little laugh. This photo has really brought her to life he thought, wondering what the story was behind it.

"Was that your house?" he asked.

"In Ohio, yes," then her voice lowered a little and her smile slipped. "Until Daddy had to go away and we had to move across the country to a horrid little house in a nasty little town." She checked herself and the beam returned.

"I was so happy there," she gushed with authentic emotion.

"Who is the little boy? Your brother?"

The woman unexpectedly snatched up the photo and thrust it back into her bag.

"Mind your own cockamamie business!" she shrieked with a malevolent glint in her eye.

"I'm sorry," Craig stammered, taken aback, "I didn't mean to upset you."

The woman huffed and puffed, turning her back to Craig and muttered a stream of angry words that he couldn't quite catch. *Undoubtedly, the bird woman was a 24 carat Sunset*, Craig thought, frustrated that he would never discover the mystery of the nervous little boy or the father's disappearance. The father probably took the photo, Craig mused, as he drained his coffee cup.

Perhaps, he was an abusive father and that could be why he "had to go away." He ceased his pointless wild speculation, and pulled out the napkin from his pocket. So he would remember to tell Pete about her and to remind him to make a diary entry, he wrote down, 'The Sparrow Lady'.

"Did you forget something on your list?" The woman's sweet girly voice had returned and the beady gaze was fixed on him again.

"Yes, wild bird food," he said, folding up the napkin and pushing it back into his pocket. She blinked several times and continued to stare. He was no longer in the mood for mentally imbalanced strangers and asked the waiter for the bill.

Craig killed some more time window shopping on Santa Monica Boulevard. He spent longest in the occult store near Fairfax, browsing through books on witchcraft and paganism, but he felt it was disappointingly tacky, having imagined an authentically sinister curiosity shop straight out of Rod Serling's 'Night Gallery'. Eventually, Craig decided that he must have been out of the apartment for two hours and headed back.

Craig deliberately made a bit of a palaver out of unlocking the door to give Pete and Candy some warning that he was back. This was clearly a waste of time as both of them were naked and oblivious; Candy sat astride Pete, her pert backside, facing Craig, was bouncing up and down.

"The return of the thin white duke!" shouted Pete, in high spirits for some reason.

"Er, sorry," said Craig, averting his eyes, "I think I was out for a couple of hours."

"Hi, Craig," drawled Candy, grinning mischievously over her shoulder. "Why don't you join in?" She wiggled her backside as she spoke which Craig couldn't help noticing despite trying to look away.

"Because I'm queer, darling, remember," he said trying hard to sound queeny, whilst walking over to the chest of drawers.

"All the more fun for Pete. He can screw me whilst you take him from behind!"

"I think Craig probably prefers receiving to giving," grinned Pete. She laughed loudly.

Craig wasn't entirely sure they were joking. He felt distinctly uneasy as he fished around for his passport, spare clothes and Shandy's number and felt his anger rising too, mainly at Pete. He had done him a favour, pissed around for 2 hours whilst feeling like shit, just so Pete could get his end away, only to come back and be ridiculed.

"Aww, are you angry with us, Craig?" patronised Candy.

"No, don't worry about me, you resume copulation. I'll just grab a few things then I'll be out of your hair," he said, his voice not quite concealing his resentment. He had to move around the far side of the bed next to them in order to retrieve his watch, lens solution and fake ID.

As he stuffed these into his knapsack they both grabbed him and pulled him on top of them. He went with the roll then turned it into a neat backwards flip, extricating himself from their grip and landing on the other side of the bed, surprising himself with his agility.

"Have a nice day now," he mocked in his crudest American accent then, hoisting his knapsack onto one shoulder, he made a swift exit before they could cajole, apologise or jump on him to restrain him.

Hot Spots

"What are you doing out here, Craig?" said a voice, waking him suddenly from another reverie about Rachel.

It took a few seconds to work out where he was. Pete had asked to be left alone with Candy for the night, and after chatting up Betsy in Piper's for 2 hours and downing several coffees in Ben Franks, he'd ended up here, around 3, on this fraying two-seater couch in the foyer of Park Sunset. The voice belonged to a moustachioed man who was leaning over the couch gently shaking him.

Oh yes; the guy with the apartment backing onto the pool, who they'd chatted with recently. David, he was fairly sure that was his name. The pieces started to click into place.

"It's 5, man; you can't possibly spend the night out here. Come and crash in my room."

Maybe he was still groggy with sleep, but at that point Craig saw no reason to reject the offer of a comfortable bed.

"Come in, make yourself at home." This wasn't difficult as the room was almost identical to Craig's current home, but a cleaner mirror-version of it. David gestured to the far side of the double bed, by the window.

"So Pete told you to get lost for the night huh."

"Something like that," said Craig. He kicked off his shoes, pulled back the bed cover and flopped onto the crisp white sheets.

"Some friend eh," said David, sitting on the other side of the bed. "At least take your jeans off."

Craig complied, slipping them off beneath the cover.

"Do you like movies, Craig?"

A strange question, he thought, *at this hour, even in the film capital of the world.*

"Yeah, I'm a bit of a buff I suppose," he said, trying to stifle a huge yawn.

"Great," beamed David, "you'll get a kick out of this then."

161

Craig looked across at him expecting to be shown a rare poster or some autographed memorabilia, but David had his back to him, leaning off the bed, fiddling with something. Then he heard the click of a power switch followed by a curious whirring noise. Craig's semi-awake state struggled to comprehend the flickering light on the wall opposite, and why the man next to him was jumping up then turning off the room light. A blurry figure appeared on the wall.

"Goddam focussing," mumbled David.

"Oh right, you've got a projector," observed Craig, adding lamely, "that's nice."

David fumbled with the machine on his bedside cabinet, which Craig hadn't even noticed as he came in, and a young blonde woman materialised from the colour and light in front of him. She appeared to be engrossed in housework, wafting a large feather duster around.

I hope this is short, thought Craig, who was feeling confused and a little resentful that he was being deterred from his sleep. Only when the doorbell rang and a burly man with permed hair, a large moustache and a toolbox appeared, did the penny start to drop what sort of movie show this was to be. At least that explained why David would be showing a film at 5 in the morning, but on the other hand, what sort of person would invite an almost total stranger into his room at 5 in the morning and show him 8mm porn movies?

The man had laid out his tools and started to repair the TV set whilst the woman climbed onto the settee to remove a cobweb on the ceiling. At this stage, Craig was not yet worried; he was merely annoyed that he hadn't even been given a choice regarding the porn.

Having spent a couple of nights in West End porn cinemas recently, (a cheap and reasonably comfortable way of passing a cold night, having missed the last tube home), Craig was not surprised when the repairman started staring up the housewife's improbably short skirt, or when instead of bashfully covering herself up, she hoist her skirt up further, inserted a couple of fingers into her knickers and began to masturbate.

"Is this standard or super 8mm?" he asked as her protruding buttocks began to swivel and grind.

"Standard 8," replied David, as the repairman unzipped his trousers to reveal a sizable erection.

"And umm…where do you buy your movies?"

162

"In a store on Santa Monica Boulevard. Why? Are you after something, Craig?"

"No, no, I was just wondering."

He glimpsed at the reel and guessed it was a 100 footer, already halfway through. So, only 3 or 4 minutes left at most. He would just sit this out then politely ask if he could go to sleep.

The repairman had by now decided that that the housewife was in more need of servicing than the TV. She was kneeling on the settee, her knickers around her knees, and her ecstatic face writhing on the elegant scatter cushions as the man lunged repeatedly at her raised, voluptuous backside.

"I presume this model doesn't have sound then," said Craig.

"It does actually, it's just this film that's silent. I do have a good sound movie here somewhere. I'll put it on next."

Damn, thought Craig, *why did I open my mouth?*

"Say, Craig, do you want a blow job?"

What! Craig's head spun. Jesus! Why me? Did I suggest I liked men, even a little bit? Did I fuck! First, the Pedro episode in Vegas and now this!

"Er, no. No thanks."

Aarrgh! Why am I such a pathetic middle-class wimp? Say what you really feel.

"Are you sure?"

"Yes," said Craig, a little more sharply, "I'm not gay."

David laughed a little patronisingly:

"You don't have to be gay to enjoy a blow job."

Yes you do, assuming it's from a man, he thought, *don't you…* He heard a clicking or snapping sound but wasn't sure if it came from the projector or inside his own head.

"Well, maybe not but I wouldn't be comfortable with it."

The housewife had now turned around and was riding the repairman. She kept arching her back melodramatically as she bounced up and down. Craig was now well and truly losing the battle to suppress his erection so he was greatly relieved when the couple disappeared mid-bounce and the trailing edge of film wove its way noisily through the gates and over the spindles.

"Hot stuff eh?" said David as he turned to lace up the film to rewind it.

"Mmm, yeah, but I'm pretty shattered actually," said Craig, laying his head back on the pillow.

"Yeah, I can't believe Pete would just turn you out like that," said David sympathetically, completely missing the hint.

"He wanted to be alone with this girl," mumbled Craig.

"Oh I see; still he could have shared some of the action with his buddy, huh."

Craig said nothing; he was concentrating on his shrinking penis, trying to hurry the process along and resolving to avoid any arousal next time around. David fumbled about in his bedside drawer.

"Aha! Here we are; *Pussy Picnic*," he exclaimed, proudly mounting a new spool and threading the leader.

Craig sighed as the inevitably bland but cheerful lift music heralded another artless 6-minute romp. The plot, such as it was, this time revolved around two unconnected couples (one interracial) who finish off their wine, and nibbles in a forested picnic area and start feeling a little frisky. Snogging soon turns into foreplay, and within a minute the usual flesh feeding (and pounding) frenzy has ensued.

"Look out for the black guy, he's enormous," warned David.

Craig started walking through the aisles of an imaginary furniture warehouse and piling up various flatpacks onto a trolley. The vision had to be extremely boring but also steady and sustainable. Although he could virtually blot out the images by blurring his eyes, he was unable to block out the cacophony of sighs, moans, slaps and squelches that rose above the jolly lift music. He tried with renewed concentration to picture various granite and formica kitchen surfaces but felt his groin tightening.

"Yes, yes, yes! Do it there. Harder!…" pleaded a female voice followed by a rapid series of series of slapping noises. It was no good; the soundtrack seemed to be hardwired to his genitals.

"Bet you've got a hard-on," whispered David.

Craig made a non-committal "unnghh" noise at the back of his throat in an indifferent a manner as possible. David then playfully pulled back the bed cover. Craig, feeling very self-conscious about the recalcitrant vertical shape of his M&S underpants, whipped the cover back.

"Oh come on, Craig," simpered David, "why don't you at least let me jerk you off."

The furniture showroom had collapsed into a heaving mass of knobs, knockers and screwdrivers. The well-endowed black man had spotted the girl on the neighbouring picnic blanket ogling him and said, "Why don't you join us, honey."

"No I'd rather not. Really," stuttered Craig, as if responding to the celluloid invite rather than to the man next to him. He felt compromised and flustered by his own arousal which David seemed to read as a green light. Had he been leading him on in some way after all?

He wasn't sure of anything anymore. Agreeing to come back here was a huge mistake so why not just leave again.

"Look, David, perhaps it's best if I don't stay after all."

David looked startled.

"No. No you must stay, I insist. I'm sorry, I'm being insensitive, I'll turn this off."

Partners had been swapped and double cunnilingus looked set to be the dessert at *Pussy Picnic* when David pulled the plug. The room seemed unnervingly quiet now the whirring and orgiastic moans had stopped. Craig wanted to leave but he didn't want to hurt David's feelings. He vacillated.

"Gee, Craig, you seem a little tense. Hey, I could give you a massage that would really relax you."

"Uh, no. I'm fine thanks." He was shackled by his own politeness.

"I'm an expert you know. I used to do them professionally."

Craig wondered if he was being a little uptight.

"Well, I…" David sensed wavering and seized the moment.

"Don't worry; I'm not going to charge you. Here, roll onto your front."

He gently pushed Craig's shoulders back until he was lying flat, head on the pillow then patted the space next to him. Craig felt the moment to protest had somehow passed. He nervously acquiesced and rolled over onto his stomach. Strong hands squeezed and rubbed his shoulders and neck.

"Bad stress knots. It's not good for you having this much tension in your body."

Craig stopped paying attention to David's words around this point and started to notice the relief in his tired muscles. After some deft chopping, his shoulders gradually loosened up. Long rhythmic strokes down the length of his back were accompanied by symmetrical kneading motions either side of the spine. All the worries, doubts, fears and negativity seemed to be flowing out of him.

He felt himself smiling into the pillow like an idiot as he gave himself up to the sheer luxury of the experience. Ripple after ripple of sensuous bliss spread through Craig's grateful body. David's voice which seemed to have dropped an octave, was somehow connected to the movements of his hands, making low rhythmic circular patterns.

The tone and repetition had quite a hypnotic effect, and as he became dimly aware that David was now kneeling astride him he was suddenly struck by the vivid image of Kaa, the snake, working his spell on Mowgli, the man-cub.

"Whoa, you tensed up again there for a second. Let it all go, that's it, relax," purred the voice and Craig followed it back to the inviting pool of soothing ripples. Then seconds, or was it minutes, later he felt a hand slip underneath him and brush his penis. His body jolted and he started to struggle.

"Oh sorry, did I do something wrong," said David.

"I'd rather you didn't touch me there," he said coyly as if naming the part might draw more attention to it.

"Sure, no problem," reassured the masseur.

Only now did the potential dangers start to dawn on Craig. What if the man now crouched over him had no intention of letting him out without getting what he wanted. His easy, pleasant demeanour and slightly effeminate mannerisms had lulled Craig into a false sense of security.

David was actually a tall, solidly built man who obviously worked out quite regularly, with powerful-looking arm and leg muscles. Whereas, in contrast, his own physique had gone from slim to thin in the last few weeks, dropping well below ten stone on his strict regime of drugs, alcohol, little food and total abstinence from physical exercise (bar walking).

Outside a police siren wailed in the Hollywood night. He was effectively pinned down at the moment, but if he played things cool he thought, and chose his moment carefully, then he could well make it to the door first. Once David went back to his side of the bed though, his exit would be blocked.

Then it occurred to him that David might have a weapon, like a knife, secreted in his bedside drawer alongside the porn. I'm being paranoid, he told himself; he didn't even know I'd be coming back here tonight. Despite this, he couldn't quite shake the idea of rape at knifepoint from his mind.

Craig tried to relax his body again as tense muscles might give away his intention to escape. He needn't have worried however; the quality of David's massage technique was such that despite everything Craig found himself enjoying it once more.

"Craig, how would you like me to teach you where a woman's hot spots are and how to manipulate them so that they are powerless to resist you?"

Craig tittered as the outlandish claim sounded like a glib advert for a new wonder diet or an anti-ageing cream.

"Seriously," insisted David, sounding slightly hurt, "this is a powerful secret that I am offering to reveal to you."

The idea that this man could be a threat suddenly seemed absurd, plus it would be a cool trick to have up my sleeve, thought Craig, suspending disbelief for a moment.

"Mmm, I suppose it could be useful," he said.

David grasped this partial endorsement and started a fine-tuned massage to the back of Craig's neck.

"So the hot spots are women's erogenous zones, are they?" he asked, enjoying the light-headed sensation.

"You could call them that but the way you open them up is what's important." This sounded credible to Craig, who's body felt like a sunflower unfurling and submitting it's petals to the nourishing rays.

He was slightly less happy about the next hot spot located around the base of his spine which was a little too close for comfort.

"This one really gets them going," whispered David seductively. As two strong thumbs pushed deep either side of his coccyx, Craig again imagined Kaa's coils tightening around him but he was frozen in a form of hypnotic trance. The serpentine fingers decreased their pressure gradually, almost imperceptibly, and simultaneously slid along either side of the triangular bone.

Craig felt himself becoming almost weightless, then started to float as the fingertips played gossamer-light arpeggios around the top of his buttocks. Craig heard a low moan of pleasure and was so removed from things that he wasn't sure if it came from David or him.

Perhaps, if it did emanate from him this was why David felt he could get away with inserting a dissonant note into his graceful melody by suddenly slipping his right hand underneath Craig's stomach and grabbing his penis. In fact, he merely shattered his own illusions. In a split second, Craig wrenched himself free and twisted violently, managing to topple David onto his own side of the bed.

"Whoa! Whoa there, little buddy. I'm sorry. I'm sorry ok; I just got carried away for a second."

"Yeah well, I've had enough. I'm tired. I just want to go to sleep," insisted Craig.

David seemed to recognise from the forcefulness of his tone that the game was up.

"Sure, Craig, whatever you say." He rolled over and turned off his bedside light. The room was now almost dark but for a thin sliver of half-light creeping through a crack in the curtains. Craig turned on his side, facing the window, away from David. It was silent for a few seconds. Then a whisper:

"I hope I didn't upset you."

Craig said, "No. Good night," with as much finality as he could muster.

David just murmured, "Sweet dreams," then turned over himself.

Craig lay there rigid, waiting for the next move or another attempt at conversation but all was peaceful and still. He decided to wait for a few minutes until David was definitely asleep before creeping out.

The next thing Craig was aware of was waking with a jolt. He was right on the edge of the bed and could feel David's body curled right up next to him. Judging from the gentle snoring sound in his ear, David was asleep. Craig was shocked that he could possibly have fallen asleep in such potentially dangerous circumstances.

He pondered clutching his trousers and shoes and running for the door, but the idea of emerging in the corridor trouserless was just too painfully reminiscent of a Brian Rix farce to seriously contemplate. Instead, he extricated himself from David's touch, sliding out from beneath an arm as smoothly and quietly as possible. In slow motion, he inched away from the bed, picked up his trousers and shoes and tiptoed to the bathroom door which was just his side of the room.

Inside, he took some deep breaths then pulled on the trousers, trying to avoid any harsh or jerky movements. He sat on the toilet seat to put on his shoes then peered around the door at the figure on the bed. All was still. He took what seemed an age composing himself but felt paralysed to the spot.

What if David was only pretending to be asleep and was to leap up barring his exit. If he ran now, he should be safe but it felt like a slightly hysterical course to take. Eventually, he opted for a dignified but rapid walk straight to the door. He was geared up for action, his adrenaline pulsing.

He was surprised that nothing happened at all. David didn't even stir as he opened the door. The clunk of the handle and click of the latch sounded absurdly loud to Craig but this was probably due to his state of mind. Then seconds later, he was outside. He was free.

He gently shut the door behind him and sneaked off to room 42. He tapped on the door expecting Pete and Candy to still be fast asleep but Pete appeared straight away. His friend was dressed but unshaven and gaunt. He almost scowled at Craig.

"Oh it's you," he remarked offhandedly and turned away. "We're just off to get some breakfast."

"Hi, honey," smiled Candy, emerging from the bathroom.

He wanted to blurt out the whole story to Pete but Candy's presence and Pete's evident bad mood blocked him. He felt he must at least bring up the bizarre and scary experience.

"Guess what, I ended up in that bloke David's room and he almost raped me." He didn't mean to describe it that way, sounding almost flippant.

"Almost? So nothing actually happened then…" said Pete in a dismissive tone.

"Well no…not really, but it was pretty frightening."

Pete laughed and Candy joined in. Then she whispered in Pete's ear; he thought he heard the words 'gay after all' and they both roared with laughter again. Craig felt angry that his still fresh trauma was only inducing amusement and snapped, "I'm going to crash out for a few hours."

Pete and Candy left a few seconds later, still giggling, and Craig collapsed on the dishevelled bed. Everything felt alien and ugly. He was shattered and little fragments of him lay scattered all over the place. The whole event with David was already fading into a surreal dream-like episode, and within a few hours it would be transformed further into a light well-honed anecdote.

Blood on the Tiles

After a couple of days spent at Shandy's, Craig had no real choice but to return to Park Sunset as she was staying over at her mum's following an operation. She had dropped him at Santa Monica where he'd spent most of the day on the beach and checking out the pier. As the journey back to Hollywood had been so long last time up Santa Monica Boulevard, Craig decided to try another route catching a bus on Wilshire.

He had then had to change and wait for another at Fairfax. As he sat sweltering on the unshaded bench, he wondered whether Candy would have grown bored and moved on. He felt a little mean-spirited hoping so as Pete was over the moon about her, but nevertheless he had a bad feeling about her.

Next to him a blonde, well-built, slightly vacant-looking teenage boy in vest and shorts was holding a basketball and chewing gum. Craig wiped the sweat from his forehead. The boy chewed his gum, bounced his ball on the ground and stared at Craig. Craig looked away, but a few seconds later when he glanced back the boy was still staring at him.

"What's happening?"

Craig didn't know if this was an actual enquiry or just a form of greeting. He wasn't sure how to respond.

"Er…I dunno."

The blank-eyed, slack-jawed stare continued, punctuated by the thud of the basketball on the sidewalk.

"What's happening?"

"Where…? Umm, how do you mean?" faltered Craig. Clearly a response was expected. He was vaguely aware of a middle-aged woman standing behind the boy, grinning in amusement.

Chew. Bounce. Stare.

"Are you a punk rocker?"

This is an easier question to deal with thought Craig, though the kid might have an antipathy towards punks. Do I look like a punk, he wondered? Certainly not by English standards but maybe being dressed in black and sporting short, slightly spikey hair was enough to qualify you in Los Angeles.

"Not really."

Chew. Bounce. Stare.

"You look kind of like a punk rocker."

Craig felt this must be what it would be like to try and converse with an alien. Perhaps, sign language would be easier.

"I mean I like quite a bit of punk music…"

"So you are a punk rocker…"

Chew. Bounce. Stare.

"No, not really…" he mumbled again helplessly. The woman behind snorted, then coughed.

"So what's happening?"

As the exchange came full circle, Craig breathed a sigh of relief as the bus drew up, saving him from this loop of cultural misunderstanding. He let the boy board first and as he sat immediately behind the driver, Craig headed for the back of the bus.

Looking out the window, his thoughts drifted back to Candy. Surely she would have located her mysterious friend, the one she was looking for in the middle of the night, by now, and be hanging out with him…. Pete would be sad she'd gone of course, but he would take him out to Piper's and cheer him up. Things would soon be back to how they were before. He noticed a poster for 'American Gigolo' showing at the New Beverly Cinema, and made a note of the screening times.

Craig was still in an optimistic frame of mind when half an hour later, he unlocked the door to their apartment. Sure enough only Pete was home laying topless in bed, smoking. But something was wrong: He barely greeted Craig with more than a grunt. A heavy atmosphere hung over room 42. There was no getting away from it, he had to ask…

"Where's Candy?"

"Gone out for a walk," Pete replied flatly.

Damn, she's still around, thought Craig. He dumped his bag on the chair then perched on the end of the bed. The curtains were closed despite it being early evening by now, though this was by no means unusual. There was perhaps even more rubbish strewn across the floor and surfaces suggesting they may have been cocooned in here since he left. Pete looked pale and tense.

"Are you OK?" he ventured gently.

Pete exhaled smoke before answering.

"Not really."

"Did you have a row?"

Pete shook his head but then seemed to nod towards the bathroom. Craig furrowed his brow and Pete repeated the gesture. Craig stood up and wandered the few steps towards the open door.

"Fucking hell!" he exclaimed as he took in the sight of blood covered towels on the floor, a smeared handprint on the wall tiles and some spots on the floor leading out of sight behind the door.

The first thought that raced through his mind was that Pete had killed Candy in a passionate rage and the 'walk' she'd taken was a euphemism for eternal sleep. Hot on the heels of this thought was the question, so where's the body? Then another thought; perhaps Candy had harmed or even killed herself, and Pete had called an ambulance. This would explain Pete's ashen expression.

Craig became aware that his heart was pounding. He took a deep breath and told himself he was leaping to extreme conclusions. The bloody bathroom was like a scene from a slasher horror movie, and as Craig had watched too many of these he was undoubtedly constructing scenarios from this mindset.

As his panic began to calm, a more realistic, if unhygienic explanation came to him: perhaps Candy had her period but had no tampons handy. He turned to Pete, suddenly confident he'd hit upon it.

"No jam rags when she needed them eh?"

Pete just stared into space as his cigarette burned down to the butt. Were there tears in his eyes? Craig was worried now, he'd never seen Pete cry before.

"She's dying."

"What?" yelped Craig, in confusion.

"She's got some disease that only affects black people... She's been throwing up blood... She's only got a few months to live."

Craig hadn't seen that coming. He felt knocked for six and had to sit on the end of the bed again.

"Blimey, that's...heavy," he mumbled inadequately.

"She thinks you don't like her," said Pete. "She doesn't want to stay where she feels unwanted..."

Craig swallowed hard. He felt pushed into a corner; how could he possibly complain about or resist a dying young woman's wish without appearing to be a complete bastard. It wasn't that he didn't like Candy, he just wasn't sure he could trust her, but now he felt guilty for feeling that way and started to censor himself.

"OK, I'll talk to her," he managed to formulate.

Right on cue, there was a tap at the door. Craig, who was sat only feet away, got up and answered it. There stood Candy, a vision of health and vitality in a fresh flowery summer dress.

"Hi, Craig, how nice to see you again. Do you mind if I come in?"

"Just come in for fuck's sake," growled Pete from the bed.

"Of course," stammered Craig, "you don't need to ask me."

"Oh but I do. This is your room and Pete is your friend. It's not for me to make assumptions."

Her voice sounded different, more serious and perhaps less southern… She hovered on the threshold until Craig felt compelled to say, "Please come in, Candy."

"Why thank you, kind sir," she simpered, finally entering. Craig closed the door behind her.

She walked around the other side of the bed and kissed Pete chastely on the forehead.

"Craig wants to speak to you." Pete's voice was still oddly flat and emotionless.

"Does he? How nice. Why don't you and me take a little walkies then, Craig."

Craig was actually glad of the opportunity to escape the suffocating air of their apartment room, and Pete who was freaking him out a bit. Plus it would be easier to talk to Candy without Pete there.

A few minutes later, the pair of them were eating Baskin-Robbins ice cream in cones, bought by Craig, perched on some fire escape steps near to Barney's Beanery.

"I really am sorry to hear about the er…what's it called again?"

"Sickle-cell. Yeah, I am kind of sad I won't ever get married or have kids and stuff but you know, I think I've kinda accepted it now."

He looked at her deep brown eyes as she sat in her demure summer dress, lapping her vanilla ice cream and thought how brave and beautiful she was.

"I'm real worried about Pete though, he ain't taking it well. You won't go off with Shandy and leave him will you, Craig?"

So his gay cover was blown then.

"Cos' I'm a little scared of his moods. He gets real intense. He said he might even…harm himself if I left…"

"Really? That's so unlike him…"

"I've grown real fond of you English boys, and I'd hate for something to happen or for you to stop being friends. If you were to stay, you could keep an eye on him."

"Yeah, I'll stay. I mean, not every night, but I won't leave."

Candy smiled a real movie star smile that lit up West Hollywood. There was also the beginning of a spectacular fiery sunset, with rich crimson streaks daubing the sky.

"Wow, this sunset is magnificent; you don't get ones like this in England."

"Oh it's not real," said Candy. "What I mean is, they say the colour of the sunsets recently is down to that volcano."

"Oh, Mount St Helens…" said Craig, having seen some TV news reports on the deadly Washington eruption that had killed over 50 people. "That's kind of spoiled it," he said with a little mournful laugh.

"Nothing's what it seems. Can I ask you something, Craig? Why don't you like me?"

"But I do like you, Candy, I happen to think you are a very brave and impressive person actually…even with ice cream on your nose."

He bent towards her and gently brushed the blob of white vanilla from her dainty dark nose. She grinned then put a hand behind his head and pulled him closer to her. He brushed her lips with his then tried to pull away but she clamped her lips to his.

He felt confused again, was this making peace or something else? Then she stuck her tongue in his mouth and wriggled it around. Again he tried to pull back but perhaps not as hard as he could have. He felt a slight stirring in his groin as her tongue darted around inside his mouth. He heard a car horn and a male voice shouting, "Get a room."

Candy laughed and pulled away herself.

"You naughty boy, Craig!"

He frowned, questioning what had just occurred.

"Relax, I'm only teasing you. But truthfully, I am so pleased that you do like me and that we can be good friends now. Shall we go back?"

He nodded and they stood up and headed up La Cienega towards Sunset, Candy holding his hand and swaying it whilst they finished their ice creams.

Crossing the Line

From a feverish 'Caligula'-inspired dream of a Roman orgy to suddenly falling from a great height; at first an abstracted weightless freefall then a terrifying 100mph crushing, hurtling descent with the desert floor rushing up towards him… A panicked gasp, then Craig emerged into consciousness that hit him like a freight train.

First, he was fully erect. Second, there were fingers or a tongue, or both, on his cock. Third, there was nobody beside him but someone was under the bedsheet, making slurping noises.

Gingerly, he lifted the sheet…for a second he felt relieved to see Candy's tight black curls on his stomach, but then he felt a horrid sinking feeling like being on a lift that is plummeting very fast. This sensation brought back the dream of falling. He tried to pull her head off him but stopped as he felt teeth snagging.

"Candy, what the hell are you doing?"

A face turned upwards to greet him with a cheeky grin and a thread of saliva hanging from her mouth.

"Good morning; I was just having breakfast in bed."

He had a hand either side of her head but this didn't stop her projecting her tongue and wrapping it around his shaft.

"No, you can't," he hissed urgently, this time managing to delicately separate her from his throbbing manhood.

"Don't you like it?" she asked, as if he'd commented negatively on her choice of lipstick or something.

"That's not the point…" he said, trying to sound stern but aware how his body was aching from pleasure denied and yearning for release.

"Where's Pete?"

"Don't worry, he'll be out for an hour or so."

"I can't possibly do this to him," he grunted, as he shuffled his body over to the edge of the bed.

Candy threw the sheet back and propping her elbow on the bed, she balanced her chin on the palm of her hand and looked at him.

"But he knows about it. He wants it to happen."

Craig felt like his fairground ride that was already turning around a vertical axis had just been spun wildly at the same time.

"What…? Why on earth would he want it to happen?"

"To keep me here. I told him he was too possessive, and he had to learn to share me or I'd go. He does think it could bring us all closer together."

A siren wailed in the distance. Could it be true? His cock screamed yes whilst part of his mind told him to wait and check the story. Why would Pete go out and leave them alone together if he is so possessive, unless he really was giving them tacit permission? But even if this were true, it didn't mean he would be happy about it. What if he never forgave Craig?

On the other hand, Candy was not Pete's property and she had shown interest in Craig too from the word go. Candy had shifted over next to him again and her tongue went back to work. He felt frozen, unable to move or act. The trouble was that indecision would soon be overtaken by biology, as her hands now squeezing his buttocks was underlining.

"I want you to make love to me," she purred as she started to slide her way up his body. "Are you not going to make a poor girl happy?"

The darker side of his soul found a trump card and played it. Remember she's dying. Can you deny her this? As she climbed astride him his conscience gave up the fight and surrendered with a groan, as his victorious body came back to life.

Cutting

By the sound of it, Candy was on the verge of climaxing again as Craig heard the key turn in the lock behind him and the door open. Instinctively, he stopped dead in his tracks although Candy continued to writhe and moan for a few seconds until Pete walked around the far side of the bed. Craig withdrew from Candy and moved over to his own side of the bed.

An Arctic chill permeated the room. Craig stole a glimpse at Pete's face, it was cold and hard, mask-like. Pete took out a Marlboro from the packet on his bedside table, walked back to the other side of the bed and sat down on the chair. He lit up the cigarette and inhaled deeply before blowing a cloud of smoke across the bed.

"You're back early, baby," said Candy.

"No, I said an hour and I've been an hour," he replied with barely suppressed malice.

"Are you OK?"

"Never been better," he spat.

"Why don' you tell us what you feelin'," persisted Candy.

"Total indifference," he said imperiously which almost brought a smile to Craig's face but he thought better of it.

Craig wanted to put some clothes on but felt unable to move. In the softest tone he could muster, he said, "Candy said you were happy for it to happen... That you thought it could bring us closer together..."

"Did she?"

"I told you 'bout this actin' like you own me shit..." Candy sounded like she was trying to be angry, but it was not very convincing.

"Shut up," said Pete quietly, with a hint of menace.

Candy mumbled something inaudible but complied.

Silence hung in the room like stalactites. Pete stared icily with furrowed brow through wreaths of smoke. Craig felt wretched. He sat upright, closed his eyes and breathed deeply to try and steady himself. The tension was unbearable.

He desperately tried to work out what to say; how to get Pete to forgive him and extricate himself from this mess. He almost launched into a full apology but held himself back, unsure if he'd be digging himself in deeper.

After what felt like an eternity, Pete stubbed his cigarette out on the wall behind him then flicked the butt across the room. He moved a few steps to Craig's bedside table and placed something small on it, then said, "I'm going out" to the room in general and left. Craig puffed out his cheeks as he exhaled. He turned his head to see what Pete had put on his little table. He felt all the small hairs on his arms stand up; it was a razor blade.

Drowning in Room 42

Craig awoke shivering from a dream where he was being ruthlessly beaten up in a toilet by a stranger. The bedclothes seemed to have disappeared, onto the floor no doubt; presumably after another night of disturbed thrashing. He curled himself into a ball, burying his hands between his knees.

His teeth started to chatter. Why was he so cold? The room was usually stuffy. Perhaps he was ill. He ran his tongue over his mouth ulcer to confirm it was still there, and the violent twitch told him it was possibly larger and rawer. *Mouth ulcers are a sign that you are rundown*, he thought.

He hadn't eaten a proper meal for days. There was a dull ache in his head, but only on the periphery in a slept-in-too-long sort of way. More than anything he felt drained, devoid of any vital energy.

He tried vainly to submerge himself once more, longing for the seamless deep of a dreamless sleep. The harder he tried to push himself down however, the more consciousness crept up in him like water slowly filling a bathtub. Reluctantly, he opened one eye to test the waters then the other. Very little light permeated the dingy room through the earth-coloured curtains.

With an effort, he craned his neck to check over his shoulder. As he expected, the bed was empty. Pete may have arisen hours ago for all he knew. He reflected that Pete hadn't said a word to him since coming back to the room and finding him and Candy in flagrante. How many days ago was that?

His brain tried to figure it out but gave up as the effort was painful. Had Craig missed yet another sunny morning in the City of Angels? Judging by this murky half-light, he may well have missed the afternoon as well and slept through 'til early evening.

Was it worth looking around for his watch? Did it matter what time it was? He sank back down and closed his eyes, but then he shivered again and realised he was going to have to sit up even if it was only to retrieve the sheet and blanket from the floor.

After a struggle with himself, he summoned enough willpower to the relevant muscles and overruled the body's solemn intent. He sat up, took a mouthful of stale, musty air and pulled one curtain aside a few inches. The greyish light made his temples thud briefly despite the lack of luminance involved. He surveyed the carnage that was apartment 42, Park Sunset.

It's like 'Nam in here, he thought. Since seeing 'Apocalypse Now' on Hollywood Boulevard a few nights ago, more and more of his world resembled Coppola's vision of Vietnam, or so he told himself because this made the darkness more romantic. He gazed around the room. The layer of debris seemed to have grown overnight like clusters of dank mushrooms.

A half-eaten pizza festered in its carton. Days old styrofoam cups festooned every surface, many of them converted into would-be ashtrays. One had leaked and was dripping onto his suitcase. Newspapers, magazines and flyers piled up on the floor. Scrunched-up clothes hung limply from the radiator and towered precariously on the chair whilst towels were discarded across the bathroom floor.

Faint shadows from the plants outside the window waved and fluttered on the sickly green walls. Something about the motion of these shadows and the green hue made him think of the seabed, albeit a filthy and polluted seabed. The notion of an underwater room revived a long buried memory of a childhood game he'd played with his sister where they had to imagine the room was slowly filling up with water and swam around looking for a way out.

I'm drowning in here, he thought to himself in a state of anxiety, *I must go up for air*. Not so long ago, the chaotic clutter of the room had felt liberating and anarchic but now it seemed stifling and oppressive. He wondered if this was just down to the degree of clutter; did one Styrofoam cup or soiled towel too far tip the balance from hip dive to squalid tip or was it down to a change in his perspective?

Craig realised that he had undergone a number of changes in the last few days and that his emotional state, and if Shandy was to be believed, his behaviour, had grown very erratic. He perched on the side of the bed, still inspecting the floor. He was finding it hard to predict his own behaviour anymore or follow his own mental patterns; as hard as following the green carpet's pattern which had almost disappeared beneath all this flotsam and jetsam.

If he concentrated and looked beyond the debris, he could picture how the pattern developed underneath but he lacked the will or energy to sustain such concentration. He was becoming disconnected from himself which frightened

181

him but he couldn't even hold onto this fear: he kept slipping away into the undulating shadows on the walls.

Sensing that this monstrous lethargy would not only swallow the whole day but possibly swallow him too, he galvanised himself and threw his body back on the bed and contracting every voluntary muscle he took a deep breath, gave a loud guttural roar and sprang from the bed in a single bound. He impressed himself with this superhuman feat, apart from the fact that his left foot had landed in something sticky. Not wanting to lose this new impetus he didn't stop to investigate but ran into the bathroom and splashed cold water repeatedly over his face.

He imposed a deadline on himself of 2 minutes to be outside the room, knowing that any distractions would fatally pull him back under. He counted down the seconds as he raced from garment to garment to preserve his focus. He remembered his money with seconds to go, but still managed to shut the door behind him with three seconds remaining.

He smiled to himself as he walked down the poorly-lit corridor. He may have been unshaven, in need of a good shower, wearing non-matching socks and generally in a somewhat questionable state but at least he'd escaped the room. Then his smile vanished as he realised he hadn't found his watch. Refusing to accept defeat and go back inside the room, he carried on towards the pool.

Outside the sky was unusually overcast and almost grey although the temperature was still reasonably warm. The small communal pool was deserted although a beach towel was spread over a lounger at the far end. Craig wondered if he should continue the impulsive behaviour and properly wake himself up with a quick dip.

He then stood there for a while, gazing at the unfeasibly bright bougainvillea and hibiscus plants fringing the pool, and thought about how he'd have to go back to the room to change unless he fancied walking about in wet clothes…he could feel his thought processes bringing down the shutters on his spontaneous impulse and thought 'I'd never do that'. Then, breaking into a grin, he said out loud "which is why I will do that!"

Kicking off his trainers, he screamed like Little Richard then dived in fully clothed. In the split second before he hit the water, Craig saw the pool transform into his underwater room and thought it had claimed him back after all, but a beat later, the hallucination vanished and in its place was nothing but the moment; the tingly refreshing here and now. He felt complete clarity and inner calm as he pulled himself through the perfect blue silence. Eventually, he had to return to the surface if only to get another lungful of air.

"You Brits are crazy!" said a disembodied voice. Craig bobbed up and looked around but couldn't see anyone.

"I thought you guys were supposed to be reserved."

A familiar tall moustachioed figure emerged from an open French window.

"Oh hi, David, I didn't see you there. We are as a rule but I'm rebelling."

"Good for you. Why don't you really kick out the jams, Craig, and share a joint with me."

"I'd love to," said Craig, hauling his extra sodden weight out of the pool, "but I have to be off."

"What? Like that? At least let me dry you off," he drawled, producing a large colourful towel sporting a cartoon tiger.

"No, no I'm fine, thanks all the same."

His shoes squelched as he hurriedly forced his feet into them. David stood at his French window feigning sadness.

"Say, Craig, we are still friends, aren't we?"

"Of course we are, David, I just really have to be going now." He was walking away as he spoke, not caring that his desperation to leave was clearly apparent. "Speak to you soon. Bye for now."

He closed the door back to the corridor behind him and dripping onto the carpet, breathed a sigh of relief. What with everything else going on, Craig had forgotten he wanted to avoid David after the other night. The whole surreal incident which Pete had merely laughed at had already sunken beneath the surface of his reality. He shivered and padded towards the lobby and Sunset Boulevard.

Baby Blue

"You're what…?"

"I said I'm pregnant," Candy spoke slowly as if addressing a child.

"Bloody hell…"

Craig turned and looked at Pete who merely stared inscrutably at him.

"Tell him the rest."

Candy frowned at Pete, then turned to Craig and took a large breath.

"Don't freak. I think it's yours, honey."

Craig's legs turned to blancmange and he sat abruptly on the edge of the unmade bed.

"But how…why…I mean…what makes you think…" His brain seemed to have joined his legs.

"It can't be mine as I never came," said Pete bluntly.

Candy sat down next to him and picked up his left hand and held it softly between hers.

"It's true," she said in a virtual whisper, "all the times we did it, he never came."

"For once, my little problem seems to have a silver lining," smirked Pete.

Craig's mind felt like a hurricane was tearing through it, ripping up anything he thought he knew. He tried to recall what he'd heard about the time it takes to get pregnant, but couldn't think straight with the wind screaming in his ears.

"But it was only a few days ago…" he just about heard himself say over the roar.

Candy smiled sweetly.

"It don't take long, baby. To be honest, I think I felt it happen at the time; I just knew it somehow. I had the same goddam feeling a couple of years ago and I was right then too".

"Congratulations, Daddyo."

Craig glared at Pete who seemed to be really enjoying his predicament, perhaps unsurprisingly given the circumstances. The storm seemed to have shifted slightly, allowing Craig a slither of clarity.

"You're not thinking of keeping it, are you?" Craig regretted his wording immediately.

Candy's eyes clouded over. She stood up and wandered around the bed towards the bathroom.

"I sure am. I got talked into killing my baby last time and that ain't gonna happen again."

The bathroom door closed behind her with finality.

Pete merely raised his eyebrows and puffed out his cheeks, then flopped onto his side of the bed and reached for yesterday's New York Times.

"I need some air," mumbled Craig, feeling abruptly nauseous. He emerged from Park Sunset, blinking in the brilliant light, disorientated, his mind reeling. He started sleepwalking east on Sunset.

How did this possibly happen to me, was the main thought buzzing around his head like a trapped fly. As he was walking past The Body Shop, the all-nude strip club, a raggedy-looking street guy asked him for a dollar. Craig swore under his breath as he pushed past him. He felt a surge of anger so strong he felt an instant need to lash out at something.

He started kicking the nearest object which was a portable metal 'valet parking' sign, shouting "Why? Why? Why?" with each kick and feeling no pain. Out of the corner of his eye, he became aware of a middle-aged, well-heeled couple staring at him.

"What are you fucking looking at?" he turned and snarled as if Travis Bickle was pulling his strings. He had a dim realisation that to them he must look like a real Sunset but he didn't care. He started walking again.

The heat was stifling. The petrol fumes were oppressive. The glare of the sun made his head throb. He had not been consciously heading for Piper's for once, but it still came as no surprise when he found himself under the familiar hand-painted happy/sad clown masks. Piper's was like the magnetic north in his internal compass.

Mimi served him a beer with her customary warmth and good humour, but he did not feel sociable, to say the least, so he eschewed his usual barstool for one of the empty booths beneath the Chicago mural. Gradually, as the beer dwindled, his anger began to dissipate and be replaced by sadness and self-pity.

There was no escaping this time; he had no control over the new direction his life was taking.

He was not ready to be a father and he did not love or even trust the mother-to-be but here he was… He sighed as he imagined his parents' disappointment, no doubt exacerbated by closet racism. It felt like a steel cage was descending, closing off all his dreams of freedom and extinguishing his youth.

He looked around him and was dismayed that his mood had transformed Piper's into an Edward Hopper painting. He downed a second beer and a third but could find no trapdoor at the bottom of his glass. Ernest was sat in the next booth along, arguing loudly with Cricket and Gregg, a chubby half Italian friend of Joe Junior, with dark ringlets, an eager puppy-like expression and invariably sweat stains on his t-shirt. However, he turned things around in his mind, Craig could not picture anything but a bleak future.

He had taken his youth and freedom for granted, but the crushing responsibility of premature parenthood felt like a judgement and a life sentence. He realised he must be a reasonably moral person as he would not be able to endure the guilt of just walking away, but right now he wished he was a less moral person. He almost gasped as he suddenly remembered Candy's terminal illness.

She might be dead within the year, so what would happen with the child then… "My child," he muttered out loud to make it feel more real. He might need to fly back to LA to take custody of him or her.

He felt he could hear his mind spinning and unravelling at a higher and higher pitch until he realised this was actually Ernest's voice that was rapidly reaching a Smokey Robinson falsetto level as he became agitated and defensive. This made Gregg and Cricket laugh even harder. Craig was not sure what they were arguing about, something about sex probably; it was usually sex on Ernest's mind.

"You're lying, old man," drawled Cricket.

"You don't believe me, huh?" squealed Ernest.

It went quiet apart from a strange scratchy noise, causing Craig to lean out of his booth to see what was going on. From this angle, he could just about make out that Ernest had ducked under the table and was scrabbling about with something. A general hush had descended over Piper's.

Craig glanced around and noticed Mimi had stopped drying a glass to stare, and at a table opposite under the New York City mural, a British Indian DJ called Neil, plus associates, paused in their dubious business discussion.

Suddenly, Ernest reappeared and with a clatter he banged something down on the table top.

"See, I told you," he proclaimed.

The bar erupted into howls, snorts and belly laughs. Craig's vision was obscured by Cricket's back so he had to crane his neck to see around him. He was astonished to see a foot and lower leg as if the Monty Python animation had just come to life. It took a couple of beats for him to process that Ernest must have been unscrewing or unattaching a prosthetic limb.

"Shame on you for mocking the afflicted," Ernest preached to the bar as a whole, failing to convey the importance of being Ernest and merely eliciting more laughter. Cricket, who seemed to have swapped his trademark mean scowl for a crooked toothy grin today, all of a sudden grabbed the fibre glass and leather contraption and ran around the bar brandishing it. Ernest instinctively got up to chase him and promptly fell over.

He hauled himself up and started hopping after Cricket, cursing him. Cricket turned and hurled the limb with surprising accuracy to Neil. One of Neil's accomplices was laughing so hard he slid off his chair onto the floor. It was as if the Marx brothers had come back to life and had decided to start a residency at a Hollywood pizza joint.

Neil called out to Gregg, and with a fine two-handed underarm pass across the width of the bar he found his target. Ernest hopped back towards Gregg but by the time he got near, Gregg had passed the fake leg back to Cricket. Just at this moment, who should enter Piper's but the one and only Bob Atcheson. Cricket ran behind Bob.

"Hey, Bing Bing, I'm gonna kick your ass!"

Holding the lower leg in an upright position from the top he swung the foot at Bob Atcheson's backside. Oblivious until it made contact, Bob span around and presumably thought he was grabbing hold of Cricket's foot, but when it came away in his hands, his expression of horror cranked up the hysteria in the bar to a new level. He instantly dropped the offending item saying, "Little brother, what have I done?" to Cricket who doubled over as if in pain, making a hideous braying sound whilst also gasping for air.

Ernest saw his opportunity, hopped over and plucked his prosthetic from the floor before solemnly intoning to Bob Atcheson.

"Robert, I expected better from you," then wheeled around and hopped back towards his booth.

With jazz hands fluttering, Bob gazed at Ernest's one leg and a look of genuine concern came over him.

"Ain't nobody gonna ring an ambulance for this poor man?"

As Mimi tried to explain the situation to Bob, Craig wiped away tears of laughter from his face, and reflected that only minutes earlier he had been in abject misery. Only Piper's he felt could possibly have lifted his spirits like this, and he decided to leave on a high.

By the time he returned to Park Sunset, it was almost dark and the boulevard had donned its glittering neon accessories. Since the legless antics in Piper's, Craig had not reverted to a depressed state but instead felt cold and numb, at a remove from the world around him.

There was an L-shaped corridor leading from the foyer area back towards their apartment. Just beyond the door from the foyer was a public phone which Craig passed, vaguely aware that somebody was standing with their head in the Perspex bubble, as he passed. As he turned the corner in the corridor, he almost collided with Pete who was leaning against the wall.

"What the hell…" began Craig.

"Shhh!" Pete cut him short with a finger in front of his lips for extra emphasis.

Pete pulled him by the arm to the wall next to him.

"She's on the phone to Uncle Leroy," he whispered.

"Who?" asked Craig, realising Candy must have been the figure he had just passed.

"Leroy, you remember, the uncle in the Mafia…" hissed Pete in exasperation.

"Oh yeah," Craig foggily recalled what he had assumed was one of Candy's tall tales about a doting over-protective uncle in New York City who also happened to be a ruthless crime lord.

They both edged as close to the corner as possible and craned their necks. Craig could just about hear Candy's voice now and then without making out anything intelligible. He was about to suggest the situation was pointless when Candy raised her voice a little and he heard the words, "he's just a kid."

Pete and Craig exchanged looks, then telepathically both peeked their heads around the corner to gather up more titbits. Candy seemed to be getting more animated, twisting and pacing the few steps that the phone cord would allow. Then she stood still and half turned towards them. They both heard her state icily, "If you do that to him, I will never speak to you again."

Craig's stomach lurched as if he was back on the Disneyland Space Mountain ride. Candy moved back beneath the Perspex bubble rendering further eavesdropping virtually impossible. They remained rooted to the spot however, until Candy hung up the phone a minute or so later.

They scurried back to their room. Pete dived onto the bed and grabbed the newspaper from the bedside cabinet, pretending to be engrossed. Craig threw off his jacket and went into the bathroom and splashed water on his face.

Candy returned seconds later, looking pensive. She nodded at Craig who was leaning over the sink with the door ajar.

"How did it go?" asked Pete casually.

"He was pretty mad when I told him. He's got his mind set on coming out here and says he's getting a flight from New York tomorrow."

Craig straightened up and stared at the frightened kid in the mirror, feeling sorry for him.

Rescue

Craig barely slept a wink all night. The tension in the small apartment had spread to his body, which felt stiff and knotted. He checked his watch one more time. 9:10, they might sleep on for hours yet.

His brain started reviewing the plan yet again. He had slipped out late yesterday evening and phoned Shandy from a call box rather than the one in the hotel. Luckily, she was in and he asked whether he could stay at hers for a few days.

He told her he had to get out of Park Sunset as soon as possible without going in to details. He was confident Shandy would not mind as he'd probably stayed over two or three nights already since things ended with Beth. She sounded surprised but not displeased with the idea.

She told him she was working an early shift at Denny's in the morning but could pick him up on the way back after work. Jamming in another quarter, he said he'd rather bring his stuff to Denny's and see her there if she didn't mind, and he'd fill her in on the details then.

Now, he had to wait for Pete and Candy to go out for breakfast, then he could pack quickly and scram. The trouble was that one of them might stay while the other went out for a takeaway, which happened now and then. He wanted to tell Pete where he was going but he was feeling very paranoid.

If and when Uncle Leroy came to see his niece and young father-to-be, he might lean on Pete for details of Craig's whereabouts. Although Pete would no doubt guess, he'd be at Shandy's place, somewhere in Brentwood, he didn't so far have the address. As far as Craig knew he wasn't aware of Shandy's surname either. He did know that she worked at Denny's on Sunset though which was the weak spot of the plan.

Candy stirred next to him but then turned over towards Pete and settled again. He sighed and checked his watch again. Craig felt exhausted now. His resistance gradually ebbed away until he slipped into a doze. A car horn brought him back to consciousness with a jolt.

The room felt unnaturally quiet. He turned over in bed and sure enough, it was empty, and the bathroom too. Damn, he didn't know how long they'd been out; he'd have to hurry. His watch said it was now gone 11.

He pulled his suitcase out of the cupboard and slung it on the bed. It didn't take long to empty the drawers of his stuff, bundling it all into the case, mostly screwed up, but it was in dire need of an iron anyway. Within 5 minutes, he'd collected all his odds and ends and done a quick check under the bed and in the bathroom. He felt bad leaving Pete without a note but that wouldn't be advisable in the circumstances. Besides, he'd see him again in a few days no doubt.

Deciding to keep his key for now, he carried his case out into the unrelenting bleached out glare of a skin-stripping LA sun. Fuck, he'd packed his sunglasses, he'd just have to put up with being dazzled. He guessed Pete and Candy would have headed eastwards towards Ben Franks whereas he'd turned westwards, but this didn't stop him expecting to come across them at any moment.

Being almost midday there was precious little shade. He'd forgotten how heavy his suitcase was. He started off lasting a 100 yards or so before needing to change hands or take a rest but after a few minutes, he was only managing about 10 yards. He wished he'd borrowed his mum's suitcase, which had two little casters built in. By the time he'd heaved it as far as Fairfax, he was covered in sweat and decided to hell with frugality and hail a cab, whatever the cost.

10 minutes later, Craig dragged his heavy load through the doorway of Denny's, thanking all the Gods for air-conditioning. He approached the centre but could not spy Shandy and his heart sunk a little. Then she appeared from the ladies room.

"Whoa, you English don't travel light, do ya?"

"Tell me about it. I can't feel the fingers on my right hand."

She came around the counter and kissed him on the cheek, then gave him her car keys.

"You might as well stash that in the trunk of my car. It's just out back."

"Thanks, Shandy, you're a diamond."

"Wait 'til you get my bill!"

Craig felt more secure and liberated with the case out of the way. He sat at the far end of the long counter where he had a view of anybody coming in, and near to the back exit in case he needed to beat it fast. He sat hoovering up a freebie breakfast, sporadically explaining the situation to Shandy, in between her serving customers.

"So you're telling me she can't possibly have known she was pregnant within two or three days?"

"No way. A missed period is usually the first sign and that's normally around two weeks after conception. Even if she'd taken a more sensitive test at a doctor's, it would have to be taken between seven and twelve days after conception."

Craig wished Shandy would lower her voice a little as a couple of nearby diners were staring, but his self-consciousness was totally eclipsed by the rush of relief at the news.

"I had a feeling it took much longer than she claimed but I didn't really know, and there was no public library in the area to check up. Also…she can be strangely convincing."

"If she lied to you about being pregnant, she was probably lying about this mafia uncle too. If he does exist, I can't see him hightailing it over from NYC 3 days after his niece got laid."

Craig nodded and drained his coffee mug.

"Unless she lied to him about the details for some reason."

Shandy waved to a customer to indicate she was on her way.

"It sounds a helluva lot more likely that she's trying to scam you, if you ask me."

"Agreed," said Craig. "Oh the other thing you may be able to shed some light on is this disease she claims to have. She says she's been given about 6 months to live."

"What's it called?" asked Shandy, already looking sceptical.

"Sickle-cell anaemia."

"OK, well that does target the black population."

"Yeah, but she claimed to have thrown up blood, and there was a lot of blood on the towels."

"Hmm," Shandy furrowed her brow, "I haven't heard of that. I know it causes pain and fatigue. I know, I'll ask Carmen over there; she's studying to be a nurse." She pointed out a petite Mexican waitress attending to a family by the front window.

A few minutes later, as Craig was finishing his second round of toast with grape jelly, Shandy brought him up to date.

192

"OK, she says you can get ulcers and bacterial infections, an enlarged or damaged spleen, and I think she called it aseptic necrosis, when parts of the bone die. She did mention possible bleeding from the eyes but she doesn't think throwing up blood would usually be a symptom."

"Another lie then!" said Craig victoriously, the sense of weight lifting from him felt truly dramatic.

"She just turned up at your room in the middle of the night, you say?"

"Yep," confirmed Craig, "and as you can imagine, Pete welcomed her with open arms."

"Despite knowing nothing about her. What other stories has she told you guys…"

"Ha, she claimed she was Diana Ross's second cousin. She freaked us out one night, telling us all sorts of stuff about our childhood…"

Shandy smiled drily, "Probably just intuitive guesswork, maybe Pete had told her some of it already. If this was after she first met you, it's possible she did some serious homework on you…but I doubt she'd have the resources."

"Oh yeah, a few days ago, out of the blue, she told us she's schizoid."

"Could be true. Could be a way of scaring or intimidating you both, if you'd openly started doubting her, like the mafia uncle thing…"

"I'm starting to question everything she's ever said now. She told me out by the pool, not long after Pete walked in on us, that he had threatened to slit his wrists if she walked out. I never asked him about it: She may have just made the whole thing up…"

Craig had to hang around until 2 when Shandy finished work but he didn't care, he was now feeling happy and light as a feather. He thought moving out of Park Sunset probably wasn't even necessary now, but the tension had become hard to bear and he was getting quite into the idea of staying at Shandy's smart, clean, well-stocked Brentwood apartment.

Losing the Plot

This should be heaven, thought Craig, looking up at the cosmic jewellery display box above him. Stars seemed to be dancing but in actual fact this was just down to the vibrations caused by Shandy riding him in her parents' open-air hot tub. Perhaps, it was the lack of friction involved in trying to screw in water or perhaps, he just wasn't in the mood but he kept losing the page.

There was a clash of sensations: the sensual balmy night air, the stars, the dope and the cool water were all combining to relax him deeply, but at the same time Shandy's splashing, thrashing, bouncing naked body was demanding a more energetic response. He forced himself to focus on the rhythm and was soon feeling his heart pumping faster and his prick harden. Shandy's groans and the sight of her heavy breasts jumping in and out of the water started to ratchet up the sexual tension.

But then he couldn't resist another peek at the night sky's beauty, and immediately he felt a powerful pull elsewhere. The rhythm faltered and Craig sensed a growing frustration in Shandy.

"Where do you keep going?" she whispered.

"I dunno," he mumbled, "sorry."

"Do you want to change positions? You could do me from behind…"

"No, this is cool," he said, feeling like a ventriloquist's dummy, mouthing his words unconvincingly.

He decided to ignore the serene distractions of the night, until he had completed the job in hand at any rate. He took a firm grip of Shandy's ample hips and applied himself to regular controlled thrusts. Before long, he was as excited as she was and on the verge of delivering a final depth charge when they suddenly heard voices, one male and one female, talking and laughing and coming closer. Then they heard the latch lift on the side gate to the garden.

"Shit, they're back early!" hissed Shandy as her body froze into an erotic underwater statue. Craig tried to freeze too but his body kept jerking with involuntary spasms, making the water lap about audibly.

"Shhh! Duck down, they'll probably go straight inside the house."

They both took a large lungful of air and ducked beneath the surface.

Craig opened his eyes but couldn't see anything through the murk. After what seems a long, while a shape emerges from the blackness. It is a woman with long wavy black hair and dark piercing eyes walking towards the man.

In the background is a curious sound like the hissing of steam. She advances a little and fixes the man with a penetrating gaze. He retreats a little, looking nervous and awkward in his dressing gown. Finally she speaks, "I locked myself out of my apartment."

She looks around his dimly lit room then back at him.

"And it's so late."

Pathetic, mewling cries are faintly audible from the grotesque and bizarre-looking baby swathed in bandages behind him. He tries to hush it by furtively placing a hand over its mouth.

"You were right," whispers Bethany, "this is a seriously weird fucking movie." She sticks her tongue in his ear. "Or is it just the acid?"

"No, it's just as weird without drugs," says Craig, and they start to giggle quite loudly. Most of the midnight movie crowd are either drunk or stoned themselves and are oblivious.

She closes the door behind her and looks away from him for some time before smirking and asking, "Where is your wife?"

He looks confused as if it has only just occurred to him that she is missing.

"She must have gone back to her parents again. I'm not sure."

The woman looks almost predatory, never taking her eyes from him as she slowly approaches. She leans in as if to kiss him then says, "Can I spend the night here?"

He looks unsure but then she does kiss him, and this seems to overcome his doubts. They are soon naked and embracing in bed but they appear to be semi-submerged in a circular pool of opaque milky liquid in the centre of the bed. An industrial drone has been building and now intensifies to a menacing pitch as the woman notices the baby's cries and looks across the room, over the man's shoulder, at a monstrous silhouette of its head and looks alarmed.

The man turns her head back towards him and continues to kiss her. Then they both start to gradually sink into the liquid, into the bed.

"Then again, it might be more intense this way," says Craig. Bethany and he dissolve into cackles again.

Seconds later, there is nothing left of them except the woman's hair, or wig, that floats on the surface of the liquid like seaweed.

Craig watched the water swirling around the toilet basin, semi-hypnotised until a loud sucking sound signified the flush was complete. He washed his hands whilst gazing absently at one of the naked pin-ups stuck to the wall above the mirror. He lowered his gaze and stared at his own dilated pupils. In the reflection, over his shoulder, he noticed a little window looking onto a solid brick wall.

"Nice view," he muttered as he splashed water on his hands.

He walked out of the Piper's rest-room right into Frenchie who was evidently waiting for him.

"Ah, zere you are. Let's go."

Craig looked a little baffled.

"Umm, where are we going?"

"Oh, shit-for-brains, my apartment, remember? I want you to meet my flatmate."

"Oh yeah," said Craig, as if he remembered anything before going for a pee.

Frenchie put an arm around him and ushered him out the back way, across the parking lot and into a dark alley which Craig could swear he hadn't noticed before. Frenchie held onto his arm as if he might try and make a run for it, singing softly in French into his ear. He felt discombobulated as well as disoriented which may have been partly the reason he didn't notice a large bag on the ground and kicked it, almost tripping over.

The bag jolted, sat up and growled at them. It took Craig a couple of seconds to realise that the bag was actually a person, wrapped in dirty blankets. His face was encrusted with filth and twisted into a snarling grimace. Before Craig could apologise, Frenchie started hurling abuse at him.

"Clear off, you feelthy animal! You are deesgusting!"

The emaciated figure got to its feet and, surprisingly tall, towered over them, staring balefully. Frenchie shrieked and dragged Craig away. They emerged from the alley into a glaringly bright road. They hurried across in front of a van which hooted angrily at them.

Next thing Craig knew, Frenchie was unlocking a door in an anonymous looking Hollywood block. They stood in a drab foyer area. Frenchie led him down an even dingier corridor and knocked on the end door on the right. A pretty brunette in a puffy white blouse opened the door and smiled broadly.

"Thees is the English guy, Ray, I told you about from the bar."

"Er, it's Craig actually," he said quietly as Michelle kissed him briefly but softly on the lips.

"Hi, I'm Michelle, come in. Would you like some wine?"

He noted the surprisingly lavish zigzag black and white floor tiles, guessing vaguely that they were in the art deco style. Frenchie mumbled something about getting changed and disappeared while Michelle led him through to a good sized living room which was full of light from the open French doors. They sat on a slightly battered sofa in front of a huge low glass table. On the table stood a carafe of white wine, next to a large sheet of thick paper, covered in symbols and delicate calligraphy in different coloured inks.

"Oh, this is an astrological chart I'm doing for somebody. It's almost finished. What sign are you, Craig?"

"Er, Capricorn," he said, trying not to sound dismissive.

"Ah, the uncapricious climber. Let me get you a glass."

Left briefly on his own, Craig tried to work out where he was and why he was here but there was a haze hanging in his mind like smog, preventing him from thinking clearly. He could just about trace events back to Piper's but everything before that was a blank. Something about the rest-room in Piper's was nagging him, but what was it?

He mentally re-ran relieving himself and washing his hands. That's it! He'd seen a reflection in the mirror of a window looking onto a brick wall, but there *was* no window in the toilet at Piper's. He wondered if it could have been a hallucination or perhaps a reflection of a poster on the wall behind him.

Yes, that must be it, he thought; the walls were covered in pictures. Mainly centrefolds, but he could also bring to mind a weird hippy-style painting of a huge cactus in a desert landscape.

Michelle reappeared with a large glass and poured him some wine from the carafe and freshened her own glass on the table. She clinked his glass with hers.

"Chin Chin. Isn't that what you guys say in England?"

She was gazing right into his eyes and smiling coquettishly, or was that just his imagination.

197

"Round my way, we are more likely to just say 'cheers' actually."

"Cheers," she mocked in Dick Van Dyke cockney, "that is a cute accent you have there, Craig."

She moved closer to him on the couch.

"Well thanks, Michelle. That is a very cute smile you have there."

These words just seemed to come out on their own. He wasn't even sure he wanted to flirt with her, pretty though she was. He had an uncanny feeling he was performing a script though he couldn't predict what was coming next. Michelle leaned towards him and kissed him tentatively.

On one level, he was taken aback and yet on another it seemed inevitable. She kissed him again and this time pushed her tongue into his mouth. Craig felt himself start to relax and reciprocate. Their tongues darted and flicked their way around each other's mouths until Craig wasn't sure which tongue was his.

Michelle pushed him back on the sofa. He assumed she was going to lie on top of him but instead she reached for his fly and deftly unzipped it. She paused to take a large sip of wine then she licked the full length of his erection in one continuous slow lick from root to shiny tip.

Things were moving so fast. Craig had only met this girl five minutes earlier but with just one stroke of the tongue, the reticent part of him surrendered completely to his seduction. Preparing to abandon himself to sensual bliss, he stretched himself out. As he did this he felt his left foot collide with something brittle, which he heard fall over and smash. There was a pregnant pause before Michelle cried out, "Oh Jesus, no, look what you've done!"

He sat up and surveyed the damage. For a second, he assumed the carafe must have been made of the finest Austrian crystal for her to make such a fuss, but then he noticed that the wine, previously held in the carafe, was now spreading across the personally designed horoscope.

"You fucking idiot!" raged Michelle, "you cocksucker, that took me three fucking days! How can I charge 60 bucks for it now?"

"I'm sorry, I'm really sorry," stammered Craig, his doubts about Michelle's mental stability growing as rapidly as his penis was shrinking. Her fury seemed to grow rather than diminish. She started stamping back and forwards in front of the window, holding up the sodden chart, screaming and wailing like a banshee.

"I don't believe it, I don't fucking believe it!" She repeated this over and over again until it turned into a sort of furious mantra. Still clutching the ruined masterpiece to her bosom she ran out to the kitchen to try and dry it out. Craig lay paralysed with shock on the couch feeling seriously freaked out by the intensity of Michelle's reaction.

Listening to the shrieks and curses coming from the kitchen, he steeled himself for a further onslaught, expecting her to burst back into the room at any second, hopefully without a carving knife. He closed his eyes tightly and laid his head back on the padded arm, feeling his heart thumping like a bass drum at a frenzied punk gig. After a while, he realised he couldn't hear anything from the kitchen. The silence was eerie.

Gradually, his heart rate started to return to something resembling normal. He thought he probably ought to leave. It was tempting to just slip out quietly without any more fuss but he didn't want to be rude and upset Michelle again, or Frenchie for that matter. Where the hell was Frenchie anyway? He lay there, eyes closed, pondering the various options and the likely fallout until, exhausted, he reached a point where whatever happened, happened.

His eyes opened and he jumped as he realised he must have fallen asleep, but for seconds, minutes or hours? Distractedly, he realised he was gazing up at an artex ceiling. Having helped his dad decorate the family lounge a couple of years ago, he was familiar with artex, but was intrigued by the unusual design.

He could not make up his mind if the pattern was stipple, swirls or broken leather as it seemed to feature elements of each. The randomness of the pattern reminded him of a barren lunar landscape. He ran his eyes slowly over the swirls resembling craters and the rocky outcrops formed by artex drips, imagining he was a lone astronaut in a small craft preparing to land. Once he was down safely he felt obliged to go for a moonwalk.

Once he tired of giant leaps and Olympian strides, he became acutely aware of the deafening silence. A vivid sense of the extreme loneliness of being the only living person on the moon started to sink in. Waves of sadness started to break over him, reinforced by the beautiful desolation stretching as far as the eye could see. Planet Earth seemed so far away, almost unimaginably distant.

Craig tore his eyes away to break the spell. Hang on…where was he? The room was bland and pastel-coloured, almost alien in its tidiness. He was lying on a bed, not a couch. Where had the glass table gone?

If he had fallen asleep, could Michelle or Frenchie have moved him into a bedroom? This room definitely looked more like a cheap hotel or motel room though. Then it occurred to him that perhaps the whole scenario with Michelle had been a dream.

Of course! That would explain the hazy unreality he had felt, the non-existent window in the Piper's rest-room, the terrifying tramp and the alley he hadn't noticed before! Not to mention the whole unlikely sexual seduction scenario! He began to wonder if Michelle actually existed at all; he vaguely remembered Frenchie talking about her flatmate while serving him beer once, but didn't recall her mentioning any names. OK, so he had fallen asleep and dreamt the whole episode but that didn't explain where he was now.

He gazed around the room, searching for clues. It looked anonymous. He was wondering if he'd be any the wiser if he looked outside when he heard a cough, coming from behind the door opposite him, presumably the bathroom. It was not just any cough but a deep male cough. He knew straight away it wasn't Pete.

He felt legions of tiny hairs stand up on his neck and down each arm. Why the hell was he in a motel or apartment room with a strange man? Could he possibly be suppressing the memory of a gay encounter? Had he been drugged and kidnapped? Crazy movie plotlines bounced around his head like a pinball.

The toilet flushed and the sucking sound galvanised him into action. He leapt up from the bed, heading for the door, then realised he was missing his shoes. He felt under the bed, nothing. Starting to hyperventilate, he threw himself crosswise back on the bed: there they were on the floor on the other side.

He scooped them up, jumped off the bed and bounded again for the door just as he heard the click of the bathroom door handle. Despite the panic, as he opened the door to the corridor and stepped out, he could not resist turning to look. Unbelievably, whoever it was, had a large towel draped over his head, still drying his hair. Most of his naked upper torso was covered and all Craig detected was a slim build, muscular arms and skin-tight black jeans.

He couldn't really even guess an age; anywhere from late teens to mid-30s. A heartbeat later and Craig had closed the door as gently as possible, to room 69 he noticed, and was sprinting away down the corridor; he wasn't in Park Sunset then, judging by the carpet and fancy wall-mounted lights. He saw a fire escape sign and followed the arrow down a narrow flight of stairs. He burst out of the heavy doors into an area full of giant dustbins on wheels.

The slanted golden light suggested it was evening. He wanted to make his way around to the front of the building to work out where he'd been but a gruff voice from somewhere shouted out "Hey!" in an aggressive tone. Immediately assuming the guy from the room was following him, he ran across a small car park, up a side alley and into a residential-looking road which didn't look remotely familiar.

Feeling too self-conscious to run, he walked briskly away, looking for some recognisable landmark. Were passers-by staring at him or was this his imagination? After a few minutes, he felt much safer though he still didn't know where he was. The sky was now a dramatic dark pink, raspberry colour.

He was entering a more urbanised area with some offices and large stores. A few neon signs were glowing in the dusk. Craig was always struck by how a beautiful sunset could transform the flattest of locations here into something atmospheric and special. He came across a bus stop opposite a supermarket and feeling suddenly weary he rested his bones on the blue bench.

He did a sweep of his pockets but only produced a few nickels and dimes. He was wondering how many blocks the sum total of shrapnel might take him when a black Mercedes pulled up a few yards in front of him. A man in a suit, with a finely trimmed beard, in his mid to late 40s, lowered his window and stared at Craig. Craig assumed he was, ironically, about to be asked for directions but the man didn't speak.

Was the man silently offering him a lift? The man's motivation became clearer when he opened his mouth wide then slowly and deliberately raised his pointed index finger to his mouth, putting it right inside then lowering it again and repeated the gesture three or four times. All the time the man's face remained expressionless as he fixed Craig with cold shark eyes.

"Fuck off!" he heard himself whine.

The car didn't move. The man's eyebrows furrowed slightly but he didn't break the stare. Craig sighed, stood up and walked on up the sidewalk. He could hear the infectious but irritating sound of 'Funkytown' playing from a car radio. Since it had hit the number one slot, Lipps Inc. were ubiquitous here.

Then from a first floor balcony, he thought he could make out the strains of Jim Morrison singing. He stopped walking and looked up at the pretty flower-bedecked balcony trying to make out the song but it was merging, or clashing more like, with the upbeat disco pumping from the car radio. He thought he could make out something about women seeming wicked then about being down.

Ah, *People Are Strange* from the second album. Simultaneously though, he could hear a female voice distorted by a vocoder singing about making a move to another town that was right for her. It was like the '60s going head to head with the '80s. The scene on the balcony above was like a '60s flashback with candles, bare feet and sandals leaning over the edge and the unmistakable smell of weed wafting down.

The car drove off with the request to be taken to Funkytown' repeating and fading in the distance. The Doors seemed to have won this particular battle and the dark purple sky intensified the moodiness of the song as Jimbo invoked faces emerging from the deluge. At this very moment, the same black Mercedes from earlier slid out of a side road in front of him.

He tried to avoid looking at the driver but couldn't help glimpsing the trim beard and the shark-eyes, reflected in the wing mirror. As the car was effectively blocking his way forward he crossed the road and hurried on in the same direction. This ugly bastard was definitely tailing him and didn't seem inclined to take no for an answer. His mind started to spin.

Could this guy feasibly be the guy from the hotel room? Craig was fairly sure he couldn't, as the brief flash he had of the figure exiting the bathroom suggested someone younger. He half thought of retracing his steps to the hotel or apartment and stalking the guy from room 69 to get some answers. *If this was a film, that's what my character would do*, he thought, but it was virtually dark now and he wasn't even confident that he would be able to find his way back.

Who was he kidding anyway; he was scared shitless and just wanted to get home, wherever that was. He'd settle for anywhere safe and familiar right now. He looked over his shoulder. He felt hopelessly lost, in more ways than one. He was seriously beginning to wonder if he was losing touch with reality.

A car hooting and someone shouting spooked him into suddenly turning off from the main road. He broke into a run and criss-crossed smaller roads a few times, just in case shark-eyes was still following him. A car he had assumed parked, in front of him, roared into life as he passed. Panicking, he turned to check if it was black, but was blinded by the headlights.

He laughed at himself when the car turned in the road and headed in the opposite direction. He told himself he was behaving in an irrational and paranoid way and needed to calm down. He found himself walking past a bar. Some jaunty Irish folk music drifted out through the open door.

He looked in at the window and had a vivid impression of bright light, smiling faces and loud banter. That's what I need, some friendly normality to sort my head out he thought, wondering if he had enough nickels and dimes for a small beer or at least a coffee. He walked in and approached the bar. The barman was chatting and laughing with someone at the other end so Craig waited patiently.

He became aware that a middle-aged man with bushy hair, seated on a barstool a few yards away was staring intently at him. Oh no, surely not another man with designs on his body! He looked around the bar, pretending he was interested in the décor, then looked back and the man was still staring at him.

Suddenly the man's face broke into a big broad grin. The noise in the room suddenly abated as if an invisible sound mixer had just faded it down, then the man said, "So whaddya know, Henry?"

Craig looked behind him, in the forlorn hope that the man was talking to someone else. He looked back into the bright full-beam smile which had a peculiar frozen quality. Craig was disturbed by the words as well as the petrified smile. He had heard them before somewhere.

He backed away from the man, whose eyes kept following him, but backed into something that fell over with a loud clatter. It seemed to be a life size wooden man, presumably a promotion of some sort. He struggled to pick it up but was assaulted on all sides by mocking laughter. He looked up and was horrified to see that everyone in the bar had been reduced to two dimensions.

A movement behind the bar caught his eye; it was the barman's hinged arm waving up and down at him, as if someone was operating it with wire. Panic overtook him again as the laughter continued to ring in his ears. He fled back into the night. He tried to keep to one direction, assuming that he must come across somewhere he recognised sooner or later.

On the other hand, what if he was in one of the many suburbs he wasn't familiar with like Anaheim or Pasadena? Adrenaline had been keeping him going but as it started to wear off, he realised he was physically and emotionally exhausted.

He found himself entering a more salubrious residential district, the houses and gardens were becoming larger and often surrounded by large walls and tall wrought iron gates. A lot of the plush lawns and bountiful gardens were illuminated by exterior lighting, green bulbs apparently the popular choice. There were fewer and fewer pedestrians around so he was starting to stick out like a sore thumb.

No sooner had he thought this than a police car on the other side of the road spotted him and slowed right down. Two officers stared suspiciously at him. He avoided their gaze and kept walking. They drove on. The sound of cicadas rubbing their legs together was oppressive and hypnotic.

There was also another repetitive whooshing sound he couldn't place. The musky scent of the California sycamores lining the street smelt aggressively cloying to him. Some towering 8 feet bushes with dark burgundy red flowers leaned over a wall to his left, suckers extending out, emitting an aroma like old wine. The whole night, even the plant life seemed predatory.

An engine purred gently behind him. He turned to face a familiar black car, creeping along at no more than 10mph, as if in a funeral procession. Craig freaked; he could not believe this man had been pursuing him all this time. Without thinking he scaled a 5-feet garden wall to his left and jumped down into the garden. He ran across the rubbery grass, setting off a security light, and scrabbled over the opposite wall.

He figured he was now in an adjacent street and to throw off the Mercedes further he crossed and clambered over a wall on the other side. This residence was palatial and the gardens featured rows of statues, impressive topiary, summer house and of course a pool. It's raining he thought, as he snaked between a group of cypress trees, but then realised he was getting soaked by one of the several automatic sprinklers which were also responsible for the whoosh, whoosh sound he couldn't place earlier.

He wondered why this sound was getting louder but then recognised the sprinklers were masking the sounds of helicopter blades. A helicopter came nearer and nearer until it was almost hovering overhead. Then a searchlight hit a neighbouring garden, and it suddenly occurred to him that this was a police chopper searching for someone. Could someone have already complained about a trespasser?

Maybe that police car that spotted him had called for some aerial assistance. Lights in the house were being turned on and a face appeared at an upstairs window. Craig took cover behind a tree. After a few seconds, the face disappeared again and Craig ran across an open space, past a fountain, towards another row of tall trees. As he did this the searchlight suddenly illuminated him and the area around him.

Panicking, he altered his course and ran towards the nearest boundary wall beyond the gigantic pool. Could he hear shouts over the sound of the helicopter or was it his imagination? What if a cop had a gun drawn and was shouting "freeze" at him? What the hell was he doing?

He thought he had evaded the searchlight so decided to just keep running until he could reach that wall. Just as he ran by the edge of the deep end, his feet slipped on the soaking grass and he toppled sideways into the dark water. He hit his head on the side as he went in. Everything started going black as he felt his body sinking.

His clothes felt heavy and were pulling him down. He was so exhausted, he just wanted everything to stop. The cold water and the silence felt good, and he wondered if he should just remain at the bottom. Then above him, he saw bright beautiful white light, dazzling, dancing, sparkling, now all around him.

Tremors

Craig sat up gasping for breath. There was no pool, no police, no sound, except his own wheezing attempts to draw breath. The scene had shifted again; he was on another bed. He recognised the room this time thankfully; Shandy's bedroom in her Brentwood apartment. But for how long? A glimpse under the sheet told him he was naked.

No sign of Shandy. He had no idea what day it was, and although there was daylight outside the window he wasn't sure this was real. He dearly wanted to believe the nightmare was over, but was terrified the carpet would be pulled out from under him if he started to believe it. His breathing gradually began to normalise, but his mouth felt like the Sahara desert, or perhaps Death Valley was more appropriate.

He was so parched he thought he may choke. Once the thought of water entered his brain it excluded everything else. He stumbled out of bed and almost collapsed; his legs were rubbery, as if he had been in bed for a week. Perhaps, he had. Leaning on the wall for support, he edged around the double bed, looking for his clothes.

There was no sign of them, and although he felt vulnerable naked, he ignored this in his desperate quest for liquid. He didn't have his contacts in so everything was blurry. The living room light was glaring and he had to shield his eyes, almost tripping over a trunk full of Shandy's old treasures. He circumnavigated the couch and made his way around to the little kitchen area on the right.

It was darker here and cooler. Ah, the sink, at last. He turned on the cold tap and thrust his mouth at the resulting jet. He had turned it on too full and it was splashing his torso but he didn't care, he must drink. Finally after having his fill, he stood upright, turned off the tap and reflected that he felt almost human.

He poured himself a large tumbler full of reserve water and made his way back to the bedroom, still a little unsteady on his pins. He sat on the bed and just as he was putting the tumbler down on the little bedside cabinet, the world tilted on its axis. The glass fell on its side and emptied its contents all over the cabinet and dripped onto the carpet. A deep rumbling filled his ears.

A framed professional glamour photo of Shandy just inside the living room fell to the tiled floor and smashed. A loose pile of books on the shelf in the bedroom fell to the floor. Something large crashed to the floor out of sight in the diner area. He could swear everything was vibrating!

Craig screwed shut his eyes, put his hands to his head, and whispered, "No, no, no", rocking back and forth on the bed. Just when he thought he was beginning to stabilise, his world was literally coming apart at the seams! He had experienced extreme mental confusion before on drugs but nothing compared to this. He could even hear voices screaming and shouting in his head.

Strangely, he could almost blank these out by pressing his hands tightly over each ear. He sat naked on the bed, rocking slightly, pondering the horrors of encroaching schizophrenia and wondering if medication might alleviate the anxiety or at least block the hallucinations. After some time, the symptoms decreased and Craig opened his eyes warily, half expecting to be confronted by a towering winged demon or the ghost of Ian Curtis.

There was nothing except a book lying open by his left foot. So some higher agency was delivering him a message, or perhaps it was a manifestation of his own troubled unconscious, acting out in a poltergeist fashion. Tentatively, he reached down and picked up the book, instinctively knowing that the first sentence his eyes fell on would be the 'message'. He de-focussed his eyes so he would not cheat and consciously choose a fitting or meaningful sentence.

He moved his eyes around the leaf waiting for some sort of signal. Nothing really happened so he just moved his eyes around in a circular motion three times then brought them into focus.

'No, people who love downy peaches are apt not to think of the stone, and sometimes jar their teeth terribly against it.'

Is that it, he thought, disappointed. He turned the book over to see who had written it. It was a paperback novel called *Adam Bede* by George Eliot. Craig had never read anything by her though dimly recalled watching an uninspiring TV play based on one of her novels. Lightweight English, heritage chick-fodder; typical Shandy-fare he decided dismissively.

Even so, he read the sentence a second time. Pondering the words, he felt the words may have a deeper level of meaning after all; more so than most of the surrounding page at any rate. He could have merely landed upon empty description or functional dialogue. He read out loud, slowly, committing it to memory.

Suddenly a phone rang. Craig's nerves were as taut as fuse wire and he physically jumped and dropped the book. It sounded real and outside himself, but so was the book. He turned and stared at the phone on Shandy's bedside table, consumed with dread.

For some reason, he feared listening to a voice emanating from his own mind as much as from one beyond the grave. He stared at the phone as it continued to ring. I don't have to answer it, he reasoned with himself; if it is a real call for Shandy then they can always ring back later.

He shivered and pulled the bedclothes tight around him. The ringing finally stopped and the tension in his muscles relaxed a little. He felt unaccountably oppressed and claustrophobic. He breathed deeply a few times then the phone abruptly leapt into life again. He felt ridiculous all of a sudden, cowering from a telephone and grabbed the receiver.

"Craig. Craig, is that you?" A friendly voice!

"Shandy, is that really you?" he laughed, relieved but still uncertain.

"Of course it's me. I was just phoning for a damage report."

"Damage?… How did you know…? I mean, was I in a bad way when you left?"

"What?"

"I was stuck in a bad dream or a nightmare. Couldn't wake up, or thought I had but then everything turned upside down again…"

"You sound disorientated, but I guess it was your first time, huh?"

"First time? Well I've been feeling flaky for a while off and on, but this was a whole new level of unreality. I think I've been given a kind of message from your George Eliot novel, *Adam Bede*, by the way, it's…"

"Jesus, Craig, lay off the white lines, you're talking gibberish! I just wanted to know if anything got broken in the tremor."

"Eh, did you say tremor?… As in earthquake?"

"Surely not even you could sleep through a tremor like that?"

A lightbulb went off in Craig's head.

"Ha ha ha ha ha! So you are telling me all that noise and vibration, and stuff was real and not just in my head?"

"Yes, Craig," Shandy said slowly as if speaking to a child, "I'm telling you it was real. I'm getting worried about you."

"Blimey, I've just experienced an earthquake!"

"Well, it was only a relatively small tremor, before you phone your friends in England and brag on about it, though we may get another; be prepared to run outside. So, did anything get broken?"

"Oh er, not much; your framed photo fell down and smashed…"

"Shoot! Anything else?"

"I don't think so, oh hang on, I did hear something smash in the living room or the kitchen."

"And you haven't even taken a look?"

"Well I thought it was just in my head, remember; I'll take a look now…"

Craig put the phone on the bed and sprang up, feeling a huge weight had been lifted from him. He couldn't see anything untoward in the living room but in the kitchen he almost trod on a sliver of broken glass. A 3D Jackson Pollock painting in glass and plastic obliterated the floor tiles.

"Oops, she won't be happy," he said aloud.

"I'm afraid you'll have to make do with takeaway coffees for a while," he said into the phone.

"Ohh crap, not my filter machine! I can't do without coffee. I'll try and pick a new one up on the way home from work. Clean up the mess, will you, and I'll see you in a couple of hours."

"OK, I'll be counting the seconds, my sweet downy peach."

Shandy chortled; "I might even take you out to the Troubadour tonight, if you play your cards right."

Lucky me, thought Craig, hanging up and laying back on the bed, still naked, contemplating the delights of a dodgy country and western band, listening to Shandy, pissed on white wine, making small talk with Arlen, her geeky waiter friend. Actually, on reflection, a cosy if potentially dull evening with Shandy was probably just what he needed to get his feet back on the ground, after who knows how long spent orbiting Neptune. Staring at the smooth plaster ceiling above him Craig had a sudden déjà vu.

"Artex!" he exclaimed. A fleeting image of a lone astronaut floated into his mind like driftwood, but then receded again with the tide before he could examine it further. "Shit!" He realised he had forgotten to ask Shandy where his clothes were.

The Woman with the Feathered Hat

Craig sat in Piper's propping up the bar on a tall red leather and chrome stool. He sipped his beer and dipped in and out of 'The Electric Kool-Aid Acid Test'. He hadn't really expected to find Pete here but was disappointed nevertheless. He was glad to catch up briefly with Mimi, probably Piper's most friendly and level-headed barmaid, before she finished her shift and handed over to Drake, who was turning into his latest obsession.

Robert Madigan also started his shift at the same time which put a smile on Craig's face, knowing he'd be in for some quality conversation and possibly even a spliff out back in the parking lot. Mimi had shocked him with news that Betsy, the pale opinionated curly blonde barmaid, had gone into rehab for her coke addiction. She'd seemed so fresh-faced and freckly innocent when they first met her a few months ago.

She can't be older than 21, he speculated. It was true she had become quite thin but Craig didn't even know she touched coke.

"Everyone's taking it. Be careful honey," warned Mimi, "this place can suck you in and spit you out."

Craig wasn't sure if she was referring to Piper's, California or the USA, but he appreciated her warm mumsy concern. Joe Senior, or Napoleon, as Pete and he thought of him, had sacked Betsy a few days ago when she was so obviously out of it, she couldn't perform even the most basic of bar duties. Instead of apologising to Joe, she'd pretended nothing was wrong.

As Drake settled in to her routine, Craig wondered if he'd exaggerated in his mind the chemical reaction between them last time. As he'd been pretty wasted on coke, weed and beer at the time it was not surprisingly a bit of a blur.

"Are you not going to say hi then?"

He looked up from his book straight into her shining dark-eyed smile.

"You weren't shy last time we met!"

Craig felt himself blush. "Um, yes hello, Drake, I do apologise for my incoherence and possibly my behaviour if it was a little forward last time." He heard himself turning stiff and dry like a BBC newsreader.

Drake exploded with laughter.

"Hey, Robert, listen to this guy; 'I apologise for my incoherence'," in a deep voice and dodgy posh English accent. "I love the way he talks!" She punched him playfully on his arm.

Robert poured Craig another Budweiser from the tap without even checking he wanted another.

"Yeah, he's a real sweetheart," he drawled and winked at him. So it seemed Craig hadn't imagined the flirtation.

"What are you reading this time?" asked Robert. Craig held up the book as a response.

"Ah Mr Wolfe," he purred, "though I have to say I prefer Kesey himself, especially *Sometimes a Great Nation*."

"Ooh," exclaimed Drake, holding up Craig's book, "he wrote *Cuckoo's Nest*, didn't he…"

"Almost," replied Robert, to avoid a complex explanation. "Why, Drake, is that another of your all-time favourite movies?" he teased.

"Oh come on, it's one of every body's favourite films, isn't it!" she replied.

"If not, it should be," agreed Craig, "Jack at his charismatic best!"

"Yeah, but it's a bit late for Drake, she doesn't usually go for movies made after the '50s."

"Are you being sassy with me, Mr Madigan?" she said with a hand on her hip, then scolded Craig for laughing, "don't you encourage him."

She moved off to serve a customer.

"Do you remember chapter 6 by any chance?" Craig asked Robert.

"Ah, not especially, why do you ask?"

"It's just that when I started the book on the beach the other day, a bloke called out, 'wait 'til you get to chapter 6!'."

"Ha," mused Robert, "then I'd guess that's the chapter when he hoaxes his own death, at least that's the part that sticks in my mind."

Seeing Craig looking slightly taken aback, he added, "Sorry if I spoilt it for ya."

Craig walked over to the jukebox, determined to stem the flow of Frank Sinatra songs. Pete had commented semi-jokily that these were a good indicator they were in a Mafia-run joint. Cricket was sitting in the nearest booth to the jukebox with his stilt-like legs protruding out sideways blocking the machine. He stared at Craig.

"Hello, old chap," he said in another painful English accent.

So Pete was right about the nickname, he thought.

"Umm, hi, how are you?"

Politeness was clearly wasted on Cricket who ignored the question and baldly asked one of his own.

"So what are you doing here?"

Craig was a bit stumped, not least because Cricket never spoke to them.

"Well I suppose you could say we're on holiday here, but I kind of think of it as just hanging out, if you know what I mean."

Cricket continued to stare.

"So when are you leaving?"

Craig smiled, trying to figure out if this was an implied threat or just an ignorant blunt remark. An image of him running to escape Cricket wielding a chainsaw flitted across his mind.

"I haven't decided yet."

Assertively, he trod over Cricket's legs to peruse the jukebox and hopefully signal that the conversation was over. Luckily, Cricket's attention span was pretty short, and he turned around and insulted someone opposite him in the booth.

Craig realised that he wanted to hear a tune that he and Pete had grown accustomed to over the months. Oddly for Craig, because it was by a jazz group, Weather Report. Craig hadn't noticed it get under his radar and he smiled as this was probably the first time he'd selected a jazz tune on a jukebox.

The song was called *The Pursuit of the Woman with the Feathered Hat,* and had what Craig felt was quite a modern sleek cinematic vibe. As he put his quarter in the slot, Craig laughed to himself as he recalled that the first time he saw Drake arrive for work at Piper's, she was wearing a feathered hat, in keeping with her '40s Lauren Bacall-inspired style. He liked the idea of Drake recognising the track as a sophisticated come-on, even though it was unintentional, consciously at any rate.

Back at the bar, he was annoyed to find Neil had taken over the neighbouring stool and was getting stuck into chatting up Drake.

"Hey, Clyde, how you doin', man?"

"It's Craig, actually. I'm fine, thanks."

"Craig, yeah, I was just trying to tempt Drake here to come along to one of my little shindigs."

"And how did that go, Neil?"

"She's really game for it, aren't you, Drake?"

Drake, looking slightly stressed, counting out some change, leant over.

"The DJ thing? Like I said, I'll have to let you know, I may be busy that night." She turned away again.

"Game," said Craig in a slightly arch manner.

"She'll be there, she's just playing hard to get; you know what they're like, man."

"They?" queried Craig.

"Chicks, especially American chicks, they're all ballbreakers right?"

"If you say so, Neil."

He tried to turn the other way and briefly glimpsed Chuck glaring in their direction, but Neil was persistent and tugged at his shirt cuff. *What on earth did Pete ever see in this bloke*, he thought; he's slimy, arrogant and lacking all awareness, and to use one of Holden Caulfield's phrases, a real phony.

His stories struck Craig as fake as his transatlantic accent. He seemed to think of himself as a cutting edge DJ and yet he looked like a refugee from 1975, with his long wavy locks and top two buttons undone to show off some wispy chest hair and that old chestnut, the gold medallion. He was invading Craig's space and was certainly not fluent in body language or he'd have picked up a message screaming to be left alone. Instead, he launched into another self-aggrandising story that had no obvious point.

"You know Alison; after the gig last night, she only started stripping in the back of the limo!"

"Who the hell is Alison?" Craig interjected.

"You met her with Pete in The Nest on Hollywood Boulevard man, you must remember, she really dug you guys…"

This disturbed Craig as he didn't hear the faintest tinkling of a distant bell. Neil might have been mixing him up with someone else or be delusional, but he sounded so sure of his story; and yet Craig would swear blind he hadn't even met Neil in The Nest, let alone Alison. He had zoned out from the story and was only concerned with extricating himself from this babbling idiot who still had hold of his shirt cuff.

Then a merciful vision; Frenchie, all tarted up and walking, or rather lurching, right towards him. Frenchie, whose real name was Catherine, had long straight blonde hair, wide cheekbones and smoky sensual grey eyes. You could tell she'd been around the block a few times but she was still attractive, with her self-possessed stereotypical Gallic insouciance.

"Darleeng, zere you are," she gushed, kissing him two, three, no four times, two on each side. Neil tried to ingratiate himself.

"Hi, I'm Neil, I think I've seen you in here before," he smarmed, offering her his hand. She blew cigarette smoke straight in his face then dispatched him like he was an irritating and pointless insect.

"Leesen Nile, I have to talk to Craig 'ere, so peess off eh, there's a good boy."

She virtually pushed him off his stool, and even Neil picked up on the vibe that he wasn't wanted, for some incomprehensible reason, managing a weak, "Catch you on the flip side," before returning to a side booth.

"Thank you, Frenchie, you saved me from a fate worse than death there."

"'Im? Ee's a boring little teet," she said, impressively capturing Neil's essence in a nutshell. Frenchie could not be bothered to conceal a dismissive attitude to others unless she liked them or thought they could offer her something. "I was 'oping you might be able to 'elp me. Michelle pulled strings and got us invites to a beeg film industry party. Zey say De Niro will be there."

"Wow," exclaimed Craig, "that sounds great. So what are you doing in Piper's?"

"I am looking for a leetle sniff first, you know. Can you 'elp me, darleeng?"

Frenchie's coke radar was impressive, he didn't even remember her being around when he scored that half gram the other day. Despite knowing she was just using him, he was fond of Frenchie and now grateful too, for getting rid of Neil.

"You are in luck," he said tapping his back jean pocket, "I've only had a couple of lines."

"My 'ero!" she said putting a hand on either side of his face, the cigarette almost singeing his ear, and gave him a white wine flavoured kiss on the lips. He dug out the wrap and tucked it into Frenchie's palm.

"Just a little, Frenchie, no more than two lines."

She was already halfway to the rest rooms.

"Three at most, ok..." he called after her.

Robert Madigan leant in and in a hushed voice said, "Just so you know, she's persona non grata around here now, orders from the top, so you might wanna put a little distance between you, if you get my drift. Only whilst in Piper's obviously."

"Understood!" he said frowning. His inner Pete was raging at him; *Are you completely fucking stupid, you could get us banned from Piper's or physically ejected by a couple of Joe's boys!* He'd heard about Frenchie getting her cards but hadn't realised the extent of her ex-communication, or considered the collateral impact.

Drake was smiling at him as she wiped down the surface of the bar in front of him.

"Are you OK, Craig? You're not overdoing it again, are you?"

"Uh no, I'm fine thanks, all under control."

Just at that moment, a loud Frenchie-shaped commotion erupted from the rest-room area. All eyes in Piper's were on her as she hurtled back towards Craig, knocking punters aside like they were skittles.

"Ees it joke or what?" she demanded, her face a wide-eyed Halloween mask.

"Sorry, what? Is what a joke?" he stammered nervously with Robert's recent words ringing in his ears.

She waved the wrap, or rather the unfolded piece of paper that used to be a wrap, in front of his face.

"I open eet in normal way," (her command of English seemed to be shrinking under the stress), "and nothing. Then I look down and see the powder in the water."

Craig's stomach lurched as he recalled struggling to re-fold the wrap correctly after his two lines and feeling that he might have been partly responsible for this crisis.

"Come, I show you," Frenchie said, urgently dragging him back to the rest rooms. She burst into the ladies room, luckily nobody else had gone to use it in the meantime, and pointed down the bowl to the powder floating on the water as she'd described.

"So you opened it up the wrong way but surely not all of it ended up in there," he pleaded, thinking of his remaining dollars he had blown on marching powder that had marched straight down the toilet.

"Look!" she said triumphantly pointing to a tiny spot on the carpet fringing the toilet. Craig licked his finger and dabbed at the spot then sucked on his finger.

Frenchie had also noticed a faint trail down the inside of the bowl and excitedly pointed it out. Craig bent down but then had a light-bulb moment where he asked himself what his life had come to, scrabbling to snort a class A drug from the inside of a toilet. He stood up straight.

"I tell you what, you take it, Frenchie. Don't worry about it, it's just one of those things."

She gasped apologies and thanks whilst sticking her head down into the toilet bowl. There were still a lot of eyes on Craig as he found his way back to his seat, or at least he felt there were. Robert Madigan whispered in a serious voice, "When I said put some distance between you, I wasn't picturing you going to the ladies room together."

He could not quite stifle a laugh. "Did she really just drop your stash down the crapper?" He could barely get the sentence out through guffaws and a tear was running down his nose.

"Yep," sighed Craig, "that's about the size of it."

Robert slapped the bar.

"That's fantastic man, you couldn't make that up."

"Unfortunately, I didn't, Robert. Please, may I have another beer?"

"Ah Hollywood," grinned Robert, "in the words of Raymond Chandler, 'Anyone who doesn't like it is either crazy or sober'."

A few minutes later, when Frenchie was long gone, his breathing had calmed down and a relative impression of normality was resumed, Craig recommenced contact with Lauren Bacall.

"I'm not sure I want to know exactly what happened there, Craig."

"I don't think full knowledge of the facts would necessarily be wise or healthy, Drake," he said, retreating back into repressed English gent role.

"There you go again," she giggled, "you should be in the movies!"

"Talking of which, Lauren, er sorry, Drake, I am dying to know how your audition went."

She asked Robert to cover for her for a few minutes then came around the other side of the bar and climbed elegantly onto, the now vacant, stool beside Craig.

"I don't think I was what they were looking for. They all said nice things, but I could tell from the look in the producer's eyes that I wasn't the one."

"I'm sorry to hear that but I'm sure there's a great role out there with your name on, probably looking for you right now."

"You're sweet," she said smiling, and kissed him coyly on the cheek. His face felt electrified and he could swear his heartbeat stuttered. "To be honest though, I am losing faith. I'm almost 27 and that's already getting old in this town."

"That's crazy," he protested.

"Maybe, but I gambled on a high rent place and now I'm not sure I can pay this month's rent let alone next month's."

"What are you going to do, find a cheaper place?"

"I may have an offer coming that will be hard to turn down. It might get me out of a mess."

Drake realised she was bringing herself down and tried to jump back into her happy-go-lucky persona.

"You're a good listener, Craig. Shame you're so young…" she said in an affected husky voice.

"Are you being Mae West now?" he asked, trying to ignore the pain between his legs. "I'm not that young, I'm 19, only seven short years behind you, that's nothing!"

She laughed and kissed him on the cheek again.

"I do really want to go and see *Nosferatu the Vampyre* with you. I think we'd have a lot of fun, but I'm not sure I can right now."

There was something implied, something hidden in this phrase but Craig pushed this thought to one side.

"Well, I think there's more than one screening and it's on late, so you'd be finished here."

He became dimly aware of Chuck again, over by the New York City mural, staring balefully at him. He wasn't sure what Chuck's position was at Piper's. He wasn't family and he didn't work here so maybe he was a business partner or associate. He obviously wielded influence as Craig had heard him berating the bar staff before.

Perhaps, he was angry about the Frenchie debacle. Drake also seemed to notice the stare and apologised but said she had to get back to work. He stole another peek but Chuck's beady eyes were still fixed on him. Craig could see why Pete thought he was a real gangster—the lean, wiry physique, the coiled physical presence, the self-assured authority that automatically generated nervous respect, and especially the icy look in the dark glittering eyes.

Only the thin moustache detracted from the image, thought Craig and funnily enough brought his namesake to mind, Chuck Berry. A faint grin flickered across his face as he visualised Chuck duck-walking across the floor. The glower grew even darker; Craig coughed and turned away.

Piper's was filling up and Craig thought about leaving. He strained over the increased noise to hear Robert Madigan who was leaning towards him whilst drying a glass.

"She really likes you, you know. You may be in with a chance there but don't gamble on it. Some things are not in our control."

"She said she really likes me?" he burst out, utterly unable to conceal his burgeoning excitement.

"Well yeah, kid, but like I said, that doesn't count for everything."

Craig's brain edited out everything except the one magical phrase, "She really likes you."

He looked around for Drake but she had disappeared somewhere. He waited for a couple of minutes, then another Sinatra tune came on the jukebox and he decided it was definitely time to leave. He asked Robert to say goodbye to Drake for him and headed for the exit, noticing Chuck was no longer around.

Floating to the door on cloud nine, Craig set the controls for the heart of the Starwood. He checked he still had the flyer in his pocket. *The Plugz and Gang of Four; it will be a great night*, he thought.

Lost in Space

As Craig walked out of Piper's, he almost collided with a large bulky figure standing stock still right outside the door, seemingly staring at the roof. Annoyed, Craig opened his mouth to moan, then he noticed the shiny bald head. Yes, it was none other than Bob Atcheson. Craig felt a surge of affection for the great bear of a man.

"Bob, it's you, where have you been?"

He walked around in front of Bob and spontaneously hugged him, whilst surreptitiously nudging him to one side of the door. Bob looked down and smiled warmly.

"Hey, little brother, Googies, right here, living history."

He took a slow deep breath then gazed up to the skies, "Take in the beauty."

Craig raised his eyes to the heavens too. Some stars were visible despite the skyglow from all the excessive and obtrusive LA light. In a moment of almost eerie synchronicity, Craig suddenly realised that the Sinatra music spilling out from the Piper's jukebox was none other than *Fly Me to The Moon*. He still felt warm inside from Drake's smiles, her words, her kisses.

"Beautiful, and sad," rumbled Bob. "Some of them stars ain't even there no more. They is so far away that by the time their light reaches us, they've already gone out. Trick of the light, you could say, my friend."

Craig just nodded, feeling moved by Bob's philosophical nugget. Bob looked him quizzically in the eyes and put an arm around his shoulders.

"Where you goin'?"

As usual when Bob spoke, Craig wasn't sure what level he was referring to.

"Well, I'm going to a gig, to see some live music… But I was wondering if I should stop off and see an old friend on the way…" He paused as Bob's smile urged him on. "You know him actually, Bob; the thing is, I did something bad and hurt him, and I'm worried I've lost his friendship for good."

Bob's visage melted into pure compassion.

"It may not be too late. That star may still burn. You may have to choose though; choose to lose someone. All we can do is try and connect with each other. If we don't, we are just lost in space…and time." He looked up once more. "It's a wonderful and terrifying world, little brother. You already know what you gonna do. Why you wastin' time talkin' to me?"

Craig felt his eyes misting up.

"Thanks, Bob."

Bob looked back down at Craig and grasped his hands in his huge paws and squeezed them. He stared deep into Craig's eyes, right through his soul and beyond…

"Bing bing. It's later than you think."

The shift into an ominous warning unsettled Craig. He extricated his hands from Bob's grip and hurried away up the Strip. Behind him, he could hear Bob crooning an old standard about the passing of the years.

It was just an old song, not a warning at all, he laughed to himself. He looked back and could just make out Bob Atcheson's large figure shuffling on the spot, outside Piper's, under the stars.

As he walked west on Sunset, Craig wondered what he should say to Pete if he was in. He was feeling anxious about Candy who would probably be with him although it seemed highly unlikely that Uncle Leroy would be sitting in the small apartment with them. He considered asking Pete to step outside and out of earshot, where he could warn him about Candy, but rejected the idea as it could just drive the wedge further between them.

No, he would simply apologise and hope that Pete came to his senses soon. He would not be long, then hurry to the Starwood. It was already almost 8:45 and he didn't want to miss the Plugz. How to say sorry though?

It occurred to him that Pete would be unable to resist hearing what happened with Frenchie and his wrap of Charlie. He would undoubtedly crease up at the story which would breach the barrier between them, at least enough for him to apologise and ask for another chance. Feeling more confident he hastened his step.

Luckily, the outer door of Park Sunset was not locked. There was nobody around. A bulb had gone out in the corridor that curved to the right, leading to their old room, so it looked even darker than usual. He steeled himself and tapped on the door.

No response. He couldn't hear voices. He knocked again, slightly louder.

"Who is it?" Pete's voice yelled grumpily.

Craig thought it best not to answer as he'd probably be less likely to open the door, knowing it was him. He thought he could hear sighing then rustling before finally the door opened a couple of inches. Craig tried not to look startled at his friend's hollowed-out appearance. Pete's eyes were sunken with bags underneath like bruises. Unshaven. Hair filthy. It smelt like he hadn't showered for a week.

"What do you want?" he said blankly.

Instinctively, Craig knew that telling the Frenchie story wouldn't work right now. Thrown off guard, he ummed and erred like a simpleton.

"Are you OK, mate? You look a bit rough"

"I'm fine."

"Are you…on your own?"

"She's not here. What do you want?" sounding more impatient this time.

"OK, I just…I just want to say I'm really, really sorry, Pete. I wish I could turn the clock back."

"You can't unring a bell," mumbled Pete. He already seemed to be on the verge of shutting the door.

"No, I guess not. But maybe, you could try to forgive me. It was a stupid mistake but we don't have to let it destroy such a great friendship."

The door was closing and Craig put his hand up to push it back a little.

"I'm going now," said Pete, exerting more force that was more than a match for Craig. He found himself once more staring at the closed door. He raised his voice so Pete would definitely hear:

"Come on, man, we are partners, like Butch and Sundance…Kerouac and Casady…Morecambe and Wise…" He heard his own voice crack. Silence.

After a few seconds, Craig felt a flash of anger and before he could stop himself, he started spewing the stuff he'd told himself he wouldn't say.

"You're letting her come between us, but she can't be trusted."

Then he shouted: "You do know she's a liar through and through, don't you. You can't know you're pregnant in two or three days, it takes two or three weeks, Shandy told me."

He paused while a man in a suit passed, looking suspiciously at him.

"I don't believe she's dying either! You don't throw up blood with sickle-cell, that's another lie! She's twisted and manipulative. You've let her inside your head. Mate."

A tear ran down his cheek. He softened his tone:

"You need to get away from her. Come and stay at Shandy's…anywhere, just get away from her or she'll drag you down."

After a few more seconds of complete silence, Craig sighed and wiped his face. He hit the door to no. 42 with the palm of his hand then turned and left.

He turned down Olive Drive towards Santa Monica Boulevard on automatic pilot, then back east towards the Starwood.

Despite an impressive set by the Gang of Four, Craig did not really enjoy the gig.

The Getaway Plan

Craig lay sprawled on Shandy's sofa, eating Corn Flakes, trying to sieve memories of the previous night through yet another hangover, onto the pages of his diary. Shandy had taken him, Phil and a photographer friend called David, to Fippers, a giant purple and blue Roller Boogie Palace at the corner of Santa Monica and Cienega. Craig had also arranged to meet up with Jeff from Sacramento, the nice guy who saved his bacon at the Starwood a few weeks back.

Craig had never been to a roller disco before, so it was a novel experience anyway, but this was punk night which imbued the evening with an extra helping of bizarre. The place was rammed with more hardcore punks than Craig had so far witnessed in the whole of LA, and the music was deafening. There was an insane level of carnage with wild drunken pile-ups on the skating rink, around the live band stage whilst strobe lights bounced off mirrors.

He recalled Shandy showing him a custom skate shop with artificial life-size palm trees and Art Nouveau murals. Jeff had invited him because he remembered Craig had wanted to see the Germs, but sadly they failed to show up. The Mau Maus did show up but didn't play for some reason.

Black Flag had the plug pulled on them after just one number, a startling burst of nihilistic rage and heaviness. Jeff was furious as he loved them. The Dadas weren't bad nor were the ubiquitous Alley Cats but the sound was muddy and distorted as hell. They had all got shredded, apart from Shandy, who had to work today, and Craig had a feeling that he blew quite a lot of dosh at the bar.

He was struggling to revive much memory of the heated debate between Phil and Jeff, and wished he could recall some of David's pointed one-liners, but despite the wild drunken abandon, Craig had felt a certain detachment throughout the evening and off and on for a few days before this. He gave up on the diary and reflected on his burnt out state.

After all the stress of the Candy saga, Craig felt like he needed to get out of the city for a while. Although Shandy had kindly helped him escape to the

223

sanctuary of her apartment in Brentwood, he still expected to run into Candy at every diner or bar they frequented. He was feeling mentally and emotionally battered and was craving some space and serenity to take stock and get his head together.

Unfortunately, the incessant gigs, clubs and drinks as well as the trip to Vegas had eaten away at Craig's meagre resources. If he didn't find some work soon, he would have no option but to kiss LA goodbye and take his return flight home. He sat and vacillated in Shandy's living room, vainly trying to formulate a plan. He had turned to Shandy's vinyl collection after feeling cheated by KROQ's 'Stooges Day' which had featured precisely 3 Stooges tracks in 3 hours.

He'd wanted to go to Death Valley ever since reading about it in western annuals as a kid (passing through it at night on the way to Vegas didn't really count) and Yosemite looked very inviting too, but they were hundreds of miles away and he couldn't even drive. Part of him wanted to go and rescue Pete from Park Sunset and Candy's clutches.

Then he could heal the rift between them, persuade Pete to hire another car and head off into the desert together on a fresh adventure. One problem with this idea was that Pete didn't want to be rescued. Another was that Craig couldn't deal with the strong possibility of running into Candy right now.

He got up to take off the Leonard Cohen record and put the first Tim Buckley album on. Shandy had impressed him the previous night with a story of how she used to meet Buckley walking his dog when she lived in Venice, not long before he left this world.

He had to admit she had fairly good taste in music, though erring to the pretty and melodic, eschewing the edgier post-punk stuff that Craig was really into these days. However, if he had to sit through one more conversation about the perfect looks of Elton John's old drummer, Nigel Olsson, he might have to eat his own fist.

He relit his spliff and looked out of Shandy's first floor window. He watched one of her shapely neighbours get into a guy's car below and it came to him; Hitching! Of course, why didn't he think of it before? Free, romantic and vaguely dangerous; the perfect way to experience the real America. He would tell Shandy that evening and leave the next morning.

*

"Umm, Shandy, I was thinking of maybe hitching to Death Valley for a few days."

"Yeah, why not. Let's go away for a few days. Forget hitching though, that's a shitty idea. I'll drive."

Hang on, thought Craig, this isn't quite what I had in mind. He opened his mouth to protest but his brain did a quick juggling act before allowing him to speak. He had been looking forward to some solitude in the wilderness but sex in the wilderness was an intriguing alternative; the love-in scene from *Zabriskie Point* flashed briefly in front of his eyes.

The hitching might be fun but it might just mean sitting at baking roadsides for hours on end with no takers. He had wanted to take stock of everything, but doubtless Shandy wouldn't shut up the whole trip so he'd probably feel just as crowded out in the desert as the city. On the other hand, he did owe Shandy big time for getting him away from Candy and putting him up, and feeding him, and keeping him in weed, and he had been teasing her a lot lately over Drake, the new Piper's barmaid he had fallen for…

OK, OK, enough! The selfish side of his brain capitulated to the never-ending list from the guilty side.

"You're right, that would be far better."

"Why the hell would you want to hitch unless you had a death wish?"

"Hmm, 'Death wish Valley'. I like that, good name for a song… Oh, you know me and my crazy notions of tapping into the random patterns to dig the real America…"

"Craig, America has changed a lot since Jack Kerouac's day."

"So, perhaps the map needs updating; it doesn't mean his methods aren't still sound."

"Sound? Running the risk of being sodomised in some trucker's layby or left in a ditch by the highway with a bullet hole in the head?"

"Don't you think you're being a tiny bit melodramatic here? I don't know if statistics are available on this, but I doubt that a significant amount of the country's hitchhikers actually end up raped or murdered."

"Oh, Craig, I love your naivety."

Craig felt his blood beginning to boil. He could just about take this sort of condescension from Pete, but not from Shandy. He told himself, remember she's well-meaning and swallowed the anger.

"Oh, Shandy, I love your cynicism."

She laughed victoriously then set about hijacking the getaway plans.

"I have a great idea where we could go. It's more picturesque than Death Valley and it's a lot nearer; only a couple of hours drive away. You'll love it. It's called The Joshua Tree."

He was about to get annoyed again then Craig realised it was a genuinely good idea. He'd seen pictures of Gram Parsons and Keith Richards there, wrapped in blankets at dawn on top of some mountain, looking for UFO's, and had often wondered what the place was like. He didn't let on to Shandy that he was keen.

"Mmm maybe, I don't know. I kind of had my heart set on Death Valley. If I agree to the Joshua Tree, will you agree to take some psychedelics with me while we're there?"

This caught Shandy unawares.

"Oh come on, I haven't done that stuff in years."

"All the more reason, my dear," purred Craig, channelling Pete, "come on, it'll be the perfect environment for it."

"Ah what the hell, OK, if it's such a big deal to you."

"Cool," said Craig, thinking he'd just try pushing her a little further. "Do you have a tent?"

"Tent? No way! I like my shower in the morning. There's a neat little motel there, right in the middle of nowhere. Don't worry, it's pretty basic, no luxury bullshit."

"Well, I'd prefer sleeping under the stars but if you insist…"

The Drive

"… And that's when I met Francois. Did I tell you about him? He was gorgeous; long dark curly hair and deep blue eyes. He was a sculptor and a poet…"

Shandy was enthusiastically recounting her travel adventures across Europe in the summer of '73 which mainly seemed to involve her sexual conquests. Craig sighed and gazed out of the passenger window, losing the will to live. He clocked a sign for San Bernadino coming up on Interstate 15.

He groaned inwardly, *We're not even halfway there yet.* Luckily, the views from Interstate 10 were enough to distract him. Once they'd finally left behind the seemingly never-ending urban sprawl of Greater Los Angeles, then the traffic thinned out and the big wide-open spaces started appearing.

Rows of towering telegraph poles stood two abreast on the right hand side of the road, stretching off into the distance. This struck him as a beautiful sight, possibly because of half-remembered scenes from cherished road movies.

"Wow."

"Huh?"

He realised he must have interrupted Shandy's flow.

"What?"

"This view, it's so…epic," he struggled.

"Oh, the telegraph poles. Nice, yeah. Anyway, so Francois turned all Gallic and surly when I insisted that I would not take part in a threesome…"

At least, there was room to stretch out his legs in this car, he thought. Brandy had borrowed a car from a Denny's colleague for the weekend as her Beetle didn't have air conditioning. On the downside, the car's cassette machine was bust so they only had the radio to listen to.

Craig had packed Shandy's portable cassette player so they could listen to music out in the desert under the stars, but the bag was in the trunk. The radio station, whatever the car's owner had selected as a pre-set, was spewing out US chart fodder between the ads. Foreigner's *Head Games* drew mercifully to a close only to be succeeded by something instantly forgettable by Bob Seger.

In his own mind, he ran over the tapes he'd selected for the trip and wondered which would suit this nascent desert landscape the best. For once his beloved post-punk music was out of the frame. It would have to be American and probably West Coast.

He had a Buffalo Springfield album which would chime well; *Surrealistic Pillow* by the Airplane which didn't feel quite right somehow; oh yes, of course, how could he forget; *Notorious Byrd Brothers*. This would resonate perfectly, with its sun-dappled, laid-back harmonising and heavenly baroque pop arrangements.

He tried to imagine the blissed-out *Natural Harmony* with its wistful steel guitar meshing with the Moog over the panoramic desert valley vistas, but the droning mundanity of the Bob Seger song kept invading the pictures. He looked across at Shandy who was still in full flow.

"… So I thought, what better place to mend a broken heart but St. Tropez."

"Shandy, sorry, I was just wondering if we could get the cassette player out of the boot and listen to a couple of tapes."

"I'd rather save the batteries until we get there. Why don't you change the station?"

"OK," mumbled Craig.

"So I decided to leave Paris and hitchhike down to the Cote d'Azure."

"Hang on," said Craig, "Hitchike? Didn't you just give me a lecture the other day on the stupidity and danger of hitchhiking?"

"Well sort of, but it's much safer in Europe. Also it was the early '70s and I was young and didn't know any better."

Craig wondered for a moment if he was just being served up colourful stories rather than rose-tinted memories as he really couldn't imagine Shandy hitching even when she was young. He realised he couldn't actually visualise Shandy at 20 at all, so he blamed the limitations of his own imagination and concentrated on the tuning dial.

Coward of the County by Kenny Rogers; a second hand car showroom ad; evangelistic tub-thumping; more country and western; an ad for a spa resort in Palm Springs; more country, more religion, more ads… Craig sighed again and gave up, returning them to the pre-set station which was now playing *Sara* by Fleetwood Mac.

"… Phillippe came on to me on the beach; I may have been topless sunbathing actually. He told me to stop reading rubbish and gave me his copy of *Iron in the Soul*. I said, 'Excuse me, Steinbeck is not rubbish…'."

Craig had seldom felt grateful for Fleetwood Mac before, not the post-Pete Green line-up anyway, but at least they helped him zone out of Shandy's saga of sun, sea, sex and Sartre.

Call of Nature

As they approached Joshua Tree from the north on Highway 62 and the desert valley gave way to massive granite monoliths, scrub, and strange jagged trees as far as the eye could see, Craig felt a strong wind of liberation blow through him. The landscape seemed to directly awaken a desire for freedom deep inside him. By the time, they pulled in at a motel in Twenty-nine Palms, this desire had transformed or solidified into a baser physical yearning. He felt possessed by a dry, scratchy, desperate hunger.

As Shandy leaned forward on the counter to sign in, he thrust his free left hand right up her skirt, squeezing her right buttock hard then roughly rubbed along the crotch of her panties. He felt her flinch momentarily but then swiftly relax and even part her legs slightly to allow him easier access. The motel manager was a slow-moving and even slower-talking old buffer who didn't look like he'd notice anything untoward unless aided by alarm bells and flashing lights.

Perhaps, if Shandy had peeled her top off in front of him, he may have been distracted from his spiel about breakfast, pool opening hours and the laundry service but he doubted it. Apart from a couple chatting outside on a bench, they had the place to themselves. With growing confidence, he hooked his thumb under Shandy's panties, pulled them to one side and slid all four fingers under the cotton.

With only minimal trouble, he managed to penetrate her with his index finger then his long finger and found her surprisingly moist already. He stared ahead at the man's large metal-rimmed glasses and receding silvery hair, as he slid his fingers in and out.

"… The Oasis Visitor Centre is open all year from 8 until 5," droned the robotic voice as Craig's ring finger joined the other two at the party. He leant in towards her whispering, "And Shandy's oasis is open to visitors right now."

She gave a muffled giggle whilst he wiggled his fingers about rapidly. There was an audible squelching sound. The man stopped speaking and Craig froze, thinking he'd been rumbled but, after a pause, the old timer merely coughed dryly and continued.

"There are only 158 desert fan palm oases in North America. Five are located in Joshua Tree National Park."

"That's very interesting," said Shandy, a slight quaver in her voice.

Out of the blue, she bent forward over the counter sticking her bum right out. For a second, Craig thought she was inviting him to take her from behind right there.

"Could I see one of your brochures there?"

He recognised her strategy and made the most of her position, grabbing a fistful of luscious cheek in his sticky fingers, squeezing and kneading it before sliding his whole hand back into the slippery wetness. Shandy had opened a brochure in front of her and was asking the first question that came into her head.

"Have the native Americans really used these oases since prehistoric times?"

This set the frustrated old tour guide off.

"Certainly, they ate palm fruit and used the fronds to build waterproof dwellings…"

Craig located the devil's doorbell as he'd heard Ernest describe it the other day and proceeded to ring it earnestly, teasing and tweaking the hardening love bud between two fingers. He increased the tempo, then he felt a shudder, then Shandy made a little moan, which she tried to disguise as a cough.

The man barely noticed this interruption to his lecture.

"Umm, which tribe was this?" she stuttered, struggling to stay focussed.

"Well, the Cahuillas periodically set fire to oases in order to increase fruit production…"

Craig was ablaze with lust. His tactile digit switched back to sliding in and out.

"They also planted palm seeds in promising locations…" the talking encyclopaedia droned on.

"I know just how they felt," whispered Craig in Shandy's ear.

"Fascinating," said Shandy rather briskly, standing back upright, "but could we have our key please. Nature calls, I'm afraid."

"Oh sure," said the man, sounding a little crestfallen at being stopped in full flow. "Number 18, just up the stairs outside and to the left."

Craig was thankful he had his bag to hold in front of him and disguise his straining erection as they passed the couple on the bench outside.

No sooner had Shandy opened the door to number 18, then Craig had pushed her forward face down onto the double bed just inside the room. He dropped his bag, kicked the door to and leapt on top of her. Shandy anticipated the next move by pulling up her skirt and burying her head in the pillow. Within seconds, he was slamming into her, his stomach slapping against her raised buttocks with each thrust.

"The door," hissed Shandy, noting that it hadn't shut properly and was now a good foot ajar.

"So what?" said Craig, with uncharacteristic abandon, "what would anyone expect to find inside except some hot desert motel sex!"

"Mmm," said Shandy wantonly, "what has got into you?"

The wilderness, thought Craig as he groaned with a deep guttural growl.

Vertigo

"Shandy, I want to thank you for bringing me here. This place is fucking outta sight, it's other worldly."

Craig grabbed Shandy by the shoulders, planted a firm kiss on her lips and bounded up another boulder.

"And it's gonna be even wilder when we get these down our necks!" he said, waving his little polythene bag of Mexican mushrooms.

"Aww, come on, Craig, you don't really expect me to eat that crazy-looking fungus?"

"Of course, we made a solemn pact. What are you scared of anyway?"

"Getting sick to my goddam stomach; those things look toxic!"

Shandy heaved herself up onto the same boulder, then mutinously sat down and pulled one of her dark French cigarettes from her shoulder-bag, lit it and took a deep puff. She then rooted around in the bag some more and produced a tiny Instamatic camera.

"OK, throw me some poses, Tarzan."

"Must we? We are on a potentially sacred journey and you want to take holiday snaps?"

"If it's so important, surely we should record the journey."

"Fair point," granted Craig, who was secretly delighted to have a chance to indulge his own narcissistic whims against such a majestic backdrop.

"Plus you do look kinda cute in your tight English pants and your pansy shirt."

"Hey," said Craig, feigning hurt as he gazed down at the clingy bright pink leopard skin-print t-shirt with cut-off sleeves, "this came from a shop on the Kings Road in '77!"

"Exactly," teased Shandy, "but I like it anyway."

Craig laughed and cocked his head whilst puckering his lips. Shandy pointed and snapped.

"I'm giving that one to Phil, he'll love it."

Craig leapt up onto a higher boulder than Shandy and gazed meaningfully towards the horizon. Once he heard the click he shifted position. He made a series of climbs and jumps, trying to look his most macho and wondering if he'd ever see the processed results. Remembering the iconic stills of Keith Richards and Gram Parsons at the Joshua Tree circa '69, he whipped his shirt off and stuffed it through his studded belt.

He sucked in his stomach muscles and tried to recreate the wasted but naturally graceful poses. He soon began to feel a little silly and self-conscious. He decided to challenge himself with a little exertion and without warning Shandy, he rapidly started to scale the large rocky feature. He felt strangely energised and in touch with his own body which he usually tended to ignore.

As the sun warmed his bare back, he felt a stillness descend upon him, or inside him, and with this, a growing physical confidence and assurance. He sprang from rock to rock with increasing ease, but less and less conscious thought, until he almost felt he was ascending on autopilot.

He heard Shandy's voice some way below him but couldn't make out the words. He was enjoying the brief oasis of solitude in which to more fully appreciate the eerie beauty of this place. Within a few minutes, he was at or near the top; there was no clear peak as such, more of a long staggered plateau.

As he hauled himself over a beautifully smooth and rounded stone the other side of the rock came into view. He decided that this was good enough and sat cross-legged, taking large lungfuls of the startlingly clean air. Shandy was not visible from there due to the angle of ascent, otherwise he'd probably have screamed down at her to take some shots of him dancing wildly at the summit.

Instead, Craig had the illusion of being the only living person for miles. The vastness and silence of the place was tangible and indescribably strange to him. The exposed granite monoliths and rugged mountains of twisted rock were testimony to the power of the earth forces that shaped this peculiar land.

"It's like being on another planet," he said out loud just to hear the reassurance of his own voice. He felt a fleeting sense of the emptiness and isolation he imagined Neil Armstrong must have felt as he set foot upon the moon. It was hard to believe they were only two or three hours outside of LA.

Craig sensed a movement behind him and span around. A black shape dived fairly low above his head then out beyond his perch into the brilliant blue yonder.

"Wow!" A sharp intake of breath as he watched the large bird of prey glide along a thermal, then dip down out of sight in front of the outcrop. He stood and clambered forward to the edge to get another glimpse of this impressive vulture or buzzard, whatever exotic creature it was. As he moved forward, he stretched out his arms and tried to imagine the sensation of swooping out across the valley.

The bird had disappeared, but more importantly Craig was greeted by the unexpected sight of a sudden drop, a gorge, beyond his boulder. A wave of vertigo swept over him, gripped his stomach and turned it inside out. The chasm could not have been more than a couple of hundred feet, but he may as well have been on Everest. He felt dizzy and sat down quickly to get a hold of himself.

His hands clenched the rock under him and he closed his eyes. He was struck by the feeling that he had been here before. No, not here, but the feeling was the same. The clenched fists brought the image into focus—a cliff, overlooking the sea somewhere. He was sat down but simultaneously being propelled forwards over the dramatic descent.

He gradually recognised the memory locking into place. Allum Bay; the Isle of Wight; the late '60s. He was sitting in a rudimentary ski-type chairlift next to his father. He gripped on to the single bar in front of them for dear life, his eyes shut tight as his dad eulogised about the wonderful view.

"Look, Craig, that's the Needles over there!"

The nausea had lasted all the way to the foot of the cliff. He had almost cried with fear, but held back and tried to cover it up so as not to upset his dad and unsettle his good mood. At the bottom, his brother and sister chattered with rapt excitement at the ride making him feel absurd and isolated.

His mother would have understood and comforted him but she had remained at the top, by the amusements, being scared of heights. He had a vague blurry recollection of the shingle, a little wooden jetty and the pretty multi-coloured cliffs but had a clear memory of dreading the return journey and wishing he didn't have to make it.

The clarity of this long-buried memory, and the way it swooped over him out of the blue startled him.

Slipping and Sliding

As sunset painted the window with tantalising crimson and orange streaks, Craig broke off from his restless pacing, drawn towards this magical ever-changing billboard on the motel room wall. He needed to be out there communing with nature in all its strange and majestic desert glory, not stuck inside a 15 feet square box with a woman in love with her own voice, wittering on about T.S. Eliot. The walls visibly pulsated then inched inwards and to think he'd thought the trip was wearing off only minutes ago.

He hadn't spoken in aeons but she hadn't noticed. A wave of desire to escape room 18 reared up in him, constricting his chest, making it hard to breathe. The voice whirred on; something about Cummings saying it all with anagrams. Craig wondered what had triggered his sense of claustrophobic paranoia.

To be fair to Shandy, she had opened up at the beginning. But now, fuelled by at least three unnecessary glasses of Merlot, she had reverted to type.

"But the words are mixed up rather than the letters: Very simplistic once you've got the hang of it. He just goes to prove that poetry is mere shorthand…"

He resumed pacing and tried to rewind the trip to see where it took a wrong turn but it was not easy with his mind slipping and sliding all over the shop. He had finally cajoled Shandy into taking the Mexican mushrooms with him back at the motel after finally tiring of cavorting about on giant boulders. 45 minutes later, a pleasurably mellow atmosphere was settling in and they were sliding down blurred conversations.

"I think you have unfriendly shoes," Shandy said.

Craig looked hurt, "Perhaps, you just have to get to know them."

Shandy's mouth emitted an extraordinary noise. It took Craig a couple of seconds to realise she was laughing. It was an odd high-pitched twittering sound. Shandy, self-contained queen of composure, high priestess of affectation, was actually relaxing and even deigning to be silly.

Her face had grown younger and almost childlike. The unselfconscious trilling sound fluttered around the room like an iridescent butterfly, and Craig became aware of a lump in his throat.

"The kettle's laughing!" Shandy exclaimed as she busied herself with her portable tea-making kit on the dressing table, perhaps trying to pass the buck out of embarrassment.

"You didn't slip it some of your mushrooms, did you?" said Craig in a grave tone.

Shandy poured the boiling water into two matching cups she had brought and stirred them.

"Oh, I think I bruised the tea-bag."

This set Craig off. He guffawed and it went on and on, eventually weakening into a chortle. He was just coming up for air when he thought of a bruised tea-bag again and the guffawing started once more. His laughter infected Shandy and before long, they both dissolved into a mess on the carpet.

"Ow, my stomach hurts," squealed Shandy, stifling another bout of giggling.

"My shirt feels sick," said Craig, quickly before his chest shook with laughter again.

At some indistinct point, Craig realised that the laughing was not voluntary anymore; he wanted to stop, it was becoming uncomfortably oppressive. He clutched his stomach.

"Help!" he gasped, "I can't stop. I might die laughing."

"Well," Shandy drawled, regaining some control, "it's a helluva way to go."

Craig became distracted by the exploding suns all around him in the carpet.

"Wow, at first I thought this carpet was just a hideous '70s throwback, but now it looks like the death of the cosmos!"

"You must have eaten more toadstools than I did," said Shandy, pulling herself up by the leg of the dresser, "it still looks like a piece of shit to me."

"Come and give me head, you desert fox!" Craig purred lasciviously, undoing his zip fly. "Oh, I dunno," he frowned, "it might be a bit too much right now."

"Let me sip my Earl Grey first and I'll consider it," she said coolly, perching on the dresser chair.

Craig crawled over to the cassette player which was plugged into a socket by the door.

"Sounds!" he shouted.

"If music be the food of love…" started Shandy in that show offy way that grated on him.

"Don't let it be prawns or I'll puke!" finished Craig.

Shandy launched into a fresh peal of giggling and spluttering as her tea went down the wrong way. Craig pressed the play button. He immediately recognised the infectious jerky rhythm of The Beat's *Mirror in the Bathroom*; he leapt up and started skanking.

"What's this?" enquired Shandy suspiciously.

"Ska innit. You don't know nuffin' Mrs…"

He flung his limbs about with increasing abandon.

"Hey, Craig, what's with the arms?" she asked dryly.

"I've always had them," he replied, attempting a running on the spot move, bringing his knees up very high, which he'd seen Terry Hall do on *Rock Goes to College*.

Shandy almost dropped her mug as she creased up with laughter again.

Sometime later, they were sitting in silence staring at Shandy's Lewis chess pieces locked in combat on the full size board. In retrospect, Craig thought his suggestion to play chess had probably been a mistake; the energy and fun had drained from the trip, along with the music that Shandy demanded be turned off as it was distracting, and a very serious atmosphere had descended. Shandy was not about to let some foreign fungus interfere with her competitive spirit.

As he waited interminably for her to make a move, he started to imagine the black squares were actually holes leading down into an abyss. He hovered over the board like a helicopter peering down into the dark tunnels. Perhaps, they were trapdoors over the bottomless shafts which slid aside automatically when a piece was taken.

Shandy's face was screwed up in concentration. He suddenly had a desire to puncture the serious bubble by making a schoolboy machine gun noise in his throat, and take out all her pieces by flicking them off the board. She probably wouldn't see the funny side of this he reasoned. How about if he accidentally slid off his chair simultaneously kicking the board up in the air?

Then finally, mercifully, Shandy moved; well, almost. She moved her hand forward purposefully but then it froze and she withdrew it again. Craig sighed, feeling the weight of eternity pressing down upon him. He pondered the indignity of surrender to the black queen just to get the bloody thing over with.

Then Shandy's hand became active again. This time, no false alarm; she boldly moved a bishop right across the board. The only problem was, she'd moved a white bishop.

"I don't believe it!" he groaned. "Five minutes of intense concentration and you move one of my bloody pieces. You are black, Shandy!"

"Oh yeah, sorry," she mumbled, replacing the bishop and sat back to resume contemplation. Craig sank into gradual reluctant acceptance that surrender was the only answer but he was dreading her crowing for days about her success, and by extension, her intellectual superiority. Just then, Shandy's face changed. It relaxed and smiled.

"Actually, Craig, do you mind if we ah…take a rain check on this?"

"Of course, Shandy," he said unable to believe his luck, "there's no shame in capitulation."

"Hey, I didn't say I was giving up."

"Well, technically, I think withdrawal from the match without mutual consent constitutes surrender." *Careful*, he thought, don't push it or she'll insist on carrying on. "But on this occasion, I'll agree to postpone the game."

Shandy said she wanted a glass of wine, and went to wash the glass on her bedside table in the bathroom. Craig lay on the bed and started scribbling down a stream of consciousness in his diary. 'Musitron. Fishbeaters. Hagfish writhing. I feel zoony. It is now 7 and no sign of land. I want this sea to go on and on. Earlier, I saw primary coloured dots in the air march into the wardrobe!'

'To be fed up with getting high is to die. I am bored with dying. Is to be completely free the butt of the ultimate joke? Or are the only justifiable barriers the self-imposed ones? Just hours ago I held no form. I was becoming lost, an alien. Los Angeles was real, not me.'

'But now amongst the unearthly rocks, the eery silence and the jagged little trees, I am alien no longer. Who blows these bubbles? The afternoon feels timeless but I fear there are not many timeless afternoons left. Are we having the trip or is the trip having us?'

A shriek from the bathroom interrupted his reflections. With images of hissing cockroaches and poisonous spiders detonating in his mind, Craig sprang up and ran to Shandy's aid. Shandy was cowering in front of the mirror as he opened the door.

"Are you OK?" he asked scanning the floor and the shower cubicle.

"I was just taking a contact out to clean it and as I looked in the mirror the pupil just expanded. It freaked me out, it looked so…organic."

"Yeah," sympathised Craig, "in my experience mushrooms and mirrors don't tend to mix well." As he spoke he could not help stealing a brief glimpse of his own reflection, and his face definitely had a disturbing greenish tinge.

He led her back into the bedroom where she quickly downed a glass of Merlot. He took pot luck on a new cassette, put it in the machine then gazed out of the window. The view was fantastic and rather unreal like a prog rock album cover. The sun was beginning to go down and there was an orangey glow in the sky.

The lazy, sinister New Orleans growl of Dr John, the Nighttripper, snaked out of the cassette player and roamed around the room. The slow, intense trance-like groove rendered the orange sky spooky. The women singing backing seemed to be chanting obscure invocations of Creole curses. Craig loved to imagine the song as a kind of voodoo séance, to summon forth vengeful zombies.

"Has Pete ever done mushrooms or acid with you?" asked Shandy quizzically.

"No, I've never been able to tempt him with psychedelics, unless you count weed. Why do you ask?"

"It's just that you two do everything…*did* everything together, but I can't picture him giving up control of himself."

That's exactly what I thought about you, Craig pondered silently.

"Weirdly though, he says he'd like to try opium," said Craig. "I think he just sees it in terms of fashion," he smiled, "and whereas he thinks hippies are a bunch of tasteless scruffs, he associates opium with classy literary types like Coleridge and De Quincey."

"And Sherlock Holmes," added Shandy.

"Er, he was fictional," corrected Craig.

"I meant Conan Doyle of course," said Shandy.

"Of course," echoed Craig smugly.

The mention of Pete had started a reaction in Craig. He sensed that the person he had been blocking out of his awareness might be about to swamp his thoughts. He stood, watching the remains of the day as a wave of emotion crashed over him.

Turning his gaze inwards he was surprised how clearly he could identify the separate strands of emotion: part sadness, part guilt, part anger, part self-pity, part loss. Overall, the result of all these strands woven together was the undeniable feeling of missing his old friend. He wondered what it might take to bridge the gap that had opened up between them.

One of Dr John's lines, about seeing his enemy at the end of a rope, suddenly lunged out of the smoky bayou murk, raising the little hairs on the back of Craig's neck, as if Pete himself had uttered it. As soon as this thought became conscious, fear took hold. Had Pete vowed vengeance? Had the mushrooms opened up a doorway through which Pete's rage and desire for revenge could stalk him?

"I kinda miss the guy, even though he can be a pain in the ass," said Shandy.

"Who, Conan Doyle?" replied Craig, obtusely.

"Pete, you asshole! Why don't you call him?"

"Cos' he's not on the phone."

"No, but you could phone the reception and ask him to bring Pete to the phone… Or at least leave a message for him."

Pete maintained his gaze at the mandarin sky as he answered flatly, "You gave him your number. If he wants to get back in touch, he'll call."

Shandy sighed. "Why do you both have to be so proud?"

"Look," he snapped, "I said sorry. I said I wish I could undo what happened. He made it plain that he didn't want me around. I'd say the ball is in his court…"

Craig's mind drifted off over the twilit clouds, back to a lazy afternoon in Piper's, where Pete was haranguing him about getting a dog for some reason.

"You should get a boxer. They are good robust dogs."

"But I don't want a dog," protested Craig.

"Alsatians aren't suitable, nor are Dobermanns or Chows. Get a boxer puppy and call him Spike. Otherwise a Samoyed. They are big white dogs, part of the husky family. They are a little rare though…"

Pete was away, organising all Craig's dog needs even though he didn't think he had any. Why this memory should rise to the top of his heightened awareness, Craig had no idea but he smiled as he recalled the typical absurdity of the conversation, and the passion Pete showed for his subject which trod a fine line between enthusiastic and exasperating. He distinctly remembered starting off uninterested and absolutely set against dogs and yet somehow within 15 minutes he was beginning to find the idea strangely alluring.

It was the same with tattoos, one of Pete's favourite subjects. Craig had never really thought about them much before he met Pete, but after several fervent tributes to the art form and the associated outsider rebel status, Craig found

241

himself won over and had gone ahead and got Cliff Raven to give him a delicate rose with a barbed wire stem on his upper arm. And yet, Pete, the big tattoo admirer, had prevaricated in the parlour, saying he couldn't make up his mind which image to choose and avoided getting one altogether.

How did this happen? Craig thought of himself as generally holding strong opinions; his parents sometimes described them as rigid or inflexible. So how come Pete alone seemed to possess the powers to persuade him black was in fact white?

Craig became aware that his eyes were welling up. Embarrassed, he shifted his position in front of the window so that Shandy couldn't see his face.

"Well, here we are," he said to distract himself.

"Where?" said Shandy, from the bed where she lay sprawled across the cover.

"That's a good question," he ruminated.

"Why?"

"And that's another," he said.

"No, I meant why was 'where', a good question?"

"Ah," he said with a slight grin, "because it seeks to pinpoint our position."

"So," said Shandy, "I'm guessing Joshua Tree isn't the answer."

"Well," he paused for a second, "geographically it is, obviously, but 'here' can be a point in time too."

"Okaaay," drawled Shandy, "so the answer you were looking for is almost 8." She sounded very certain as she looked at her wristwatch.

"Is it?" He wasn't sure if time was passing slowly or if he'd lost an hour or two. Time did not feel real but more like an abstract concept, which he supposed it was.

"Perhaps, the answer is not a time as such but a place reached, a sort of stage of development," he mused, his own words sounding distant and strange to him.

"Ohhh, I get ya! 'Here' was a metaphor," smiled Shandy, with satisfaction.

She is feeling surer about everything whilst I am feeling more and more doubt, he thought.

He frowned and turned to face her. She lay diagonally across the bed with her head on a pillow, staring up at the bland white ceiling.

"So, here we are," he said once more; a slight harshness in his tone.

"Again," said Shandy blankly.

"No. That was then, this is now. Now...then..."

"What's the difference?" Shandy asked, shifting her gaze from the ceiling to his face.

"A subtle movement or change between one and the other," he said, his eyes piercing like a bird of prey.

"What change?" said Shandy in a voice that betrayed curiosity and maybe even a little concern.

He looked away and started to pace between the dressing table and the door and back again.

"One change, or maybe it's not a change but the effect of a change, is that stage I usually reach on a trip where words start to unravel and lose their meaning. They seem laughably inadequate to express what's going on and worse, they start to feel like barriers separating us from direct experience. Do you know what I am talking about, or are these words just random sounds to you?"

He was aware his voice was sounding jagged and edgy, and fast too, speeding up. He paced back to the dressing table.

"Of course I know what you mean," slurred Shandy, as she clumsily banged her empty glass down on the bedside cabinet. "You are referring to the gap between the real world and the symbolic world of words." She was off, quoting Eliot and expounding pet theories about poetry.

Craig felt her torrent of words was suffocating him. He paced backwards and forwards like a caged animal, praying for silence so he could breathe again.

"But the words are mixed up rather than the letters. Very simplistic once you've got the hang of it…"

Hold on, thought Craig, *I'm having a déjà vu*. He could have sworn he'd experienced this moment before. The rational side of his brain told him that Shandy could well be repeating herself under the influence of mushrooms and red wine, but the irrational side of his brain told him that he was stuck in a time loop. She'll say something about shorthand in a moment he thought to reality test the theory.

"He just goes to prove that poetry is mere shorthand…"

Aaaarrggghhh! It was true. He was trapped in some godforsaken Twilight Zone scenario, doomed to play itself over and over and over.

He put his hands over his ears, screamed then rushed at the door, flung it open, scrambled down the stairs and tore into the freedom of the wilderness just as night was falling.

Am I Craig or Not-Craig?

Shandy's bewildered protests faded into the distance. Luckily, there was a full moon which illuminated the ground in front of Craig. The relief was immense having broken the loop and escaped that room, to be alone and free, out in this wide open space. The silence was deep and boundless.

The stars, my God the stars, he thought and flopped down on the ground, on his back to appreciate their splendour. He'd never seen them shine so brightly before. He'd also never seen so many stars at one time before; the night sky was alive; packed with radiant glittery points, in contrast to the emptiness on the ground all around him. The moon seemed to have coated the Joshua Tree in glow-in-the-dark paint; an ethereal pearly white sheen which was almost as effective as daylight and far more atmospheric.

The mysterious beauty made him shiver and he was glad he'd swapped his sleeveless t-shirt for a sweatshirt earlier; although not cold there was a distinct coolness to the evening. He sat up and scanned 360 degrees. Back in the direction he'd come from, in a slight hollow near to the motel, he could make out a solid shape.

Intrigued, Craig stood up and walked back towards it. Only when he was almost on top of it, could he discern that the odd shape was in fact a noticeboard.

Thanks to the moon, he was able to make out most of the contents. There was a map, some health and safety advice for desert environments and some information on local flora and fauna, all laminated and faded from the sun. The rest of the board was covered in scraps of paper with handwritten personal messages, mostly attempts to meet up with friends or recriminations over failed attempts: 'Louis, where the fuck were you? We waited at Jumbo Rocks until 2! Suzy'; 'C. See you at Split Rock tonight, same place as last time. Bring Mary Jane with you! J and M'.

Craig assumed this was a reference to weed. There were a couple of ancient Indian sayings or proverbs: '… We do not inherit the Earth from our ancestors, we borrow it from our Children'. It was the sort of wisdom you'd expect to find on a greetings card back home where it would probably provoke cynicism but still being high on mushrooms and in this ancient place, where native Americans had lived or travelled through for thousands of years, he found the words curiously affecting.

This was especially true of a neatly typed piece entitled 'Hold On'—'A Pueblo Indian Prayer' despite the large pencil drawing of an erect penis over the top of it:

'Hold on to what is good,
Even if it's a handful of Earth.
Hold on to what you believe,
Even if it's a tree that stands by itself.
Hold on to what you must do.
Even if it's a long way from here
Hold on to your life.
Even if it's easier to let go.
Hold on to my hand.
Even if someday I'll be gone away from you.'

His eyes were drawn to the right hand edge of the noticeboard, to what looked like a circular beermat. He had to peer very closely to make out the small spidery black writing: 'Your children will come at you with carving knives'. Craig shuddered. He was fairly sure he'd come across these very words before in a newspaper report, spoken by Charles Manson at a parole board hearing, which was surprisingly not successful.

He could not help wondering what sort of person would write this on a beermat and pin it to a noticeboard in the desert. He moved his head as near to the mat as possible and realised that the little blob of ink underneath was actually a symbol. Craig could not be a 100 percent sure but it looked to him like a swastika.

A few inches to the left of this someone had simply written 'Gram RIP. I miss you bro'. *Of course*, he thought to himself, *Gram Parsons died of an overdose here at a motel in Joshua Tree, maybe at our actual motel…*

After another minute or so, he was tired of decoding barely legible messages and wandered away from signs of human habitation, lured by bizarre moonlit shapes in the distance that looked like the work of a surrealist sculptor, or madman, but were in fact entirely natural. He felt a sudden surge of energy even though it was now several hours since they took the mushrooms. Craig started to run.

His body felt so light it was like being on a planet with barely any gravity. When he jumped in the air, it was in slow motion. Instead of depleting his energy, running seemed to be reenergising him. He bounded from rocks and dodged creosote bushes, breathing in huge lungfuls of clear clean air.

Around Craig, the arid landscape itself pulsed with vital energy. Ecstatic, he kept looking up at the sparkling jewels in the night sky. The stars were growing brighter and brighter. He began to spin in circles with his arms outstretched, turning the sky into a dizzy celestial carousel ride.

When he finally dragged his eyes back down to earth, the desert floor was alive with peculiar small dancing trees. Like him, they all seemed to have outstretched limbs, some with many elbows. He somehow knew these were Joshua trees and there were dozens, no, hundreds of them cavorting and swaying around him; it was like a huge open air rock festival, only silent.

A nearby Joshua tree was holding out its outstretched arms towards him in invitation. Craig approached and bowed graciously.

"May I have the honour of this dance?" he asked, channelling Jane Austen.

He clasped the ends of each furred arm and yelped. The dry prickles were like clusters of metallic green spikes, much sharper than he'd anticipated.

"Please accept my humble apologies," he offered, loosening his grip. Then the nocturnal desert waltz whisked them up and transported them.

*

We danced through different realities and a consciousness that is eternal. I became one with this eternity and knew that I was this pure consciousness. The absolute opened up like a desert flower, bathed in the mysterious half-light which gave everything an unearthly clarity like a De Chirico. I knew without doubt that Craig was just a vessel, but I was the breeze that blows through it.

I had reached a place of deep concentration that was somehow incompatible with action. I realised the full meaning of the words 'Being, not Doing'. The transfigured desert landscape I was drifting through was my inner world, full of myth and archetype. It was a relief for Craig to be out of the way for a while; needy, neurotic Craig with his feelings and his judgements.

His melodramatics in the motel room and all his cartoonish thoughts and behaviour now struck me as immature. It wasn't that I didn't like him; I had compassion for his humanity, but now found him too confining. Like a thinly drawn character in a novel, his limitations kept him anchored in a formulaic reality. I on the other hand, 'not-Craig', was no longer seeing through his merely-human eyes and had transcended his boundaries.

I walked towards a vertical pile of massive boulders that looked like a crude totem pole constructed by a giant. Craig's perception would have stopped there. I stopped, breathed and listened in awe to the ancient story of these rocks.

A million years ago, or more, molten liquid heated by the continuous movement of earth's crust oozed upward and cooled while still below the surface. It developed a system of rectangular joints. Some sets resulted from the removal, by erosion, of miles of overlying rock. I watched ground water percolate down through the joint fractures, beginning to transform hard mineral grains along the path into soft clay, whilst loosening and freeing grains resistant to solution.

I saw rectangular stones slowly weather to spheres of hard rock surrounded by soft clay containing loose mineral grains. I could visualise flash floods washing away protective ground surface. As they were exposed, the huge eroded boulders settled one on top of the other. How did I know all this stuff? It was as though my brain had access to a huge encyclopaedic computer system.

I glided further into the desert. A few centuries later, I came across a shallow depression. In the middle of this were the remains of a campfire. There was the inkling of a remaining ember left suggesting the place had only recently been vacated. I knelt by the ember and gently blew at it which raised a pleasing pinkish glow then gathered up a few small unburnt sticks and propped them around it.

Whist carrying out this age-old task, I noted a small spider on one of the sticks. I watched him cross onto the hand holding the stick and then progress up the forearm. Craig would have instantly shaken it off. I merely reflected that there was no difference between the arm and the piece of wood; either to the spider who traversed both or to me, who can see the spider's point of view.

I did not try to restart the fire because I was cold; in fact I was only distantly aware of any physical sensations. I did it so I could sit and watch the flames. Whereas Craig would have lacked belief and probably have given up after a minute or two, I gradually, and seemingly without effort, coaxed a small fire into being.

Before long, I am gazing at and through the flickering orange tongues of flame. One of the pieces of wood with glowing fragments of bark resembles the mosaic-like scales of a snake. A flame hisses as if granting this image life. I sit observing the magic mushroom lantern show through Craig's eyes but also one step removed.

While I can see a helter skelter in the fire, I can simultaneously appreciate how the particular shape of one flame wrapped around another, conspires with lens, retina, optic nerve and visual cortex to conjure up a recognisable form from the random flame generator. There is also of course the hidden part; the mysterious psychodynamic process determining which image is chosen to project out from Craig's free-associating psyche onto the fiery inkblot.

As soon as an image is identified it is gone; cavorting dancers, Planet Mars, a willow tree, a bat…one regenerated into another by the campfire kaleidoscope. The pictures start to speed up. The stream of consciousness becomes a torrent. There is barely time to identify an image before it is superseded. As one blurs into another, I sense Craig's dizziness and a jolt of anxiety that causes him to close his eyes and give his brain a break.

The effect of this intermission is limited as his eyes can still see the fire through closed lids. The pace of the imagery is slowed temporarily but soon gathers pace. There is a curious difference to the quality of the pictures now; with eyes open they were like crude sketches but with eyes closed they are more vivid, more detailed, three-dimensional.

There is a complex hedge maze, followed by the inside of a domed Cathedral roof, illuminated by shafts of brilliant sunlight. A forest of Corinthian pillars is chased away by a peacock, with a thousand impossibly blue eyes in his tail feathers. There is a relentless painterly beauty to this phantasmagoria, but no obvious personal meaning.

No sooner does this thought occur when a memory-laden image jars the pretty slideshow: 'a hand dropped a razor-blade onto a cluttered bedside cabinet'. Hypnotic patterns of reflected light playing upon the underside of a Venetian bridge followed by an intricately woven kilim festooned with lion and bird symbols give no time for reflection. I intuit a message of some sort is being deliberately drowned out by striking images from Craig's memory banks or perhaps archetypal images from the gallery of the collective unconscious.

A shadow moves across a lunar landscape made of artex. A mountain man stares sadly as large insects devour pieces of food entangled in his beard. I smile at the distracting sight of a school of red fish, all frantically flapping their dorsal fins in unison. I become aware of a rustling, scraping noise somewhere on the periphery beyond the campfire. I am relieved that the dominant visual sense is not being allowed complete control as the imagery was threatening to become formulaic.

A sudden sigh, or at least an exhalation of breath, freezes Craig's blood. I perceive a presence nearby. Maybe animal, maybe human…maybe something other. I feel Craig's fear spread like an ink stain, or a carved bloody swastika. It threatens to obliterate all clarity.

Although I know it could be a trap of the mind, I open my eyes. At first, all is darkness outside of the dwindling flames. Consciousness hanging by a thread. Breathe. Hold on. 'Hold on to what you believe. Even if it's a tree that stands by itself. Hold on to what you must do'. Be still and pay attention.

Gradually, some ghostly half-shapes start to materialise, become distinct in the darkness. A Joshua tree reveals itself; spiky but reassuring. Is this tree speaking to me? A tree spoke to Craig before, in a way; a way that he could apprehend. Is Joshua Tree, the place, now attempting to reveal a secret to me, not-Craig, who might be able to grasp or fleetingly understand a vital truth?

But wait, another living presence looms out of the murk. 20 yards or so away, still as a statue, tensed and yet relaxed. Two ears pricked up in silhouette. Powerful coiled energy in some sort of feline or canine shape, a cougar or bobcat, even a wolf, or perhaps just a coyote?

I catch a hint of a rank smell. Unfamiliar breathing sounds frame the yawning hush. This silence grows deeper and deeper. Then it is broken open by what Craig perceives as a crackle like radio static, which presages a gruff raspy voice. I perceive a message either through sound waves, telepathic transmission or an inner projection, urging Craig to look into the fire.

As I follow this instruction, a strange thing occurs; Craig's consciousness grows as mine diminishes until they meet in the middle, both present together in a fragile interdependent bond. Until now, one or the other held sway as in cognitive illusions like the Rubin vase where a perceptual 'switch' is elicited between seeing either a vase or two faces, but never both together.

But now, somehow, both Craig and not-Craig are present at the same time. At any moment, he or I threaten to become dominant but fleetingly the two become 'we'. In this vibrating state of mind-flicker, we perceive in the flaming embers, a vision of a man and a woman laughing together beneath a tree covered in pink blossom. The creature or entity beyond the fire, in a hoarse scraping voice, commands us to pay attention.

We both understand instantly that the man is Craig and the woman is Rachel. The scenarios shift very rapidly; walking on a flat beach, having sex on a white rug, watching a black and white film together in the back row, tears over a meal in a poky kitchen. The images change quickly and the moods connected with them range from ecstasy to painful longing, and a myriad more in between, but behind these, in the background, more consistent emotions are evident; sometimes full blown happiness, sometimes just contentment, but a prevailing and profound feeling of fulfilment.

They are joined in the visions by a new form, that of a beautiful baby girl. Images of breastfeeding, kisses beneath a rabbit mobile, a buggy ride in the park to feed the ducks, speed by, quickly followed by another baby girl, different but equally beautiful. Rachel reading a bedtime story in funny accents to howls of laughter, sad school drop-offs, a cake with several candles and a sparkler…

"Do you understand?" asks the grating voice.

We both know without a shadow of a doubt that we are witnessing, or experiencing, a series of moments from Craig's future life. Cheering a chubby angel in the Nativity play, a rare and special romantic meal out, Rachel teasing him about pulling out grey hairs in front of the mirror, then Craig's father's funeral. The feeling of fulfilment does not waver even in such moments. A grandchild, a boy, is smothered in kisses…

Suddenly Craig cries out, "No more!" and wrenches his head away from the flames. The fragile bond is broken and not-Craig is gone. Tears stream down Craig's face.

"There is more," rasps the voice.

"I've seen enough," chokes Craig. "Thank you, I am truly grateful but I don't want to know everything."

He is intensely moved and also shocked that his dream-girl actually falls for him, and astonished that they can build such a stable and rewarding life together. The joy of these shared moments travels right to his very core, but he realised he could not bear to see her death. He may have died first and the epiphany may have stopped at this point, but for some reason he feels this is not the case.

Craig's head is still turned away from the dwindling flames, his chest wracked by sobs, when he again hears what sounds like a burst of radio static then what may or may not be a creature bounding away. He turns and looks and thinks he may just catch sight of a dark shadow disappearing in the distance but he cannot be sure.

The spell was broken. The heightened atmosphere was dissolving quickly like a dream on wakening. Craig warily glimpsed down at the embers but there was just a fading glow from a bunch of charred logs. He felt acutely sober all of a sudden, more sober than perhaps he'd ever felt before. He noticed the first faint trace of luminance in the sky.

Had he really spent the whole night out in the wilderness? For the first time in several hours, he thought of Shandy and felt a pang of guilt for just abandoning her. He shivered and ushering his tired and heavy bones into a standing position, he headed off in what he hoped was the general direction of their motel.

Loose Ends

Craig stood at the end of the quiet cul-de-sac off Carmelina Avenue, staring at the Hacienda-style property in front of him. There was something familiar about the L-shaped building, with white adobe walls and red tiled roof, though he had probably only seen it in black and white photos or news footage. He wasn't sure if a mental image of a body on a stretcher being wheeled out the house to an ambulance was real or imagined.

On the drive back to Brentwood from Joshua Tree the day before, Shandy had mentioned that Marilyn Monroe's house, the one she died in, was just a few blocks away from her apartment. This had piqued Craig's interest, so, armed with a map of the stars' homes that he bought in his first few days in LA, together with a more detailed conventional map, he found on one of Shandy's bookshelves, he set off around noon, to find 12305 Fifth Helena Drive.

It had only taken 30 minutes to find. He remembered telling Pete just a few months ago in The Hog In The Pound near Bond Street, about a sensational article he'd read about JFK and Bobby Kennedy being implicated in Marilyn's death. According to the article, they had both had affairs with her and supposedly she was threatening to hold a press conference and reveal this to the world.

The article claimed that Bobby Kennedy, who was Attorney General at the time, visited her Brentwood home the night she died and when she refused to play ball, he had her killed, in a plot possibly involving her psychiatrist and a famous actor. She was either injected with barbiturates or given a drugged enema, thereby snuffing out the life of arguably the biggest movie actress in the world.

Until now, Craig had found the revelatory allegations almost titillating, but standing here at the site of her death, in a mindset still altered by events in the desert just days ago, he felt simple sadness at the death of a beautiful and clearly troubled young woman. The murder plot may have just been a conspiracy theory; she may have committed suicide, but either way, it was an undeniably sad loss.

Craig felt disconnected walking back to Shandy's. Since the night of the epiphany, as he'd started mentally labelling it, Rachel was never far from his thoughts. Since he'd arrived in the US, before that even, he had been consciously suppressing thoughts of her, as to do otherwise seemed a pointless and doomed waste of time that could really screw him up, if he let it.

However, the visions he'd been granted by the Mexican mushrooms and the Joshua Tree, of a future with Rachel, and having children together, were so powerful, detailed and convincing, that he allowed himself to believe that he may after all have a chance with her. Perhaps, the boyfriend that her mum informed him of on the phone, didn't last long, if he was genuine at all. He had to at least try one more time to reach out to her. After all, what did he have to lose?

Only a few days ago he was besotted with his latest crush Drake, with the Lauren Bacall thing going on (even asking her out while high on coke and pcp and she'd said maybe, let me think about it) but now his heart was elsewhere, eclipsed totally by a vision of the girl he'd tried so hard to forget.

His more thoughtful, less egotistical, disposition continued back at Shandy's. She wouldn't be back from work for a good couple of hours. He put on her Fred Neil album, filched some quality writing paper from her desk, and started writing to his mum and dad. He realised he'd only phoned them once early on and sent a couple of postcards in almost 5 months.

The act of writing to them made him feel closer to them, and there was an ache in his chest by the time he was done. It was only so long before his mood of guilt, regret and reflection brought him back to Beth. He had procrastinated for too long. He reasoned that he couldn't phone her as she'd still be at work so he'd better write, but he knew really that cowardice and fear of confronting a distraught and tearful woman was what really lay behind his decision.

However, he did find that the process of elucidating his thoughts slowly and carefully on paper allowed him to control and hone what he expressed. On the phone, he would probably have burbled and blundered and forgotten vital elements. He apologised, described his own painful position and explained why he felt the split was ultimately for the best. His decision had stayed firm since the night in Park Sunset after he opened up her little red envelope.

He thanked her for all she'd done for him, struggling to convey just how grateful he was and how much he cared for her and still desired her and how the decision was not an easy one and how he might come to regret it. He only became aware that he was crying when a tear dropped onto the page. He screwed up this version like the previous one but his third attempt hit all the right notes.

He ended by saying that he hoped one day when the dust settled that they could be friends, but how he understood if she could not accept this. He was already missing Beth, and he hadn't even left California yet. Craig lost all sense of time, immersed in deliberation. The key turning in the lock brought him down to earth with a bump.

"Hey, sorry I'm late, I went somewhere after work."

Late? It felt like Shandy was an hour or two early. How long had he spent on his bloody letters? Shandy was carrying in a heavy bag of shopping and talked as she went into the kitchen and unpacked it.

"No problem. How was work?"

"Oh, same old shit. I have to study for a law exam tonight, by the way. But the thing is, after work..."

Craig appeared in the kitchen to assist in unpacking duties. Shandy was staring at a huge packet of crisps.

"The thing is..." he prompted.

"Darn it, I picked up the wrong flavour potato chips. Will you eat these?"

"Yes, Shandy! What were you saying?"

"Oh, so after work, I dropped by Park Sunset to see Pete..."

"Oh yeah..." said Craig, his tone suddenly wary.

"Well, we haven't spoken in almost two weeks. I wanted to check he was ok."

"And...?"

"And he's not ok. I mean, I don't think he's ill, but he just wasn't himself. *She* was there, glaring, barely saying a word. It's like she's got him under a goddam spell."

Craig knew just what she meant, he could picture the scene in detail.

"He was so cold and rude, and she'd just sit and snigger. The place looked like a pigsty and smelt like one too," Shandy said, brushing some crumbs from the work surface into the pedal bin, as if to underline the difference.

"Did he say anything about his plans?"

"Yeah, he said they were moving out in a day or two to a place downtown, belonging to a friend or cousin of hers. I asked for the address but he just said we don't have it yet. I did leave him my number again."

Craig put the juice away in the oversized fridge.

"I said Craig wants to talk to you, and his reply was there's nothing to talk about. They didn't want me there. To tell the truth, I couldn't wait to leave."

Craig sighed.

"I know, I should have run it past you before going, but…"

"No," said Craig, "I'm glad you did, thank you, but it looks like I'll be going home without him."

"Going home? So you've decided then…"

"I think so," he nodded, "I'm out of money, and I can't keep living off you."

"I'm OK with it. I'll tell you when I'm not."

Craig spread his palm and lowered it in a gesture that may have looked like he was quashing dissent.

"No, I think the time has come. It was a nice dream, but I think it's over."

Shandy pursed her lips and said with a steely edge to her voice, "Can you put the rest of this away. Like I said, I have to study tonight."

She walked to the bedroom and pointedly shut the door behind her.

Great, another woman I've upset, he thought. It hadn't even occurred to him that Shandy might be broken up by his decision. Their relationship was so twisted up with sarcasm, one-upmanship and mutual wind-ups, with sex thrown in of course, that he took her for granted and failed to consider her feelings beneath all the games.

He returned to the living room area and sat back down on the couch where he'd been writing.

"Looks like another one is in order," he mumbled to himself. One by one, loose ends seemed to be getting tied, or untied, except for the big one, which he was again putting off. A young woman in a residential suburb of north London, 5000 miles away would be sleeping, oblivious to the fact that she held the key that could either unlock his future or shut him away in solitary.

It occurred to Craig that his decision to go home could not have been hinging on whether Rachel would give him another chance, as this was still up in the air, and yet the experience at Joshua Tree felt life-changing, including witnessing his own future unfold with Rachel. Since that night, things had turned on their head. For instance, he no longer wanted to move to America and he no longer detested England.

In fact, he was missing it more than he could have imagined. He sat and cleared his mind for the task ahead. *One strong joint was required*, he thought. For musical background, he felt in the mood for an album of Chopin piano music, which was unusual for Craig. No voice or words to distract him from writing the most important letter of his life; to pull out every writerly stop to persuade a girl that his love for her was so great, that it would be criminal for her not to give her heart in return.

La Cienega Waved Goodbye

Craig decided not to finish his coffee as it tasted a little gritty. He fished out a couple of quarters and left them next to the half-empty cup. He sighed and wondered if he should hold on a little longer in case any Piper's regulars were about to show up.

This was so different to how he had pictured his farewell scene. He had lain awake imagining various combinations of Piper's characters all hugging him, slapping him on the back, wishing him all the best and telling him they'd miss him. The common thread in every permutation was Drake who either tearfully pleaded with him to write or locked him in a silent but passionate embrace.

In yet another version, she produced a suitcase and announced she was coming with him, but even within the realms of fantasy Craig felt this option lacked credibility.

The sense of deflation was almost overwhelming as he looked around in vain once more for the familiar faces. Apart from an old white guy that he'd seen Ernest talking to a few weeks back, sat in front of the still unfinished New York City skyline, he recognised no one. The smattering of anonymous customers looked strangely bleached of character. All trace of eccentricity, perversion and flamboyance seemed to have been wiped clean and replaced by regular people.

It wasn't right, especially on his last day: Piper's just wasn't a place for Mr Jones. Craig felt abandoned even though it was he who was jumping ship. He longed for just one final Sunset encounter; one of Ernest's preposterous tales; one of Bob Atcheson's Buddah-like grins; one of Travis's sexist boasts; fuck it, he'd even settle for one of Cricket's lopsided psychopathic leers. But no, instead, he had an uptight middle-class man lecturing his wife on palm trees.

"Surely you realised that they aren't indigenous to Los Angeles, that they were all originally imported."

Craig felt obscurely disappointed on overhearing this, as he'd been hugely impressed by the range and exoticism of LA's palms. He glared at the pompous little man and felt unreasonably angry. He felt like shouting, *So what, your hair obviously isn't indigenous to your fucking head! What third world dive do they import cheapo rugs like that from?*

He looked away and sighed again. He felt the same way the other day when he'd heard that the totemistic Hollywood sign was in fact just a decaying advertisement for a real estate development. The sunburnt barmaid, who he'd never seen before, was chatting to a young guy in a suit, "…it's really sad, he was like, so talented."

The guy said, almost gleefully, "Yeah well, it looks like he's a goner now. 90 degree burns all over they reckon… If you play with fire, you know what they say…"

The barmaid noticed Craig looking at them and smiled broadly at him.

"Can I get you anything else, honey?"

Craig said, "No thanks, except…umm, I was wondering if you could give Drake a message for me."

She walked over and picked up his cup and tip.

"Drake? I'm afraid she quit a couple of days ago. I've just started in her place."

"Oh," said Craig, looking visibly shocked, "Did she get a part in a movie, do you know?"

"Uh, I don't think so. Joe just told me she decided to move in with someone called Chuck, so I guess she doesn't need the money anymore."

Chuck! She'd moved in with Chuck of all people. Presumably, he was the source of the offer she talked about, which would be hard to turn down.

"Hold on, are you, Clay?"

"Craig," he said.

"Yeah, Craig, she left something for you behind the bar."

She left him briefly then reappeared brandishing a long cylindrical tube. She handed it over then returned to her duties. Intrigued, he examined it more closely. He noticed a message in biro scrawled down the cardboard just beneath the lid. He had to hold the tube up horizontally to read it, like it was a telescope. It read: 'Sorry we never made it, Craig. It would have been lovely to get to know you better. When you look at this, think sometimes of what may have been. Love, Drake x.'

He smiled sadly and began to tease out the thick paper content, unfurling enough to discern it was a poster for *Nosferatu the Vampyre*. An appropriate farewell gift he thought returning it to the tube and replacing the lid. He stood up to go.

"Come back real soon," chirped the barmaid.

Craig thought it pointless to tell her he was leaving the country in a few hours. In fact, he suddenly couldn't wait to put Piper's behind him. The vague sense of disappointment had solidified into a strong feeling of rejection. The indulgent nostalgia for Piper's people seemed to vaporise at a stroke.

He couldn't get outside quick enough and was determined not to look back. In his rush to exit, he knocked his knee on the jukebox by the door. He was outside blinking in the sunlight by the time the pain reached him. He hopped around rubbing his knee, grimacing, then kicked the puny non-indigenous palm tree that stood mocking him.

As he stood upright something caught his eye. It was the painting of the happy/sad jester masks on the high fanlight window. He hadn't really paid it much attention before but suddenly it was communicating to him, 'Look at this'. From high above the street, he looked down at the rather pathetic, puffed-up Malvolio on the sidewalk and for several moments didn't recognise himself.

He was clearly the one presently modelling the tearful mask but was also being shown that it was just a mask. He wanted to indulge in his feelings of anger, hurt, and self-pity but his focus was being shifted; directed to a different, more fatalistic level of awareness, a wide-angle lens view of a world that encompassed the positive and negative in an objective light. To think he wasn't going to look back!

Piper's had other ideas and possibly one last life lesson for him. He grinned to himself and embarked on one last walk up Sunset Strip.

The Imperial Gardens restaurant and the Chateau Marmont looked as elegant as always but somehow more remote. A little further on, Craig was struck by the seediness of the The Body Shop on the other side of the road. He recalled Pete and him pausing outside with their suitcases for Pete to take a fag break after checking out of the Travelodge. This seemed like a lifetime ago.

Onwards past dear old Carneys and the red and yellow striped umbrellas, shading the picnic tables outside, where they had so often sat and watched the world go by. He looked at the incline that rose quite steeply behind Carneys. It was one of those scrubby almost-wild looking patches of land that served as a reminder of the early days of Sunset Boulevard when it was just a scruffy dirt trail that served to connect the studios and Beverly Hills.

As he passed the Argyle opposite, he wasn't struck by the beautiful art deco lines and curves for once, but by the sad deterioration and ravages of time. He realised that the clock was ticking and he was never going to bluff his way inside and up to the roof as he and Pete had planned for months, to take in the stunning view over West Hollywood.

As he inevitably found himself outside the entrance to Park Sunset, Craig knew he had to try. Even though Pete had told Shandy that he was moving out several days ago, plans may have changed or been delayed. The outer door was unlocked so he walked straight in and through the gloomy corridor to room 42.

He held his breath as he knocked. If Pete appears, what would he say? How could he persuade him to let bygones be bygones, drop everything and go back to England with him? *I'll just have to wing it*, he thought to himself as the door opened. His heart sank at the sight of a thin, nervous-looking bespectacled man in his 40s.

"Yes?"

"Sorry, my friend was living in this apartment, but I guess he must have moved out."

"I guess so. I just moved in a few days ago."

"I don't suppose he left a note or anything…"

"No, nothing but the cleaner would probably have picked it up. You'd need to speak to the manager."

"Yes, ok. Thanks and sorry to bother you."

Craig rejoined Sunset Boulevard and continued his journey. He looked up to check out the huge billboard poster of Angelyne. Every time he and Pete had passed the gaudy peroxide goddess of the city, they carried out a private little ritual, singing together the chorus of The Doors' LA Woman.

He was already murmuring the words to himself when he realised that she was missing. The billboard was stripped down to its essentials of scruffy-looking naked wood and scaffolding. Then to the left of the hoarding, he spotted Angelyne's head dangling in the air. It was suspended from a crane.

Craig couldn't help feeling a little sad for Angelyne whose luscious mouth was torn and hanging off in shreds. For some reason, he had a mental flash of Sharon Tate's bloody, battered corpse sprawled across the ground.

She had been on his mind a lot since the mountain man's story on the greyhound. Only last week, he had insisted Shandy take a detour, returning from a friend's, to take in the old crime scene at Cielo Drive. He swallowed hard and looked the other way.

A couple of blocks further up, Craig paused in front of some newspaper stands to rest for a moment as he was feeling drained and sweaty in the relentless heat. It was a particularly airless day with not the slightest whisper of a breeze. He was surprised to find himself looking forward to the cooler, and probably wetter, climate waiting for him back home.

Despite all his recent jibes and put-downs about England's weather, he recognised a deeper pull from his homeland, a deeper bond than he would have believed possible, or admitted to himself, a few months ago. One of the newspapers, probably the LA Times, had a big front page spread on Richard Pryor who had almost died, in a fire after freebasing cocaine. So this was what the barmaid and the suit had been discussing earlier.

He remembered Chuck just a few days ago, spreading the gospel about the joys of freebasing and he shivered a little at the prospect of what sort of world awaited Drake. He was battling to process her choice of lover. He guessed she must need the money very badly, to risk her safety and well-being. He noticed that he did not feel jealous or possessive about her, only concerned as a friend.

Craig turned away with a sinking feeling in his chest. A small cluster of people gathered in the parking lot of the Comedy Store, drew his attention. A fat long-haired man in a waistcoat, was holding forth about something to four of five younger men who looked spellbound. The man laid down, spread-eagling himself on the cement ramp between the Store and the Hyatt. He heard the words, "…and he landed right here." Craig wondered vaguely if the man was a comic; if so, it did not sound like a very amusing routine.

He knew subconsciously that he was not far away from the intersection with La Cienega. The quasi-sacred space was calling him one last time. He smiled, recalling a recent conversation with Robert Madigan when he'd raved about the poetry of the ubiquitous Spanish names in California, and had picked out La Cienega as a prime example. Robert had roared with laughter and said, "Yeah, real poetic man, you know what it means? The goddam swamp! Hahahahaaaa!"

Despite the disappointing translation, Craig's mouth dried and his palms started to sweat as he neared the junction. It's only a bloody road, he told himself, but his body was telling him a different story. Who knows what the Navajo or the Cahuilla people may have used this spot for hundreds of years ago?

It had always felt like a sort of portal to him; a magical invisible gateway slap in the middle of urban Hollywood. Absurd, and yet he still believed it to be true. Perhaps, if it really was a gateway, he needed to pass through it if he wanted to leave this land of dreams. Perhaps, it would not let him pass, telling him that he belonged here now and could never really go back.

He felt as taut as the phone wires overhead by the time he reached La Cienega. He stood on the sidewalk and his eyes panned across the featureless suburban grid that dropped away in front of him, nothing. He waited... Is this it? The tension melted away and was usurped by the same sort of empty but objective state as before.

He gazed at the horizon but defocussed his eyes. Gradually, he became aware of a brown layer in the air, hanging over the entire skyline. For a second or two, he thought it must be a trick of the light or a problem with his eyes but then he felt an irritation in his throat and coughed. At the same moment, it occurred to him that he was experiencing the smog directly for the first time.

Pete and he had been constantly told about it, warned about it and bored about it, ever since they arrived but neither of them had actually seen it or felt its effects. Consequently, they had stopped believing in the smog, except in an abstract sort of way. Now Craig could see it clearly, and even thought he could smell it and taste it in his throat. It looked, smelt and tasted ugly, just as everyone had said it did.

He stared at the criss-cross patterns in front of him and below him. They looked like a circuitboard his dad had once shown him. The lines stretched off towards infinity in every direction. He felt queasy. Was this going to be like a bad trip riposte to the good trip moonlit magic carpet ride that Cienega offered him before?

He thought of Duane, the Lost Boy with the blue balloon: Little Boy Blue. Why was he lost, wondered Craig?

"I want to go to London soooo bad."

Duane's phrase surfaced and echoed in his head. Maybe Duane had been hovering around La Cienega as he also sensed it was a gateway, and he desperately wanted to escape from LA:

"LA's the pits, baby."

Maybe the time just hadn't been right for him to leave then. Craig somehow knew he would be presented with a more concrete omen as his conscious mind doubted everything that he perceived in states of heightened awareness. He heard a rustling noise to his left.

Everything nearby looked blurred and he had to manually focus pull in order to see the young black man with ratty-looking dreadlocks rifling through a trashcan. He saw instantly that this was the same figure that Pete had pointed out on their first day at the Travel Lodge, and then seen fairly regularly since; either looking through the trash or wandering the Strip aimlessly, talking to himself.

Once Pete and he had labelled the guy a 'Sunset' and added him to their collection, they only seemed capable of seeing him as a colourful character in their own post-Beat narrative. It was almost a shock for Craig to detect the real person behind the fiction. He looked at the scraps of sticky paper or tape that had attached themselves to the man's dreadlocks.

He noticed how painfully thin the man was, and wondered if he had a family somewhere. Out of nowhere, a quotation from George Elliot, provided by an earth tremor, ripped open a small hole in his mind. "No: people who love downy peaches are apt not to think of the stone, and sometimes jar their teeth terribly against it."

If Los Angeles is a downy peach, thought Craig, *then I definitely forgot about the stone and jarred my teeth badly on it.* The man looked up at Craig:

"What are you starin' at, bro? Ain't you never seen no one look for their dinner before?"

His manner was confrontational but not aggressive.

"Sorry, I was just…waiting for something."

"On vacation huh?" said the man. "Looking at you, I'd say maybe the vacation's over, if you get my drift man."

Craig thought that the man was probably younger than he looked, possibly around the same age as Duane. Another Lost Boy, but his words spoke so directly, clearly and unequivocally to Craig that he wondered if he'd made them up himself.

"Yeah, I hear you, man. Time to go home."

Then as if the omen wasn't weird or concrete enough already by now, the man said, "Home. Bing Bing."

Bing Bing? Had the man really just used Bob Atcheson's mantra? Craig pondered briefly whether this was a more common catch-phrase than he'd realised, but his rational mind knew when to accept defeat. Bob had just spoken to him through this derelict figure rooting through the trashcan.

This was quite appropriate really considering that Bob's job was supposedly collecting up the trash at Universal Studios. So his favourite 'Sunset', no, make that his favourite American, hadn't forsaken him after all. He was telling Craig it was time to leave now. He decided to give Dino's Lodge, The Tiffany Theatre, Le Dome and the other Strip landmarks up to Doheny, a miss.

He did have a pang of regret at not setting eyes one more time on the huge iconic yellow Tower Records store, where he'd bought *Metamatic* by John Foxx and *Rescue* by Echo and The Bunnymen and also heard the tragic news about Ian Curtis. Craig looked up at the blue sky high above the smog. There was a thin white line, a vapour trail, like someone had scratched across the baby blue paint job with a car key.

He looked down at his watch and realised that the sands were indeed running out as there was less than 3 hours until his departure for Heathrow, and he still had to get back to Shandy's. Hopefully, she would still be up for driving him to LAX. The man had given up on that particular trashcan and was heading west up Sunset. Craig yelled out, "Hey, Bob!" The man turned around in surprise. "Thanks for everything, man. I love you!"

The man laughed, "You're crazy man, go home." Then he headed up towards Ben Franks restaurant in hope of richer pickings.

Into the Sunset

It turned out that Craig had already met Doug, Shandy's husband, at a couple of gigs, albeit 26 years earlier which both of them just about recalled. He was a bit of a silver fox, with still boyish features. He seemed like a pleasant guy, and they all made mostly small talk on the drive from the airport, about the flight and catching up on the basics like job, family, and bands seen recently.

Shandy was looking good for her age (mid 50s), he had to admit although she was still sporting the same hairstyle as in 1980, which did not look quite so suitable in 2006.

In no time, they had reached Culver City, which was unrecognisable, in a good way from the unfortunate first port of call back in 1980.

"So, it took a funeral to get you to come back to LA!" she said, as Doug found a space in the parking lot behind the crematorium.

"I suppose so," answered Craig, "but thanks for the invites over the years anyway."

Shandy had come over to London a couple of times in the '80s and they'd met up, but not since she got married. Craig had changed into his black Hugo Boss suit and black tie in a rest room at the airport, and was already missing the air con, on the short walk from the car to the funeral home. They traversed the tranquil landscaped lawns at the front towards a striking A-frame façade.

The funeral home interior was deceptively modern and elegant with a lot of straight lines and angles. They were shown in to a lounge area with comfortable but smart-looking couches, armchairs and low coffee tables, but before they could relax, somebody else appeared and asked them to come through to the chapel.

They walked through an aisle of churchy dark wooden pews, beneath bronze chandeliers suspended from a high ceiling, towards the focal area, a pentagonal shaped recess with a tall inset pentagonal window looking onto a mature garden. Craig was suddenly stopped in his tracks by the sight of his old friend circa 1980, blown up and grainy on a wooden easel to one side of the recess, in front of an unfurled American flag. He looked moody, unshaven but handsome, wearing a slightly scruffy checked shirt.

"That was one of my snaps I gave them to use," whispered Shandy.

"You captured him well," he whispered back, having forgotten there was a touch of the young Jack Nicholson about Pete in those days.

The sense of loss which had evaded Craig so far, hit him like a hammer. His legs turned to jelly, and his vision was blurry. He was relieved to follow Doug's lead and sit down on the left side, a few rows back.

There were only a couple of others present so far; an elderly woman and a middle-aged woman in the front row on the right. As the elderly woman turned her head a little, Craig instantly recognised the profile despite the ravages of time.

"Do you reckon they are family?" asked Doug.

"Yeah, the older one's his mum," affirmed Craig. "I'm not sure but the younger one might be his sister," he mused out loud. Pete and she never used to get on, so Craig only had the chance to chat to her briefly a couple of times and he could not connect his distant memory with this slim figure in black.

"His pa died a few years ago apparently," said Shandy.

"Oh really, I didn't know that," mumbled Craig.

Pete's dad had always been a quiet, shy presence, whenever he'd visited their Finchley home. His mum though had always been a very warm, welcoming and maternal lady, although Pete was usually embarrassed by her, and forever ushering her rudely out of earshot. Craig felt a shiver of guilt as he stared at the old lady's wispy white hair.

Does she blame me, he thought, for suggesting the trip to America in the first place, or for coming home without him? He'd almost phoned her a few times when he first returned home, to express his concern for Pete's well-being, but always ducked it in the end. He hadn't wanted to worry her, possibly unnecessarily.

As he gazed at her, he became aware of her head bobbing up and down, and wondered if she was coughing for a moment, before realising that she was sobbing. As the female who was probably Pete's sister, put a comforting arm around her shoulder, Craig felt a deep wrenching pain in his chest.

A few more people were drifting in to the chapel, none of whom he recognised, but as the service started, Craig estimated no more than fifteen, and some of those may have been staff. The service was perfunctory and impersonal. The lacklustre minister had clearly never met Pete, and gave the impression of not really being very interested in him either.

Craig zoned in and out through the haze of hymns and prayers, on automatic pilot, mirroring Shandy and Doug whenever they stood up or sat down. He stared at the image on the stand, feeling it was odd that Pete was being cremated in a foreign land, his picture in front of the Stars and Stripes, but then again, he had loved it here, much more than Craig in the end. He had spent more of his life in the USA than England, so it wasn't odd really, this was his home.

Craig's mind revisited the well-trodden path of self-blame and guilt for his actions in Park Sunset, or rather his lack of resistance, over two and a half decades earlier. He imagined how the outcome could have differed if he'd rejected Candy's advances or if he'd made a better job of apologising and asking to be forgiven: Or if he'd allowed Shandy to drive him downtown to where Pete and Candy moved to and try to patch things up. Pete's life after Craig came home, remained a mystery to him.

"There is a time for everything, and a season for every activity under the heavens; a time to be born and a time to die, a time to plant and a time to uproot, a time to kill and a time to heal…"

The drawling words of the minister restored Craig to the present moment, not for their soothing message of acceptance, but for their familiarity… Shandy turned to him with a small grin and in unison they pronounced, "The Byrds!"

There was an absence of any personal recollections although the woman who was probably Pete's sister, did read out a short poem, her crisp English vowels making it sound classy but remote.

They had to be on the home straight now, Craig thought. He couldn't wait to escape the formulaic banalities and find a bar with Shandy and Doug. The sledgehammer symbolism of the curtains closing on the coffin failed to elicit the usual waterworks for Craig; probably due to the dreadful quasi-spiritual funeral muzak. Pete would have loathed it as much as him, and Doug, judging by the pained expression on his face.

Presumably, hopefully, Pete's family hadn't chosen the soundtrack or surely they would have opted for a deep soul or gospel tune, or maybe a melancholy jazz score, something vaguely on Pete's wavelength.

As they filed out of the chapel a few minutes later, Craig realised there was no escaping the minister who stood at the back door, next to Pete's mum and sister, earnestly shaking everybody's hand. He noticed a young Hispanic-looking woman in the back row who seemed to be staring at him as he passed, which seemed a little odd. He mumbled "thanks" to the minister and pressed the flesh, feeling like a phoney, but relieved the ordeal was over. Sheepishly he approached Pete's mum, "Hello, Mrs Lawes, you probably don't remember me..."

She grinned and interrupted:

"My mind may be on the wane, Craig, but of course I remember you."

Relieved at her friendly tone, Craig found himself hugging her.

"I'm so glad you were able to make it," she said.

"So am I, but it's so desperately sad..."

She sort of pulled away as if she could not allow her real emotion to emerge again or it might break her. He took the hint and turned to Pete's sister.

"Hello, Craig," she said with a surprisingly warm smile. He kissed her on the cheek, mumbling that he was so sorry.

As they filtered back into the comfortable lounge area where drinks and dishes of sandwiches and savoury snacks were laid out on tables, Shandy asked what he thought of the service.

"A funeral service constructed by robots, no doubt following an algorithm," he replied caustically. Doug sniggered and said "you nailed it there." Shandy looked serious and he thought for a second he might have offended her.

"Yeah, if I was his mum, I'd be tempted to ask for a refund," she said. Craig smiled, he had forgotten the deadpan expression that accompanied Shandy's putdowns or witticisms. "OK, one of you, find me a dry white wine, while I go and powder my nose," she said in an attempt at a posh English accent.

Doug and him struggled to find any beers and had to ask a serving girl who found some un-chilled bottles out the back somewhere, and Doug sipped at a glass of white wine.

"That'll have to do," he said, and they sat down on one of the sofas and started devouring Doritos from a bowl in front of them. Doug looked up at the ceiling's asymmetrical long sloping beams.

"Jeez what's up with all these angles, man, it feels like we're in a funhouse or something."

"Or a German expressionist horror movie," added Craig, thinking, oops, that was a poncey reference in front of an American, and one he barely knew, but Doug was clearly no cultural slouch; "ha, yeah, like Dr Caligari..."

Craig asked Doug if he remembered meeting Pete back in the day.

"Once or twice yeah, he was a funny guy as I recall."

Over Doug's shoulder, Craig noticed the female from the back row was now hovering awkwardly, gazing at them but then looking away.

"Hello there," Craig said, to alert Doug to her presence as much as anything. He swivelled round.

"Oh hi, can we help you?"

The long sloping lines over her head accentuated her fidgety awkwardness.

"Erm hi, sorry to bother you," she spoke with a slight lispy accent, "but I wonder if one of you is Craig?"

Doug grinned and pointed at Craig using the index fingers on both hands.

"Er yes, that's me," he said, wondering who on earth this could be. She was probably in her late 20s, with a luxuriant head of thick black curls cascading over her shoulders and was the only person present not in traditional mourning attire.

"Hi, my name is Josefina. I work as a volunteer at the hospice where Mr Lawes came. I get to know him a little in his last days."

"Oh right, I see, please sit down," Craig said gesturing to the space next to him on the couch.

She looked hesitant for a moment, before smiling and taking up his offer.

"He was a quiet man, he looked sad, and I speak to him often as he not have many visitors. He was a very nice man I think, though the more we spoke, the more he became, umm how you say…" She blushed slightly.

"Inappropriate?" suggested Craig.

Josefina's dark eyes twinkled.

"Si, yes, inappropriate, but in a funny way, not horrible."

"Sounds like he hadn't changed that much," commented Craig.

"I think he has some problemas in his life, like with alcohol, but on his last day he talked to me of happy times with his friend Craig. He smile a lot then, but it may be the morphine. He asked me to come to his funeral. Then he gave me something and said if Craig happen to come, to give it to him."

She fished in her purple shoulder bag and pulled out a brown paper bag and handed it to Craig. He coughed and struggled to say thank you due to an obstruction in his throat. At this point, Shandy returned and looked slightly frosty, seeing this young woman sat down with Craig and her husband.

Craig wanted to ask her more about Pete's final days, and the stories he'd told her but Josefina sprang up, afraid she had offended Shandy in some way.

"I am sorry to intrude, on such sad occasion."

Doug said, "Hey, you don't have to go, stay and have a drink."

"Yes, please do," added Craig.

She said politely, "Thank you but I must go. I am sorry for the loss of your friend."

She smiled then disappeared behind a small group of people then seemed to vanish altogether like a magic trick.

"So I leave you two alone for 5 minutes and you make a move on a poor Mexican girl, half your age!" It was hard to tell if Shandy was teasing or not.

"Hey, I'm innocent," protested Doug with his hands up.

"We're both innocent," said Craig and related Josefina's story.

"So what's in the bag, Craig?" asked Doug.

"I can't imagine," said Craig, before pulling out a battered paperback copy of Kerouac's 'On the Road'. He recognised the cover straight away as he had given the same book as a gift to Pete back in 1979 when he was trying to inspire him to join him on the big American quest. Was it the same actual copy?

"Second hand Kerouac eh," said Shandy.

"I think I might have been the original owner…" Craig replied, opening the book, revealing on the title page an inscription in biro. He held it up to Shandy. "Yes, see, my handwriting."

"So, why did he want you to have it back? Is it like thanks, but no thanks?" asked a baffled-sounding Doug.

Craig frowned. "I don't know. He used to love the book, it became a kind of sacred text for us…"

"Maybe he went off it later on and wanted you to know he was rejecting the message…" mused Shandy before sipping her wine. "Urrggh, this sucks!"

"Hmm, maybe," said Craig, flicking through the book. Some pages had the corner turned down and a couple of paragraphs were marked with asterisks. He turned to the back and there on the inner sleeve was a brief message. He could still recognise Pete's handwriting.

"Actually, the contrary, I think," then he read aloud: "Hi Sal, shame about the bump in the road but all part of the trip, man. Thanks for sharing the adventure. Bing Bing. Love, Dean."

His voice cracked at the end. So Pete had forgiven him. He could feel 26 years of guilt, doubt and shame start to evaporate.

"Wait, who's Dean?" asked Doug. Craig let Shandy explain this was a character in the book, who was actually a pseudonym for Neal Casady, who was a friend and kind of muse for Kerouac.

Craig felt suddenly lightheaded and a bitter-sweet mood enveloped him. Why didn't Pete let him know things were OK between them? All this wasted time, they could have resumed their friendship… Or was this a deathbed realisation? So many questions…

"You guys had a bit of a falling out, didn't you?" Doug said, still trying to put the pieces together.

"Ha, you could say that," weighed in Shandy. "I always said you guys could work it out," then she reined in her triumphalism a little, adding, "shame it's come a bit late…"

Craig swigged down the rest of his lukewarm beer.

"What do you say we go and find a decent bar and get smashed…"

"Sounds great, but I'm afraid I have to go back to work," said Doug.

"I can drive us to a bar," said Shandy, "but then I won't be able to drink much more."

Craig thought she wouldn't have let a detail like the drink-drive laws get in the way in the old days, but he was relieved they were in a different, more responsible era.

"Maybe we could go for a few tonight, Craig, if the jetlag doesn't get you first," suggested Doug.

After driving to work, Doug got out, then Shandy took the driver's seat and Craig moved up front. Shandy turned to him as she turned on the ignition.

"I was thinking you'd probably want to go back to Hollywood for old time's sake…"

Craig's face lit up.

"You read my mind, Shandy!"

"Yeah, well that's not hard, it's like reading Peter Rabbit…or the National Enquirer."

"Bloody hell, you make me sound like George Bush," he laughed.

"Huh, don't mention that asshole," she grumbled.

"I remember when we thought Ronald Reagan was a calamity!" Craig reflected.

Shandy reached the slip road and after waiting for 20 seconds she figured they'd been waiting long enough, and swung out into the traffic, causing a squeal of brakes and angry hooting.

"Well at least your driving hasn't changed."

She shot him a steely look but he thought he detected a slight twitch around the corner of her mouth.

Driving west on Sunset, some of it looked almost unchanged. Passing Carneys, the converted train carriage, transported him right back to 1980 with surprising force, leaving in its wake, a feeling of nostalgic melancholy. Craig already knew that Piper's had tragically closed down a few years after he'd left LA, but he still wasn't prepared for the sick feeling in his stomach as they drove past Crescent Heights; the whole block where Pipers had once stood, alongside the Bottom Line Club, was indistinguishable, utterly transformed, home to a monstrous Virgin megastore.

He felt angry as if the developers had launched a personal attack on him, ripping out a crucial part of his youth. He realised Shandy was talking to him but his brain could not process her words.

A little further on, they passed Ben Franks, on the other side of the road. At least, this was still standing and the memory of Pete and him, drinking coffee, high as kites, sat at the counter, chatting to a gaggle of transsexual prostitutes, jumped out at him. Shandy turned left off Sunset just after this. After a couple of blocks, she turned left again onto Santa Monica Boulevard, going east.

As soon as he spied Barney's Beanery, Craig realised this was where she must have been aiming for. They had spent a couple of riotous evenings there with Pete and some of Shandy's friends back in the day. She found a fortuitous parking space nearby and they walked back past a vaguely familiar IHOP.

Shandy found a free table by the window and Craig went to the bar. He ordered a Bass beer and a glass of Chablis and politely explained to the barmaid that his accent was English not Australian. His mind wandered back to Debbie and Carol, the two 30 something Barney's barmaids who, in 1980, had scored the Mexican mushrooms for him.

He had found it deeply odd, but also kind of thrilling, to overhear Debbie referring to him as 'jailbait' to Carol. He could still picture Debbie's deep tan and cropped, bleached-blonde hair. The only thing he could remember about Carol was that she spent 3 years in the LAPD, although this did not seem to present an obstacle to a little drug-dealing on the side.

Finding his way back over to Shandy's multi-coloured padded booth, he sank gratefully into his seat, realising how tired he was. They raised a toast to Pete. Shandy was then very keen to hear all about Lisa and the two girls, and he showed her a few photos on his phone.

He in turn enquired about her son who was already a teenager, although he would soon be meeting him face to face, back at Shandy and Doug's.

"So, how often did you see Pete over the years?" asked Craig, cutting to the quick.

"Not a whole bunch," she replied. "I tried but he didn't exactly encourage my visits if you know what I mean. I told you before about the couple of times I turned up at that shitty dive downtown…"

"The place he moved to with Candy?" he queried. She nodded.

"That bitch made it pretty clear she couldn't stand me being there. Pete kowtowed to her; you remember how that played, right?"

"Unfortunately, yes… Then what?"

"Jeez, I miss smoking in public," she said disgruntedly, pausing to sip her wine. "So, I went back a few months later. She'd left shortly before that and he was in a real state."

"I remember you telling me about that in London," said Craig.

"He barely let me in the door. The place looked like a bomb had gone off. I was real worried about him, and made him take my number. I almost pleaded with him to call me if he needed anything."

"Then next time you went, he'd gone, is that right?"

"Uh huh, a few weeks later. Of course he'd left no forwarding address. So that was pretty much that, for years…until I got a call out of the blue. He was steaming drunk, kind of friendly, talking about the old times, but I could tell he was really after a handout."

"And did he get one?" asked Craig, genuinely unable to predict which line Shandy would take in such a situation.

"I decided to give him a one-off 'loan' (making ironic quotation marks with her fingers), of 500 bucks, but told him it would never happen again."

"And you delivered this loan in person?" Craig zeroed in on Shandy's words.

"Yeah. I took Suzie, a friend with me though as I was actually a little nervous. He sounded so out to lunch, and a bit shifty to be honest, and I wasn't sure I knew who he was anymore. He was holed up in a godawful fleabag motel that literally had roaches on the walls."

"He was dirty and unwashed, stinking of booze, at like midday. I remember hearing someone else in the bathroom, throwing up. I didn't hang around, I gave him the envelope full of cash and we got the hell out of there."

"Phew, that sounds heavy," Craig murmured with furrowed brow, sitting back in his seat. "When did you hear from him again?"

"I did put all of this on Facebook you know," she said spikily.

"You know I don't follow any of that social media bollocks." Craig could not quite conceal the note of irritation in his voice.

"Luddite!"

"You could have emailed me…"

"Pah, email!" Now it was her turn to sound exasperated, "Who uses emails any more, outside of work… Anyway, I didn't hear from him again until literally a few months ago, out of nowhere. He sounded like a changed man. Calm, sober, thoughtful even. He wasn't like the Pete of old, he sounded more serious."

"He'd phoned to thank me for the loan, as if I'd just given it to him, rather than 10 years earlier. He said he wanted to start paying me back in instalments. I told him to forget about it, that I earned decent money these days and didn't need it, but he insisted. It was quite sweet in a way… Hey, if I give you the money, can you get the next round in. I'll just have a spritzer."

Craig sighed and said, "Shandy, I'll buy—you guys are kindly putting me up remember, and saving me a packet."

"Take the money, Craig," she said in her firm no-nonsense way, pushing a 20 dollar bill across the table. It felt futile to resist, so he picked up the bill and headed back for the bar. She could still be controlling and infuriating, spinning out the story, keeping him dangling.

As the same waitress was getting his drinks, Craig had a mental flashback, and scanned the framed pictures and memorabilia behind the bar and on the walls. Thankfully, he could see no trace of the notorious 'Fagots (sic) Stay Out' sign that used to be proudly displayed behind the bar as well as adorning packs of Barney's matches. He wondered when the owners finally saw sense, or more likely, caved in to public pressure.

This hateful message had probably sprung out of a defiance brought on by defensiveness at being virtually the only heterosexual joint left on LA's 'Queer St'. He vaguely recollected being told that the bar used to get away with it due to the deliberate 'humorous' misspelling. He had found it genuinely shocking to witness such naked homophobia in the heart of progressive LA, as relatively late as 1980, but he reflected that it hadn't stopped him frequenting the place.

Craig wondered if he had allowed the glamour of the rock 'n' roll mythology of Barney's Beanery to blind him to the ugly truth; stories like Jim Morrison getting so drunk, he just took a piss on the floor, or Janis buying her final drink here before going back to her hotel and taking a fatal overdose. He felt a twinge of guilt for not even considering boycotting the place at the time. His thoughts drifted back to Pete and he wondered how heavily into alcohol he had got, given Josefina's comment earlier, as well as Shandy's vivid description of the fleabag motel.

When he found his way back to their booth, Shandy was concentrating on texting. He sat patiently looking out the window and noticed a filthy looking young man sitting on the sidewalk opposite with a handwritten sign in front of him, presumably begging.

"Pete actually agreed to meet up for a coffee." Shandy suddenly resumed. "He suggested a new place in Santa Monica as it was near to where he worked. Turns out this was a community addiction and mental health clinic."

"I wonder if…" started Craig.

"Yeah, so did I," interrupted Shandy, "and we were right, he did get treatment there a few years ago. Then he volunteered for a while; giving something back I guess, and he wound up getting offered a part-time admin job. As ever he managed to ask most of the questions and fielded most of mine…"

Craig smiled in recognition, "but he did reveal that he had hit rock bottom with alcohol and had some real mental health problems with paranoid delusions and stuff."

"Poor guy," said Craig, but what he was actually thinking was, my best friend turned into a 'sunset'.

"But he told me he'd come out the other side of it and was trying to get his act together. He seemed quite serene, almost philosophical. I wondered if he might have been born again and asked if he'd joined the church, but he just smiled and said that wasn't for him."

"There was a bit of small talk, then he paid the bill, gave me an envelope with a hundred bucks in and proposed meeting up again in a few more weeks. Then he was gone and I never saw him again." Shandy sounded plaintive as she wound up her account.

"Did he look ill?" Craig remembered to ask.

"Not really, just older. From what his mum told me at the funeral, he phoned her for the first time in years then kept up regular contact. She said he'd known he had lung cancer for a few months, which may be partly why he started getting back in contact with family and old friends."

"Settling accounts…" mused Craig.

"Maybe," said Shandy. "Talking about Pete's mental health problems, how are you faring in that respect, bearing in mind you were acting pretty fucking weirdly before you left LA, and not just when you were high."

"You're right, I almost did lose my mind for a while back there. Some sort of 'breakdown' was the consensus I remember. I was put on tablets for a few months, and things just gradually settled down and I stabilised, or got back to normal as my mum called it. I was lucky I guess."

Craig had felt fine for so long, well over 20 years now, that it felt strange being reminded of this phase. In 1980, he had consciously feared that he might turn into a 'sunset' if he stayed in LA but as it turned out, Pete seemed to have suffered this fate instead.

"Do you remember, in Joshua Tree, going on and on about the epiphany you'd had where you'd been shown the future, in which you married that ballerina and settled down with her and had kids together?"

"Rachel, yes, how could I forget?" he grinned.

"I told you it was just a hallucination, but you wouldn't believe me."

"Funnily enough, I still don't believe that. I know the fairly central element that I got back with Rachel and spent my life with her was wrong but in everything else, the vision, or whatever you want to call it, was spot-on. Images of both my daughters being born and growing up, and my dad's funeral… Even some moments with Rachel seemed to come true but just with Lisa, not Rachel."

Shandy, the cynic, was having none of it.

"Sounds like random generic stuff to me. Two kids, both girls; that's what, a one in three probability. Your dad dying, sad though it is, is statistically likely to happen once you hit your forties…"

Craig raised his hands, fingers wide.

"I hear you, Shandy, but it's not just the bare facts of these things, but the look, the texture, the detail…"

"Sure," she said sardonically through pursed lips, "detail like Rachel not being Rachel, but actually being Lisa…"

Craig laughed and let his frustration go. It was plain that he was not going to persuade Shandy in a month of Sundays that he'd experienced a mystical vision of the future. He doubted it himself too sometimes.

Entirely feasibly, he had just had an imaginary trip through his future stoked up by psilocybin, but there was a clarity and force behind the 'message' that he believed was real, whether it was communicated by a mysterious Joshua Tree entity or an inner voice from an elevated consciousness. The point was that he felt it had saved him from mental, emotional and spiritual collapse by painting a forceful and convincing picture of an alternate, more positive, path that awaited back home.

"What did happen with Rachel, and her pedestal, when you got back?"

"Very little. I managed to persuade her to meet me, in a wine bar, and I told her I totally believed we were destined to be together. I was excitedly trying to convey the essence of my epiphany but without freaking her out. She didn't even let me finish before interrupting and telling me she was afraid she had fallen for somebody else at her dance school."

"Obviously it felt like the world was ending and I was totally crushed, but I weirdly seemed to bounce back quite quickly and within a couple of months I met Lisa through a friend of a friend, at a party. I fell in love at first sight…"

"Of course you did," said Shandy.

"You could say, bearing in mind this was the '80s, that there was a 'total eclipse of the heart'."

Shandy ignored this, obviously finding a throwaway pop reference beneath her, and instead zoomed in on the epiphany.

"Even if the whole vision in the desert thing is a crock of shit, I have to say you are in better shape and seem happier now, so maybe it's for the best that you went home."

Craig was pleased to hear some generosity of spirit in these words since, back in London decades ago, she had admitted that she had really fallen for him back in 1980. He could now understand that she had probably felt a little hurt and resentful that he chose this ballerina he barely knew over her, and didn't even return when the vision failed to materialise. He was relieved that she had clearly got over him long ago, so now they could just be friends, albeit competitive ones, with no awkwardness.

"I am pleased that you seem to be in a good place too, Shandy. You dig Doug and Doug digs you!"

"Oh please…" she protested.

He lifted his glass of Bass and Shandy raised her spritzer and they clinked glasses.

"Here's to ongoing friendly Anglo-American relations…" he said. "To a 'special relationship' in fact."

"No. Here's to us!" she countered emphatically.

"Fair enough. Here's to us," he echoed.

Coda

Daylight was already beginning to fade as the plane took off from the runway at LAX, bound for London. Craig decided against watching movies as he was looking forward to catching a few hours' sleep if possible. He was glad he had a window seat. Sitting next to him this time round, in contrast to the outward journey, was a petite, reserved English lady in her 60s, a good omen he felt.

It felt much longer than 3 days that he'd been gone and he couldn't wait to get back and see Lisa and the girls again. He reached for his hand luggage stuffed under the seat in front, and pulled out the dog-eared copy of *On the Road*. He felt he ought to read it one more time as Pete had gone to the trouble of returning it from beyond the grave. He sensed he wouldn't get very far this evening though, as his eyes were already struggling to stay open.

He flicked to Pete's message at the back and read it again. He smiled and thought to himself that perhaps, this is what closure feels like. He looked out the window and rested his eyes in the fluffy rolling cumulonimbus clouds and the soothing salmon-coloured light.

There was a spectacular view of the sea from the white clifftops. He walked through the large semicircular amphitheatre carved into the earth at the top of the cliffs. The audience had taken their seats and there was an air of hushed expectation. He was lucky to find a vacant seat only a few rows from the front. There was a very serious and proper atmosphere that made him feel out of place.

A tall thin gangly man in morning dress appeared and announced solemnly, "This evening's sunset will now commence. It is entitled 'Beyond Laws'."

At this moment, Craig realised why he was here. The conductor clicked his batons together then turned to face the sea and sky. He made a dipping motion with the sticks and the fiery red balloon on the horizon proceeded to sink beneath the calm surface. There was a smattering of applause.

Golden rays shot from the point of the sun's exit, painting the underside of clouds, yellow and orange. The batons straightened then flung themselves skyward as a ray burst through the cloud like a Saturn Five rocket. There were a few gasps amongst the crowd.

Golds were gradually replaced by rose pigments, increasing in splendour, moment by shining moment. The subtly darkening canvas was briefly turned radiant from horizon to zenith and Craig fancied he could make out the curvature of the earth.

Applause grew stronger and some shouted out compliments. The conductor started flinging his batons around with wild abandon, like a zealous sorcerer's apprentice, and the hues changed to ecstatic crimsons and purples, spreading high up to the cloud-vaulted dome. Then the conductor pointed to the west, and a solitary line of birds appeared in silhouette.

Someone cried out, "Look bluebirds!" which attracted some mocking laughter.

They slowly glided across the epic stage set, underlining the vastness of the cloudscape. Craig knew this sunset was being personally performed for him. He felt removed from the formal crowd but hemmed in. He ached to be free like those birds. They seemed to pull the blissful radiance with them, leaving darker shades in their wake; more elegant but also sad.

The conductor's previously frantic gestures had slowed to an adagio. As the birds disappeared to the east, gentle waves lapped shorewards far below and there was a suggestion of a long slow drawn-out final chord, a closing of the heavy purple drapes. A few whoops heralded a sudden outbreak of frenzied applause which turned into a standing ovation.

Craig had been deeply moved by the beautiful display, but defiantly remained seated, irritated at what he perceived as the false behaviour of the crowd, who just seemed to be rigidly adhering to conventions.

Then Craig noticed for the first time a row of people in judges wigs seated on wooden chairs to the left of the conductor. One by one, they all held aloft huge cards with numbers on which were all either 9s or 10s, causing an even louder reaction from the crowd.

Then, the conductor who had remained focused on the sky, made a sudden final flourish and projected both batons upwards together and threw his head back, with what seemed to be a laugh. All the crowd, including Craig, had been distracted and thought the show was over but in the meantime a huge proud Corinthian column of cloud, hundreds of feet tall had been forming, illuminated by the last glimmers of the dying sun.

It unmistakably resembled an erect human phallus, even down to the foreskin, and a couple of small cirrocumulus clouds drifted past the tip, suggesting an ejaculation. Craig exploded with laughter.

The applause died away to be replaced by loud mumbles of discontent and even some boos. One judge protested and lifted up a new card with a 2 on it. A portly bearded man near to Craig pronounced loudly, "Pah, it should have been called 'Beyond Taste'!"

Nearly everyone had sat back down or was trying to leave but Craig now stood up and started applauding wildly, shouting "Way to go, man! Yeah" to the obvious displeasure of those around him.

There was a lurch and Craig's eyes opened, looking shocked.

The lady next to him, smiled and said, "Nothing to worry about, dear, just a little turbulence."

He managed a grin, and rubbed his eyes to try and wake himself up. What a dream! What a sunset! He had an overwhelming sensation that Pete had just sent him a glorious final anarchic message via a dream. He had heard it was quite common for recently bereaved people to experience visitations from deceased loved ones in their dreams shortly after death.

Although Pete did not appear in human form in this dream, the whole sunset theme, the title, the pandering to Craig's love of transcendent visual beauty, only to undermine it, the irreverent puncturing of pretension, shocking a load of dull, stuffy people, was pure Pete Lawes.

The plane lurched again, dropping a few metres. The lady next to him looked away from her magazine to steal a glance at him, and check he was OK after the last time. He smiled broadly to reassure her, then all of a sudden the little hairs on the back of his neck stood up. The headline of the page the woman was reading was 'Bingbing'. He thought this is just too bizarre, I must still be dreaming.

He could see she was looking at the in-flight entertainment magazine, so he plucked his own copy out of the pocket in front of him and flipped impatiently through the pages…then yes, there it was, the headline 'Bingbing'. It turned out to be a profile of a Chinese actress called Fan Bingbing who had starred in a TV costume drama series called *My Fair Princess* and starred in *Cell Phone* the highest-grossing film of 2003. He'd never heard of her, but was glad to find there was some logical underpinning to this absurd, surreal moment.

Craig flashbacked to his last day in LA in 1980, which was actually a year before Fan Bingbing was born, to what he'd believed was Bob Atcheson speaking to him through a young black street guy, using the same phrase, and now Pete was using it, via some trashy freebie magazine. He pictured how Lisa was going to look at him when he told her this story, and probably call him a fruitcake.

He didn't care, he was now at a stage in his life when he'd stopped questioning himself and could fully accept that reality did not operate the way he had been brought up to believe. He sat wanting to say goodbye in style to Pete somehow, as he was evidently still present, then it occurred to him. He would ask the stewardess if it would be possible to get a Tequila Sunrise.

The End